Books of Merit

BLIND NIGHT

BLIND

Cordelia Strube

Thomas Allen Publishers
Toronto

National Library of Canada Cataloguing in Publication

Strube, Cordelia, 1960–
Blind night / Cordelia Strube.

ISBN 0-88762-141-4

I. Title.

PS8587.T72975B55 2004 C813'.54 C2003-906635-5

Editor: Patrick Crean
Jacket and text design: Gordon Robertson
Jacket images: Kristen Sjaarda (girl); Ben Graville/Photonica (sign)

Published by Thomas Allen Publishers,
a division of Thomas Allen & Son Limited,
145 Front Street East, Suite 209,
Toronto, Ontario M5A 1E3 Canada

www.thomas-allen.com

Canada Council for the Arts

The publisher gratefully acknowledges the support of the Ontario Arts Council for its publishing program.

We acknowledge the support of the Canada Council for the Arts, which last year invested $20.3 million in writing and publishing throughout Canada.

We acknowledge the Government of Ontario through the Ontario Media Development Corporation's Ontario Book Initiative.

We acknowledge the financial support of the Government of Canada through the Book Publishing Industry Development Program (BPIDP) for our publishing activities.

08 07 06 05 04 1 2 3 4 5

Printed and bound in Canada

For Carson

BLIND NIGHT

1

My dog has narcolepsy. That's what made him impact-resistant. I'd just given him a spicy sausage. Two seconds later he'd dropped to the floor, legs sprawled, head lolling around. Logan was digging in her sand turtle and accused me of doping him on purpose. I said, "I can't help it if gourmandise makes him sleepy. What am I supposed to do, never give him treats?"

"What's gourmandise?"

That's when the truck hit. It felt more like a quake actually. The deck splintered under me, the back wall of the house buckled, the screen door popped off its hinges, whacking the amorphous Stanley, who torpedoed into Mrs. Pawusiak's tulips. I knew she'd get hysterical, she orders them from Holland, plants them in symmetrical patterns—I doubt she's had a shit in years. Anyway, I remember thinking Logan will never forgive me if I killed her dog with a sausage. That was foremost in my thoughts, that the sausage had finally brought retribution for my sins.

I don't remember being hit myself. I remember Logan's screams, and scrambling towards her, stumbling in mud because it had been raining for days, tripping over a Hula Hoop and landing inches from her. She'd stopped screaming and was staring without blinking at the burning house. I tried to pull her away but she was riveted, watching her world end. I lifted her with adrenaline-fuelled strength and ran to the back of the yard, feeling her skinny legs dangling around me. She didn't ask to be put down, didn't say anything, glass was shattering. Her grip on my shoulders tightened, hurting me, but I wasn't letting her go. Sirens wailed. All my life I'd listened to sirens rushing to somebody else's disaster. Now they were coming to mine.

You wouldn't believe the leeches who appear at a disaster scene within minutes. Insurance adjusters, not from your insurer but independent dweezles who claim they'll help you get more money out of *your* insurer if you let them represent you. "What's the cut?" I asked.

"Eight per cent," a nimrod in too-short pants told me.

"Forget it."

"Okay, seven."

Then Stanley woke up and started barking, scaring the assorted leeches because he's a Doberman, and Logan squirmed away from me so she could hug her dog and assure the too-short-pants dude and his associates that Stanley only attacks at her command. Which is untrue. Stanley has no concept of "attack." I think he thinks he's a rabbit. The truth is, he's a reject. One of my clients is a breeder, and in-bred Dobermans are narcoleptics, so she destroys them or gives them away. I thought a fierce-looking dog would come in handy. Nobody has to know spicy sausage knocks him out.

Meanwhile the house continued to crack and crumble and smoke was spiralling out of various orifices, reminding me that our strawberry-scented candle from the dollar store was lit. Logan had insisted I buy it because she likes whipping her finger in and out of the flame, proving she's immortal. Then there was this bang, the truck engine blowing up or something, and the firemen told us to move back, move back. Mrs. Pawusiak bustled out huffy in her Maggie Thatcher wig. I waved, hoping to distract her from the tulips.

What's bizarre is, I don't remember feeling anything. You always hear stories about people running back into fires to rescue high-school yearbooks, wedding dresses, quilts their grannies made, paint-by-numbers pictures they did when they were eight—crap they've accumulated over the years that make up who they are. I felt no urge to do any of that. I've never been big on possessions. I've never had enough closet space. Any time I consider buying anything my first thought is, Okay, so where am I supposed to put it?

The reality of the thing hit when the lobotomized truck driver limped over and said he was sorry about a thousand times. I said, "How could you run over my house?" I mean, it's not a busy street, it's not like we live beside an off-ramp of the 401. He just stared at me with the eye that wasn't swollen shut, blood leaking out of his nose. A beefcake paramedic led him away.

The firemen really soaked the place. I kept expecting them to start stripping. Kristos, my no-brain boss, hired a male stripper in fireman's togs to dance around the salon. But these firemen looked pretty serious gripping their hoses, and not about to wiggle their tushies or gyrate their pelvises. Which I thought was a shame; if your house has to incinerate, the least you deserve is a show. Even after the fire was out, they kept hosing things down, I guess to make sure there wasn't a stray spark lurking somewhere. It wasn't till then I remembered the photographs. Logan's babyhood, toddlerhood all gone. And her first shoes. Even though I'm not one to get teary, it shook me up that her little purple shoes were torched. Fortunately, a cop with attitude was distracting me by asking questions for his report. And the insurance dweezles kept hovering, plus a scrawny guy stinking of Old Spice who assured me that he was *the man* to call for "emergency enclosures." For a thousand bucks he'd "secure" my house, meaning he'd nail chipboard over what apertures remained standing. "Your insurance will cover it," he promised me.

All I wanted was to go inside my home, broil a couple of spicy sausages for my daughter and myself, and hit the sheets. This was the impossible dream I was dreaming at that moment. Something that minutes before had been a given—confining in its predictability—had been torn from me. Which brought Payne to mind, when he stole Logan, yanked her from my arms, pulled on her baby limbs so hard I feared he'd dislocate her shoulders and hips. She was screaming, I was screaming, tears stung our cheeks, but the newtbrain would not release his grip and I knew he'd tear her apart before he'd let her go. And it wouldn't bother him that he'd killed her. What mattered was that he'd taken her from me.

To this day I want him plugged with bullets. And I want him to touch his gushing wounds in that way movie actors do and say, surprised, "I'm bleeding," to which I would reply, "Yes, rodentbrain, and you're going to die a torturous, *slow* death."

I got her back but it took a while and a lawyer who billed me for listening to him breathe. She came back to me skinny. My cherub was gone.

So these were thoughts I was having while watching my house collapse, until my daughter tugged on my arm. "Mum . . . ? Where are we going to go?"

"Go . . . ?" Her knees were sandy, her hair—that she won't let me brush because she insists she can do it herself—was matted at the back.

"We have to go somewhere," she said.

It took me a moment to absorb that we were homeless. The attitudinal cop noticed that my head was bleeding and drove us to the hospital, where, after waiting for three hours, a numbnuts with icy hands shone lights in my eyes, performed a few other tricks, then pronounced that I was concussed. Which didn't surprise me because I'd been developing the kind of headache that makes you want to slam your skull into rocks. But something else was going on, I told him. "My vision's weird."

"Your vision?"

"I can't read signs. They look Chinese or something."

We went to my father's. He wasn't happy to see us. He's never forgiven me for becoming a hairdresser. All he does is watch television and eat deli meats. He gave Stanley some Black Forest ham, which knocked him out. We camped in my old bedroom, whispered into darkness. It was then Logan began to understand her loss: all her stuffed toys—especially Donkey—and her collection of plastic animals carefully accumulated over her short life. "They must have melted," she whimpered. I felt her cheeks for tears, wiped them with a Kleenex. When she was three, she'd always ask me to wipe her tears with a Kleenex. I didn't know what to say, where to begin; I couldn't say we'd get her another Donkey—I got him on sale, he's probably been discontinued. I promised we'd live in a hotel with a pool until they rebuilt our house. I told her she could decorate her room with any wallpaper she wanted (I loathe the stuff and had resisted her pleas till now). I curled my body around her and felt my heart beating into her spine. She said the Lord's prayer because she's decided that God does exist.

When her breathing got heavy the way it does when she's out, I listened to the sounds of the house—a click here, a creak there, my father's foot on the stair, the bathroom fan, the taps as he brushed his teeth, the toilet as he flushed—and I felt small, infantile. Back home again.

My father's snores sawed through the wall, driving me bats. I went downstairs and looked for something to eat besides deli meats, found some individually wrapped cheese slices. I enjoyed peeling the cellophane off them but thought it was weird that the cheese was grey. I ate it anyway. I could still hear my father's snores, which reminded me of how much I hated him, how I wanted him dead, and I concluded that this wasn't healthy. I think I'm a very angry person. I can just be driving along, just driving, and I'll think of some septic ulcer like my father, or Payne, or my grade-eight teacher who always made me read the messenger parts in class when I should have been reading Lady Macbeth, and I'll suddenly shout "Fuck you!" Nobody can hear me of course; I guess it's a cathartic thing. I've watched other people alone in cars and they can get pretty animated. Maybe we're all shouting "Fuck you!" Anyway, I had to get away from my father's snores because I started thinking about holding a pillow over his face, bagging him and stuffing him in a Dumpster somewhere, moving in and redecorating. Instead I went down to the basement and sat in the windowless room crammed with crud he's too cheap to throw out. When I was little, he'd lock me in with the crud. I'd have to bang on the door until someone let in the light, usually my mother, who I considered weak and needy because I'd caught her screwing Uncle Wally. It was bad enough that she'd married Lester-the-fascist, then to go and spread her legs for Wally-the-pinko/unemployable was more than a daughter could bear. I wrote her off. Then she died. This wasn't fair. Because it left this void, this airless, suffocating place where I no longer existed. She'd contained my history, wiped my butt, kissed my hurts, phoned even though I didn't want to hear from her—my loser mother with the Miss Clairoled buttercup-blonde hair. "*I'll* colour your hair," I told her again and again. "No, no," she'd say, "I don't want you to go to any trouble."

I didn't want to hear from her because she always wanted to know if I was all right, which I never was, although I never admitted this. I made like everything was hunky-dory, tutti-frutti.

I only started being all right after she died. Then I missed her calls. The phone sat mute for days. Nobody wanted to know if I was all right.

A few weeks after the funeral I told the fascist about the pinko. I was hoping to cause him pain, anguish, the kind he'd caused me. I'd been keeping the secret for years, mostly to protect my mother, but also because I believed it was a weapon so powerful it would nuke Lester in an instant, and I wasn't sure I was ready to have him mushroomed. I still needed him to be a bad guy I could hate, blame, curse. But one night, when he wouldn't get off my case regarding my brief career as a shoplifter, I launched the missile and watched as he carefully folded a slice of salami and popped it in his mouth.

"She was getting it on with Uncle Wally when you were out of town," I said, to be more specific.

He chewed steadily, king of the bovines. "Don't you think I knew that?"

I was out of ammo, defenceless.

"Nobody's perfect," he said and started folding a slice of smoked turkey.

That's certainly been my experience. The question is, how unperfect does it have to get before you jump the bus? I suppose it's possible that his love for my mother was so outstanding, so invincible, undying and all that that her nooky with Wally held no meaning for him. Or maybe Lester was getting it on with other tile reps on the road; there must have been a chickybabe or two singing the praises of marbleized linoleum. Or maybe he hated himself so much he felt deserving of an unfaithful wife and didn't care as long as she kept him supplied with deli meats.

Kristos, my no-brain boss, insists that all women want to marry their fathers. He says all his girlfriends want him to act like Daddy. "How's Daddy act?" I inquired while he was doing a fluff 'n' puff on one of his rich sowees.

"A deektator, you know what I'm saying." He drummed his chest. "The *alpha dog*. You see it all the time. A nice girl, you theenk 'she want me to be nice, take her nice places, buy her flowers, maybe a little chocolate' and all she want is for you to freakin' push her around."

"That's twisted," I commented, hoping that I personally did not want to marry my father and be freakin' pushed around. It's not outside the realm of possibility, as I have a habit of going after those strong, silent types who half the time are stupid, which is why they're silent. A social worker at the treatment centre told me I took substances because I had an absentee father and my mother bottle-fed me. She said I had "internalized feelings of rejection." She was a real keener, fresh out of Freud school. I listened to her long enough to get a fix, then said I had to get going. She said, "You've sealed up the crack. There was a chink in your armour and you sealed it up. What are you afraid of?"

"Everything," I replied, then explained that my meter was expired and I was afraid of getting a ticket.

But that got me cogitating on chinks, holes you take drugs to fill up. Or anyway, that's what you think you're doing. The truth is, you're just punching more holes. You take shit, you become shit. No great mystery there.

Sometimes I think I've "internalized" my mother. She's this little dried-up carcass inside me. During treatment me and a few other junkies sat in the lounge watching a documentary about how a lot of us start out as twins in utero until the dominant twin absorbs the weaker one, kind of morphs him into his body. "So some of us are walking around with shrivelled-up siblings inside us," I announced in case they'd missed it. "Maybe we hate them and are trying to poison them with substances." Nobody sitting around with dry mouths bought this hypothesis. It worked for me though. Only in my case, it was my mother. She's still there, never speaks, just does the quiet reproach, martyr thing.

She never even told me she was dying.

For this reason I tell Logan everything I'm thinking, so she won't have to imagine what I'm thinking.

What scares me is how I've come to rely on her. I put my head on her tiny shoulder and draw strength from her. You're not supposed to suck strength from your kid, *you're* supposed to be the shoulder to lean on. When she was four and I was freaking out because I had carpal tunnel syndrome so badly I was dropping combs, she put her arms around me and said, "Don't worry, Mum, you'll get better."

Sometimes I'm scared I'll end up shrivelled inside her. Already it's obvious she has more strength than is good for her. Losers will lean on her till she breaks. My goal in life (the social worker said I had to have one) is to be around to pick her up when she falls. Because it's going to happen.

2

"What are you scared of?" Logan asks. Her mother's been jumpy all day, and blinking a lot, and squinting at the phone book and the notes she keeps scrawling on Grandpa's pad.

"Who says I'm scared?" McKenna rubs her eyes again.

"You're even sweating."

"I'm busy."

"You never sweat."

"Don't bug me."

So far none of the hotels will take Stanley, and McKenna's getting steamed. "What do you mean you don't accept pets? Are you telling me if Celine Dion showed up with twelve cats you wouldn't give her a room?"

Logan starts doodling on the pad.

"What are you writing?" McKenna asks.

"No way does Celine Dion have twelve cats."

"How do you know? Maybe she does."

McKenna asks her to read out another phone number because the print's too tiny. She let Logan stay home from school today, which is awesome except that she's been talking on the phone all day to insurance people she calls parasites. But Logan is relieved that she doesn't have to go to the stinking after-school daycare where Curling Ellsworth hogs the TV, cranking the volume so Logan can't concentrate on her space project. She doesn't get why Dotty doesn't tell him to turn it down. Dotty's a wimpoid and scared of Curling because his father's a lawyer and is always suing people. He even sued a daycare when a baby choked to death on a piece of apple. Since then, Dotty's always been careful about providing "age-appropriate" snacks. They never even get popcorn anymore because Dotty saw on the news that some baby choked to death on an unpopped kernel that got stuck in its throat and swelled up after seven days. "We don't want anything like that happening to you lot," she tells them.

"We got one!" McKenna shouts, slamming down the phone. "It's even got a pool. It's outdoor so I don't think they've even put water in it, but in June you'll have a pool."

Logan starts making a paper airplane. "We're going to be there till June?"

"Well, yeah, they can't build our house in two weeks, sweetpea."

"Is it far?"

"It's by the lake. I'll have to drive you to school. That's no problem. It's a motel, right, not a hotel. So it'll be like our own little cottage."

"Do I still have to go to Dotty's?"

"What's wrong with Dotty's? Is that Curling kid bothering you again?"

"Nope." Logan flies the plane into one of Grandpa's dead plants. There's no way she's telling her mother about Curling cranking the volume because any time Logan admits to something bothering her, her mother phones people: Dotty, Curling's parents, the school principal. It's totally embarrassing. Logan's not even telling her about Mr. Beasley hanging around Dotty's, handing out Maple Buds and Smarties and making the kids sit on his lap. Even when they cry he makes it sound like it's their problem. "What a fussy little girl," he says. Dotty just married Mr. Beasley. They're both from England and think kids should have good manners. Dotty is constantly telling the kids to hush up and be polite to Mr. Beasley. Logan thinks he stinks of dead rats and has flat eyes like the fish in the tanks at the supermarket.

Her mother drives through two red lights on the way to Shoppers World.

"You just ran two red lights," Logan observes.

"I did not."

"You did too."

"I did not."

"You did too."

"Here we are." They park in the lot, stop in the Bun King for bagels, then head into Zellers to buy clothes since all theirs were burned.

Besides being jumpy and squinting all the time, McKenna keeps bumping into things. What's even weirder is she starts choosing clothes that don't coordinate, like an orange fleece top and brown jeans. She never puts brown and orange together, says it makes her think of fast food. "They're brown," Logan points out.

"They're grey."

"They're *brown*."

"Logan, I'm really tired, let's not fight, okay?"

So Logan lets her mother buy pale blue socks and two pale pink T-shirts with smiley faces on them (normally McKenna despises smiley faces). Next she lets Logan choose whatever she wants for school, without looking at the price tags. This is highly unusual; her mother always checks price before product. Logan considers getting some Barbie clothes. McKenna's never let her have them before because she hates Barbie's "hard tits" and "anorexic legs." But after thinking about it, Logan decides that Barbie's pretty retro, really, the only reason to buy Barbie clothes would be to piss off Brittany and Molly, who think they're so cool with all their Barbie junk. What Logan really wants is a pair of overalls with tons of pockets, and a new baseball cap and a polar fleece top with a hood because her ears get cold. What Logan wants is never to have to go to school ever again.

"Can we get some toys?" she asks. Normally she would never ask so directly. Her mother rarely buys toys from Zellers because she hates Walt Disney and plastic and "being brainwashed" by advertising. Her mother usually buys Logan stuff she can "*do* things with." "What's the point of a toy that just sits there?" her mother always asks. So when McKenna nods consent, Logan, her eyes spinning, cruises the toy aisles. She's always wanted a Mr. Potato Head, even though she knows she's too old for it. And she's been yearning for the flowerpot music box with the dancing daisies. You press a button and they dance around to "In the Mood." Normally her mother won't buy her toys that make noise because she says they make her feel like Big Brother is watching.

"What about Play-Doh?" McKenna asks. "And we should look for animals. And maybe a teddy. Or what about a doll? This one pees, moves her head and shakes her rattle."

"Gag," Logan says. She's not crazy about dolls, usually she strips them naked and leaves them lying around until her mother says, "This baby's naked, don't you think you should put some clothes on her? She'll get cold." Like the doll's alive.

Logan focuses on the plush toys. There's nobody like Donkey, no donkeys, period. Just loser bears with dumb ribbons around their necks.

"This one's cute," McKenna offers.

Logan searches the shelves, pushing aside rabbits and Teletubbies, dogs and cats. "They all look retarded," she announces finally.

"Really? What about a bunny? This one's nice."

"Puh-leeze."

"Okay, well, we'll shop around, another day."

"Can I get some plastic horses?"

"Whatever, monkey, but we've got to keep moving, to get to the motel and settle in."

Logan grabs a cellophane-wrapped box containing a "Champion" mare and foal with a tiny apple you can feed them, and hay and a brush for their manes, and a flowerpot. "Look, Mum, the mare's head bends so she can smell the flowers."

Her mother's staring up and down the aisle as if she's lost.

"Mum, look, there's a brush to comb their manes."

"Nice. Do you want that? What about a Hot Pocket Etch A Sketch? That would give you something to do."

"Cool," Logan says, hopping on the end of the shopping cart and appraising the load. "We're buying all this?"

"If you want it."

"Yeah but . . ."

"No buts. We're starting over, sweetpea. What about a ball so we can play?"

"A beach ball for the pool."

"Great idea. And a drawing pad, and markers. Lego. Stuff you can *do* things with."

3

It was the ocean in the moose painting that tipped me off. Standing ahead of us at the Zellers checkout was a tiny Filipino girl buying a seascape that was grey. I thought, How weird to paint an ocean grey. This was after marvelling that anyone of their own free will would buy a painting from Zellers. The tiny woman clung to its fake wood frame as though afraid someone might snatch it from her. I figured she was a dental assistant, she had that unobtrusiveness about her. But then I noticed that the moose standing on the shore was black. A black moose, I thought. What kind of psycho paints a *black moose*? And the mountains rising from the ocean were even more leaden than the sea. Then it occurred to me that the painting looked grey because the lights were out and I wondered why no one seemed to mind, why no alarm systems were sounding. Logan was busy examining candies and sneaking packets into the cart. "I wonder why the lights are out," I commented to the Filipino girl, who only looked away. Behind me a sausage-fingered woman, wearing black lipstick, was gripping a foot massager. "It's weird that the lights are out," I said to her.

"What lights?"

"In the store."

At this point her face had faded; all I saw was black lips. "There's no lights out," the lips advised me.

"There's no lights out, Mum," Logan groaned, grabbing some licorice.

"That's enough now," I said. "Don't come crying to me when you get cavities."

"I don't get cavities. Dr. David says I have beautiful teeth." She displayed her teeth, grinning widely, and even her teeth looked grey. Where a front one was missing, I saw a black hole. "You're sweating like a pig," she told me.

"It's hot in here."

"No, it isn't. Maybe you're going to have a heart attack or something. Maybe we should go to the hospital."

"I'm not going to the hospital."

Driving in the dark, both the red and green lights looked black.

"Logan, is the red light on top?"

"Is what?"

"Is the red light on top?"

"Of what?"

"The traffic light."

"Duh." She was sucking on a Tootsie Pop.

That's how I drove, guided by the positioning of the lights. A terror was rising in me, but I kept gulping it down. Drive, just drive, I told myself, when you wake up the door will be open. Because sometimes it was. No one ever owned up to granting me freedom, but one thing's certain, it wasn't Lester because he'd ask me where I'd been and then say, "Make yourself useful." The stinking old fart would forget he'd locked me up. But that's forgivable; it's his disinterest in Logan that makes me want to stuff him in the Dumpster. She has nobody except me, her deadhead father and her wingnut uncle who tolerates her when she doesn't argue but otherwise prefers to jump off planes or skyscrapers. So a nice grandfather, one who remembers Christmas and her birthday, wouldn't hurt. Lester looks through her as he looked through me, and I feel the rejection all over again. Logan, being a trooper, doesn't complain. That's just who Grandpa is.

She reminded me that we needed dog food. In the supermarket, grapes looked like olives, mustard looked like mayo. I had to read labels. At least I can read, I realized, no more Chinese. This was a good sign, I figured. The darkness too will pass.

"I like this tiger," Logan announced in the toy and useless crap section.

The tiger was grey and black.

"Can I have it?" She hugged it to her chest.

"Of course, angel."

At the checkout I noticed she'd sneaked some Swiss cake rolls into the cart. I didn't object. Our world had changed. Thank God for Interac, I thought as I swiped my card, because sorting bills would be a problem.

The thing about drugs is that you swallow them, snort them, inject them because it's something that makes you feel better that you tell yourself you can control. Unlike people.

It's something you tell yourself will fill that dungeon inside you where decaying corpses lunge at you shouting things like You stupid fuck, You asshole, You no-good useless twat. The drugs rain down on the corpses, forcing them into nooks and crannies where they can't be seen or heard and you float free, for five minutes.

But every junkie knows that the corpses multiply, become louder, a huge chorus calling you fuckhead, moron, idiot, dipshit, loser. More of those chemical substances "under your control" are required to muffle them. And it goes on.

The keener Freud-fresh social worker told me I was depressed because I was "a child abandoned too early by a mother too absorbed in her own image." I thought that was interesting. I mean, there's no question my mother looked after her appearance, to please Wally-the-pinko, I presume. Although she kept it up even after he got chewed by the giant snow blower, so I don't know. She abandoned my father too, I guess. Although, as far as I can make out, he deserved it. He wasn't there, and if he was, he was watching TV, masticating deli meats. I think he's a very angry person. Maybe it's a genetic thing.

I remember fantasizing about setting his feet in concrete and pushing him off a bridge, watching the bubbles surface.

Once, while messed up, I interrogated him about bombing people. He'd always been so proud of being a pilot—I mean, who isn't, it's like they're *la crème de la crème* of murderers in uniform. I chased him around the yard shouting things like "You must have killed babies, women, children, how could you do that?" He was picking up twigs so they wouldn't choke his lawn mower. I was convinced, being coked out, that I was on to something, that momentarily he would reveal some essential aspect of his being and I, being full of profound thoughts, would offer him insights into how to cope with his guilt. Just before he yanked the starter cord he said, "You forget."

I think he's done that his whole life. Which is one way of dealing with things; you got a problem, forget about it.

"Stop, Mum!" Logan shouted. "It's a crosswalk."

I slammed on the brakes to avoid mashing a woman with osteoporosis so severe she couldn't look up from the stripes on the road. The only way this woman could see sky was if she did a somersault. I said to myself, You think *you've* got problems. In the short term I always find the old there's-always-somebody-worse-off-than-you argument works wonders.

Logan was bouncing the new tiger on her knee.

"What are you going to call it?" I asked.

"Tiger."

The social worker told me that the lack of recognition I got from my father made it impossible for me to make demands because I was scared they wouldn't be met, so I stopped expressing my needs and was in this endless state of grief, except I didn't know what I was grieving for. And she kept going back to the mother thing. She said "children seek out a mother's gaze." If her gaze is empty, if she turns away her head, the child is "shattered," lost in limbo, thinks she must do something to win her mother's love but she can't think what. Eventually the child decides it's no use, there's nothing to be done, she's good for nothing, might as well stay depressed. I think there's some truth in this, although I'm a little tired of mother-bashing. Especially now that I'm a mother.

"Mum, why're you looking so weird all the time?"

"Weird?"

"Like you don't know where you're going?"

"I know where I'm going."

Anyway, the social worker's theory was that I was taking all these substances to replace mother love. But, since I didn't know what mother love was, I'd settle for what I could get—men with problems. I'd desire these turds, work myself into a frenzy believing that finally I was really *feeling* something, finally I was going to be recognized, accepted, adored, then poof, the smoke would clear and I'd see that he was just some poor schmuck wanting to get laid, with free haircuts on the side.

The only addiction I'm currently allowing is caffeine. And my daughter. Without seeing her face, feeling her warmth, watching her growth, I'd be dead. She freed me from drugs by implanting herself in my uterus. Her father, the substance I wanted to absorb so he couldn't get away, left her with me, and for this I am daily thankful. Although at the time, becoming drug-free was like being carved repeatedly with knives.

The aforementioned deadhead was already at our motel, waiting for us, strutting around the parking lot. "What the fuck happened?" he demanded.

"How did you know we were here?" I inquired.

"Lester. He says you burnt your house down for the insurance money."

"I should burn *his* house down." I opened the trunk. "Help carry at least."

"Is he alright? He was singing 'Irish Eyes Are Smiling,' like loud, like he was trying to drown me out with it."

"He's old."

The motel room had air breathed by too many people over too many years, and stains on the carpet, and zigzaggy wallpaper that was making me dizzy.

"Are you going to tell me what happened?" Payne demanded, jangling his car keys.

Logan jumped on one of the double beds. "A truck ran over our house, you should've seen it, it was awesome. Dad, how come you didn't call me Saturday? You said you were going to take me to a movie."

"Sorry, Lo, got tied up."

"Doing what?" she asked, because only she can.

"Business, hon."

"On Saturday?"

"Payne," I interjected. "Can you leave us, please, we have to get settled." The amazing thing was, he looked dull to me, dirty. Even though I can't stand the fucker I usually enjoy looking at him. He takes great care of himself, is always perfectly groomed, wearing the right clothes. He regularly checks himself out in mirrors, makes little adjustments. Usually, even though I hate him, I want to jump him, run my tongue up and down his neck. But now he was grey. His naturally blond hair had no sheen, his skin looked like clay. The only part of him that looked normal was the black leather jacket that cost more than what I spend on Logan's wardrobe in a year.

So I had this power, suddenly, because usually looking at him is painful. Like staring at that little stone house in the south of France you know you'll never own because a cup of coffee costs five bucks there. But you can't stop thinking about it, dreaming of a happy life in a vineyard.

"Get out," I said. "Call Logan later." I tore a page off a grungy calendar with the Lakeview's number on it.

"I can't believe you're staying here," Payne said. "This is like a . . . a total dive. I can't have my daughter staying here."

"It's the only place that'll take Stanley," Logan explained.

"Jesus, McKenna, I mean who lives here, like there's probably drug dealers next door or something. I mean, talk about living next to temptation."

"I can't believe you said that. How *dare* you say that. Get out. I'm not fighting in front to her."

He looked around me the way you look around strangers in train stations. "Logan," he said, "you can always stay with me and Sheena."

"I like it here, Dad. And Sheena's scared of Stanley."

"Don't bring the dog, for chrissake, you can visit the dog here."

"I like it here, Dad. The TV's bigger than ours."

"Sheena's got a fucking huge Panasonic." He glanced at himself in the mirror above the dresser.

"Don't use that word in front of her," I snapped.

"I know that word," Logan said.

"I know you know it, I don't want you to use it. Get out, Payne, I mean it, or I'll call the cops. You have no right to be here." He only figured out she was his daughter by doing the math (must have been hard for him) and noticing that she looks exactly like him. That's when he stole her from me, leaving me dislocated, hysterical, fumbling, scared. I couldn't stop crying. I told clients I had allergies. After I got her back he occasionally made vague attempts at offering money: "Do you need cash? I don't have much but I can spare a few bucks." I decided I didn't want any of his greasy money he makes selling time shares or whatever else he's got going because I didn't want him to have a way back to her. In court I would simply say we were never married, did not cohabit, he has done nothing, zip, zero, zilch. Think of him as an anonymous donor. A good fuck.

Logan had picked up a Bible and was flicking through it. "Curling Ellsworth uses that word all the time."

"Curling Ellsworth is a moron. Bye, Payne." By this time I was literally pushing him out the door, leaving sweaty fingerprints all over his leather jacket.

"Call my cell," he advised me, actually looking relieved because, once again, I was freeing him of responsibility.

"Sure, whatever." As if I would. I slammed the door and watched him scoot in his leased Beemer.

"He won't call," Logan said, knowing he would let her down as he has done more times than should be legal.

"Do you think Dad has another girlfriend and that's why he didn't call on Saturday?" She's on to her second Swiss cake roll. I can't stop her, can't take her fun away now that her home is gone.

"I don't know, sweetpea. And I don't care."

"Yes you do."

"No I don't."

"Yes you do. Especially if they're younger."

"Can we turn the TV off?" It's been driving me nuts. It's not just that I'm only seeing black and white, it's that I don't know what things are. The shadows confuse me, it's too contrasty, I can't tell what's real and what isn't.

In the paper there was a story about some guy who went blind after a head injury. He had a computer chip or something implanted in his brain that enabled him to see shapes. They had a picture of him with an electrical cord sticking out of his skull.

I keep blinking, thinking next time I'll be able to see better. It's not happening. I'm in that stinking room again, only this time nobody's opening the door.

At first the light hurt. I'd squint, hold my hands over my eyes before peeking through my fingers.

I wish my mother were around. Contrary to the social worker's theory, she could be there for me, if the pain was physical, a bruise or a sprained ankle or something. She'd know about it even before I mentioned it. Sometimes I wouldn't mention it because then she'd get fussed, swaddle me in bandages and force aspirin down my throat. Even less obvious ailments, like indigestion, or headaches, blisters, she always knew. But emotional pain, that erodes your spirit, she didn't want to know about. The first time my heart was broken she said, "Honey, there'll be other men." When you're heartbroken there is only one man. The rest are worms writhing underground, you can't even see them.

I thought I'd never get over Payne. Now he's grey. A statue for bird shit.

I've often wondered what happened to my mother after Uncle Wally got sucked into the snow blower. Police suggested he was trying to clear something away from in front of it and was pulled into the blade. My mother found his body, never said anything about it though, I guess because she wasn't supposed to be obsessed with him. But something must have died in her, a piece of her heart must have atrophied. I know a chunk of mine degenerated after Payne. I can live without it. It's like anything, you get injured, you compensate. Keep moving, that's the important thing.

"What're you thinking about?" Logan asks. She's got black goop in the corners of her mouth, chocolate.

"Tomorrow, getting you to school."

"That's not what you were thinking about."

"Yes it is."

"No it isn't."

"Logan, can we not fight, I'm so tired."

"I'm not." I can see she's buzzed on sugar. "Can I watch *The Unforgiven*? It's on next."

"There's violence in that. You know I wouldn't let you watch that at home."

"It's different here."

It is different. It's horrible. I can imagine the bad sex that has taken place on this bed, the vomit that has spewed on the carpet, the bits of potato chips lodged in corners beyond the reach of the vacuum cleaner. Already I had to rinse a pubic hair down the drain. Stanley, the cause of our current digs, licks my hand, hoping for a sausage. "None here, pal. Just your regular chow." I point to the bowl.

"Can't he have one of my cocktail weenies?" Logan asks, already pulling one from the jar.

"He'll go to sleep."

"No problemo." She feeds him several and he's out.

"There's horses in *The Unforgiven*, Mum. I want to see the horses. I promise I won't look at the violent parts."

I have no strength to fight. I close my eyes, hoping to see colour. I try to *remember* colour, go somewhere colourful in my mind. I used to do this in the windowless room, stare into darkness and go places I'd never been: Puerto Vallarta, Las Vegas, the Côte d'Azur, Acapulco. Places I'd seen sparkle in my mother's travel mags. I'd imagine warm waves washing over me, sandcastles, beach balls, ice cream.

"It's going to be alright, Mum. There's a pool, I saw it, it's really cool. It's even got a diving board."

"You've got to brush your teeth after eating all that crap, even though it's different here." Inside my head I see only fog.

"Okay."

"Promise?"

"I promise."

"I'm so sleepy, baby, I've got to sleep."

It's as though someone's thrown a lead blanket over me; I can't lift my limbs, open my eyes. Can't even think straight. Let's hope they don't find me dead in the morning.

4

Normally Logan resists bathtime because it means bedtime, but as her mother is unconscious and therefore not very interesting, and as this bathtub's pink, she's decided to have one and put all kinds of stuff in it. She's poured most of the little bottle of shampoo into the running water to make bubbles. And she's unwrapped the little soaps and the shower cap, which she's wearing, although really she should wash her hair because it stinks of smoke.

It was the shattering of the windows that spooked her the most; she kept expecting shards to fly off the house and stab her mother, who was gripping her so tightly she could hardly breathe. And the explosion. That hurt her ears.

The Unforgiven wasn't great. There weren't enough horses, for starters. Logan couldn't believe the whores didn't take the free pony from the cowboy. It was definitely violent, her mother wouldn't have liked it. Especially at the beginning when the whore got her face slashed. That was gross. And the whipping. Logan doesn't mind shoot-outs, but whippings freak her out. She couldn't watch. She surfed to see if anything else was on but it was pretty boring; hospital shows. Why do people always want to watch hospital shows? Logan hates hospitals, there's always sick people in them. Like last night there were people moaning and coughing and barfing. And that psycho who kept shouting at God and picking at scabs all over his face. You don't see that on TV.

Logan's been talking to God herself recently. She doesn't understand why he let the truck run over her house. She's not complaining or anything, she just doesn't get it. She hopes it's not because he's angry that her mother doesn't believe in him. Her mother used to believe in him, a long time ago. McKenna hasn't explained to Logan exactly why she gave up on him; she says it's personal and that everybody has to work out their own deal with God.

Logan suspects it has something to do with God being male. Her mother thinks that most men are newtbrains, and doesn't see why God has to be male. "Because Mary gave birth to Jesus," Logan explained.

"But it was immaculate," McKenna argued.

"What's immaculate?"

"She didn't need his penis to get pregnant." Her mother has always used the proper words for what she refers to as "sex organs."

"But if God was female," Logan pointed out, "he could have had Jesus himself."

"So then why isn't Mary God? Since she had Jesus."

"Because Mary was human. God isn't human."

"Maybe that's what I don't like about him," her mother grumbled.

Logan presses her palms together and prays that tomorrow her mother will be normal. In return, Logan will obey. She also prays that they catch the cheetah poachers. The dirtbags snatch cubs from their mothers when the babies are only three weeks old. If the cubs don't die in transit, the poachers sell them, starving, to businessmen in the Middle East who only let them out when they want to watch them kill gazelles.

She's stopped praying that her parents will get together again because she doesn't think this would be appropriate. But she has prayed that Curling Ellsworth would get hit by a car and she knows this is wrong and may be why her house got hit by a truck. Curling has two parents and a little sister and a motorized car he can drive plus a remote-control Monster Truck and a huge collection of Beanie Babies. He's always asking Logan to have sex with him, even though she calls him "toad," and he's always setting fire to caterpillars and bugs with his Bic lighter, or cutting worms and snails in half on his "slaughtering slab." These are sins in Logan's opinion.

She pulls off the shower cap and holds her head under water.

Curling doesn't have a pool, she realizes. She'll have to tell him about hers, then say he can't come over.

The other thing she asked God about, which she knows may have been inappropriate, was if he could get rid of Sheena, like not kill her or anything but make her move to France or somewhere. Because they're never going to France. Her mother went to France when she was younger and always says they'll never be able to go there because it's too expensive. A cup of coffee costs five bucks there.

Anyway, Logan figures she shouldn't have said anything about Sheena to God. It's just she's sick of her dad's girlfriends. They always want to smear lipstick on her and go to sucky movies. And during the movie they hold her dad's hand and it's like totally icky.

Why else would God be angry with her? Oh, she stole Curling's pencil with the pumpkin-head eraser on it. She needed to erase something and knew, if she asked to borrow his pencil, he'd tell her to suck his dick.

These aren't big sins in Logan's opinion. She didn't torture a pomeranian. A girl at school got arrested for burning a pomeranian on a barbecue. That would be a good reason for God to total a house.

She squeezes shampoo into her hand and works it into her hair. Maybe she'll take the foal to school tomorrow, it's small enough, she can fit it in one of her pockets so Miss Spongle can't see it, and the apple and the hay and the flowerpot and the brush, they'll all fit in her pockets.

She's also praying for the beluga whale dying in the Niagara Falls marine park. They brought her all the way from Russia. The park's owner said the whale showed no sign of disease, just stopped eating. It's obvious to Logan that the whale must have been depressed about something—being trapped in a tank, for example. When Logan gets depressed she has difficulty eating because it feels as if her gut's stuffed with marbles.

She steps out of the tub and pulls the plug. She's not going to think about home, since it's toast. She starts towelling off. Normally her mother would do this. Normally they'd snuggle in bed and read books. They forgot to buy books.

Logan pulls her new dinosaur pyjamas out of the Zellers bag. She doesn't have scissors, which means she'll have to sleep with the tags on and they'll be scratchy. Her mother can tear tags off with her teeth but Logan's afraid to wake her because she's been acting so weird. It was sunny today, not a cloud in the sky, the kind of day her mother normally won't shut up about. "Can you believe how blue the sky is, monkey?" she asks repeatedly. But today she didn't say a word, just kept squinting and blinking. And when they were driving to the Lakeview, the sun was setting; a big fireball sinking into the darkened city. Normally McKenna would say, "Look at that sunset, sweetpea, it's pure gold, this moment is pure gold." She'd stop the car and they'd watch and she'd talk about Greek gods and how stupendous skies should make humans humble.

Logan remembers her teeth. She promised to brush her teeth. She feels around in the bag for a brush and toothpaste.

She knows that her avocado plant got torched. She grew it from the pit. And her grapefruit seeds that were starting to sprout. Miss Spongle told them to put them inside a glass against paper towel, and to always keep the towel moist. Logan was the first person in class to have a seed sprout.

She turns out the lights, hugs Tiger and gets into the bed beside her mother's. It's made really tightly; she has to pull back hard on the sheets. And the comforter is stiff, not like her duvet at home. She lies back and listens to noises next door, the TV and somebody coughing. A door slams and she hears someone in the parking lot, then a car starting. The lights shine in the picture window even though the curtains are drawn.

It will be nice to have a new house, especially after they put up wallpaper. Maybe they can find some with dinosaurs on it.

She misses Donkey, remembers the feel of her against her chest, the tufts of her mane that would tickle her nostrils. She rolls on her side and tucks the covers around Tiger, who she has decided is a girl. She kisses her between the ears. "Don't be scared," she tells her.

5

It's like being in one of those war movies, standing in bombed-out Berlin. The dweezle stinking of Old Spice was right, the place has been vandalized. I guess smoke- and fire-damaged goods are saleable commodities. I keep remembering things that are gone, things you wouldn't normally value, like a can opener that works, the blender, sharp scissors, knives.

The city called this morning and told me to clean up the "refuse," insisted that I was posing a health risk by not attending to my premises. "Excuse me," I said, "there is no premises."

"Steps must be taken," the bugbrain with nasal congestion informed me.

I relayed this message to the parasite insurance guy, who located the inspector who appraised the wreckage yesterday. It turns out they've decided to demolish the place. This is the last I'll see of it, the house that knows me better than any human. I signed the purchasing agreement the week after I quit cocaine because Logan was inside me. This house has watched me shake, twitch, jump at shadows, clench my teeth so hard my head throbbed. Becoming drug-free, I twiddled so much hair off my head, I had to wear trendy little hats to cover bald patches. This house's walls have listened to my tears and screams and generalized "Fuck yous." It has been my prison and my Alamo. Now it fits under the heading of "detached private dwelling impacted by aircraft or land vehicle."

Apparently my insurer is chasing the trucking company's insurer for cash (subrogation, they call it) but the adjuster insists that this will not have any effect on "restoring the house as it was." As if that were possible. No more hundred-year-old oak trim, stained glass, friendly ghosts. Maybe I'll get a toilet that flushes properly. That would be cause for celebration.

A busted TV, a fridge and an old mattress lie in a heap on my front lawn. I guess a burned-out house screams *Free Dump!* Mrs. Pawusiak is going to have a bird.

This morning, for a moment, when I switched on the bathroom light, I thought I was completely blind. All I could see was blotches floating in front of my eyes. I must have screeched or something because Logan was there in an instant.

"What's wrong, Mum?"

"Nothing," I said, gripping the sink, feeling for the taps. I closed my eyes, opened them again, closed them, opened them. I started to see the outlines of things, then dimensions. I'm not blind yet. I called my GP, who referred me to an ophthalmologist, who has a waiting list three months long. I asked for another one, phoned only to learn that he too had a waiting list months long. When you say, "This is an emergency," the receptionists become even less receptive as pickles shoot up their asses. "The doctor's very busy et cetera et cetera . . . go to your local Emergency."

I managed to work, even though my hands were shaking and I kept thinking my reflection was somebody crowding me. It didn't look like me because the person wasn't wearing colour. So I'd get jumpy, looking over my shoulder at this ignoramus of personal space requirements, about to tell her to buzz off, then realize it was me. Hooped earrings are a problem, I keep getting my fingers caught in them because I can't see them. Clients don't like to hand over earrings because they're part of their look, they feel naked without them. Meanwhile I'm ripping their ears off, saying "Sorry" every two seconds. *Nothing* is easily identified, every label has to be scrutinized. French noticed this. I told him I was looking for a carcinogenic ingredient I'd read about, wanted to know if we were using it. This muzzled him; we don't want clients knowing we're putting toxic sludge on their heads. I've been managing with regulars because I make a habit of marking everything on a card and dating it, leaving no room for error. But if some stranger walks in wanting to go red, I'm going to have to fake a seizure or something.

I'm even dreaming in black and white. Saw my mother in her perky red blazer only it was black. She was projectile-vomiting into the toilet in my father's house. I kept waiting for her to get off her knees, but grey fluid continued to spew out of her mouth. I tried to think of something useful to do or say but my tongue was clogging my throat and my knees felt lubed. I've been trying to figure out if this is some kind of repressed memory. Sandrine, at the salon, has been seeing a shrink who hypnotizes her and digs up all kinds of nastiness, like her sister trying to cut off her toes with pinking shears.

Mum wore the perky red blazer during her Wally period. Did she experience projectile vomiting after witnessing the snow blower incident? Did I barge into the bathroom (she always accused me of barging) and find her heaving, then proceed to forget about it? As my father regularly forgot he locked me in darkness? Is forgetfulness a genetic thing?

I took LSD once. It made furniture move in threatening ways. I barricaded myself in a corner, under a table. This colour-blindness is a bit like that. Shadows lurch at me, trip me up, appear cavernous. Food looks fierce, disgusting, dead. My flesh is rat-coloured, as is everybody else's. In hairdressing it's important to comment on what your clients are wearing, say things like I just *love* that outfit, you look *faaabulous* in aubergine, *amaaazing* how it brings out your eyes. Hairdressing is 75 per cent showmanship and 25 per cent skill. On your good days you can sell a bald man a brush. Today, fumbling around in shadows because Kristos keeps the place softly lit so clients notice highlights but not wrinkles, I said I was hung-over—a standard excuse for being spaced out. Partying all night is expected of hairdressers, most of them think they're rock stars, most of them are queers who can't keep their peckers in their pants. Red-eyed and tousled, they show up at work reeking of body odour. Their clients don't mind a bit, they'll take all kinds of abuse from a man. In fact, the more he shouts, "What did you do to your hair, use Sani-Flush for conditioner?" the more the gals like it. French, whose chair is next to mine, regularly insults his clients, and they all want to look like him. He cuts their hair like his hair, all day long. Currently he's into the Mod look, flopsy bangs—Beatles but carefully mussed. So these women come in looking like women and go out looking like Ringo.

So I'm hoping there's some flexibility there, that I can fake it for a while. Except that I have to keep going into the can and sitting in the dark because, with the lights out, my eyes don't have to work so hard. I figure my headache has to do with my brain working over-time trying to figure out what things are. I can't recognize anything at a glance anymore. Even towels are a problem; I can't tell the dirty ones from the clean ones. Same with smocks; I started wrapping a hairy smock around one of those girls who brush after every meal. "Might I have a clean smock?" she asked, looking ready to pass out. *Everything's* unfamiliar. It's as if I'm in a foreign country, only it's no fun this trip. Nobody seems to be noticing though, and I keep smiling. I told Ruby, the slut of a receptionist, to send me more cuts. She sniffed to indicate what's in it for her? She's top tart at the moment, Kristos has been banging her in the back room between cigarettes. The poor fuck doesn't know she's been stealing his money, crumpling receipts and scoring the cash to pay for her Volkswagen Beetle. Receptionists are all-powerful, unfortunately, because they decide who gets what client. They expect bribes, preferably Cartier watches. I cough up a cappuccino for Ruby once in a while but that's my limit. I've been cutting hair for seventeen years, I've seen a few Rubys go by. Even so, watching the gay boys hand her prezzies they get from groupy clients—theatre tickets, fruit baskets, booze—and noticing their bookings sky-rocket puts me in a mean frame of mind. The ass-munching bitch has no idea that, should the necessity arise, they would scalp her fur.

I've been trying to decide when and if I should advise Kristos of my predicament. He's been busy doing updos for a wedding: chignons, French twists. The maids of honour looked fifty, and the blushing bride over sixty. Kristos has this trick of making them lean forward in the chair while he's brushing so their faces are inches from his balls. Then he gets them to sit up, flipping their hair back so they're eye to eye with his nipples, gold chains and hairy chest. They love it. And when he moves around, leaning into them, no one ever says, "Would you mind keeping your jewels to yourself."

Herbert, one of my regulars, nearly brought on a seizure because he said he wanted "a change"—overall colour with red highlights and lowlights. "I'm feeling flirtatious" was how he put it. He's queerer than a three-dollar bill but not offensive, doesn't have that I'm-gay-and-you're-a-hag attitude. I kept him talking so he wouldn't notice me jumping at shadows and fumbling around. Sweat was trickling down my armpits while I mixed some coppery reds for him. Hair colour isn't rocket science. The boxes are numbered, you squeeze the stuff out of a tube, mix it with peroxides you measure with a beaker. It's not like I have to *create* colour. Still, there's guesswork involved, and timing's crucial. Anyway, Herbert was so into telling me about a genitalia-art video that I don't think he noticed my stumbling. "It's really hard to be original with genitalia-art," he advised me. "The big challenge facing genital artists is visual discrimination because, let's face it, penises, unless they're deformed, tend to look alike. The same goes for vaginas." I assumed my "how interesting" expression while struggling to fit papers on his head. The word *genitalia* got French's attention and he immediately wanted to know where he could see the video, then, to impress, informed Herbert that one of his clients has an original Picasso which he, personally, had seen as he was invited to his client's son's bar mitzvah. This got them talking about botched circumcisions. "Some rabbi lopped off a penis," French informed us, fondling the seven earrings tracking up his right ear, "and they tried to raise the kid as a girl, pumped him with hormones, dressed him in pink. I mean, *honestly*, how Draconian."

Kristos felt a need to contribute here. "So you think he'd be better off a man with no prick?"

"You'd be amazed what's being done with plastic surgery these days," French said.

Kristos shoved his blow-dryer into his holster. "A plastic cock? What can you do with a freakin' *plastic cock*?" He winked at one of his fifty-something bridesmaids, who blushed.

At the end of the day I had no idea how Herbert's colour looked. I kept smiling so he'd keep smiling because if you look scared, they panic. I spent a long time blow-drying so he could adjust to whatever I'd done. The cut was good, more layered than usual, which gave him a bit more lift. All of a sudden he jumped up and I thought he was going to start screaming or refusing to pay or something. Instead he kissed me. "You are a *genius*," he said. I felt like I'd missed the plane that crashed.

I walk to the back of what was once my house, trying to remember to breathe. I hoped to find something to salvage here, something for Logan. But everything's grey, black and gnarled. And there's a smell of death. We could be dead.

I spot the sand turtle, empty it, shove it in the car.

The lobotomized truck driver has been charged with careless driving. He'd been driving for fourteen and a half hours. Under federal trucking laws that's one and a half hours longer than is legal. I feel for the guy, he was probably just trying to make a few extra bucks. We've all been there.

Mrs. Pawusiak scurries out. "How coot zis happen?" she demands. "Can you believe it? How coot zis happen?"

"Human error," I offered.

"You coot have been killt."

"We weren't. Did you happen to see who dumped the garbage?"

"You shoot zank Got." Her husband was a cab driver who got stabbed to death outside a Pizza Hut. Ever since, she's been a churchgoer. She told me she's willed her estate to the church and her miniature poodles.

"If you see anyone dumping garbage," I say, "please call me." I scrawl the Lakeview's number on the back of a dominatrix client's card.

Mrs. Pawusiak flaps her hands around. "You can't leave it like zis."

"They're going to 'doze it tomorrow. You might want to keep an eye on your tulips." She's completely paranoid, thinks I stole her delphinium. She's acting concerned because she doesn't want to live next to a dump.

"Zank ze Lort you veren't insite," she says.

I'm hearing squeaks coming from the garbage heap. I lift a corner of the mattress. Underneath is a plastic bag that's moving.

"Rats," Mrs. Pawusiak gasps.

I open the bag and discover three furballs. I lean closer to figure out what they are. They don't have ratty tails. Only one of them is breathing. I scoop it up and feel it shiver in my hands. Its eyes are still closed. We're both blind.

"It's a kitten," I tell Mrs. Pawusiak. She stands back as though the tiny animal might jump out of my hand and go for her throat.

"What colour is it?" I ask.

Mrs. Pawusiak eyes me suspiciously, as though I'm planning a tulip heist.

"What colour is this kitten?" I repeat.

"Grey. It doesn't look grey to you?"

"It does." I kiss the kitten gently on its tiny head. I'm so pleased it's grey, that I'm seeing it like it is, that I don't have to imagine how it is. Although, at this point, I can't even imagine in colour.

Mrs. Pawusiak scrutinizes the garbage. "A bat man who coot do such a zing."

I tuck the kitten into an inside pocket of my jacket. "I guess the litterer didn't want to clog his toilet." Against my heart, Fuzzball begins to purr.

6

They're back in Emergency because her mother says her head's still hurting. There's some psycho screaming really bad words—some words Logan doesn't even know—and flailing his arms around any time somebody goes near him. McKenna says he's a heroin addict, says he's probably on methadone, smoked some crack and is ODing. Logan knows her mother used to take drugs, before she was born, when she went to France and during her biker period. Her mother says some people have addictive personalities, which doesn't mean they're bad people, you just can't rely on them unless they quit, totally, forever. She says Logan's father is addicted to sex and spending money and that's why he doesn't show up most of the time. "Don't take it personally, sweetpea," McKenna says. "He can't help himself, he's weak. It's not that he doesn't love you." Although Logan suspects that her father doesn't love her, especially now that she's older. When she was younger and cuter he'd take her places and pick up girls. He used to say, "Nothing draws chicks like babies." Now that Logan's "a smartass," they rarely do anything except go to movies. And he always takes one of his dipshits along.

Even so, she misses him, wants her dad. Other kids have them.

The only other kid Logan knows who has a single mother is Amber, who's black and taller than all the boys. Amber hates her father, says he's a no-good son-of-a-bitch deadbeat, says he never makes his payments and her mother would like to see him busted up. Logan is glad that McKenna doesn't say horrible things about Payne. She always insists that it's up to Logan to decide if she wants to see him, that she doesn't have to. Once, when she was younger, her father lost her in a mall. He phoned McKenna to come and help him find her. Logan was sitting in the photo booth, spinning around on the stool. She had no idea she'd lost her father. McKenna got all the security guards in the mall looking for her. The guy who found her in the booth smelled of cigarettes and had yellow teeth. Her mother was apoplectic and wouldn't leave her alone with her father for eons after that. But being with her father with her mother around was a drag because McKenna was always sniping at him. He'd get sulky and wouldn't buy Logan nearly as much stuff as when they were alone together, so she asked please please please could I be alone with Dad? She overheard her mother say to her father, "If you let her out of your sight, I will cut off your balls." So he's been pretty careful. Logan finds keeping an eye on him is the best policy. Because he does get talking to people, especially girls.

An old lady on a hospital bed in the corridor keeps moaning, "Oh my God it hurts," and "Lord help me," but nobody's paying any attention to her. They're too busy looking after guys in handcuffs who keep showing up with police officers.

"Why do the nurses look after the prisoners before the old lady?" Logan asks.

"Because the cops are on a clock," McKenna says.

The old lady starts wailing.

"I wonder if she's going to kick off," Logan says.

Her mother shakes her head. "It's probably just a broken hip. It won't kill her."

"Can I peek at Fuzzball again?"

McKenna opens her jacket and Logan gently strokes the kitten's head. They've been feeding her cream from an eyedropper they picked up at the drugstore when they were walking Stanley. Logan warned her mother that cats weren't permitted in hospitals, but McKenna said that, after what Fuzzball had been through, there was no way she was leaving her alone.

"She's asleep again, isn't she?" McKenna asks.

Logan nods. "I'm so glad she's a girl." They'd checked, McKenna had spread her legs and said, "No balls. Good."

Ever since Logan can remember, her mother has told her that boys are stupid, which is why they push and shove and can't concentrate. Ever since she can remember, McKenna has told her that if *anybody* bothers her she must look them in the eye and tell them "BACK OFF!" Logan has done this and for the most part remained bully-free. Although there was one newtbrain who kept pulling on her ponytail, but she took care of him by stabbing his hand with her pencil. He cried and told on her, and Miss Spongle reported the incident to the principal, who phoned McKenna. Her mother didn't give Logan a hard time about it, she just asked why she'd stabbed the boy with a pencil. "He was always pulling my hair," Logan explained. "It hurt." McKenna told the principal that if he couldn't keep boys from pulling her daughter's hair, she personally would come down to the school and stab them with pencils.

But Logan has to believe there are some smart boys out there, with decent concentration spans. She hasn't met any, but she hopes to because she wouldn't mind getting married one day and having a family, since she doesn't have one. Her mother met a smart man in France called Armand who knew how to make cheese and fix scooters—both tasks which require concentration. But he was already married. McKenna says that although most boys are stupid, it's important to keep an open mind because a smart one might turn up one day. What's bothering Logan is that even though she's told Curling Ellsworth to BACK OFF, he's still on her case. Today he informed her that his father has a gun and that he's not afraid to use it. He said his father hunts bears. "That's retarded," Logan said.

"My father's got balls."

"What's that got to do with killing bears?"

"It's got to do with don't fuck with me or my dad."

"Why do you use that word all the time? Can't you think of another word?"

"Why can't you like take a Valium," Curling said, giving her the finger before looking for more slugs to slaughter.

Sometimes Logan feels there's just too much wrong with the world, the weight of it presses down on her.

Once when she was visiting her father, she discovered him with his head between Sheena's legs. Logan knew about giving head because Curling Ellsworth never stops talking about it—that and blowjobs. So Logan knew what was going on—which didn't make it any less disgusting in her opinion—but Sheena started acting even more retarded than usual, scrambling around looking for her panties. Payne just wiped his face and said Logan should knock first. "There's no door on the living room," Logan pointed out.

"Don't be a smartass."

What Logan's noticed is that as long as she acts girlish and says please and thank you and may I all the time, her dad tolerates her. This gets pretty boring.

"Come on, monkey," her mother says. They follow a doctor through swinging doors, then more doors. The doctor's backside is as big as a barn door. That's how McKenna describes clients who want skinny haircuts. They come in with photos of skinny models and say they want to look like them. She says the ones with the biggest backsides always want the skinniest haircuts.

While McKenna explains what's wrong to the doctor, he blows air in and out of his lips as though he's been running and has another relay to go. Logan finds this distracting and hopes Fuzzball doesn't hear it and wake up and start squeaking. The doctor holds up different pamphlets and asks McKenna to name the colours. She says they're all grey, different shades of grey. The doctor sighs as if McKenna is being a bad girl and he just doesn't know what to do with her. He wipes his forehead a couple of times, sucks in his lips, pushes them out again and tells her she has to have a CAT scan. He sends them back into the waiting area, where two baby twins are screaming. Their parents pass them back and forth between them like footballs. The psycho's still shouting bad words and the old lady's still begging the Lord to help her. A nurse with a humongous mole tells McKenna to follow her but doesn't look too excited about Logan tagging along. "Wherever I go, she goes," McKenna says.

"She'll have to wait outside for the CAT scan," the nurse responds. "You don't want her getting radiated."

This freaks McKenna. "Who's going to look after her?"

The nurse with the humongous mole volunteers. While they're waiting she asks Logan retarded questions about school. Logan tries not to stare at her mole while she worries about Fuzzball getting radiated, growing an extra toe or something.

They have to wait around a few more centuries for the doctor to look at the x-ray. The psycho's still shouting and the old lady's still moaning. Beside Logan two zit-faced teenage boys are ogling each other's pizza slices. "You got extra cheese?"

"Guess so."

"It looks like it, man. You got like fuckin' tons of cheese. That's fuckin' great. I should've asked for extra cheese."

"I didn't ask, man, he just gave it to me."

"For two ninety-nine?"

"Guess so."

"Fuckin' awesome."

With pizza in their mouths, they start comparing movie stars' earnings. "He gets like twenty million a picture, man."

"Fuckin' bad, man."

"And now he's fuckin' some Spanish chick."

"Fuckin' A."

There's no question that boys are stupid.

All the doctor says after they follow his backside through the doors again is that McKenna's CAT scan was normal and that she should see an ophthalmologist. When McKenna explains that she can't get in to see one for months, he says they have an eye clinic at St. Mike's and that he will refer her. Then he says, "There is such a thing as hysterical colour-blindness."

"I'm not hysterical."

"You've had an accident, you're in shock."

"I don't think I am. I mean, it's a drag, you know, to have your house flattened, but it's not the end of the world. I mean, we're alive."

"See an ophthalmologist," he repeats.

Logan runs out into the cool night air and does two cartwheels on the grass.

My mother was put in an isolation room with special purified air. Even the anemic food they set in front of her which she couldn't eat was purified. We were only allowed quickie visits while the chemo and total-body radiation destroyed her immune system, leaving her with zip to fight infection. We had to wear gloves, gowns, hats and masks. She couldn't feel our touch or see our faces. She vomited for days, went into a swirl of vertigo, constantly thought she was falling. She lay rigid, with her eyes squeezed shut, keeping her head still, and barely spoke. After a couple of weeks her hair fell out, her mouth blistered, her bowels ulcerated and her blood counts dropped. She got pneumonia, required oxygen and megadoses of antibiotics. She died before the bone marrow transplant. I was supposed to be the donor. I was the perfect match. I was supposed to save her.

All that time she was in the torture chamber, I wanted to ask if she'd ever loved me. I needed to know this before she died. I couldn't understand how you could not be wildly crazy about your child. I still don't understand it, especially since I've had Logan, who is more important to me than breathing. But Mum lay wasted, in agony, and I knew I couldn't ask, that there would forever be this hole where mother-love was supposed to be. Not even Logan can fill it.

I watch her intently colouring and feel as if I'm losing her. She's leaving me behind in this stained, shadowed place.

"Look, Mum, magenta," she says of one of her new crayons. I smile dully in a dull world. Usually I love new crayons—their smell, rainbow colours, perfect nibs. Usually I get as excited about them as she does. Now they're just so much wax.

How am I supposed to tell her I can't see the green of her eyes, the pink of her skin, the honey of her hair? How am I supposed to tell her she's the colour of a rat?

From the moment I knew she was inside me, I was freed of the kind of loneliness that leaves you cold in hot rooms. Now it's back. We're on different planets.

"Are you really colour-blind?" she asks as the chicken fingers arrive. I was hoping the restaurant would distract her. She loves eating here because they have a treasure chest full of junk toys. Just take *one*, I always tell her, which she does.

"I don't know," I reply.

"You told the doctor everything looks grey."

"It's probably temporary."

"Was he ever a porker." She shoves about ten fries in her mouth.

My mother died alone. My father didn't even phone me. My brother was jumping off a mountain in Switzerland. I got to the hospital and found her bed empty, knew it could only mean one thing.

I'd been terrified of the extraction—the big needle they stick into your pelvis to suck out the cells. Staring at her empty bed, I felt guilty for having been afraid.

Fear's useless. You stand there frozen with shit in your pants.

"Can we feed Fuzzball some chicken?" Logan asks.

"She can't eat solids yet, she's just a baby." I feel something wet against my chest. Fuzzball's piss.

A fat-assed politician's wife phoned the salon today to chew me out for cancelling yesterday. She was booked for colour and insisted I was the only one who could do it right. She's one of those clients—and there are many—who, when told their hairdresser is dead, would respond, "So who's going to do my hair?"

I told her to go fuck herself. I wouldn't normally do this, there's no question that my nerves are fried. Ruby immediately reported me to Kristos, who got freakin' mad. I told him about Ruby stealing cash. You take a swipe at me, I swipe back. So she's history. She doesn't bring the salon money, *I* do. Maybe he was bored with stuffing her.

Anyway, I've got to get some fighting spirit where this eye problem is concerned instead of standing here frozen with shit in my pants.

"Is it scary?" Logan asks.

"What?"

"Being colour-blind."

I try to meet her stare without flinching. "Not at all. And anyway, we don't know that I'm colour-blind."

"You look spooked."

"I got hit on the head, that's all, I'll get better. How was school?"

"Curling's dad is suing a doctor because he cut flab off a lady's butt but she got fat again anyway. The doctor says she was eating too much ice cream."

"Has Curling been bothering you?"

"Nope."

"You tell me if he bothers you."

"He's got a gun."

"Curling does?"

"His dad. He shoots bears."

"Curling told you that?"

Logan nods. "So maybe you shouldn't go over there again and make a scene."

"I didn't make a scene."

"Whatever, Mum. Just please don't, okay? I want a chocolate sundae, please please please."

While my mother was dying without telling me, disintegrating and never leaving the house but still phoning to ask if I was all right, I was straddling toilet seats, cutting cocaine on tank lids and snorting between appointments. This isn't lovable. But she didn't know, didn't know that I'd started hitting in my arms, that when I came down hard I'd take Valium, smoke dope. That my nose bled, that post-nasal drip was a constant in my life. "Damn this cold," I'd tell my oblivious clients, who had eyes only for themselves. It was easy to be background. Lying's easy. Telling the truth presents problems.

Once when she phoned, I'd just snorted some garbage from a dealer who'd flooded the cocaine with Borax. My nostrils were glued. "That cold sounds terrible," my mother said. I tried to confess, said I was taking drugs. She responded that I must make sure to buy only brand names, that the generic drugs weren't to be trusted. She said she had to run because the Bay was having a scratch 'n' save day. She loved shopping. Maybe that's why I hate it. Those endless hours standing around, watching her try on outfits. That little pirouette she'd do, the over-the-shoulder glance to assess how it fit in the back.

While she was dying without telling me, I was busy with Diana dos. *Everybody* wanted to look like Di. But they'd never come right out and say it, they'd hem and haw about how they wanted a change, a new look. I'd put on my attentive face and suggest, "A variation on the Princess Diana theme?" Their eyes would ignite and I'd go to the back to mix Di's colours, which I'd stapled to a card for easy reference. But first I'd go to the can for a snort.

Occasionally I'd get a harpy who bitched that she didn't look like Diana after the do (forgetting that she herself weighed four hundred pounds). So I'd put on my concerned face and do a few mirror tricks to show off the most Di-looking bits. French and I have this routine. If one of us gets a client who wants to suck blood from a turnip, the other will jump in and exude over the do. This was crucial during the Di period. "You remind me of somebody . . . ," he'd say, fingering his diamond pinkie rings (gifts from clients) to suggest he had to think about it. "I know. Princess Diana. You remind me of Princess Diana." That (a man's word) would usually silence the turnip-suckers. They'd waddle to the front desk, and I'd speed to the can for a snort. My record for Di dos in one day was nine. I was getting rich. At two hundred bucks a gram, I had to.

What a waste, waste, waste. Maybe my mother knew it, smelled it on me. I offered *her* a Di do, figured it would be a nice change from that relentless flip. The woman was a fifties hostage, chained to rollers.

All this time I knew I wasn't worth loving, and that my mother was only phoning to confirm that I wasn't dead, and to offer helpful hints regarding career changes. I told her I didn't have time to look for a career, I was too busy making a living. She, who'd never had a job, had this idea that I should be an interior decorator—like there aren't enough of those. I disappointed her, the shopping queen, which is why I faked having a fabulous life and told her nothing of my reality. A resentment builds when you can't speak the truth for fear of condemnation. You get walled in, you can't move. You scream in silence.

After the funeral, Lester told me if I wanted any of her things I'd better come and get them, otherwise he was going to give it all to charity. Not only were the closets crammed with her clothes but I found bags of stuff under beds. Many of the items had never been worn, were still tagged.

Logan rummages in the treasure chest and pulls out a small jigsaw puzzle.

"What's it of?" I ask her.

"Can't you tell?"

I shake my head.

"It's an octopus, and starfish and stuff." She holds the puzzle inches from my face.

"Nice," I say, although it's all grey squiggles to me.

I'm trying to work on the list of claims but Logan's got the TV blaring. She's watching *French Kiss* on the movie channel because she wants to see France.

There's something really disturbing about trying to remember what you once possessed that's currently a slag pile. You get twitchy remembering stuff you'd forgotten that suddenly you can't live without.

I feed Fuzzball more cream with the eyedropper, stare down at her trusting, mousy little face and wonder what colour her eyes will be. When she can see, she too will leave me behind on planet smog.

"Look, Mum, she's in Paris!"

I stare at a grey Meg Ryan looking lost. The winding streets are familiar to me, but the buildings and shadows merge.

"Look, Mum, the Eiffel Tower, she walked right by the Eiffel Tower without seeing it."

I sit on the bed beside my baby, pull her to me, kiss the top of her head. Smell her. She still smells the same. If I close my eyes and just feel, smell, listen, *stop looking*, maybe I can feel part of her world again.

8

"I smell cat pee," Logan says.

McKenna's got her eyes closed, not like she's sleeping but like she's in pain. She's not even watching the movie. "She's gotta go when she's gotta go."

"Are you going to sleep with her?"

"Of course."

"What if you crush her?"

"I slept with you when you were tiny and I never crushed you."

"When will she open her eyes?"

"I don't know. In a week or so, maybe. Normally her mum would lick them open. Fuzzball's going to have to figure it out by herself."

The movie's pretty boring. Logan doesn't see what's so great about Paris, it just looks crowded. And she doesn't get why the air-head is chasing her husband after he told her he had another woman and didn't want the airhead around. That would be like being forced to play with Curling Ellsworth. Dotty's always trying to get the kids to "play nicely." Like *nice* is even in Curling's vocabulary.

Something weird was going on today with Mr. Beasley. He was yelling at Dotty for some reason. She was crying and then sulked in the kitchen for like an hour, mainlining Oreos. Katey peed her pants and Mr. Beasley took her to the toilet, giving Curling the opportunity to beat up on Russell who's skin and bone and only interested in fibre optics. "Leave him alone," Logan warned, "or I'll tell Dotty."

"I'm not scared of that *bovine*," Curling said.

Logan wasn't exactly sure what "bovine" meant.

"Mum. . . ?"

McKenna keeps her eyes closed. "Ummm."

"What's bovine?"

"Cow." She opens her eyes. "Did somebody call you that?"

"Nope."

"If somebody calls you that, you tell them you've always admired cows as they produce milk which is crucial to our survival on planet Earth."

"Nobody called me that."

"Okay." She closes her eyes again. "I picked up your sand turtle. It's in the car."

"When're they going to start building our house?"

"Soon."

The airhead walks past the Eiffel Tower again.

"Can we paint it purple?"

"On the outside?"

"Lilac. That would be nice."

There's knocking at the door. McKenna doesn't open her eyes.

"There's somebody at the door, Mum."

"I know. Leave it."

"It might be the police or somebody."

"It's nobody. Nobody knows we're here."

"McKenna . . . ? I know you're in there."

"It's Dad."

Her mother's eyes pop open and she swears under her breath.

"I'll let him in," Logan offers.

McKenna jumps up. "No, you won't." She flings open the door and stares at him.

"Hi," he says.

McKenna continues to stare at him, wearing her concrete face. Logan always fears this expression because anything could be under it: explosives, live wires, molten lava. When her mother's wearing her concrete face, Logan tries to look busy. She grabs the champion mare and starts to comb her mane.

"Can I come in?" Payne inquires.

"No."

"Come on, Mick, it's raining out here."

"Mum, don't you think we should let him in? He'll catch cold."

"Hi, sweetness," Payne says to Logan. McKenna steps back, allowing him entry, then slams the door.

"What are you doing here?"

"I brought these," he says, handing a 7-Eleven bag to Logan. She pulls out two bags of marshmallows.

"You brought us *miniature marshmallows*?" McKenna demands. "What are we supposed to do with *miniature marshmallows*?"

"Give me a break, McKenna. I only had five bucks on me."

"Oh, out, out, out, I want you out!"

"Mum, can't he stay for a bit? He can watch the movie with me. You're not watching it."

McKenna groans and leans her forehead against the wall.

"The truth is," Payne admits, "Sheena threw me out. I think it's over."

"Hurrah!" Logan shouts, jumping on the bed. God *has* answered her prayers, he *is* listening. Maybe this means he'll terminate Curling Ellsworth.

McKenna faces Payne. "So what are you doing *here*?"

"I came to make sure my daughter was alright in this dive you've set her up in. What's the movie, honey?"

"*French Kiss*. It's totally boring but it's set in France."

He looks at McKenna. "It's set in France and you're not watching it? Aren't there any scooters in it?"

"Very funny."

Logan points at the TV. "Look, Mum, they're going to Nice. You love Nice, that's where you met the cheese guy."

"It smells of piss in here," Payne observes.

"Mum found a kitten at our house."

"Maybe you want to get it a litter box."

"Maybe you want to mind your own business," McKenna snaps.

Logan hops up and down on the bed, waving the marshmallows. "You're not supposed to fight in front of me, remember?" Stanley starts barking.

"It's a frigging animal shelter in here," Payne says, checking himself out in the mirror.

"So what did you have in mind, Payne?" McKenna asks. "Why don't you fill me in on your plans."

He shrugs. "I'm maxed out on my cards. A cheque's in process."

"So you plan to stay here?"

"Just for a night or so. Till she cools off. It's her place, right? I can't force my way in there."

"It'll be fun, Mum. Like a sleepover. There's lots of room here, Dad. And the bathroom's totally cool. It's got a movie-star mirror in it."

"Oh I *love* those," Payne says.

"And a pink tub!"

"Are you kiddin' me? Fantastic. We got to get you some fantabulous bath toys. Maybe tomorrow we'll go shopping."

"With no money?" McKenna crosses her arms.

"Like I said, a cheque's in process."

"I'd like one of those wind-up dolphins," Logan says. "Those are excellent."

"Then we'll get you one, peachypie."

"Here's the deal," McKenna states. "On the floor. Get blankets from the motel. *We* take priority in bathroom usage."

"No problemo."

"Look, Mum, the airhead's in a vineyard! And there's a little stone house. Mum, look! Is that like the one you'd buy if it wasn't so expensive?"

McKenna squints at the TV. "Something like that, honeybun."

"I like our house better," Logan says. "Especially after we paint it purple. And you know what, Dad? We're putting up wallpaper."

"Oh I *love* wallpaper," Payne says.

McKenna lies on her bed in a fetal position and puts a pillow over her head.

I watch him sleep, remember lying beside him, my arms gripping his ribs, my forehead pressed between his recently pumped lats and traps—the human shield. He seemed superhuman because he wasn't a druggie, and everybody else I knew was. We were weak, took drugs to be accepted, whereas he didn't need to be part of a crowd. This seemed like strength to me. He even tried to get me to go to rehab, like it was that simple, like you could walk through the doors and get cured. He'd never known self-hatred, was too busy gulping protein shakes, checking out how his ass looked in leather pants. But he didn't snore and this scored major points in my book. A good lay, maintains good personal hygiene and doesn't keep you awake while his glottis flaps around.

In the dark the clay look isn't a turnoff. In the dark I want to wind myself around his lats and traps, surround myself with his flesh. He owns that piece of me that fit so neatly inside him. You don't show that to many people, and the ones who see it never forget it. They have that on you. They've seen you naked, vulnerable, pathetic, needy. In lust. And you hate them for it. Because you want that self back. That's private. The veneer you give away, but the blood and guts of you, you want that private. Sometimes, when we're fighting, I'm thinking he's thinking about my blood and guts, and getting off knowing he's had that kind of power over me. A power I didn't have over him. Because he was busy chasing pussy while my knees were shaking just thinking about him. The man does not know how to feel, has no interest in it, doesn't make him look good. Women are just another outfit to him and he wants a lot of them, preferably young in spandex because *they* make heads turn. And there'll always be more of them because he'll spend whatever cash he's got and they'll think, *Wow, he's so gallant, with most guys you're lucky if you get a coffee.*

I wish I could stop hating him. It's pointless, draining, suffocating.

I think if he wasn't the father, if he didn't own that piece as well, I could probably stop wanting him impaled. But the fact that he's there—still—causing trouble, interfering, makes me unable, *completely* unable to forgive and forget.

He left me in a pool of my own vomit. I'd drunk a bottle of scotch and smoked dope to soften a landing after taking too much crap because he hadn't called when he said he would. I knew he was out with the tightass bitch who called me disgraceful, which I was. He's always gone for the ones who put on airs, with mouths tighter than cats' asses. Educated. Like they went to community college and learned how to file.

This bitterness is bad news. Everybody knows the bile shoots up your throat into your brain, leaving you just plain nasty, like my father.

Time to shower. Leave the bathroom lights out, give the kitten a sponge bath because she has no mama to lick her clean.

I constantly have other people's hair on me, under my nails, in my belly button, between my toes. Daily I shed other people's hair. Towelling off, I still find foreign strands clinging to me.

I barked at one of the assistants today, another thing I wouldn't normally do. She's a bit strange—maybe slightly retarded—didn't deserve the abuse. But she's slow to sweep and it drives me nuts.

I'm ankle deep in hair before she tunes in. She's pregnant again, she told me, this will be her third abortion. I think my jaw dropped. I mean, how do you let yourself get pregnant *three* times, which is why I think she might be retarded. Anyway, I explained as nice as pie that if she didn't get off her ass and sweep, she wouldn't be able to afford an abortion. That's when the sob show started. French got all concerned, offered her Kleenexes while zinging me dirty looks. He's a sweep-slouch himself, and professional slob. I'm always cleaning up his debris because it's always creeping over to my side—used capes, brushes, combs, papers. And he wastes product, overmixes, uses the wrong peroxide, too much neutralizer, too many towels. We've lived side by side for years now. Hostile neighbours.

Anyway, while he was busy comforting Little Miss Spread-her-legs and taking his twelfth aspirin of the day for his chronic margarita hangover, his client got burns on her head because he left the mix on too long. I took pleasure from this, *his* error, which suggests that the bile has already shot up my throat into my brain.

Payne switches on the light, catching me naked. "What are you doing?" I screech.

"I didn't know you were in here, the light's out."

"I prefer the dark."

"It's pitch black."

"Just get out."

"Mac, I need to whiz."

"Wait outside." Drowning in white blotches, I fumble for the switch and turn it off.

He saw me naked. Not the body he used to know but this newer version, with the elasticized waist. This isn't fair. He, of course, still works out constantly and doesn't have a pucker on him.

"I'm sorry," he says outside the door, "I didn't know you were in there. How was I supposed to know you were in there? It's four o'clock in the morning, for fucksake."

"Use the parking lot," I croak, strangled by my ugliness, my stupidity, my blindness.

"McKenna . . ."

I lock the door for emphasis. I will hide in here. In the dark.

10

Logan gets a ride to school in her father's BMW. This has never happened before. She makes him stop beside the schoolyard, then keeps him talking so he doesn't drive off right away. She wants Molly and Brittany to see that her dad drives an expensive car. He asks about lunch hour, says he'll pick her up, they'll go to Mickey-dees. "That would be excellent," Logan says, then quickly kisses him on the cheek—which she never does—hoping that Molly and Brittany are watching.

"We should spend some time together, you and me," her dad says.

"Just us?"

"Just us."

"Cool."

Then he takes off and the kids are filing inside. Probably didn't even see him.

Miss Spongle has them making thermometers out of construction paper, cutting aluminum foil for the mercury and estimating different temperatures around the world. When Logan takes this opportunity to mention that this is the twenty-sixth consecutive year that the planet has been warmer than usual and that world scientists are warning that the consequences for the human race will be dire in as little as twenty years, Miss Spongle snatches Logan's thermometer and gets everyone to look at it. "Look at how neatly she's printed the numbers," she says. Logan feels them looking at her, not the thermometer, and hating her for always getting things right, and not giving a rat's ass about greenhouse gases. "And perfectly spaced," Miss Spongle adds.

Logan stares out the window and tries to believe that really really one day she will no longer have to go to school. Or Dotty's stinking after-school daycare.

Nina, the porker with the endless supply of chocolate bars and chips hidden in her desk, quickly shoves something in her mouth, which Miss Spongle sees. "Nina, how many times do we have to go over this? No food in class." She holds out her hand. Nina passes her some of her stash, although Logan knows there's plenty more where that came from. Molly and Brittany snicker, and Oscar, the boy Logan stabbed with a pencil, makes oinking noises.

At lunch hour Logan stands by the fence closest to the street to ensure that her father doesn't miss her. Her legs get tired but she's afraid that if she sits, he won't be able to see her. She shifts her weight from one foot to the other, and hops a bit to prevent pins and needles. Her stomach rumbles because normally she buys lunch in the cafeteria. Molly and Brittany are skipping rope with a posse of other girls. Logan thinks that skipping is completely retarded, almost as retarded as hopscotch, although at least with hopscotch there's numbers involved, and taking aim. Logan always wins, so nobody likes playing with her. And then there's all the stupid boy games, which are even worse: throwing balls, hitting balls, bouncing balls. *Yawn*.

McKenna always says she doesn't think that she, personally, learned anything in school—except about being beaten up. She says, if it weren't the law, she'd take Logan out of school. She says that if she'd learned something in school—and didn't have to work for a living—she'd home-school Logan. But Logan isn't wild about this idea. School's boring but she doesn't think being with her mother twenty-four hours a day would be so hot. Her mother gets too fussed about things. Math problems, for example. She'll panic the second she sees numbers. "You know what I'm like with math," she'll say. Logan likes numbers, totals. Summing things up. Numbers don't lie.

Her mother wouldn't come out of the bathroom this morning. Her father kept knocking on the door but her mother said she wouldn't come out until he was gone. She let Logan in to brush her teeth but wouldn't let her turn the lights on. "Why not?" Logan asked.

"It hurts my eyes."

"How am I supposed to see anything?"

"*I* can see."

"Mum, there's no windows, there's no daylight or anything."

"There's light from under the door."

"There is not."

"Alright, fine, turn on the lights."

When Logan did her mother groaned like somebody'd clubbed her or something, then covered her eyes with her hands.

The bell goes. Lunch is over and she hasn't eaten and they have art this afternoon. She considers feigning sickness and getting the office to call McKenna. But then her mother would get all worked up about Logan being sick, and her mother's acting so weird anyway she doesn't think this would be appropriate. Better just to paint a bowl of fruit or something.

She looks up and down the street one last time. For a minute last night she thought her father loved her. When he called her peachypie. That's what she thought. Just for a minute.

11

In the course of a normal day, Asian hair is to be avoided because it's tough, wears you out, snaps back at you, in your face, up your nose, even crawls into your pores. Colour-blind, Asian hair's the cut of choice, because it's black and straight. What you see is what you cut. I'm doing a whole busload of it. They're going to Niagara Falls. *Nihao*, I say to them. *Nihao*, they say back.

I took Fuzzball to my eyebrow-scratching vet this morning to make sure she wasn't going to die on me. He weighed her, fingered her, scratched an eyebrow and deduced that, before I found her, she'd probably been without food or drink for forty-eight hours. He instructed me to feed her an overpriced feline development formula every three hours. After each feeding, I'm supposed to rub her butt with a damp Kleenex to stimulate, as he puts it, "elimination." "She's been peeing on her own," I told him.

"You want to keep her regular. Their mothers lick their sphincters to make them eliminate. And to clean them, of course. Feed her through the night, every three hours. She's very underdeveloped, think of her as a preemie." He checked her ears for mites.

"Are you saying that if I don't feed her every three hours, she'll die?"

He scratched. "It's a possibility."

So that's what I've been doing, mixing the formula, drawing it into a syringe and pumping it into her. The good news is that she loves it.

"Is it normal for her to sleep all the time?" I asked.

He nodded. "Like any newborn."

"Is it normal for her paws to be furless?"

"Yes."

"When will she start looking like a cat instead of a hamster?"

"Three weeks or so, if all goes well."

She's making her squeaking noises again. Fortunately she's being drowned out by French yabbering to one of his groupies about some fruit bar he went to, and Kristos playing his all-time favourite Sonny and Cher CD. "It's a classeec," he assures us, singing along to "I've Got You, Babe." I check my watch. It's feeding time.

The parasite insurance guy called to tell me that someone has been dumping on my property and that the insurance company cannot be held responsible and therefore will not pay the cost of clearing the garbage. I told him I'd take care of it, that they should just get on with building my house and sending a cheque for living expenses. I don't know what adjusters do all day—sit around drinking java, dreaming up excuses for not paying insurance claims. I said, "How hard is it to approve a seedy motel? It's not like we're staying at the Park Plaza." He said he'd look into it. That made me feel a lot better.

Little Miss Spread-her-legs isn't talking to me, or sweeping around my chair. I'm going to have Asian hair crawling in every orifice. My client's going on about a vacation she had recently during which she was pursued by a married man. She found this shocking. I try to look shocked. One night his zombie-drinking wife tucked in early, leaving him alone with the Chinese girl. Sitting at the bar, he "put his face close" to hers. She told him this was not acceptable. He responded, "People *do* kiss, you know."

"But you are married," she reminded him. My thought was, Why didn't you just belt the dirtball? But these girls are polite. She left the bar, took refuge in her room, wandered out onto the balcony, and what do you know, the dinglepuss was standing on the neighbouring balcony, stark naked. "When are you going to take *your* clothes off?" he shouted over the roar of the air conditioner.

"He ruin whole vacation," she tells me. I appear saddened as more of her hair shoots into my eyes.

Payne called, said he was taking Logan to lunch. He's being nice to her so I won't boot him out. Maybe having lunch with the dullard will make her feel special for five minutes. Maybe it's good that Sheena has turfed him. Logan won't have to compete with pussy, at least not for twenty-four hours. I have a hunch I have to loosen up on the Payne deal and not ban him from the premises. Because I know from experience she'll spend her life yearning for Daddy, *believing* in Daddy, even though his affection is as changeable as his rubbers. And she'll probably let her lovers take over where he left off. I know it took me forever to figure it out. I was sitting around his messy apartment, after he'd split for some important meeting with a girl in spandex, thinking I should get off my butt and clean, since he didn't know the meaning of the word—or better yet, do something with my life, which was spinning around in such tiny circles any minute it was going to shoot up my ass—when I realized he expected me to clean up after him. Actually, I don't think he consciously expected it. If you'd asked him if he thought his girlfriend should clean his toilet he'd say, "No way." I'd already posed the question, "Who do you think cleans up around here, the toilet fairy?" He'd said that he personally didn't care about mess, never used to think about it until I started showing up regularly. Mess was my problem, he told me. I invented it so I could have something to nag him about. Wow, we're talking woman seeking penance for losing Daddy's love. We're talking damaged.

I don't want this for my daughter.

My next client isn't Asian, unfortunately, and tells me that she wants "a completely different look." I consider suggesting she put a paper bag over her head. Instead I hand her some styling magazines to browse. "See if there's something that strikes you," I say, knowing that she's expecting miracles, that people who want completely different looks want completely different lives. Before zipping into the back room to feed Fuzzball, I take a quick gander at my list and see that I've got two fluff 'n' puffs and an updo before I can pick up Logan. The hoping-for-miracles client is going to take time since I don't even know what colour her hair is, and lots of stroking, meaning my baby's going to be left waiting again. I stop in the can and turn off the lights, feeling a panic attack pending. It's bad enough that Logan has me for a mother; with screwed-up eyesight I'll be completely useless. I keep hoping she'll meet a decent friend, someone from a good home where she could go after school instead of Dotty's shelter for the dysfunctional. What's a lawyer's kid doing in a budget daycare anyway? Shouldn't the prodigy be somewhere expensive where his genius can be explored, his unique talents cultivated? I said this to the numbnuts when I went over to his palais to tell him to get his kid to lay off mine. Mr. Ellsworth said, "Do I detect snobbery? Do I detect an innate resentment of those who have succeeded where you could not?"

I nearly flattened him. Logan was in the car, bouncing up and down to get my attention. The prodigy was nowhere in sight, must have been hiding somewhere, with his finger up his nose, trying to locate his brain.

I walk into blinding light again. French is telling his exploding-implant-in-airplane story. It's one of his favourites.

The hoping-for-miracles client points to a shot of an anorexic model with an asymmetric cut which suits the anorexic's angular and fat-free face. "Something like this," the jowly client says. I put on my pensive, considering face, feel her hair, compliment her on her natural colour—even though it's all grey to me—because if she wants highlights, I'm toast. "I think we can work a variation on that theme," I tell her.

12

Her mother's late again. Everybody else has been picked up. Logan waits inside Dotty's front porch, watching rain splatter into puddles and form rivers in the cracked front walk. Dotty's gone shopping so there's only Mr. Beasley, stinking of dead rat. He stands behind Logan, with his hands on her shoulders. She can feel his crotch against her back.

"Not a day for playing outside," he observes. Logan doesn't respond. She doesn't want his hands on her shoulders or his crotch against her back but, if she tells him this, he'll get testy and call her a fussy little girl. She's already in trouble with Dotty because she was chewing gum she got from Nina in return for writing the temperatures on her thermometer. The after-school kids aren't supposed to bring gum to the daycare because the little kids can choke on it. Logan was very careful not to chew in front of Dotty, but she forgot about Curling and his big yob. "That's *verboten*!" he announced, pointing at her mouth.

Mr. Beasley offers Logan some Smarties. "No, thank you," she says.

"Don't you like candy?"

"Not before dinner."

"Oh, what a good little girl." He pats her head.

Logan sees her mother's car and gets ready to bolt, but Mr. Beasley restrains her. "Give us a hug," he says, bending down. She does, quickly, holding her face as far from his as possible.

Her mother pushes open the car door from inside. "Get in, honeybun, sorry I'm late. You don't have your raincoat. Let's go get you a raincoat."

At Zellers her mother insists that a red raincoat is black and keeps asking Logan if she's sure she wants a black raincoat. Next McKenna buys a baseball bat. Logan's never seen her mother play baseball. Normally her mother despises any game that involves chasing balls. "What do you want that for?" Logan asks.

McKenna shrugs. "I just want one."

"Why, though?"

"I might want to play sometime."

"You never play."

"Logan, just give me a break, alright? Are you hungry? I want to cook you a proper meal tonight. Spaghetti. Wouldn't you like some spaghetti?"

"That would be excellent. And garlic bread."

"You got it."

They stop at the Bun King for a baguette and Danishes, and croissants for the morning. But then they drive to Grandpa's. "Why are we going here?" Logan asks.

"We need pots and pans. He never uses them."

Grandpa doesn't answer the door. McKenna bangs on it, calling, "Dad!" They see him peer out the living-room window. He opens the door just a crack. "What now?"

"Can we borrow some pots and pans?" McKenna asks. "There's zip at the motel."

He says nothing but lets them in. On his TV a shoot-out's in progress; guys in leather jackets scramble around cars. It's very loud, and Logan starts to turn it down. "Don't touch that," Grandpa shouts, farting one of his poisonous farts. He always acts like somebody else farted and he's just an innocent bystander. Before his dog died, he blamed the farts on him. Once Logan asked her mother why her grandfather farted all the time. McKenna said he farts when he gets excited. Logan doesn't think Lester knows the meaning of excited. He's always crabby. Like right now she can hear him in the kitchen grumbling about the pans. "I need that one," he says.

"What do you mean, 'need it'?" McKenna argues. "It's got dust on it, you never use it."

"How would you know what I use?"

"Dad, all you eat is deli meats."

"And pie," Logan offers, joining them, noting a pie on the table. He only eats the middle, digs it out with a spoon. Logan remembers when he was shitting blood. Her mother chewed out the doctors at the hospital because they kept shoving things up Grandpa's butt. After that, McKenna warned him that he had to eat fibre.

Her mother pulls out another pan.

"I need that," he says.

"Okay, why don't you tell me what you don't need?" She rummages in the cupboard. "There's a zillion pans here, Dad, you can't use them all."

"Aliminium gives you Alzheimer's," he says.

"What about the egg poacher, can we take that?"

"Take take take, what else are you going to steal from me?" He spoons some pie. A blueberry sticks to his chin.

"This isn't stealing," McKenna points out, "it's borrowing. I'll give them back when we get set up in the new house."

"What's wrong with the old one?"

"It burned down, remember?"

"That's a good story, you stick to it." He eats more pie. "Earl Pempers torched his own hardware store and look where it got him."

McKenna stands, a pan in each hand. "Why are you so horrible? For one second can you not be so horrible? My daughter's here. She's hungry. I need to cook her dinner."

He waves the spoon, dismissing her, sending a blueberry across the room.

At the Lakeview her mother tries to make dinner but keeps discovering she's missing ingredients, ingredients they had at home. She keeps saying, "Oh well, we can do without that," until she realizes that they don't even have garlic so she can't make garlic bread, which is Logan's favourite. She decides to fry them an omelette instead but slashes her thumb cutting onions. Logan doesn't notice this right away because her mother doesn't swear or anything, just stares at her bleeding hand.

"Run it under cold water," Logan orders, but her mother doesn't move.

"It should be red," McKenna says.

Logan grabs her mother's hand and runs it under the tap. "Do we have any bandaids?"

Her mother pulls her hand away from the water and holds the thumb inches from her face. "It should be red." She starts squeezing the wound, making more blood pour out of it.

"Stop it!" Logan shouts, grabbing a dishtowel and wrapping it around the thumb. "Stop acting so weird."

"Am I acting weird? I'm sorry."

"We don't have any disinfectant or anything."

"I'll be alright. Don't worry, lovey, I'll be fine."

There's no way her mother will be fine. She looks like she's been invaded by the body snatchers or something. She goes into the bathroom and turns on the taps, which means she's crying and doesn't want Logan to hear. McKenna doesn't turn on the light and it weirds Logan out that her mother is crying in the dark. She switches it on, causing her mother to shriek, "Don't do that!" Logan quickly turns it off again.

"I'm sorry, monkey. It's just that the lights hurt my eyes."

"I don't understand why lights hurt your eyes all of a sudden."

"I don't either. It's something to do with the concussion. I'll get better."

Logan leaves her in there, doesn't know what to do about her, doubts she is going to get better. There's a knock on the door and her father's voice. Logan looks to see if McKenna is coming out of the bathroom. "Dad's at the door," Logan informs her. There is a pause before McKenna says, "Okay, let him in." It surprises Logan to hear this response. But then she didn't tell her mother that her father didn't show up for lunch. She didn't tell her because she knew she'd have a cow.

The first thing he says is, "Sorry, peachypie, about lunch. Did you grab a sandwich?"

Logan looks to see if her mother has heard this, which she has because her eyes bug out as she looks from Logan to Payne, from Payne to Logan. "Didn't you guys have lunch together?"

"Couldn't make it," Payne explains. "Car trouble."

"Car trouble?"

"You don't believe me? Call the garage."

"So you mean she was *waiting* for you? You didn't phone the school?"

"I don't know the name of the school. What the fuck happened to your hand?"

"You couldn't take a *cab*?" McKenna demands. "What's the matter with you?"

Logan doesn't want to be here, she wants to be home with Donkey and her plastic animals.

"I thought maybe we could all go out for dinner," Payne says. "You feel like going out, peachypie?"

"Step outside, please," McKenna says, wearing her concrete face.

"What?"

"Outside. *Now*. Logan, we'll be back in a sec. I just need to talk to your dad in private for a minute." She pushes him out the door. Logan hurries to the window and watches them through the venetians. Her mother keeps shoving her father until they're on the other side of the parking lot. He looks around, as though afraid someone's watching. McKenna starts jabbing her finger into his leather jacket. Logan opens the window a crack to hear better.

"You can't do to her what you did to me," her mother says. Her father mutters something. He keeps holding up his hands and shrugging. "She'll *forgive* you!" her mother shouts. "She will *always* forgive you. That's who she is." He says something else and starts to walk away. Her mother chases him and starts pounding his back. He turns around and grabs her wrists. She struggles for a minute then goes limp, just hangs there like a rag doll. Mr. Bluxom, the hotel manager with the wandering eye, approaches them and says loudly, "We don't tolerate domestic violence here." McKenna stands and mumbles something. Apparently satisfied, Mr. Bluxom nods and walks away, looking over his shoulder to make sure they don't go at it again. They stand very still, as though if they move they'll fall off the planet. After a few minutes, McKenna starts speaking, very quietly now. Logan returns to the swirling carpet to exercise her horses. She offers the mare the apple, and considers eating one of the Danishes they bought, since she hasn't eaten all day. But she's not really hungry. She has that stomach-stuffed-with-marbles feeling. She thinks of the Russian beluga whale again, starving herself to death. What Logan's noticed is that when things go wrong, they can go more wrong. You'd think there'd be a stop to it, that only so many things could go wrong. She presses the button on the dancing daisies music box and watches them pop up and down and twirl to "In the Mood."

13

I've suddenly got night vision. Even through my dirty windshield I can see the coons picking over the garbage dumped on my lawn. And Mrs. Pawusiak's Virgin Mary squatting in the tulips.

I finish my coffee and insert another Edith Piaf CD.

Non, je ne regrette rien!

My house is history. Just so much airspace.

I keep trying to breathe deeply, think of nothing, quiet the racket inside my skull. But as usual I'm chased by memories I don't want. They're rooted deep in my brain and I'm constantly stumbling over the little shits. I can be thinking about something else entirely and then *oops*, I'm ambushed by that toxic memory again.

This watch, for instance. Payne gave it to me, it's got an inscription on the back: *with oodles of love, Payne*. Like what is that supposed to mean? Even at the time I thought it was lame, but I was so thrilled he bought me something; I thought, Gee, maybe this means he really loves me and is committed and will start cleaning his own toilet. I didn't even like the watch. After he dropped me, I stored it in a drawer (didn't throw it out because I knew it cost a few bucks). I replaced it with a Swatch that lasted about a year. I tried Timex, then a Cardinal. They all broke down while his gaudy Seiko went on ticking in the drawer. Burnt out from watch-shopping, I put it back on. Every time I strap it to my wrist, I see his face.

Quand je suis dans tes bras . . .

My shoplifting career, what was that about? I'd lift things I didn't even want. Like herbal teas. There's an upscale coffee joint near the salon which burns us for cappuccinos and stale pastries. I'd slip a box of camomile into my pocket while the attitudinal staff were busy frothing. I stacked the boxes in my kitchen but never drank the stuff. I liked the look of the boxes, very flowery, with meaningful phrases printed on them like, "Saying nothing . . . sometimes says the most." That was Emily Dickinson. My favourite was Martin Luther's "Faith is permitting ourselves to be seized by the things we do not see." Bugged out, I could ponder that one for hours.

Three hours are up, time to feed Fuzzball. Fortunately, with x-ray vision, I don't need light to measure her formula.

I was caught stealing wrinkle cream from a drugstore. Actually, it was called "revitalizing cream." I felt I could use revitalizing but didn't believe the goop would work, and decided it was criminal that it cost thirty-nine bucks. So I pocketed it, did my usual nonchalant browse of magazines, then headed casually for the door. On the sidewalk, an action-hero security guard grabbed my elbow and said, "Come with me." I tried acting surprised, but he wasn't having any. He hauled me to the basement, sat me on a folding chair and started writing his report. When he asked for ID, I pretended to look for it in my purse, then said I must have forgotten my wallet at home. I wasn't seriously messed up but definitely scatty, kept blurting things like, "Oh, I must've forgotten I had the cream on me," or "Oh, I guess I just got distracted reading magazines."

"The police will get your name if you don't give it to me," he said flatly. "Show me your ID. I'm allowed to grab it off you if I want. I'm being nice."

I handed it over, smiling meekly.

"There's nothing you can do," he added, looking closely at my driver's licence, which made me wonder if he could read. "I caught you red-handed."

I tried to think of bribes: free haircuts, the ten bucks I had on me, a blowjob? I had reservations about this option.

A police officer arrived, short, squat and pent up. He took down the particulars, worked the phone, asked more questions, bonded with the security guard, then said, "You understand you could go to jail for this?"

"Yes," I murmured, trying to remember if I had any substances on me. I hoped my lipstick wasn't smudged and my mascara wasn't crumbling because the ugly truth is, pretty girls get better treatment. I was wearing a short skirt and crossed and uncrossed my legs a few times.

The action hero and the squat cop huddled briefly, then turned to me. "The store is going to be nice to you today," the cop said. "They're going to let you go."

"Really? Oh thank you so much, that's . . . that's way cool." I was in dire need of a snort, was getting jittery.

"You're free to go," the cop said.

"Okay. *Fabulous*. Thank you *so* much." I think I backed out of the room.

So no more shoplifting. One of the calls the cop made was to Lester, don't ask me why. Maybe he wanted a character reference. Don't suppose he got it. Anyway, I've never heard the end of it.

A guy in a trenchcoat, walking something short and hairy, stops and inspects the garbage on my lawn. His mutt has a good sniff. What are *they* doing out at three in the morning? He reaches into the pile and pulls out a busted lamp. He holds it up, appraising it, then tosses it back on the pile. His dog pisses on it.

Something weird's going on with my hands: things don't feel right. I don't know if it's because they're grey or what. Hair, in particular, is giving me the creeps. A hairdresser is supposed to feel a client's hair, note its shape, texture, weight. It all feels dirty and slimy to me, full of bugs; I don't want to go near the stuff. What's scary is I'm pining for a snort. Little Miss Spread-her-legs was passing around liquid ecstasy, didn't offer me any of course, since I'm supposedly reformed and her foe. But I wanted it. Instead I had to listen to Sandrine talk about getting her aura cleansed. She's already had it healed, now she's on a maintenance program. She's very impressed with the aura-healing folk at the Gentle Breeze Association because, she tells us, they've "*really* researched aura healing" and "*really* believe in it," so much so that they cashed in their RRSPs and sold their houses to invest in aura-healing tools. The gist of the thing seems to be that we all have these holes in our auras. If we clean our auras, we get rid of the holes and stop attracting other people with holes in their auras. According to the Gentle Breezers, nothing attracts a pot-holed aura like another pot-holed aura. Sandrine cites herself as an example. "I keep getting into these abusive relationships with guys with holey auras. It's like the holes *magnetize*. So now that I've healed the holes, I won't attract them." Which got me pondering the magnetic force of my own personal holes, and how they could use a good clean.

The cleansing/healing process involves sitting in a circle with other dirty people and passing around the tools. For maintenance, there are tools you can buy for your home or office that last a lifetime. Sandrine has taped one to the mirror by her chair. It's a laminated card, a steal at seventy bucks. She says she won't know for thirty days if it's working, but a couple she met at Gentle Breeze told her that the card totally changed their business. She only does five heads a day, so she could use a change. The truth is, on my bad days I want to be Sandrine. Most losers figure out they're losing ground and become humble and thank you for cleaning up after them. But Sandrine's always learning and getting enlightened and is therefore, in her own mind, a superior being. This delusion has its merits. It's a lot more fun than self-flagellation, which is my modus operandi. Today, for example, she was above the clouds because her painting teacher, Victore, spent an extra two seconds discussing her oeuvre; probably had his hand up her skirt. She told a client with a recent eye job that Victore advised her "to look at the light in Sargent." He said he'd bring in a book for her. Sandrine was all excited about this prospect. Meanwhile I was dragging my ass around thinking about survival. I mean, I envy this girl.

The sad, sad thing is, I was a mediocre art student once. I fell into hairdressing because I developed a cocaine habit. I was a mediocre art student obsessed with Francis Bacon. I *felt* like a Francis Bacon.

There he is, the little weasel. I grab my bat, lunge out of the car and charge across the street. "What the fuck do you think you're doing?" I shout. The weasel looks at me as though he just woke up. He's holding two rusty paint cans he was planning to pitch. I wield the bat. "Get the fuck off my yard!" For a couple of nanoseconds he just stands there and I'm thinking I'm going to have to slonk this guy. He's a dwarf, which is handy, because I'm not exactly an Amazon—standing straight is a challenge for me, I'm usually walking around bent over as if about to examine someone's hair. But pumped on adrenaline, I figure I can make fast work of this worm. He starts speaking some language I don't know and Mrs. Pawusiak comes scurrying out. "Vat's goink on?" she demands.

The weasel scrambles into his beat-up stationwagon, still gripping his paint cans. I keep jabbing the air threateningly with the bat. I'm actually enjoying this. It's like I have control again for five seconds.

"Who vas zat?" Mrs. Pawusiak inquires.

"The kitten killer."

"You shoot call za police."

"He won't be back. Go to bed, Mrs. Pawusiak. I'm having this dump cleared in the morning."

I check my pocket. Fuzzball dozed through the whole thing.

Back at the motel I find the father and daughter asleep with the TV still blaring. I switch it off. She's in her dinosaur pyjamas, cuddling her tiger, resting her head on her dad's chest. He's wearing a cotton sweater I remember wearing as a negligée. On my little girl's face is a look of peace.

I shower in the dark, use Q-tips to dig around for Asian hairs up my nostrils, in my navel. I use tweezers to extract one from under a fingernail. There's no point in trying to sleep as I have to feed Fuzzball every three hours. I wish I had my art books, my Rembrandt portraits. They always look as if they're about to tell me something wise. Whenever I panic, I look at the suffering in Rembrandts and tell myself it could be worse.

The thumb's still hurting. Maybe it'll get infected and kill me, free me from these black holes. Father and daughter will wake up and find me lockjawed and he'll figure out he has to take care of her, love her, hold her, forever.

I try to get comfy on my squishy bed. The comforter is a one-hundred per cent manmade-material jobby that could double for plywood.

I've never been a Sargent fan myself; all those little girls, what was that about?

I look at them again, the loves of my life in their cocoon, and think only, How can I tear them apart?

14

Logan looks up at the jaws of the Tyrannosaurus rex, which she knows means tyrant lizard in Latin. Miss Spongle tells the class that it was possibly the largest predator of all time, that it stood forty feet tall and weighed over six tons and lived in North America sixty-five million years ago. Logan knows all this because her mother has taken her regularly to the museum for years. Logan's favourite dinosaur is the Apatosaurus, which means deceptive lizard. It was a seventy-foot plant-eater and weighed about twenty-five tons. It lived about a hundred and fifty million years ago.

She sniffs her hair because it still smells of her dad's perfume. Her mother doesn't wear perfume because she says people come into the salon doused in it and she nearly gets asphyxiated. But Logan likes her dad's perfume. They went to McDonald's for breakfast. He had to borrow some money from her mother. McKenna didn't want to go because she's not a breakfast person—not a morning person, period, in Logan's opinion. Whereas her dad is fun in the morning. They sat in the window in the sunshine and ate their Big Breakfasts and Logan told him about how nobody knows exactly what happened to the dinosaurs. He said, "They died off, didn't they?"

"Yeah, but nobody knows exactly what killed them. If it was an ice age, or if a huge rock or a block of ice from outer space crashed into Earth. It's possible the dust and smoke from the explosion plunged the world into darkness for millions more years."

"Isn't that something. I always thought they just gobbled each other up."

"They weren't all predators. And they didn't all live on Earth at the same time. There were millions and millions of years between some of them."

"That's a lot of years," he remarked. "Can't get my head around that many years."

"Humans are just a speck in evolution."

"Is that right?" He squeezed more ketchup onto his hashbrowns.

"We'll go the way of the dinosaurs eventually."

"Not too soon, I hope."

"If we keep chewing up the environment, it'll be in the next hundred years."

He pointed his plastic fork at her. "How did you get to be so gloomy? I don't remember you being so gloomy. Where's my giggly girl?" He slid his hand under his T-shirt and started making fart noises in his armpit. This used to make her laugh. She tried to laugh because she felt that she was disappointing him, but it wasn't funny and people were looking at them. Next he started talking about taking her to Disney World one day. She's not interested in Disney World. She'd like to go to Africa before all the animals become extinct.

A girl, wearing what McKenna would describe as corpse make-up, sat at the table next to them, sipping black coffee. Logan noticed her father noticing her. At one point he asked her the time. He never wears a watch and is always asking girls the time. He tried to keep the corpse girl talking but she didn't seem too interested.

"We better get you to school, peachypie," he said. His car was still in the shop so they took a bus. It was crowded, meaning they had to stand, which Logan didn't mind because her father held her hand to keep her steady. She didn't want to leave him and tried to think of how to suggest she not go to school, that they spend an entire day together. She could take him to Riverdale Farm and show him the new piglets and the baby chicks. But he seemed distracted by the time they got to the schoolyard. He didn't even kiss her, just patted her head and said, "See you later, alligator." She tried to stall him by explaining the difference between alligators and crocodiles, but he wasn't listening. And then the bell rang.

But Logan was glad to go on a school trip because it got her out of the building, which she believes is sick. She saw a documentary about sick building syndrome. People get headaches inside them, and faint and barf and stuff. Logan always feels sick in school because of the poisonous air inside it. When she advised Miss Spongle about sick building syndrome, Miss Spongle just said that Logan had an active imagination and that she shouldn't worry so much.

What Logan noticed last night, when she was resting her head on her dad's chest, is that his heart beats way slower than her mother's. McKenna's sometimes sounds like a trapped bird. Her dad's is steady.

This morning her mother looked crazier than ever because she went to bed with wet hair. It was sticking out in all directions. Payne just stared at her.

"What are *you* looking gobsmacked about?" McKenna demanded.

"Nice do."

"You really irritate me."

Payne smoothed his own hair. "Did you sleep at all last night?"

"I had to feed the kitten."

"Every three hours is a bit much, don't you think? I mean, it's not like it's human."

"Who asked your opinion? Just shut up, alright?"

This is what Logan means by her mother not being a morning person.

Curling Ellsworth is behind the playhouse pissing on ants. He isn't even embarrassed when Logan sees his penis. "Suck this!" he says. Logan ignores him and would go back inside if Mr. Beasley weren't hanging around making the kids search his pockets for candies. Sometimes, after they find them, he sticks out his big yellow tongue and makes them feed him the candy. Logan climbs the tree, wishing Emma were here. Emma used to come to Dotty's daycare before she got cancer. Logan and McKenna went to visit her in the hospital several times during her treatment. Emma's father was always around, setting up tents or blowing up balloons, juggling Nerf balls. Parents of the other children in the ward always looked scared, but Mr. Feather was always playing with Emma because she *wanted* to play, she didn't want to act sick. At Halloween, he put cotton wool on pencils, pretended they were ghosts and did a little puppet show beside Emma's bed. By then she was bald and skinny and it hurt her to laugh. That was the last time Logan saw her.

They ran into Emma's father a year or so later in the supermarket. He seemed happy and was holding a new baby. It bothered Logan that he was happy, and that Emma had been replaced.

But when she dreams about the kind of father she would like to have, she thinks of Mr. Feather.

She spoke to God this morning regarding her parents. If he's trying to bring them back together, that's okay, but she advised him that it would be good if her dad got paid. Because her mother's really stressed about money right now, as they haven't received anything from the parasite insurance guy. But Logan told God it was nice to see her parents touching, even though they were fighting. She's never seen them touch before. That was nice.

15

I've waited five hours in this shithole hospital. The fluorescents are driving me nuts. I tried hanging out in the can with the lights out but old-lady Ex-Lax junkies kept banging on the door. "Is there anybody in there?" they croaked.

"Yes," I bellowed, but they must have been deaf because they went on banging.

I keep nipping downstairs for boiled coffee because sitting in the waiting area is brutal. It's crammed with people with eye problems. Some wear patches, bandages, some have Coke-bottle glasses. They're mostly geriatric and constantly ask each other how long they've been waiting. "Oh I've been here since seven-fifteen this morning."

"Is that so? Goodness gracious."

"What can you do, can't be helped."

"That's the way it goes," another concedes. They're so frigging docile. I'm about to decapitate one of the whitecoats. What gives them the right to make us wait like this? I've missed five appointments, told Kristos it was an emergency but explained no further. He was twitchy because his dry cleaning wasn't ready and the Nazi car he wants to buy isn't available with leather seats. It has to be specially ordered. "They advertise a freakin' *special edition* then tell me 'no'? What kind of beezness eez this? Could be seex weeks, he tells me. I was so mad, I lost speech. I pay you two hundred thousand freakin' dollars and you make me wait? What eez this?" The rich sowee he was colouring kept nodding and saying, "Isn't it awful?" When he paused to breathe, she got in *her* story about the trauma her husband suffered ordering a Jag. I was perming Angeline, formerly Angelo, my transy client who uses blush to create cleavage and takes so many hormones he's bloated into muumuuland. His perms take forever because he wants to look like Julia Roberts but doesn't have the volume.

"All I want," Kristos sighed, "is to be a shepherd."

"A shepherd?" The sowee would have looked surprised but she'd been Botoxed into oblivion and was no longer capable of facial expression.

"I could seet under a tree, mind my flock, eat a little bread and cheese."

"Drink vino from a gourd," I offered. This was his cue to display the shepherd's crook he bought in Crete. He likes to keep it handy to give clients the impression that he's earthy and not after their cash.

Anyway, this got me thinking about lies. When you're distracted by colour, you don't notice them much, or anyway, they're easy to ignore. In black and white, you see the bare bones of things; the dullness, meanness, cheapness. Cut flowers, for instance—especially exotic ones—I've always loved them, their texture, smell, colours. I look at them now and all I can think is that some Colombian woman was paid fifty cents to harvest them, and in the process exposed herself to pesticides that will harm her and her unborn children.

"Do you like it?" Angelo/Angelina asked me re his/her muumuu. "It's from Indonesia. Isn't it divine?"

All I could think was, You probably paid over a hundred for it while the woman who made it got a buck. "It suits you," I said.

"Aren't the colours totally Gauguin?"

Angelo/Angelina has told me how he has suffered from being a boy who wanted to be a girl. And I know I'm supposed to tiptoe around his sex change and pretend he's a girl. But the fact is, being female involves more than cutting off a penis and mainlining hormones. The fact is, he's living one big lie.

The other fib this morning came out of Little Miss Spread-her-legs, who claimed that she was gangbanged by the Russian mafia last night. I suppose there's a remote possibility that she's telling the truth, although in my experience, rape victims don't want to talk about it. This chick's even describing the Russians' haircuts.

"What were you doing hanging out with the Russian mafia?" I asked, since no one else was. French and Kristos fired me how-can-you-be-so-insensitive looks. "Are you involved with drugs?" I persisted.

"Mac," French exclaimed, hands aflutter, pinkie rings sparkling, "can you lay off her for one minute?" By this time I was knee-deep in hair and desperate for a sweep. "*Honestly*," he went on, "you can be so heartless."

Coco, who styles high-end call girls, made his cat-fight sound and clawed the air with his paw. He's been taking Prozac and has developed a tongue-darting mannerism and a taste for spiky boots. "Mac has a personal vendetta against vulnerability," he said, and out darted the tongue in search of flies.

"Never expect sympathy from one woman to another," Kristos of the wealth of knowledge informed us.

I looked hard at the little princess. "Did you phone the police?" This started her boohooing again. All the boys went "ooooh." I have a feeling I'll be doing my own sweeping into the next millennium.

What do you know, it's my turn. A nurse with pencilled eyebrows leads me into a little windowless room and asks me to sit on the examining chair. She takes notes while I explain the burning-house incident. We do the old eye-chart test, covering first one eye, then the other, and she remarks that I have twenty-twenty vision—as though this is news to me. I explain about the colour problem. Her pencilled eyebrows squiggle. She doesn't comment but hurries out, closing the door in which I note there is a small square window. This comforts me; the room isn't entirely windowless. In minutes, two Asian whitecoats with bad haircuts peer in at me. I feel like the dumb white folk exhibit. They go away, then come back for another gawp. Finally they open the door and present me with a little binder. "Identify colours, please," the shorter one says.

"Grey," I say.

"Can you read the number?"

"Twelve."

He exchanges a look with his comrade, who's wearing the kind of delicate specs you know cost five hundred bucks.

"Continue to identify colours and numbers," the shorter one says.

I explain that I don't see any other numbers and that it's all grey to me, but he insists I look carefully at every page. I resist an urge to hurl the binder at him. While I try to describe the different shades of grey, the four-eyed numbnuts checks things off on a little piece of paper.

They leave me alone in the room again. I switch the lights off.

This is all too familiar.

Why, I used to ask myself, didn't Lester lock my brother, Tait, into the windowless room? Was this sexist, or was it because he couldn't get to Tait, who decided, when he was six or something, that he was adopted and therefore not related to the people who were allegedly his parents? He could go for days without speaking to any of us but got great grades, so nobody bugged him. I tried talking to him, even tried shouting at him to see if I could get him involved in family politics. Nothing seemed to register. He hugged pillows, not people, carried them around the house. I figure he's slightly autistic because, even as an adult, he's been unable to form relationships with anything except technology and the gear necessary to B.A.S.E. jump. What's that about anyway, leaping to possible death from buildings, antennae, spans, earth? Is that what he's got to do to feel, to know he's alive? When I asked him if he would be Logan's guardian in the event of my death, he replied, "Sure." I wondered if he knew what this would entail. I said, "You'd have to get a nanny," then explained about my life insurance, et cetera. He nodded, then went back to reading some manual.

The Asian boys return with an older one with a better haircut. He speaks curtly to me as he puts drops in my eyes and instructs me to rest my chin on the brace of the periscope thing. He tells me to look this way and that, pulls my eyelids down, rolls them up. He reminds me of the Korean boss I had when I was a Santa's elf, has the same fascist eyes, wired glasses and zest for shouting orders. We elves had to look busy non-stop, keeping the kids smiling, taking the photos, selling the parents on package deals, setting up the castle, taking it down, working the cash register. All for minimum wage. I've always wondered what Santa was making, sitting on his duff.

Next, the boss fits what looks like a miner's helmet on his head. The boys switch off the overhead as he shines his helmet light through a lens he's holding in front of my eyes. I wait for the interrogation to begin but he doesn't speak to me, just shouts medical lingo to the numbnuts, who busily take notes. Finally he puts all his gadgets aside and makes eye contact with me for about a millisecond. "There is nothing wrong with your eyes."

"Then why can't I see colour?"

"You've had trauma to the head. You should see a neurologist. I'll refer you."

"You mean I'm brain-damaged?"

Suddenly he got shirty, like my Korean boss when I discovered him fondling an elf.

"There is such a thing as hysterical colour-blindness," he tells me.

"I'm not hysterical."

"You're in shock."

"I'm not."

"See a neurologist." He marches off, followed by the twins. I hightail it out of the hospital in I-can't-believe-this-is-happening mode. In the square I smell spring but can't see it. Lilac flowers appear bulbous against grey leaves, apple blossoms look like fungi spreading on branches, tulips look like scattered garbage. I take refuge on a park bench, pick up a stray newspaper because it's black and white. I read my horoscope: *You're ready to have some fun now—you're feeling saucy, spunky and hey nonny nonny. You want to pull out all the stops. Get out there and hustle and get your life in order. Think about your long-term goals. You have a wonderful opportunity to reflect on your values. Remember, happiness is wanting what you have!*

A kid in Gap jeans begs me for money. I give him some change because I don't want to argue.

It's gone now. The curtain's down.

I can't live like this, fumbling in the dark.

Yes, you can, you have a child.

16

Logan doesn't usually mind her mother playing Jaques Brel on the car stereo. It's when she sings along that it's disturbing. And if Logan asks her to stop, McKenna gets pathetic. "Can't I sing?" she pleads. "It's healthy to sing. Please, monkey, can't I sing?"

There's no question her mother's driving ability is taking a nosedive, although McKenna seems oblivious to this fact. She's swearing at other drivers even more than usual. She even swears at a crazy old lady who stomps in front of their car. The old lady's wearing a baseball cap and a miniskirt and keeps shouting, "What are *you* looking at?" at people who aren't even looking at her. She halts in the middle of the road and kicks one leg straight out front then sideways.

"What makes people nuts?" Logan asks.

McKenna stops singing. "Different things."

"Like what?"

"Sometimes there's a chemical imbalance in the brain," McKenna says, watching the old lady kick behind her a few times. "Sometimes horrible things happen to people that make them crazy."

"Like what?"

"Loss. Losing what really matters to you."

Scowling, the old lady marches to the side of the road, allowing cars to move around her.

"What's the most horrible thing that's ever happened to you?" Logan asks.

"Losing you."

"Did *you* go nuts?"

"Oh yeah."

"Oscar at school's pretty crazy. He's on Ritalin. I wonder what happened to him."

"People don't have to stay crazy. Sometimes they get better."

"You did, but you weren't really crazy though. You were just a junkie." Logan rests her feet on the dash. "You're not going crazy now, right?"

"Right."

The fact is, her mother did look pretty crazy in the supermarket, squinting and complaining that the fluorescents were killing her. She made a big deal about getting exactly what they needed to make spaghetti, and had a cow when she saw that the baskets for baguettes were empty. "Who's responsible for baked goods?" she kept asking employees, who scattered. When she finally cornered one, he went to look for baguettes and didn't come back. Fortunately McKenna forgot about him while she was taking forever to pick the vegetables because she had to finger everything and ask Logan which peppers were red and which were green. But Logan's looking forward to supper, and walking Stanley, and her mother promised they'd play rummy.

She sees her father before her mother does. He's holding a helium balloon. Logan glances quickly at McKenna, who's preoccupied with parking and studying the grocery receipt. "I can't believe that came to sixty-nine bucks," she says. Logan waves to her father, who's charging towards them with the balloon.

"How're my girls?" he says, slapping the roof of the car. McKenna doesn't move.

"We're fine, Dad."

"I was worried about you guys. It's past eight."

"We went shopping," Logan explains.

"I brought you a balloon, honey." Logan knows he got it for free because it's got Globo Shoes printed on it. "I thought maybe we could all go for dinner tonight," he says. "*My* treat."

"Did you get paid?" Logan asks, wondering if God has answered her prayers again.

"I've got some loose change," Payne says.

Logan waits to see if her mother gets out of the car. She doesn't. Personally Logan is starving and wouldn't mind eating at a restaurant because at least then she wouldn't have to wait. "Can we go out for dinner, Mum? I'm pretty hungry."

In one swift movement her mother whips out of the car and faces him over the roof. "Where did you get the money?"

"McKenna, do I ask you about *your* personal finances? I don't think so."

"Does this mean you don't have to squat with us?"

"Not exactly."

Logan pokes her head out the passenger window. "I feel like pancakes. Could we go to the Golden Griddle?"

"Pancakes," Payne says. "What a fantabulous idea. I *love* pancakes!"

Logan hears her mother throw her keys at her father. "Get the dog."

Stanley is chained to a bike rack outside the plate glass window. Logan keeps waving at him so he won't feel left out. She fed him one of her buttermilk pancakes, which she thinks he enjoyed, although he didn't fall asleep, which means he wasn't over the moon about it. Being with her parents isn't great. Her mother's wearing her concrete face and staring down at her buckwheat pancakes like they're turds.

"Aren't you eating?" Payne asks her.

"What?"

"Eat some grub, girl."

"Stay out of my face, alright?"

Her father has already asked the dipshit waitress for the time and she's given him two coffee refills. She's wearing a name tag that says Cindy. Payne's been calling her Cynthia with an English accent, which makes her giggle. She's got what McKenna would describe as "major jiggle factor." A birthday party's in progress two tables over. They keep singing retarded songs like "If You're Happy and You Know It" and "Old Macdonald Had a Farm."

"Mum, is Fuzzball sleeping? Mum . . . ?"

"What?"

"Is Fuzzball sleeping?"

McKenna peeks in her jacket. "Yup."

"I can't believe you're keeping a cat on your person," Payne says. "What's Kristos think about it? Eau de Chat."

Logan's been thinking about the oldest rhinoceros in Europe—a thirty-nine-year-old named Susi—who got put down yesterday. She was in failing health and had poor eyesight. Logan doesn't see why they had to terminate her. Doctors don't kill people just because they're in failing health and have poor eyesight. Susi was captured and brought to the zoo from Africa when she was four. That's a lot of years in a cage. No wonder she was sick.

"So," Payne says, rubbing his hands together, "what say we go to a movie?"

Logan looks at her mother, who hasn't moved in five minutes.

"I have homework," Logan says. "We should probably just go back to the Lakeview."

The birthday crowd blow whistles and ooh and aah about a blue cake decorated with cowboy hats that the jiggle-factor waitress has brought out. Logan hates birthday parties, pinning tails on donkeys and playing musical chairs. She doesn't like noise, and people kissing her and telling her to smile for the camera. And she doesn't like the cheapoid party favours that the mothers pick up at the dollar store that you're supposed to get all excited about. Since Emma died, Logan hasn't been to any birthday parties. Nina, the foodaholic, has invited her to hers but there's no way she's going.

Her mother still hasn't moved.

"Did you know," Logan says to break the tension, "that horses' hooves are really toes?"

"Are you kiddin' me?" Her father pours more syrup on his pancakes.

"They're the only animal with just one toe."

"*Un*believable." Her father tries to get the attention of the dipshit but she's busy cutting the blue cake.

"Horses were on Earth sixty million years ago," Logan elaborates. "Then they were only as big as a dog."

"Is that what they teach you in school?" her father asks, still trying to get the dipshit's attention. "What about spelling, arithmetic?"

"They don't call it arithmetic anymore."

"Whatever, why aren't they teaching you that?" He starts waving his coffee cup around and mouthing "Cynthia."

"They teach me that," Logan says, understanding that she's failed him again.

"What's six times six?" he asks.

"Thirty-six."

Her mother snaps out of her coma and stares at him. "What's seven times twelve?"

"What?"

"You don't know. You have *no brain*. Don't you *dare* talk down to her. Logan, we're out of here."

At first Logan feels badly about leaving him behind, but then, as she's untying Stanley, she sees the dipshit pour her father more coffee. He winks at her and says something that makes her giggle.

"Will he ever stop looking at girls?" Logan asks.

"Men never stop looking at girls."

"Even when they're like really old?"

"Especially when they're really old."

"That's so icky."

Her mother feeds Stanley one of her buckwheat pancakes. "Time for walkies, big boy."

17

Can't sleep. Thought of killing him over the pancakes, jabbing my fork into his jugular, watching black blood spurt out. But she was there, his little shadow, hoping to please, and I knew that dead he'd haunt her even more than he does now.

I'll bet money he's doin' the waitress on a futon in her room above a pizza joint. No doubt her stuffed teddies are spectators.

I smell dope, smelled it last night but thought maybe I was imagining it because I had substances on the brain. Somebody's rolling doobies around here. I breathe deeper.

Longing, what's that about? I used to long for Payne even when I was with him. The Freud-fresh social worker told me that "in passion there is only an endless, insatiable wait." It was around this time I noticed her facial hair and recommended electrolysis. But I thought that was interesting: "in passion there is only an endless, insatiable wait." Meaning you're sitting around pining for the numbnuts, then he shows up and you're still waiting for something to happen. It doesn't but you figure it might next time, if you play your cards right. The fact is, you can't play your cards right. The fact is, you're not even in the game. After he takes off, you sit staring into the space he left behind sticking pins under your nails because you didn't play your cards right. Your self-loathing becomes a kind of religion. You visit the shrine daily and lament. You could hang on to that vacancy forever, because it's all you've got. At least it's something you can count on, looking forward into the unknown. Now there's a challenge.

She's asleep, hugging her tiger, and I want to be that stuffed animal. In her arms I'd be safe. I have a feeling she doesn't feel safe in my arms anymore. I have a feeling she doesn't feel safe anywhere now that her home is charred ground and her mother's losing bolts. I'm trying to act normal but there's no question grocery shopping is a bit weird—having to smell everything. She said, "Quit sniffing, Mum!" So I stopped, I did, so what if the cantaloupe tastes like cardboard, what's important is that I look normal. That's the secret to survival, I figure, act normal and they'll leave you alone. I've never been able to pull it off.

I had a formerly normal client today I've been cutting for years. He used to sell photocopiers and fax machines, was one of those guys who majored in normalcy and isn't-life-swell energy. I'd say "How are you?" and he'd say "Awesome," then start whistling some jaunty tune. Now he rarely leaves his house, thinks that the rodents in his backyard are giving him instructions and that people, myself included, have green ears. But his wife drags him out for haircuts every few months so he can vegetate in my chair. While I worked on his head, Kristos ranted about his vaporized Special Edition Nazi car. "First they tell me eet's in freakin' transit, then they tell me eet's in freakin' Germany. I say to the skullhead, what kind of beezness is this? I tell him you better get me a loaner or I'm gonna talk to my lawyer."

None of this registered on the formerly normal salesman. When I was finished I had to prod him loose. What made *him* crazy?

Speaking of insanity, on my first Fuzzball wake-up call, I saw Mommy dearest sitting on the chair by the phone table. I stared at her, feeling every pore on my body dilating. She was wearing her perky red blazer, only it was black, and she was nodding at me as if I were talking. After I figured out that I was definitely not dreaming, that she was definitely there, I said, "Hi, Mum." She went on nodding as if we were having a chin wag and I thought, This is weird, a deaf ghost, a *crazy* ghost who's hearing what I'm not saying. But, I told myself, she *is* your mother, it's not like it's somebody you killed coming back for revenge. Alicia—who OD'd in my presence—now there's a ghost candidate. Even though it wasn't my fault because I didn't introduce her to drugs, didn't know she was mixing. She was a street kid turned assistant who'd suck off any dirtball for a hit and had already destroyed one nostril with cocaine. I felt sorry for her, was being generous, providing sterilized needles so she could bypass the nasal problem, not to mention AIDS. Of course as soon as I figured out what was going on I called 911. It's amazing how once dead, a body really looks dead. In minutes the skin flattens, turns that special mix of indigo and ochre.

"Do you mind if I feed the cat?" I asked my dead and deaf mother. She didn't respond. I fed Fuzzball anyway, had to walk around the ghost to get to the formula, expected to feel a cold breeze or mist or something but didn't. When I looked back, she was gone.

Logan used to ask me what happens after we die. I told her we become mermaids. She didn't buy it.

Sandrine, who believes in reincarnation, came back from a funeral today upset because she was the only one who cried. I said, "Nobody was crying because they're all on Prozac."

"Your cynicism," she responded, "comes from hurt." Then Coco of the Prozac addiction and spiky boots did some tongue-darting before insisting that *he* still cries.

"When?" I inquired.

He thought a minute, caught a couple more flies. "When Olympic girl skiers win. It's so touching. They worked so hard for their country."

"What about when they lose?" I asked. "Or bust their legs?"

He tweaked his handlebar moustache. "That doesn't make me cry."

"That's because you're on Prozac," I argued. "You're caught up in the race. You don't care about the people who fall off the mountain. Drugs have blowtorched your humanity."

"For a former junkie," French intervened, swallowing his sixth aspirin of the day, "you certainly put on airs."

"Too many margaritas last night?" I ask him. "Maybe you want to ponder the word *addiction*."

Kristos gave us one of his shut-up-and-make-nice stares because he had a new client and didn't want her to know what fuck-ups we were. "You look like Sophia Loren," he told the bag of fat as he squeezed her into his chair. He always tells his older clients they look like Sophia or Brigitte or one of the Laurens. He states the lie plainly as though it's obvious, adding a little Mediterranean shrug. I've often wondered if he ever has a moment, even a second, of self-loathing. I doubt it. His mama raised him to believe that God created man, then woman to service him. She phones the salon six times a day to make sure he's eaten some goat.

They're starting to twig to my frequent toilet visits. "Is Montezuma revenging?" French asked.

"Bladder infection," I lied.

"Bladder infections don't make you pee," Little Miss Spread-her-legs said. "I get them all the time."

"So what are you doing in the can," French persisted, "if you're not going wee-wee?"

"Masturbating," I said. That shut them up briefly. I resumed listening to another regular who's been engaged about fifty times and finally married a bugbrain four years ago. I did an updo for her on the wedding day. When the bugbrain showed up, I assumed he'd come to fix the plumbing. "This is my fiancé," my client told me proudly. I lost speech, as Kristos would say. Anyway, two babies later he skipped town. She came home last week and found a note with "I've left you" written on it.

"That's original," I commented, noticing that she couldn't stop chewing her cuticles. She told me it was okay because she'd already started dating—a guy just like herself. She said it's like looking in the mirror. She said at least she can make him laugh because she knows what makes her laugh. Then she uttered this forced, strangulated, last giggle on the gallows. I'd say next time I see her she'll be on some kind of S.S.R.I., sucking back a few flies.

It's hot in here. I check my baby, then sit outside on a crappy lawn chair and sniff for dope emissions. "I'm *not* a baby," Logan started telling me when she was three. "I'm a *girl*." Being a girl, I have to say, sucks rocks. Twelve-year-olds come into the salon and tell me they don't like sex but do it anyway because it makes them popular. Flabbergasted, I ask if their parents know about it. "No way," they gasp, "we do it after school before they get home from work." I can't cope with the thought of Logan spreading her legs for some dweezle in a baseball cap. Maybe they take the baseball caps off when they're raping girls. Doubt it. Humping with hat head can't be too cool.

Actually, the thought of her being touched by anyone makes me want to swing a tire iron. I'm hoping I'll grow out of this. It's just I know every inch of her body, every mole. I've nursed and cared for it. Guarded it. No one will respect it as I have.

I'm getting spooked by my own body parts. I'll see this grey thing lying on me and start to squirm before figuring out it's my hand. No amount of shaking is connecting them to my body. This morning I thought somebody else's arm was on my pillow.

If I'm going nuts, which seems likely, I can't crack in front of her. I have to keep it together in front of her.

In the dark I see for miles. There's a black cat gnawing at garbage on the other side of the parking lot. Deadheads with number-one buzzcuts slink in and out of one of the units and speed off in foreign cars—maybe one of them's Kristos's Special Edition. I figure they're the source of the jang. The tenant's probably a distributor, camping out for a while, paying Bluxom to keep his eye wandering in the other direction. The door of my neighbouring unit swings open and there's the tub-o'-guts himself. He shuffles down the parking lot to the office. Seconds later a woman, stinking of drugstore perfume, exits the same unit, sits on a crappy lawn chair and lights up a cigarette. I don't move because if she hears me I'll have to make chitchat and pretend I don't know she's Bluxom's muse. I stay invisible while she kicks off her fuck-me pumps and starts muttering to herself, flicking ash off her chintzy peignoir. I can't make out what she's saying other than the occasional "fuck you, asshole." She's venting as I do in my car. My breathing sounds loud to me but she's too worked up to notice. Then she starts to sob, fierce, retching sobs that rip holes in the night.

Everybody's got a story nobody wants to hear.

18

Logan enjoys going up in the plane with Uncle Tait because it makes the world look manageable. He flies it once a month to keep his pilot's licence, rents the plane by the hour from the airport. It's expensive so they're never up for long. He likes to take off and land a lot. She watched him jump off a building once. Her mother didn't know about it. It bothered Logan that her uncle was spending all that cash on seeing if he could kill himself when he could have been donating the money to the World Wildlife Federation. She wondered how this jumping to near death stuff was any different from her mother taking drugs or her father being a sex addict. She wondered what it was about being an adult that made a person need to take or do things that would stop them from feeling. Although now that she's older she can see how not feeling has its advantages.

"The moon is 238,906 miles from the earth," Tait informs her. He always says things out of nowhere that have no connection to anything. "And its surface," he adds, "is barren and filled with craters created by the impact from meteorites."

"Can we fly over my house?" Logan asks.

"It burned down."

"I just want to see where it was."

It hasn't been a good day. This morning her mother was weirder than ever, shaking her hands and showering in the dark. She put on different-coloured socks and a pale pink smiley face T-shirt. She's been freaking out because they don't have any clothes and she doesn't have time to shop. She started ranting about how she *hates* shopping, like Logan doesn't know this. Logan just kept quiet. McKenna nearly rammed a garbage truck on the way to school. She said she didn't see it because it was grey, which of course it wasn't but Logan didn't argue.

Last night she discovered her dad's suitcase under her bed. She didn't mention this to McKenna because she knew she'd have a turd about it and stuff it in a Dumpster or something. The suitcase means he'll have to come back, which doesn't bother Logan. She, personally, isn't angry with her father, and she isn't sure her mother should have told him that he has no brain. That was rude. Her mother always tells Logan not to be rude.

Also, McKenna said she saw a black pig in the parking lot. She was in hysterics about it, told Logan to hurry up and get dressed so she could see the black pig. Logan saw no black pig. "It's staying at the motel," her mother insisted. "I saw it come out of one of the rooms."

"Can we just go to school?" Logan pleaded.

School was no better. Miss Spongle was talking about the use of irrigation in dry climates like it was a miracle of science and got testy when Logan countered that it wastes water and is therefore no longer efficient in a modern world that is draining its rivers and aquifers. Miss Spongle had just had her bangs trimmed and kept tugging at them.

And then, at lunch, Oscar tore Nina's dress and shouted that she had udders. Logan knew that if McKenna were there, she'd have kicked Oscar's ass. But Logan stood by doing nothing. She didn't like herself for this. Afterwards, when Nina was crying, she gave her a Kleenex.

It was nice that Uncle Tait picked her up from school, meaning she didn't have to go to Dotty's. And she enjoyed the baguette sandwich he bought her, but when she mentioned Susi—the terminated rhino—all Tait said was, "She'd become a liability."

"What do you mean?"

"She was costing the zoo money."

"Because she was sick?"

He was carefully extracting a black hair from his sandwich.

"We don't kill people just because they're sick and going blind," Logan pointed out.

"Maybe we should." He laid the hair beside his baguette and studied it. "Not mine" was his only comment. Then he stared out the window in what McKenna calls his Heathcliff mode. A girl with smeared eyeliner, chewing a baguette, was watching him. Girls are always staring at Tait but he never notices them.

"There's your house," he says, turning and tipping the plane so she can see the pit where her home used to be. All of a sudden she feels as if she's falling out of the plane; her head drops forward and she slaps her hands against the window. All her life she has had that house. Other kids have been forced to move because the landlord was upping the rent, or because their parents got transferred, or divorced. Logan's always had her house. Now there's a hole, a crater, like on the moon—impacted by a meteorite.

"Would you like to see my new rotator saw?" Tait asks. "It cuts perfectly round holes in anything, ceramics, metal, wood. Only one seventy-nine American."

Tait's always buying things on-line. He bought a non-stick cooking set that he shows Logan every time she goes over even though she told him that the fumes from non-stick coatings kill canaries and therefore can't be too healthy for humans. McKenna says that

Tait has no feelings, but Logan is beginning to like this about him. She's sick of feelings.

When he drops her off at the Lakeview, her mother is making spaghetti and garlic bread, and seems almost normal except that she's still shaking her hands and looking over her shoulder. "What are you looking at?" Logan asks.

"What do you mean?"

"You keep looking behind you."

"I do?"

"Like you think there's somebody there."

"That's weird." Her mother rubs her eyes again.

Vance, the dog walker, shows up to get paid. He's got a nose that's bent sideways and only one ear. He said a dog chewed off the other one. McKenna pays him, but he loiters. "It's like I always say," he tells them, "never trust a dog. Man's best friend until you do something pisses them off."

"Do you know anything about the black pig?" McKenna asks him.

Vance makes a sound as if he just got burned. "That pig is one mean piece of ham. You want to stay clear of that hog."

"Are pigs allowed here?"

"Bluxom'll take anything if you pay him enough. One time he had a guy with poisonous snakes."

The thing about Vance is that Stanley likes him, and he doesn't like just anybody. They went through a number of dog walkers at home before they found a retarded boy named Scuff. McKenna says that Stanley is anti-intellectual. She got Vance's name from the bulletin board in the laundry room. He lives in the apartment complex across the street.

"That pig," he says, "is clean. She bathes him daily so she says. And he's house-trained. But I'm tellin' ya, don't let him see you with a granola bar, you'll be missing fingers. He goes hog-wild over Cheez Doodles."

It relieves Logan that there *is* a black pig, that it wasn't a figment of her mother's imagination. Last night she dreamed that her mother was bald. When she told her mother that she was bald McKenna said, "I am not bald." They went shopping and everybody was staring at her mother and McKenna kept shouting, "What are *you* looking at?" just like the crazy old lady who was kicking in the street.

McKenna stirs the spaghetti sauce. "Did she consider getting a dog?"

"She has a husband who beats her and is allergic to everything so she wanted a pet that was hypoallergenic. The pig's the ticket. No fur. It's nice as pie to her so she says. Nicer than the husband."

"Where's he?"

"Out and about. She's had restraining orders against him, makes no difference, he tracks her down, cuts her phone wires so she can't call the cops. He wants to kill her so she says. So she moves around, no fixed address. Hard-to-find places that'll take a hog. It's like I always say, don't go getting any pets unless you want trouble. Same goes for kiddies." He winks at Logan. "No offence, sweetheart."

McKenna holds the door open for him. "See you later, Vance."

After supper they play hearts and rummy.

"Why is it called the Lakeview when you can't even see the lake?" Logan asks.

"It's over there somewhere." McKenna discards a queen of diamonds, which Logan immediately snaps up.

"Past Vance's building and all the houses," Logan says, laying down a set of queens.

"Yeah." McKenna takes a card from the deck. "We could probably walk there."

"It's probably private property."

The phone rings but McKenna says, "Don't answer it." She watches it like it might explode.

"It could be Dad," Logan points out.

"Do you want talk to him?"

They continue to stare at it until it stops ringing. Logan isn't sure she wants to see her dad right away, particularly if he's hanging around with the jiggle-factor waitress. Letting him get it out of his gonads is probably the best policy. Her mother's awfully quiet, so Logan tells her about the shark that died of shock after a naked man jumped into its tank at an aquarium.

"What was he doing jumping naked into a tank?"

"Publicity. He's on TV. He could face criminal charges."

McKenna had bought them more clothes while Logan was up in the air with Tait—really gross colours. She'd held up a sweatshirt. "The salesgirl said it was purple, sweetybun, isn't it purple?" Logan couldn't bear to tell her that it was a bright fluorescent purple that normally she wouldn't be caught dead in. The same with the neon pink and the slime green. Logan just said, "Thanks, Mum," and figures if she wears them under her overalls it won't be a total disaster. But for herself her mother bought only black clothes. "This is black, isn't it, monkey? The salesgirl said it was black." It all was except for a shirt that looked navy to Logan. "I think that's blue," she said.

"Really? That bitch. I'm taking it back."

Logan takes another card from the deck. "When will they start building our house?'

"Soon, love. They're ordering materials."

"Did you get a cheque today?"

"He says it's in process."

"That's what Dad always says."

"You win again," her mother says and starts shuffling the deck.

"Where do you suppose he's sleeping?"

"I don't know. He's a big boy, he'll figure it out."

"Do you think he's staying with that waitress?" Giving her head, is what Logan's thinking.

"Anything's possible."

"I wouldn't want to sleep in other people's beds all the time."

"Me neither."

"What if they fart and stuff?"

"I hear ya." McKenna hands the cards to Logan. "Your deal."

19

"Did somebody die?" French asked me.

"I'm mourning for my life," I said. Kristos felt the need to tell me that frigid Greek women wear black, and Coco suggested that, if I was trying to do Edith Piaf, I'd have to drop a few inches. Sandrine complained that being around black weakens her energy.

I was terrified because first off I had a new colour client. Fortunately, she turned out to be one of those crows who can't stop cawing about how young they look even though they're a hundred. She told me in detail what products her former hairdresser had put on her hair and what she didn't like about them. I knew the product line, sidled over to French to get his opinion about what would work on Mrs. Rip van Winkle. We often do this for show, make the client think that *two professional* stylists are seriously consulting over her stunningly unique case. We make remarks like, A few honeysuckle lights will really brighten, bring out the natural wave, her cheekbones, whatever. In a case like Mrs. Rip's, forget natural colour, she's been white for years. So it's a question of which products to use on the previous colours. French was helpful because Mrs. Rip expressed great interest in his genetically engineered descended-from-snow-leopard cats that cost a thousand bucks each. He's named them Scott and Zelda so people will think he read a book once. Mrs. Rip was impressed and distracted, which gave me time to work out a plan. "They are *exquisite*," French said about six hundred times re his cats. He was sporting his silk pyjama look, which works when the elastic in his waistband isn't shot. We'd been trying to pin up the pants but his gut kept interfering. He had to hang on to his PJs while yabbering about Scott and Zelda. Anyway, after I'd applied Mrs. Rip's colour and put the heat lamp on her, I made a break for the can to sit in darkness and feed my descended-from-garbage cat. That news about the earthquake—the father listening to his tiny daughter die under the rubble for three days—was still rattling my bones. I could see him pulling at the rocks, bloodying his hands, screaming for help until he had no voice left to assure his baby that Daddy would save her. *Three days.* No heavy equipment was available, they were digging up bodies all over the place. How did he know she was dead? When she no longer cried? I may be trapped in this colourless hell but it beats an earthquake. And those Chinese refugees trapped in a hermetically sealed container on a boat, watching their babies suffocate, then each other. That packs a punch. So I'm feeling better overall about my situation.

Little Miss Spread-her-legs deigned to wash Mrs. Rip's hair because she wanted the tip. Meanwhile I swept up the ten feet of hair around my chair. Sandrine was eating sprouted grains while enthusing about the studio apartment she found, said it was a karmic thing, said she'd been reading a book called *How to Find Your Spirit Guides* and it was really giving her new directions.

After the blow-dry I was smart and crafty with the mirror, showing off the best bits, and Mrs. Rip left a happy camper. The rest of the morning I faked it with regulars, and now I'm doing a fashion shoot, which is the best thing possible for me in this condition as it's all styling. Kristos often gets work from this photographer who has a long greasy ponytail I want to snip. His name's Murtoch and he's Irish and thinks he's ever so cute and doesn't hesitate to dope his models if they're willing. If they don't want hard stuff, there's always plenty of booze around. This makes easy work for the hairdresser because everybody's out of it, including Murtoch. It's catered and usually I stuff my face, but, as all the nibblies look like grey slime and dog doo, I just sit back and drink Evian. Maybe I should market the Colourblind Diet—*You'll never want to eat again!*

The makeup girl is having a hard time covering the tracks on the anorexic's legs. The model, sucking on cigarettes, acts like she has no idea how those marks got there. The hair's easy because Murtoch likes his models to have that I-just-got-fucked look about them. But I have to use gallons of spray to make the loose strands stay loose in the right places. My nostrils are getting plugged with the stuff.

I've been trying to figure out what to do about Payne. I'd be more than happy to push him in front of a bus but it's Logan I'm worried about. It's obvious she misses the meathead. For the rest of her life she'll blame me for chasing him away, hurting his feelings, damaging his self-esteem. Why doesn't he just get the clap and die? Then I could say in no uncertain terms that he brought it on himself.

"Mac. . . ?" Murtoch calls. "Can you give us a tad more lift, love, a bit more puff? She's looking a bit used."

I slap on my professional eager-to-please isn't-fashion-photography-the-coolest expression. The model tells me she slept in a bathtub last night. I don't ask for details. "Must have been uncomfortable," I comment while fluffing her up. She keeps yapping about her split ends and the mini-quiches she can't stop eating. Because I don't abuse her, she thinks I'm her new best friend.

"Alright, let's have another go," Murtoch says.

Logan referred to our new dog walker as stupid this morning. I said, "Don't call people stupid," which makes no sense as I call people stupid all the time, which must be where she gets it from. You have this child who spits your words with even more venom than you do, because she's learned the refrain from you and you're supposed to be smart. And you can't admit that you aren't smart, that you're actually a bugbrain with attitude. So you try to ignore your little creation's foul mouth. She called me stupid once. She was almost four. I'd given her a skipping rope that turned out to be too long so she demanded another one. I said it was rude to demand something right after someone had given you a present. "You're stupid" was her response. I thought maybe I'd heard wrong and said, "What did you say?"

"You're stupid."

It was as if she'd pitched a baseball at my gut, because I'd heard it all before, from Lester, *You're stupid, how can you be so stupid, why are you so stupid?* It was happening all over again, only this time I had to provide for the offender for the next twenty years. I started to cry, didn't want her to see, of course, busied myself with a mop. She knew there was a problem because there was a chill around us we'd never felt before. I tried to drive it out with the vacuum cleaner. When I switched it off we looked at each other, two adversaries trying to work out a deal. I told her to apologize. She did. It sounded hollow; cheap words. I resumed my chores because I didn't want to make a big deal out of the thing. She was just trying it out, testing. She didn't know my history. But an innocence was gone and I knew it wasn't coming back.

The fact is, no matter what you do you're going to screw up somewhere. Giving her too much stuff, for instance. I never got shit as a kid, it was a classic go-play-with-some-dirt kind of upbringing. So I loaded Logan down with crap because I felt guilty that she had no dad, no siblings, no stay-at-home mom. Then one day I happened to notice that she was a spoiled brat. My little angel couldn't get enough, no matter how much Toys "R" Us landfill I dumped on her. So that was it. She was around four so I felt I still had a chance to make amends. Presents are for birthdays and Christmas, I'd tell her. We don't get presents just because we want them, and you can't *ask* for presents, they're supposed to be surprises. Pretty meagre—it felt like shoving her in front of a train. I had to look away at times because the disappointment on her face made my fingers itch for my wallet. I think it was worth it, though. She's a better person for it. Maybe.

I pick up a newspaper, check my horoscope. *Family matters are important, as is your private life. Childhood memories may surface. Take time to contemplate your early environment. Look at it with today's maturity and understanding.*

That's the thing, you're supposed to evolve, right? Mature, mellow, whatever. I still want to kill people.

Lester used to force me to eat, even the fat on the meat. He'd watch to make sure I got it all down. If he caught me slipping it to the dog, he'd drag me kicking and screaming to the dungeon. The thing is, I've put Logan in her room when she's done something so deliberately nasty I felt I had no choice—it was either that or club her. But I never left her in there for more minutes than her age in years. And the room had a window. So, try as I might, I can't excuse the fucker for what he did to me. During my five minutes in art school I read about Kaspar Hauser, that boy who was discovered in a dungeon in Germany in the nineteenth century. I was bugged out, of course, so completely identified with him. He was called the Lost Prince of Europe because it was believed he was the son of Napoleon's adopted daughter. He was switched at birth with a dying kid by some countess because she wanted her oldest son to inherit the throne. When his jailer let him out, Kaspar had no beef with anyone because he didn't know any better. Daylight blinded him, he developed eye infections and pains in his legs and feet because he'd never learned to walk. He couldn't speak properly except to say that he wanted to "be a rider the way my father was"—he had this idea he had a father but no idea who he could be, except that he rode horses. People thought Kaspar was a fake and treated him like shit, put him in a prison where he cried for days. All he wanted was to go back to his dungeon where he'd sat on his butt and played with a toy horse and a ribbon his dirtbag keeper had provided. He never saw his keeper, just referred to him as "the man with who I have always been." He figured the man had been good to him because, when he woke up, there was bread and water and the dirtbag had emptied his bucket of shit. The kid lived on bread and water. Never enough water, according to him—he was always thirsty. Anyway, he gets out in the world and, once they decide he's not faking it, he's like a freak show and everybody wants a piece of him. They feed him all kinds of nosh he can't stomach because he's accustomed to bread and water. He gets sick and depressed, burned out from being a museum piece. But by this time he knows there's a sky out there, and grass and trees and flowers. He's seen the moon and the stars—lights in the sky, he called them. So he's screwed. Can't go back, can't go forward. And he, who was once so trusting, learns to hate "the man with who he had always been" for cooping him up so long. He becomes fearful and suspicious like the rest of us. They brainwash him about God so he starts to fear him as well, worries that he's not being a good Christian. His only comfort is horses. He never learns to walk properly but loves to ride. Some lord had him killed in the end, had an assassin lure him into a deserted garden by saying that he had news of his mother. He stabbed him in the chest.

Anyway, it makes you ponder how we instill our fear and loathing in our kids. They have no choice, they live and breathe it. Kaspar was free of malice without septic ulcer parents and teachers to influence him. So until we get our act together, Junior doesn't stand a chance. I feel that all the time with Logan. The ugly truth is, when Kaspar got out he had no defences either, so people took advantage of him. The ugly truth is, I'm poisoning my daughter so that no one can take advantage of her.

The first time she said "fuck" I felt this door clanging shut. "What did you say?"

"Fuck."

"Don't *ever* use that word. That's an ugly word. Do I ever use that word?"

"Yes."

It had to happen.

Kaspar saw no colour for those sixteen years he was locked up, didn't know what colour was, didn't know there was night and day. You don't miss what you don't know. If I'd been born colour-blind, I'd be content in smogland. I have to go back there somehow, into the windowless room. See in the darkness, look at my fears. Before I get stabbed in the chest.

20

Her mother doesn't hear the knock because Django Reinhardt's blaring on the portable CD player they just bought. Plus she's frying chicken and is steamed because she's already had a fight with Mr. Bluxom about the oven. One of the elements doesn't work, which means she can't grill anything. McKenna told Mr. Bluxom that she can't cook on the stove every night because it would mean dying from inhaling grease-laden vapour. Mr. Bluxom reminded her that it was a motel, not an apartment house, and that she wasn't supposed to be living at the Lakeview long term anyway. "What's that got to do with the oven?" McKenna argued.

"You're lucky I put up with your dog," he responded.

"What are you talking about? You keep pigs here, and snakes."

"You're welcome to leave anytime" was all he said. He was wearing an undervest—wife-beaters, McKenna calls them—and his rolls of flab oozed in different directions depending on his arm movements. Logan wondered what he did when he showered, if he lifted the layers of flab to scrub underneath. He stank like a toilet so she suspected he didn't. Anyway, he wasn't scared of her mother, which is unusual, most people are. Even Curling Ellsworth's dad looked nervous when she was shouting at him on his lawn.

So now McKenna's freaking because the chicken isn't completely thawed, says she'll have to burn it on the outside to cook it on the inside. And there's no fan to suck up the chicken fumes, meaning it's getting hard to breathe.

"Mum. . . ? There's somebody at the door."

"Tell them I don't want any."

Logan peeks through the venetian blinds. "It's Grandpa," she observes, but her mother doesn't hear, she's too busy squinting at the chicken and prodding it with a fork. Grandpa keeps pounding so Logan opens the door. He's wearing one of his golf hats. He never plays golf but always wears the hats.

"You living in a whorehouse now?" he demands.

"Excuse me," McKenna says, "did we invite you here?"

"Flesh being bought and sold all over the place."

"How would you know?"

"First you burn down your house, then you take your daughter to a goddamn whorehouse. You thinking of starting a business, something you're good at?"

Logan doesn't understand why her mother puts up with her grandfather. Last year she bought him an air conditioner because he was always complaining about the heat. McKenna had it delivered and installed in his bedroom but he never used it. He put it in the storage room in the basement.

Logan smells the chicken burning. And one of Grandpa's poisonous farts, which must mean he's getting excited. When Vance shows up for his cash, Grandpa practically shouts, "This one of your customers?"

"No way," Vance says. "I cut my own. It's like I always say, never pay for what you can do with your own two paws."

"He walks our dog during the day," McKenna says loudly, "when I'm working for a living."

"Nice dog," Vance offers. "Never judge a Doberman by it's cover."

"Chicken's burning, Mum."

"Shit."

"Watch your tongue," Grandpa says.

McKenna slides the chicken onto plates and drops the skillet into the sink.

"That's *my* goddamn frying pan," Grandpa tells her.

McKenna turns on the tap, the pan hisses. She turns off the tap and leans against the counter like a boxer against the ropes about to get back in the ring.

"It's nice here, Grandpa," Logan interjects. "The bathtub's pink and there's a pool and everything. And the mirror has movie-star lights on it."

"Can't you see what you're doing to her?" McKenna asks him, nodding towards Logan.

"I'm not doing anything to her, the bastard was cursed from the start. You couldn't keep your legs crossed then and you can't now. A goddamn tramp."

At the speed of light, it seems to Logan, her mother has hurled the frying pan at her grandfather. It misses him, hits the wall and bounces feebly on the swirly carpet. Vance, looking worried, feels for his missing ear.

"Take your frying pan and get out," McKenna says in a voice Logan has never heard before. It reminds her of that exorcist movie she promised her mother she wouldn't watch but did anyway. She didn't think it was all that scary. The special effects were totally retro.

Her mother grabs the greasy frying pan off the swirly carpet and shoves it into Grandpa's gut. "Get out. Don't come back."

"You were bad news from the start," he tells her. "Looking for trouble the minute you were born. And she's no better. Born in sin."

"Out!" her mother screams, pushing him with both hands. Vance flattens himself against the wall in an effort to keep out of the way. Stanley wakes up and starts barking. McKenna and Grandpa continue to shout at each other in the parking lot. He calls her a slut and she tells him she wishes he'd drop dead. McKenna kicks his car as he drives off. She comes back in looking as if she's lost the fight and will never fight another. She pulls some cash out of her wallet and gives it to Vance. He stuffs it in his pocket.

"Most appreciated."

McKenna says nothing, just stares at the chicken as if it's from outer space.

"See you guys a little later on," Vance mutters, hurrying out. Logan closes the door after him.

McKenna rubs her eyes. "Come have some dinner, monkey."

"Is it cooked? We don't want to get salmonella."

"I can't see if it's pink. You tell me if it's pink."

Their elbows stick to the plastic tablecloth as they examine the chicken. "I think it's okay," Logan offers.

"Good. I overcooked the veggies. Do you still want some?"

"Sure." Logan has no appetite but eats to comfort her mother. Sometimes they don't talk and it's fine because there's nothing to say. But tonight the silence feels uncomfortable, as though they're trapped in an elevator pretending they're not worried.

"What did he mean when he said I was born in sin?" Logan asks.

"You shouldn't listen to him, love, he's a crazy old fart. He doesn't know what he's saying."

"A sin's when you do something against God's will."

"Who told you that?"

"Mrs. Pawusiak."

Her mother shakes her head. "I'm worried about this God business, alright, I mean, don't get all worked up about it."

"I'm not. I just don't understand how I could be born in sin. I was just a baby, I didn't know about God's will or anything."

"Newtbrains came up with the sin concept to control other humans," McKenna explains. "If there is a God, I don't think he or she set down a bunch of rules and said if you don't do this you'll get punished. Dirtbags 'sin' all the time and get away with it. Eat something, honeybun."

"Maybe that's why he burnt our house down."

"Who?"

"Because I was born in sin."

"Forget that, alright? It's meaningless. Your dad and I never married, that's all. According to the rules the newtbrains set down, if you're born out of wedlock, you're born in sin."

"That's not fair."

"Religion isn't about fair. It's about control. If there is a God, I don't think he or she condemns babies."

"Grandpa said I was cursed."

"Yeah, well, he's an idiot."

"He called me a bastard. You call men you really hate bastards."

"Sometimes."

"He must really hate me, then."

"Sweetpea, bastard is a name for children born out of wedlock. For some reason people also use it to describe scumbags. It doesn't *mean* anything."

"I'm a bastard, then."

"It's a stupid word. He's a stupid man. He's always been ignorant, and cruel. I don't know why I let him near you. I shouldn't have let him near you. He doesn't deserve it. Never again. That's it."

"Does that mean we're never seeing him again?"

"Never."

Logan spears a piece of broccoli but can't bring herself to put it in her mouth. "I don't feel very well."

"Do you want to play cards?"

"I think I'll just have a bath."

"Okay."

"The wall's dented from the frying pan. Mr. Bluxom's going to have a cow."

"We'll move the chair in front of it."

Logan has discovered pink in her chicken but doesn't mention it because she doesn't think her mother can handle it right now. Instead she says, "Did you know that a little boy shot a little girl today? He told her he didn't like her and shot her."

"At your school?"

"No, but everybody was talking about it. The bullet went right through her body and collapsed her lungs. Miss Spongle said that at the very least they should have child-safeties on guns."

"She's right." Her mother chews on a chicken leg but doesn't appear to be enjoying it.

"That's a sin," Logan points out. "To shoot somebody."

"It's a bad idea, no doubt about it."

"Do you think he'll go to jail?"

"He's too young. I don't even think they can charge a kid that young."

"You mean Curling Ellsworth could shoot me and get away with it?"

"Why are you having such violent thoughts, sweetpea? Curling Ellsworth isn't going to shoot anybody."

"He's got a gun. He told me. His dad hunts bears."

"So he says. He's probably lying." Her mother leans across the table and squints at her. "Has that little shit been threatening you?"

Logan realizes that she shouldn't have mentioned Curling because it will only mean her mother will charge over there and razz Mr. Ellsworth again.

"He's been bothering you again, hasn't he?" McKenna persists.

"Nope."

"Are you sure?"

"Yes. I'm going to have a bath."

Logan holds her head under water and tells God he can drown her if he wants. All her life she has told herself that she was a child of a single-parent family. She would have liked to have had a proper father but it wasn't something she freaked over. There are things in life you can't do anything about, no matter how hard you try. Logan understands this. Her mother doesn't. Her mother has no concept, hasn't figured out that sometimes shit happens. Like Emma dying. Her mother was always trying to find a reason for it. "Why does a little girl have to die when there's all these septic ulcers around?" She even said this to Mr. Feather when they met him in the supermarket with his new baby. He looked uncomfortable, as if he'd rather not talk about it. "It makes no sense," her mother insisted. Mr. Feather shrugged and stared at a stack of Tide. "How can you ever recover from that?" McKenna asked. Logan couldn't believe that she was being so personal. Green slime was trickling out of the baby's nose. Mr. Feather kept staring at the Tide.

"You can't recover from it," McKenna concluded.

"Yes, you can," he said. "You have to." Then he said he'd forgotten something and left the checkout line. Logan knew he was lying, and that they'd never see him again.

She is aware that in order to drown she must inhale the water, although she's not exactly sure how to do this because it will feel weird. But her ears are exploding and she decides it's now or never. She lets the air out, thinking about the little girl with the bullet holes in her chest. Miss Spongle explained that she didn't die instantly like on TV shows. She said it was important to understand that this was real, that the little girl suffered as her lungs collapsed. "Imagine having a plastic bag over your head and not being able to take it off," she said. That's a little like what Logan's currently feeling. What was the little girl thinking while she was being starved of oxygen? Maybe she figured she'd be better off dead, because she was born in sin. A fatherless child. A bastard.

The bubbles caress her face as they float to the surface. She gives one final puff of air, as though she's blowing out birthday candles, then allows the water to flow into her nose, her mouth. She tells God she's sorry.

21

It's one thing to do CPR on dummies so you can be a lifeguard and get a tan. But try giving it to your child. I can't breathe, just gasp; can't control my exhalations. The only pulse I feel is my own, jerking me around. I can't even see her because tears are pouring out of me onto her face.

I got the water out of her, grabbed her, laid her on the floor. Her skin is grey, but she's always grey to me now.

I remember the dummy, its hard plastic face and staring eyes. I'd fix my lips on it after halitosis-Dougie had slobbered all over it.

Open the air passage, block her nose, blow, pump her ribs, count it out. Blow again, pump harder, break her xiphoid if you have to.

Breathe, baby.

God, I'll believe in you if you give her back to me. You can blind me, burn me, cut off my arms, my legs.

Feel her neck again. I think it's there, she's there. Blow again, wait, give her a chance. Breathe, baby.

And she does, coughing at first, looking up at me as though she doesn't want to be here.

"Thank God," I say and hold her to me, just hold her, wait for her to put her arms around me but she remains lifeless, staring, like the dummy. "What were you doing, sweetiebun? Talk to me, lovey. Please." I'm thinking brain damage. I'm thinking our life is over.

"I'm okay," she says, still limp.

"What were you doing, love?"

"Drowning."

"I know, but why?"

"I don't know."

"You must know." I find myself shaking her.

"That hurts."

"I'm sorry." I loosen my hold, but if I let go she'll roll off my lap onto the tiles. "Can you sit up?"

"Yeah." She does, my drowned kitten, my beautiful naked girl.

"Let's get a towel around you."

"These towels smell weird."

"Bleach."

"I wish we had our own towels."

"We will."

"Have they started building our house yet?"

"He said next week."

"Maybe we could camp there."

"It's going to be pretty mucky, once they start building."

"Can we go there now?"

"Now?"

"I just want to see it."

"It's not there."

"I just want to see our yard."

"Okay. Get some clothes on."

I brought blankets. We're camping out in the back seat. I can't stop shaking. She's asleep, with her head against my chest, her arm around my waist, not letting go. I'm her life preserver.

Can't stop crying either, now that she can't see me. I try not to sob, to heave my chest. Her hair's still wet. I kiss the top of her head, smell her. She almost left me. There was this crack in the earth I was falling into, could feel my body surrendering.

This God business, what's that about? When I was a kid I think maybe I believed in him for about five minutes. I had to believe in something. I never asked him for favours though. He wasn't my pal, just somebody to watch out for.

Does she believe in God because she can't believe in her father? Or mother?

My daughter just tried to kill herself.

Or was she just fooling around? Kids do that, hold their heads under water until they black out.

You try to kill yourself when hope is this dried-up well you're sick of sticking your head in so you throw yourself down it.

She can't have no hope already. She must have been fooling around.

I don't understand what's with Lester. Does he hate me because he sees himself in me and he hates himself? Does he imagine that by extinguishing me he can purge himself of himself? And why destroy my daughter, who has done him no harm and has always drawn him birthday cards?

And why did he come here? He never even visited our house. Okay, maybe once to make sure it wasn't nicer than his. "Some neighbourhood you've found yourself in" was his comment before he started grumbling about supposed termites in the rafters. "You can see them from here?" I asked. He didn't answer, just started kicking my foundation, said my footings were rotten. Which got me worried, of course, that's his mission in life, to rattle me. I phoned the house inspector, who assured me that there'd been no sign of termites and that the footings were under the foundation, you couldn't see them unless you dug down. Thanks, Dad.

I guess he came by to snoop. Or maybe he was after the insurance money I supposedly scored for torching my house. Was he expecting a handout? *Here's a couple of Ks, Dad, don't you worry, there's plenty more where that came from.* Seriously, I want the buzzard dead. I'm tired of trying to find a place in my life where he can live. He takes up too much space, makes too much noise. Die already.

I stare at Mrs. Pawusiak's Virgin Mary. Why a virgin? It's so completely twisted. And what happens to her? Her son gets crucified. So we worship her because she suffers and doesn't whine, meaning the ideal woman gives birth to a son, never has sex and weeps silently over the death of her baby.

I can't believe in God. I know I said I would but we all make bad deals when we're up against the wall.

She rolls over so that her head is in my lap and her face turned skyward. Unconscious, free of anxiety, she has the face of a marble angel. I produced an anxious child by being anxious. Even though I tried to hide it, she always knew and she's paying for it— old beyond her years. I'll be bleaching her grey by the time she's twelve.

I stroke her forehead, then hold my fingers against her neck again. Such a delicate pulse, brushing against my fingertips like a fish. I remember when she was inside me, that fish-in-a-bowl feeling as she slithered around.

Does this mean I'll have to watch her now, around knives, tall buildings, fast cars, subway trains? She must have been fooling around.

Lester used to call my platform shoes whore-heels. That's when it started, I was thirteen or something, sprouting breasts and pubic hair, bleeding, trying to fit in. I shrugged him off but it still hurt, made me feel dirty while I hung out at the Dairy Queen.

"Cover yourself," he used to say. "You look like a hooker."

Sexually repressed, I guess he was. Since he wasn't getting any. Mom was saving it for Wally.

I've got to feed Fuzzball, who slept through the CPR proceedings.

And the weed thing, what's that about? He goes out in the yard with his weed killer and zaps 'em one by one. Why can't he just pull them out? Is he scared to touch them, get his hands dirty?

I don't remember him ever touching me. I was that dirty in his mind. Me and the ants. He freaks over ants, chases them with Raid. I used to have to sweep up their tortured, writhing bodies. After my mother died, little green worms swarmed her roses. Old Lester got out the Raid, killed the roses.

Maybe he's queer and doesn't know it, has spent his life repulsed by women but too scared to enjoy men. So he tortured the women available, wife and daughter.

Coons are going at Mrs. Pawusiak's garbage. She puts bricks over the lids to keep them out. The bandits just lift them off, have a weight-lifting party. French was in a flap because his genetically engineered, descended-from-snow-leopard cats were startled by coons last night and now think that *they* are coons.

"They just will not stop snarling at each other," he fretted. "I have to keep them in separate rooms."

"How can they think they're coons?" I inquired.

"Their eyes look a bit coony. I mean, they're descended from snow leopards."

"I realize that. Does that mean they have no brains?"

He stopped talking to me for a couple of hours, which was refreshing.

If Logan was trying to kill herself, it isn't registering. I'll have to ask her about it. She must have been fooling around.

What's the über-asshole doing now, after traumatizing my daughter? Is he pleased with himself? I gave that whoring bitch what for, he's thinking, she won't be back in a hurry, stealing egg poachers. Next she'll take the goddamn toaster. Lying good-for-nothing slut, she'll take the skin off your back if you let her.

An East Indian client of mine (black hair) was in today telling me about practices in her childhood village. She said that men poured kerosene on bitches' nipples and watched as the dogs chewed themselves to death. Another big attraction was tying cats' tails together and wagering on who'd get mauled to death first. French was horrified by this. "Honestly," he gasped, "how could anybody be so cruel?" But I didn't find any of it surprising. Lots of guys get their rocks off being cruel. My dad, for instance.

It's always bugged me when people whine about their parents and then say, "But I *love* my parents." Is there some law saying you have to love your parents? They're just people, with more holds on you than most of the dirtballs out there. They get you down and kick the shit out of you. I'm sorry, but I think as soon as you can feed and clothe yourself you should say, "See you in the next life." Otherwise the resentment you feel towards them turns into this rotten twisted thing oozing sludge into your veins. I had this client a couple of weeks ago, a whiner, but the kind who, after telling you how hard her life is for two hours, immediately says, "But it's alright, I'm not complaining," then starts whining again. Anyway, this was before I went blind and was therefore able to do multidimensional colour. It took a while. So I had to listen to her kvetch about her twenty-one-year-old daughter who was home from college and wearing slutty clothes and listening to sleazy music and just generally being uncooperative. They had a showdown in which the daughter accused the mother of being a prude with no sense of humour, an old crone and a mega-torment. The mother's line of defence was that she'd let the girl's boyfriend sleep over. She revealed this to me like it was the ace in her deck. "I let them do what they want," she told me, "I don't ask questions." Of course I knew she'd probably hovered outside the bedroom door but I nodded sympathetically while putting papers on her head, and thought, The girl is twenty-one, let her go. She might come back if you take the chains off her.

Will *I* be able to do this? I'll be fifty-something, hoping for an invite to the seniors' dance, freaking on the scales at Weight Watchers. Nope. I'll probably hang around, beg to sit in the back of her sport ute. "I won't bother you, honeybun. You just go about your business. Don't forget to buckle up."

Why's my mother haunting me now? Or was she always there but invisible in colour? Why does she want to know now what she didn't want to know before? Because the tragedy of my life can't touch her in ghostland? Where were you when I needed you, Mother? It's not like I can cry on your misty shoulder. I have to be honest with you and admit that I'm finding you a bit spooky. Like my life's complicated enough.

I should drive to the Lakeview. But I don't want to disturb my baby. Besides, my mother might be there. I avoided her in life, might as well in death. I stick my head out the window and look up at the stars—lights in the sky, as Kaspar said. I feel lucky she's alive. I feel lucky.

22

Logan kneels by the bed and looks at her dad's suitcase again. She's been wondering what's in it—money, maybe, wads of cash. If it was just clothes he wouldn't have hidden it under the bed. Maybe it's drugs and the police are looking for it. On TV suitcases contain either wads of cash, bags of cocaine or gold bricks. She's tried shoving it. It's not very heavy, which indicates it can't be gold bricks. She'd open it but she's scared her mother will return and catch her looking at it. McKenna is at the office giving Mr. Bluxom a hard time because only one of the washers is working. She says the dryers must be from 1952 because it takes six hours to dry a pair of underwear. Mr. Bluxom doesn't like her mother. When he sees her coming he squeezes behind doors.

If her mother finds out her dad is keeping luggage here she'll have a bird and probably torch the suitcase or something. Logan likes having it around because it means her father hasn't left forever.

"Monkey," her mother calls through the window. "Come check out this pig."

Her mother is stroking the black pig, even though Vance said it was mean. The pig's owner is wearing cut-offs so tight the flab on her thighs bulges out from under them.

"This is Allanah," McKenna says, "and this is her pig, Charleton."

"Hello," Logan mumbles, keeping an eye on the pig. "It's not very large."

"He's a miniature. Don't be scared, he's nice as pie."

Personally, Logan doesn't want to pet the pig. But since McKenna's been trying so hard to be fun and act like everything is normal, Logan feels obliged to pet the pig. It feels bristly.

Logan appreciates that, more than anything, her mother wants to provide her with a normal childhood. But it seems to Logan that this just isn't possible and maybe it would be preferable to become gypsies. There still are gypsies in Europe. She saw a documentary about them. They make their children beg, which isn't appropriate but it must be fun to travel all the time. Like right now, if they had a trailer they could leave Mr. Bluxom behind, and take Stanley—the gypsies keep dogs in their trailers. And Logan wouldn't have to go to school or Dotty's stinking daycare which would be excellent.

"Allanah knows how to make balloon animals," McKenna says. "She said she'll make some for us. Won't that be fun?"

"Sure."

"Why the sad face, cutie?" Allanah asks.

Logan stands straighter. "I'm not sad. What do you do about his fecal matter?"

"Stoop and scoop, just like the dog people. It's not as smelly as a dog's what with him being a veggie. And he just loves the bath, splashes around like a two-year-old."

"Allanah is a clown," McKenna elaborates. "She does supermarket openings and stuff."

"That's nice."

Allanah winks at her. "I'm a mean juggler." Logan can see how she could be a clown. She's got rubbery lips and eyebrows that pop up, and a goofy way of bobbing her head when she talks.

"You guys should come over later," Allanah urges. "Do you want to see Charleton sit?"

"Absolutely," McKenna says.

"Sit, Charleton," Allanah commands. The pig doesn't move. He looks bored, like he'd rather be in a pen with some other pigs. "Charleton, *sit*." Alannah holds up a Cheez Doodle. "Sit and you get a Doodle."

The pig sits. "Good boy." Alannah gives him the Doodle.

"Wicked," McKenna says.

"He's as smart as any human I know," Allanah assures them.

Vance shows up for his cash. "What do you say, buddy?" he asks the pig before telling McKenna about some dog food specials down at Pet Valu. "You want I go pick some up for you?"

Logan has a feeling that Vance wants to be friends with her mother and this bothers her. Scuff, the retarded dog walker, minded his own business. Vance follows them inside and advises them about his connections at Pet Valu. "It's like I always say, it's not *what* you know, it's *who* you know. I can get you maybe ten, twenty per cent off."

Logan notices that a corner of her dad's suitcase is poking out from under the bed. She quickly shoves it with her foot.

"They offered me shares, right," Vance continues, "but I said Pasadena, I got better things to spend my money on. It's like I always say, if you want to get rich you either got to manage a lot of people or a lot of money."

McKenna hands him some cash. "We haven't eaten yet, Vance, we'll see you later."

"You're right there, definitely."

She closes the door after him and starts shaking her hands.

"Why do people keep talking to us?" Logan asks.

"It's a small community, we're better off getting to know them. We're kind of living in each other's backyards."

"When's Mr. Bluxom opening the pool?"

"He promised the weekend."

"Fantabulous!" Logan shouts, jumping on the bed.

"Yeah, but you're not going in unless I'm watching."

"Oh, Mum."

"Oh, Mum nothing. Are you going to talk to me about what happened last night?"

Logan's been waiting for this. Her mother has no concept of letting things go. Everything has to be grabbed, shaken, turned upside down and inside out. "What do you mean?" she mumbles.

"In the bath. What was that about?"

"Nothing."

"Were you fooling around?"

"Yeah." Logan hops to the floor and kneels beside her champion mare, offers her some hay.

"Why would you fool around like that?" her mother persists.

"For fun."

"It's fun to almost drown?"

"It's different. I just wanted to see what it felt like."

"What did it feel like?"

"Drowning."

Her mother slumps on the end of the bed.

"It's okay, Mum. I'm not going to do it again."

"Promise?"

"Promise."

Her mother looks small and pathetic suddenly, like a little girl who's been left behind. "It really scared me, baby," she says. "I was so scared."

"I'm sorry."

"Don't be sorry, just don't do it again. And forget what Grandpa said, alright? He's a sick old weasel, doesn't even know what he's saying half the time. He wanted to hurt me. It had nothing to do with you."

"Why would he want to hurt you?" Logan exercises the foal.

"I've never been able to figure that one out."

"Parents aren't supposed to hurt their kids."

"They do though, sometimes without even knowing it. I've hurt you before."

"Like when?"

"When I've put you in your room."

"That's when I was bad." Logan places the horses face to face so they can nuzzle each other.

"You weren't bad. You were frustrated because I wouldn't let you do what you wanted."

"I was rude." Logan allows both horses to sniff the flowerpot. "*You* were rude when you told Dad he had no brain."

"I was."

"That hurt him, I bet."

"I doubt it. I don't think I can hurt him."

"Why not?"

"You can only hurt people who care about you."

"Why doesn't he care about you?"

"I don't matter to him." McKenna stands. "We have to do stove-top again. Do you feel like a stir-fry?"

"Okay. I'm going to do homework."

While Logan works on her space project, she considers what her mother has just said. If you can only hurt people who care about you, that would suggest that her mother cares about Grandpa, since he hurt her. It probably even means she cares about Payne, since he upsets her all the time. That's if being hurt and being upset are the same thing. Both make you cry and stuff.

Her mother sits on the toilet seat while Logan is in the bath, covering her eyes with her hands because as usual the lights hurt. Logan knows she's hanging around to make sure she doesn't try drowning again.

"What's on your mind?" McKenna asks.

"Nothing."

Her mother looks at her, holding her hands above her eyes as though shielding them from the sun. "Something's bugging you."

"Nothing's bugging me." Actually Logan's thinking about the ten-metre fin whale that was killed in P.E.I. because they couldn't move her. She was only ten years old; whales can live to be a hundred. Logan doesn't get how entire lakes can be filled in or made, huge buildings can be built or demolished, but man can't get it together to move a whale.

Normally she talks to God in the bath but she can't with her mother present. She already asked him to forgive her for trying to kill herself. She knows it's a sin because a man on their street shot himself in the head with a nail gun and Mrs. Pawusiak said it was a sin. Logan doesn't really understand why it's a sin, if you've sinned already and are punishing yourself by drowning or whatever. She's having trouble with the whole sin concept anyway, because people who are evil—Curling Ellsworth, for example—just go on being evil. It's not like they get punished or anything. And Mr. Beasley, he's really horrible to Dotty even though they're married. He calls her lard-ass. Dotty asked him to mow the grass today and he said, "Do it yourself, lard-ass." Then he was playing Simon Says and making the kids do things with their bums, or "bottoms" as he called them. "Simon says touch your bottom. Simon says wiggle your bottom. Simon says stick your bottom up in the air." Logan stayed clear of him. He called her princess, which she knew meant he thought she was stuck-up. She finds herself wishing he'd get run over by a truck but then remembers that she wanted such a fate for Curling and instead her house got hit.

"Please tell me what you're thinking about," her mother says, with her hands shielding her eyes.

"School tomorrow."

"That's not what you were thinking about."

"I was wondering if I got all my homework done."

"You always get all your homework done."

Logan squeezes the facecloth and lets the water dribble over her knees. "A guy tried to row across the Pacific but he got gangrene. They had to amputate his toes."

"Gag."

"It's going to be hard for him to walk."

"I'm sure, but let's face it, who asked him to paddle across the ocean? I mean, get a life."

"I guess he thought it would be a challenge."

"Yeah, well, life's full of challenges, you don't have to go looking for them."

Logan leans back in the tub and covers her face with the cloth. As she inhales she feels it cling to her nostrils. "Are you still mad at Dad?"

"Was I mad at him?"

"You're always mad at him."

"Do you want to see him?"

"He said he was going to get me some fantabulous bath toys." Logan takes the cloth off her face and hangs it over the side of the tub.

McKenna gropes around and grabs a towel. "You tell me when you want to see him, and I'll find him." She holds it out. "We'll get you some bath toys tomorrow." She keeps blinking. "Come on, sweetpea, it's late."

"I'd like one of those wind-up ones."

"Then that's what we'll get."

"A whale would be nice."

Her mother dries her hurriedly. Normally she wraps her in a towel and gives her a big hug, but tonight she drapes it around Logan's shoulders, pulls the plug and hurries out of the bathroom. Logan knows it's because the lights are hurting her eyes.

As she puts on her dinosaur pyjamas, she notices that McKenna has draped scarves over the bedside lamps. "Is that okay with you, monkey? Can you still see?"

"It looks weird."

"It's easier on my eyes."

Logan gets into bed with Tiger. "We keep forgetting to buy books."

"Right. That's terrible. We have to make a list."

"I forgot to brush my teeth."

"Up you get."

Back in the bathroom, while brushing her teeth, Logan notices that her hair is even messier than usual. Normally her mother would have insisted on combing out the tangles by now. It would hurt but at least Logan wouldn't have to listen to Curling's rat-nest jokes. Logan reaches for a comb and tries to run it through the sides but it's too matted. How could her mother not notice?

Logan has a feeling that nothing, absolutely nothing, will ever be normal again.

23

Somebody's looking in the window. I grab the bat and hide in the shadows. I unscrewed the bulb above the door because it's been bugging me and I can see better without it. I check the lock—it's a no-brainer, a credit card could jimmy it. My heart's banging into my ribs because if it's some messed-up junkie looking for dope, a baseball bat isn't going to stop him.

"Logan . . . ," he whispers.

Of course it's him. Who else? What's his plan, to steal her again, hold her ransom? He taps the window gently.

"Peachypie . . ."

I look to see if she's heard. She's right out. I open the door slowly and stand just inside it, in the dark, so he'll think it's her.

"Lo . . . ?"

I wield my bat and hiss, "What the fuck do you think you're doing?"

He jumps about ten feet, then tries to act like he wasn't scared out of his designer jeans. "For fuck's sake, McKenna."

I chase him down the lot a bit. He runs with his arms over his head. This is fun.

"Would you quit that?" he asks. "What's the matter with you?"

"What's the matter with *you*? No pussy tonight? No place to lay your shrunken head?" I'm managing to keep my voice down, don't want to alert Bluxom. "Did Miss Jiggly Jugs boot you out after just two nights? That must be some kind of record."

He lowers his arms. I jerk the bat to make him raise them again.

"Am I supposed to punch a clock with you or something?" he asks.

"Yes. If you want to bunk here. Definitely yes. So your daughter can count on you for once in her life."

"I just want my case."

"Your what?"

"My suitcase. There's a case in there."

"In our room?"

"Are you deaf? Yes, in that dive there is a suitcase which belongs to me."

"How did it get there?"

"I talked to the manager, what's the big deal?"

"The big deal is that you did not ask permission."

"To stash a case? Man, you are so bitter. You need to get laid, Mac, I'm telling you, you're turning sour."

I jerk the bat again; up go his arms. "Where is it?"

"Under her bed."

I find the case and hurl it out the door. What a pisser it doesn't fall open; it would have been special to see his garb mopping up oil. The rodent snatches the bag and skibbles to his car. I consider slonking the Beemer but this would only complicate matters. "If you'd woken her," I tell him as he's shoving the case into the back seat, "she'd have thought you'd come to see her. How do you think she'd have felt once she found out you were just after your luggage?"

"It's my clothes, I need them, what am I supposed to do?"

"Get out, just go."

"I'm going. Just back off with the bat, alright?"

I realize I'm still holding it like a club and he's scared I'm going to thwack his car. I step closer to it. He vrooms out of there without looking back. I think of the five thousand times I stood on street corners searching passing cars for him because he said he'd "be there in twenty." And how stupid I felt when the twenty turned into thirty, forty, fifty. When he did show up I didn't reproach him because I wanted him to love me, put his hand on my knee, want me. To care. This is what he's doing to Logan, the love-starvation diet. He tosses her a bone and she gnaws on it till her gums bleed.

I'm so weary suddenly, can hardly keep my head up, feel like it's crushing my spine. I prop it up against the Lakeview. The truth is, I'd like to put it under the tire of a bus. I'm tired of thinking, trying to work it out. It doesn't work out. No matter how much you "work it out" there's always something tripping you up.

Payne.

I used to make excuses for him. His mother walked out on him when he was nine, leaving him with a dad who couldn't keep his pecker in his pants. Payne had about sixty mommies; meanwhile his biological one married the bottle. Sad stories aside, how can you do to your kid what your parents did to you, add to the big stinking assembly line of polluted childhoods? When I get really pissed at people, I try to imagine them small. Because the kid's still in there, hiding behind the attitude. If you can spot him, with his runny nose and scabby knees, you can usually forgive him for stepping on your face. Other times, like with Payne, all you want to do is slip a grenade in his pants.

Back in the room, Mommy dearest is waiting for me, nodding like I'm talking, looking worried as usual. I want to yell at her. Instead I say, "Hi, Mum," and start assuring her everything's fine, tutti-frutti, before I remember she's a mirage.

I sit on the bed by Logan, notice that her eyes are slightly open. "You awake, kiddo?" She's looking straight at Grandma.

"What's going on?" she asks.

"Nothing."

"I heard something."

"Probably just the wind." If she was seeing the old lady, she'd be demanding her ID by now.

"Why aren't you in bed?" she asks.

"I've got to feed Fuzzball." I kiss her forehead. "Go back to sleep, love." She rolls on her side, gripping the tiger, tightening her jaw, preparing for a good teeth-grind. When the dentist told me that she grinds, I thought, Right, another one of my attributes she gets to inherit. Can't she be free of *any* of my bad habits? As her life unfolds I see mine, and I can't fix it this time either.

I tuck her in and go back outside, to avoid Mother. It seems she's big on that chair. I moved it to hide the dent in the wall, but she's still on it. She has to be the result of some weird eye thing. I mean, I can't tell shadows from substance anymore. My neck aches from driving hunched over the wheel, trying to figure out what's a shadow and what's a human who'll sue me if I hit him. Tree shadows on tarmac look like pools of water or oil or something, I'm constantly fighting the impulse to swerve around them. I was so busy trying to figure out what a tree shadow was yesterday I nearly got mashed by a cement truck. The numbnuts driver gave me one of those "woman driver" scowls. Logan's been complaining that I'm driving too slowly. I just keep pointing out speed limits and insisting that I've decided to become a law-abiding citizen. On the way to the daycare I was convinced that a bundle of rags was a dead cat. I halted traffic so I could move it to the side of the road. "It's a dead cat," I kept shouting at the honking drivers. I only figured out it was rags when I was five feet from it. I pulled into the Gerrard Square parking lot and scrambled onto the pedestrian ramp that spans the GO Train tracks. It's a good place to scream when a train goes past, especially mid-week when there's nobody around. I saw *Cabaret* when I was eight or something, snuck into the theatre because it was restricted, and was deeply influenced by Liza Minnelli screaming her head off under a train bridge. Ever since, I've been in search of good screaming venues. The Gerrard Square walkway isn't bad, although not exactly thirties Berlin. Contemplating throwing myself on the tracks provided diversion. And I had a good scream when I saw that the GO Train wasn't green anymore.

Anyway, it's easier at night, out here with the coons, when everything is supposed to be grey. There's the usual action down at dealer central. I sniff for weed but all I get is car exhaust, as one of the boys has left his Audi running. Fuzzball must be growing because the weight of her is starting to bug my shoulder. She still fits in the pocket though, her little nest. The jacket smells of her. If I get it cleaned she'll be homeless. A hundred years ago I adopted another orphaned cat, had to hide her from Lester of course. He found out eventually and locked me and the cat in the dungeon. He didn't strangle her though, actually got used to her, called her "the kitten" even when she was twelve. Her story was that a neighbour who worked at the food terminal found five deserted kittens on a load of yams. The mother cat must have been out hunting for food when the truck took off. Binkie, my kitten, would go crazy around yams, even regular potatoes. I'd put one on the floor and she'd roll around on it, rub up against it, lie on it. It was the closest she could get to her mother.

The door of the neighbouring unit swings open and out comes Bluxom, hitching up his pants. As he trudges towards the office Mr. Charm spits.

Next comes his floozie in her coffee-stained peignoir, glass in hand. She takes a swig and I smell rye. My sense of smell is becoming a problem. It's as though my nose is compensating for the eye deficit. Which is fine around fruits and veggies but not so special around garbage. Or rye. But if I move she'll see me, and know therefore that I know about the Bluxom liaison.

I'm also developing bat ears. I'm hearing babies crying a block away, dogs barking on the other side of town, car horns, buses, sirens, air conditioners, stereos, Bluxom farting next door. The hyper nostrils come in handy at the salon because I can identify products without scrutinizing labels. But out in the world, the racket and the stench get a little overwhelming. Makes me want to hide in a windowless room. Kaspar was hypersensitive when he first escaped the box, not just to light but to magnets that were in toys people gave him, and metals. They weakened him. And the smell of meat made him sick, and all the other fatty morsels people kept stuffing in his face. His keepers forced the meat on him and eventually he got used to it. Which makes you consider how sensitive we all are, fresh out of the womb box, and how the contaminated environment desensitizes us in no time. I have a client who adopted an orphan from Russia. The kid was two when she got him and completely wired. He'd smash his head into walls and all the cute crap she'd buy him. Finally she consulted a shrink, who advised her that the kid had spent his life in an orphanage and wasn't able to handle Disneyland. He was conditioned to stare at blank walls, ergo it was crucial to strip him of all the gizmos and let him sort himself out. He did. He's now a consumer demon like all the other kids.

"Jesus Murphy," the floozie declares. "I didn't see you."

"It's dark," I point out.

"What you doin' sitting there in the dark?"

"Meditating."

"Is that so? Well, you gave me a fright, I can tell you."

"Sorry."

She has a face that's seen too much, and no sparks in her eyes. She was a baby once. Now she's sucking back rye, banging Bluxom.

"Nice night out, anyway," she comments. And I'm feeling for this woman, because not only has she seen it all but she's getting slapped around by Mr. Charm's flab. I'd like to come right out with it and say why are you spreading your legs for that dirtbag?

"I'm an insomniac," she confides. "Always have been, four hours a night tops, the rest of the time I'm seeing only the bad news."

"I hear ya."

"Are you an insomniac?"

"Just lately. I have to feed my kitten every three hours." I show her Fuzzball.

"Isn't that the cutest thing? Makes a nice change from that pig. Where does she get off keeping that pig?"

"Her husband has allergies."

"Yeah, right. Have you see him around? She says he wants to kill her. I'd say he doesn't want to go anywhere near her."

"Or the pig." Now that I can make noise I adjust my chair to the reclining position. Maybe a miracle will happen and I'll drift off out here in the breeze. Listening to her is easier than the endless tape inside my head.

"Did you hear about that fella threw acid on his wife's face?" she asks me. "Drove to the police station, smashed up her car, then turned himself in. He'll get off easy. Meantime she's disfigured for life."

"Heinous."

"Yeah, well, goes on all the time. And the bastards get off with a year."

Speaking of bastards, I want to say, do you happen to know if Bluxom intends to fix the washers? "Have you been here long?" I inquire.

"As long as Burt'll have me. Nobody else is offering me a couch. I got fired, see, had to leave my old place."

"What do you do?"

"Stripper. My ex-boss says I'm too old. Look at these legs, better than girls' half my age." She shows me her legs and they *are* good. I can't speak for the rest of her. "It's discrimination. I've filed a complaint with the Human Rights Commission."

I'm almost asleep, should get up and get into bed, but then I'll be awake. And my mother's in there.

"There's no birds here," the stripper observes. "Used to be birds at my old place. How do birds sleep, anyway?"

"In trees." Can't keep my eyes open.

"Yeah, but what keeps them from falling off?" Ice rattles as she drinks. "Or getting eaten by coons?"

"I think coons prefer prepared foods."

I stumble into the no man's land of dreams.

24

Her mother slept in a lawn chair. This is disturbing. Next she'll start digging around in trash cans and shouting "What are you staring at?" at people who aren't even looking at her. She stinks of Fuzzball and only remembered to shower because Logan reminded her. Logan likes the cat, just thinks her mother's getting a little over-preoccupied with it. She's not even talking to Stanley anymore. Logan's been careful to give him extra treats and hugs but she doesn't know how he's going to feel once he figures out that the cat thing's permanent.

She came to Nina's birthday party only because Uncle Tait wanted to jump off a building and could only spend the morning with her. Saturdays are her mother's big day at the salon, so Logan has to spend it with either Uncle Tait or her dad if he's available.

The party began with girls fighting over who got to use what glitter tattoos. Molly and Brittany started wrestling each other over the heart-shaped ones. Nina's mother let them use her makeup so they all got painted up. Now they're in their bathing suits running around the sprinkler, screaming.

"What, you didn't bring no bathing suit?" Nina's mother asks.

Logan shakes her head. Nina's mother is even fatter than Nina, wears bicycle shorts and talks constantly on her cell phone. She ordered pizza with it—pepperoni and double cheese. When Logan said she didn't want any, Mrs. Cairney said, "What, you don't eat no meat?" Whoever Mrs. Cairney's talking to on her cell phone can't be saying much because Mrs. Cairney just goes on yammering about the birthday party and how she has to get to the store to pick up lottery tickets.

All Logan wants is for Mr. Bluxom to fill the pool. She's actually been praying that he fill it before her father returns for his suitcase so that Payne will see it and want to get a tan.

Curling Ellsworth starts chasing the girls in the bathing suits around the yard. He flails his arms and barks.

Nina's mother, still on her cell, hands out freezies. Logan tries to avoid staring at Mrs. Cairney's legs but she can't help it because they're so veiny—one big mass of blue rivers. Logan wonders what would happen if she jabbed one with a pencil, if the blood would gush out or spurt in a steady stream, and how long it would take for Mrs. Cairney to bleed to death.

"You're a serious one," Mrs. Cairney says, handing Logan a freezie. "Not exactly the life of the party."

All her life people have called Logan serious because she doesn't act retarded. It's like if you're not doing what everybody else is doing there's something wrong with you. In Logan's opinion, there's something wrong with everybody else. They make too much noise, for one thing. She has to keep covering her ears to block out the girls' shrieks. And there's no way Curling's normal. Like right now he's trying to bite a glitter tattoo off Molly's leg. Mrs. Cairney thinks it's cute and talks about it on her cell phone. "Boys will be boys," she says.

Logan's decided that, if the pool isn't filled when she gets back to the Lakeview, she's going to speak to Mr. Bluxom personally. Because if her mother asks him about it again, he'll definitely go ballistic.

The really awful thing is that Molly and Brittany have been making fun of Nina behind her back and Mrs. Cairney hasn't even noticed. They keep puffing out their cheeks and walking like Nina. Earlier they were snickering about her dress, which is too tight and makes her look like the pink toilet roll cover in Mrs. Cairney's bathroom. Logan doesn't understand why Nina invited them.

Mrs. Cairney leans back in her plastic chair, tipping the front legs and balancing on the back ones. Logan waits for it to collapse. Mrs. Cairney laughs into the phone and her entire body wobbles. The back legs look ready to buckle, but then Nina asks about the cake again, if they can eat it yet. It's huge and pink and has Barbie shoes and matching purses stuck all over it.

They had to buy Nina a present last night. McKenna, bumping into things as usual, suggested Disabled Barbie but Logan explained that Nina had every Barbie going. "I bet she doesn't have a crippled Barbie," her mother persisted, stumbling over an Exersaucer.

"There's no way I'm giving her a crippled Barbie."

"She's still got hard tits and anorexic legs."

Instead they bought some accessories because Nina's always complaining that she loses Barbie's shoes. Which must be why Mrs. Cairney has plastered the cake with them. It's store-bought and tastes like sugared sponge. Mrs. Cairney hands out party favours, which Logan recognizes from the dollar store. She tries to look enthusiastic about the plastic rings and bracelet. She wishes they'd turn the music down. Curling sits beside her with his water pistol. "El cheapo," he says, tossing the pistol on the ground and going for more cake. Why did Nina invite Curling Ellsworth? Is it because she has no friends but wanted a party anyway? Is it better to have just anybody around rather than nobody at all? Nina doesn't look too happy, except with the cake. Maybe Mrs. Cairney invited everybody so that Nina would get presents. There certainly are a lot of them. While Nina unwraps, Curling does rabbit ears behind her head and Molly and Brittany giggle. Mrs. Cairney doesn't notice because she's still on her cell phone, eating pizza. She pulls off pepperoni and feeds it to her two dogs, who she calls babies.

Logan doesn't know what to do about McKenna. It's embarrassing being with her. In stores she keeps her distance so people won't know they're related. Apart from the hand-shaking and bumping into things, McKenna's started to talk to herself. She'll announce what something is, once she figures it out. "Oh, those are eggplants," she'll tell the whole store. "I thought they were squash." People are always staring at her. And it bothers Logan that she's always wearing black. Usually her mother wears colourful clothes, she calls herself "a colour freak." People see her and say, "I could never wear that colour," but McKenna can. Logan misses her colours. Her Hawaiian shirts were burned in the fire, she had a bunch of them decorated with parrots, flamingos and toucans. She wore them in winter to brighten things up. Now it's almost summer and she's walking around in black. From a distance Logan doesn't even recognize her. Normally she can spot her a mile away.

Next they have to play fat bat. Curling and Brittany choose teams. Logan and Nina get picked last. Logan despises fat bat. Playing catch is bad enough but having to hit the ball then run to some stupid marker is just plain torture. She strikes out, then claims that her ankle hurts. Mrs. Cairney brings out a tub of sidewalk chalk. Logan tries to look busy drawing dogs and cats, pigs and rats on the patio stones. "Aren't you the little artist?" Mrs. Cairney remarks. The girls shriek as Curling Ellsworth hits a home run. Logan covers her ears, then starts to draw a whale.

25

Pixie, the new receptionist, has been too busy servicing Kristos to notice that she has overbooked. She doesn't seem to get the time requirement for perms and colour, therefore clients are waiting and cranky. My first, a chronic dieter, got shat on by a bird on her way to the salon and spent half an hour in the can wiping it off her blouse. This put me behind from the get-go. Plus, nipping into the can for eye relief is backing me up. I made the mistake of looking in the mirror and saw that it wasn't me staring out at me, more like the Wicked Witch of the West. I've had a stream of Asians, which is good except they've been chatty. One of them gabbed at length about some guy she met at church. "Whenever he sees me with other people," she told me, "he interrupts and asks if I'm leaving and if I'm leaving with him. Does that seem like strange behaviour to you?" I put on my concerned-while-thinking-about-it face but didn't venture an opinion (I always avoid opinions around clients), which gave her the opportunity to preach about her church and how she likes to keep the words of God close to her. During the blow-dry she circled back to the guy topic and made a point of saying that he was white and blond. "And he always sits next to me even if I'm with other people. Does that seem like strange behaviour to you?"

Next up was her friend who complained about her luggage, her Japanese husband and prices in Hong Kong. "It's not like when you go to Italy and can get Prada for cheap."

By this time my eyes and hands were aching from cutting Asian hair, and I had to feed Fuzzball. Pixie was in the can painting up so I hurried to the back room, where Sandrine was standing on one leg with her arms over her head and her palms pressed together. She told me that she was changing her name to Akabar per her yoga teacher's instructions. Kristos sauntered in to call his skull-head car dealer and hit the roof when they told him there was no car. "First you tell me it's in a dock in Halifax, then you tell me there eez no *freakin' car*? What kind of beezness is this?" Sandrine went in search of gingko biloba, and I took the opportunity to break the news that I couldn't take on any new colour clients. Kristos looked at me as though I'd just told him his mother was doin' the mailman.

"Are you crazy?" he gasped.

"No, I just can't see colour."

"What do you mean, you can't see colour?"

"I mean I'm colour-blind. It's shock or something. From the fire. Probably just temporary." I was trying to act like I wasn't freaked but my guts were contorted.

"I've lost speech," he said, working out the dollar figures. "You're my top colourist."

"Well, I'll just have to be your top cut and stylist for a while. I can still do regulars."

He pounded his fist into his chest as though he were having a heart attack. "You won't make money."

"That's *my* problem. Send the colour clients to French and Coco. And Sandrine could use a few clients." I didn't want him to see I was scared shitless, so I filled a glass at the tap and watered the sickly African violet some groupie gave French.

"Sandrine's too slow," he moaned.

"At least she doesn't burn heads. All she needs is practice. Just tell Pixie not to send me any new colour clients." I picked off some dead leaves.

He clutched his head. "This is terrible news."

"Look at the bright side. I'm building an Asian clientele. I seem to be doing something special for them."

"The Chinks take forever, you need wire cutters."

"They spend money, and there's a lot of them."

I left him a ruined man. He's spent the rest of the day limping and threatening to start smoking again even though he only quit three days ago. My current client drove in from the burbs and says she's not feeling well, which I know from experience means I can't make her feel any better. While wiping snot from her nose she tells me she wants a new hairstyle. My motto is, if they're not feeling well, don't give them a new hairstyle. Chances are, when you're done, they'll look in the mirror and start boohooing. So I *pretend* to give her a new style, flash my scissors, lots of combing and flourishing of the blow-dryer. I try a different flick up. When I'm done I tip the mirror, showing the "newest" aspect of the do. She goes away glum but not hysterical. I hide in the can until Coco starts kicking the door with his spiky boots. "What's going on in there?"

I exit, smiling sweetly before facing a bag of waste I've been doing for years. She's British and regularly expounds on North America's failings. When she gets really rancid I say, "What's stopping you going back to England?" This shuts her up for about five seconds because she was booted out of the U.K., sued, disgraced. I don't know her well, wouldn't want to, but even from our hair-related interactions I know she lies. She's always having a "drink the other night" with somebody important, always on the verge of some big deal that never happens, always off "on business" but then I see her sitting around Starbucks for days. I have no idea what she lives on. She spends serious coin on her hair though—all-over colour, perms, lights, cut and style—so I put up with her. But she has a nasty habit of snapping at me for no particular reason. I seem to rub her the wrong way just by breathing. So mostly I zip it. But today she's decided that there is no global warming, no homeless problem, no child poverty, no toxic waste overload, no water shortage, no nuclear threat. Because my bullshit radar has been enhanced by vision problems, I start to lose it. "Have you read the paper lately?" I ask her.

"You don't *believe* what you read in the paper, surely?"

"It beats *People*," I say, because she happens to have it in her hand.

Fortunately Kristos intervenes regarding his car with the dead-cow seats. "They're going to give me *next* year's model at this year's price." He drops his blow-dryer into his holster like a cowboy who's just shot somebody.

"When?" asks French, who's cutting a woman to look like French.

"Could be a few days."

Coco's tongue darts. "More like weeks."

I notice that Little Miss Spread-her-legs has swept under everybody's chair but mine. She's wearing a vinyl miniskirt that rides up her thighs. "Excuse me," I say for the fourteenth time, "would it be possible for you to sweep under my chair *once* a day?"

"She swept under your chair," French says, popping Advil number nine. "I saw her."

"She did not." I grab some of his refuse that's been breeding on my counter and shove it onto his.

"Territorial, are we?" he comments. He's wearing about fourteen bangles which keep jangling at me.

"Would you mind looking after my hair?" the British bag of waste snaps. I want to slonk her. Instead I shove the broom handle into Little Miss Spread-her-legs' hands. "Sweep," I order.

The boys chime in, "Would you lay off her, Mac. A friend of hers died at a rave last night."

"Quelle tragédie," I say.

"She did," the dipshit insists. "She was doing ecstasy and her body got overheated and dehydrated with all the dancing and that, so she died."

"So what are you doing here, if you're so upset? Shouldn't you be at a funeral?"

"Honestly," French interjects.

"Honestly nothing," I say. "Kristos, she sweeps or I'm outta here."

He holds up his hands. "Okay, okay. Sweep, darling, otherwise there's too much trouble."

And she does, like she's under water. If I had the time I'd snatch the broom and do it myself, but the bag of waste is getting riled. No tip today, not that her tips are worth sweating over. What I don't understand, have never understood, is why some people act like assholes for no apparent reason—just to be assholes and make people who aren't assholes miserable? I've tried to convince myself that they're actually miserable, which explains why they want everybody else to suffer. But it doesn't wash, because they thrive. They don't get sick and die. The non-assholes do. I've noticed this. Like that little girl Emma, why did she have to die while this bag of waste goes on sucking blood? I do a half-assed job of a blow-dry, no mirror tricks, and head over to Pixie to write up the bill. The bag of waste takes her time removing herself from my chair. I ignore her and head for the can for some respite, splash cold water on my face before realizing that this will smear my eyeliner.

I think the problem with being a non-asshole is that you identify with the weak, which weakens you, because you never lose sight of how fragile it all is. The assholes figure they can chew up the world and everyone in it. The assholes think they're invincible and chant "survival of the fittest" while trampling the non-assholes.

I have this client who's so over the top in the asshole department, it's all I can do not to cut off his ears. He's in the garment industry, which means he pays women and children in third world countries fifty cents to sew his Petite and Tall Girl lines. I happened to mention the pollution over there, how we Westerners should take some responsibility for it because we industrialized first and therefore got first dibs on contaminating air, land and water. He just shrugged and said, "Get a bubble."

"What?"

"Get a bubble, create your own biosphere. It's where it's going to go." He was dead serious.

So the assholes have this vision of the future in which they'll live happily under glass while the non-assholes perish. What they don't understand is that they need the non-assholes not only to produce their crap but to buy it.

I've met his kids. They're evil, they come in for flavour-of-the-month styles, then gripe about it.

I have this image of Logan and me, pressing our emaciated, dehydrated, oxygen-starved bodies against the asshole's bubble, watching his satanic kids bopping on floaties in his custom-made freshwater lake. They stick out their tongues and thumb their noses. After a few minutes one of his cloned six-foot-four guards, wearing an oxygen mask, nudges us with his baton and tells us to move on.

What keeps me going are people like that girl who lived in a tree for two years to prevent the logging company from destroying the forest. That would take some guts, staying up there while beefy logging guys threaten you with chainsaws. I see Logan doing something like that. She has it in her, if it doesn't get beaten out of her.

It took me a long time to accept that she was going to be an outsider like I'm an outsider. I wanted her to be a happy, bouncing kid who stepped on ants and watched *Barney*. The Barney crowd—the ones who chanted "I love you, you love me, we're one happy fa-mi-ly"—smelled *different* on her and shut her out. She who had so much wanted to play with other kids learned to avoid them, and despise them. Until Emma.

Pixie taps on the door with her Bic. "It might interest you to know that your next client has arrived." I sit on the toilet seat, covering my eyes with my hands. I'm not sure I can keep this up.

One of my fears in the mother-like-daughter department is that I took drugs because it muted assholery. A septic ulcer could snarl and spit and I wouldn't even notice. World news stopped getting to me, I stopped caring about children dying of starvation, AIDS, TB. I saw only as far as the next snort. And stupid shit became important, like listening to a scratchy Beatles album and understanding that John was warning us that he was going to get shot.

I try to look sharp for my last client, a school principal who, according to her, is being put through by some parents who want her to harness the bullies who keep tormenting their son. She also has carpenter ants eating her house and biting her in her bedroom, so I feel some sympathy for her. But she makes like the parents are overprotective, that the kid should be able to look after himself. "He has to learn," she says. "I think some kids just have victim written all over them." My thought is, Does that mean it's okay to stomp on their faces? How many geniuses can we name who were sickly kids? Chopin, Blake, Orwell, Chekhov, Alexander Graham Bell. I mean, do we really want a world in which we all play ball?

I refuse to force Logan into holes she can't fit.

But I feel her loneliness, because it's my loneliness. When the little girls in Barbie clothes reject her, she tells herself she doesn't care, but she does. She gave me the power not to care because my feelings for her were so huge, so unprecedented, nothing else mattered. I didn't know what a feeling was until Logan. I'd kill for her.

But she's swamped in mother-love. Feeling is no news to her, ergo I can't protect her from the Barbie clones as she protects me from the assholes. I'm only her mother, and we all know how that one goes. As the years wear on, my space in her life will shrink, she'll stop returning my calls. And look for something to fill those holes. Men, substances, aura-healing tools.

I cash out and hustle to a handy overpriced toy store because I'm determined to find a wind-up whale for her. I stare at a wall display of wind-ups, trying to decipher tigers from lions, jeeps from boats, monkeys from rabbits. Two women with fried perms butt in front of me and start fingering the monkeys. "Everybody said they were, like, the perfect couple," the frizzier one remarks.

"So did you," responds the other, who must be using dollar-store conditioner because the perm drags.

"They looked good together," the frizzier one says. "You just never know." She winds up a duck. "At least Deb and Bob are still together. They're having a lawn sale." The duck's feet flap. "That's so cute. All Mikey's toys are battery-operated. I call that sensory deprivation. I was thinking of getting him a robot, really cute, but I hate battery-operated, the batteries, like, die and then what are you supposed to do?"

A hundred years ago there was a girl on our block, not nice, one of those bossy leaders of the pack. She had a battery-operated blue yapping poodle, which I kicked. It had to go, the witch was running it night and day. I tried to make it look like it was an accident because I didn't want the witch to sic her gang on me later. I said I was sorry, but the next morning there was dog shit all over Lester's pesticided lawn, which he made me stoop and scoop. Anyway, I hated this girl, wanted her dead, imagined the ways. Then her father drowns at their cottage. Right off the dock, he dives down after a fishing lure and doesn't come back up. This shook the neighbourhood. We all went to the service. I saw Sabrina walk past her dad's casket, saw her choking with tears and thought, I have to be nicer to this girl, maybe I'm wrong about her, maybe her gang didn't dump the dog doo. That night I tried to imagine what it would be like to have your father alive one minute then dead the next. I thought it would be great in my case, but I understood that Sabrina had loved her dad; they used to bowl together. So I felt sad for her. I saw her on the street a few days later. She was sitting outside the corner store sucking on a freezie. I said, "Hi," and tried to smile. She said, "Go fuck yourself."

That was when I figured out people don't change. Outfits, hairstyles, cars, houses. But the bile inside, however it got there, whether they were born with it or whether it was funnelled into them, it just keeps circulating.

I look at my daughter and try to tell myself she doesn't have to end up like me, tell myself she could still be prom queen, a brain surgeon, or just happily married with kids. I tell myself not to draw conclusions. I tell myself it could go either way.

No easily identified whales. I start experiencing something like claustrophobia staring at all the plastic. I grab something fishy and wave it at the salesgirl. "Is this a whale?"

"It's a dolphin."

"Do you have any whales?"

"We're out." She's wearing leopard skin and has acne. All I see is spots.

"What colour is this?"

"Excuse me?"

"What colour is this dolphin?"

She stares at me like I'm a boat person. "Grey. They come in blue or grey."

I buy it, get out of there, walk straight into a lightbulb-changer's ladder. He ejaculates vile words at me. My brain must be short-circuiting from having to compute what everything is. Suddenly the whole street is just one big jumble of moving objects. I aim for what looks like a phone booth. I slam the door behind me and lean against the box with my back to the street. I grip the box, press my chest against it, even though it stinks of a thousand fingerprints; at least it feels real, I know what it is. Within seconds someone raps on the door with an umbrella. "Are you using the phone?" It's a queer in a deerstalker.

"What does it look like?"

"It looks like you're not using it."

"Looks can be deceiving."

Another queer in a deerstalker appears. "Are you going to be long?"

"Hours." I pick up the receiver and punch some buttons.

"This is a public phone."

I start babbling into the mouthpiece that stinks of a thousand mouths.

"She didn't put money in," the first queer observes.

"You didn't put money in," the second confirms.

I start pretending I'm arguing with a lover who happens to be screwing somebody else, which brings Payne to mind: how he's destroying my daughter. I start shouting and bouncing around and kicking the glass. The queers back off, leaving me alone with my toxic memories, which have spun me back to when Logan was almost one and I took her to Music Babies thinking it would be nice for her to sit with other babies and beat drums or whatever. She wanted none of it. "Car?" she kept saying, meaning let's get in it. I tried to restrain her, tried to fit in with the stay-at-home moms sitting cross-legged in their track suits. They stared at us, forcing smiles, while their spawn sucked on pacifiers. "Car?" Logan said louder, beginning her pre-tantrum wiggle. We got in the car.

We will always be outsiders. That I dreamed for one second that she might be one of them, welcomed into the kingdom of normals, shows how far gone I am. And now she has a mother who can't see straight and talks to ghosts. I look down at the ground. There is nothing beneath my feet but bog. I stumble out, blinking into the unending greyness, gripping the black or blue dolphin, my tiny offering in the face of disaster. Somewhere there is my car.

26

"Where are you going, kiddo?"

"I have to talk to Mr. Bluxom."

"Why?"

"I have to." Her mother hasn't even noticed that she's spilled coffee down the front of her shirt.

"Is it about the pool?"

"Just let me do this, okay?"

"Monkey, I can't let you go and talk to him alone. He's slime."

"You spilled coffee."

"Where?"

"On your shirt."

McKenna gets a J Cloth and starts wiping everywhere except where she spilled. Logan takes the cloth from her and wipes up the coffee.

They both go see Mr. Bluxom. He's sprawled on the couch in the office watching TV, eating Pringles and drinking Diet Coke from a full-size bottle. He's wearing his wife-beater. Sweat drips off his flab.

Her mother promised she wouldn't say anything, but Logan's accustomed to McKenna saying things and finds herself at a loss for words.

"You want ice?" Mr. Bluxom asks. "It's in the bin."

"No, actually," Logan says. "I wanted to ask about the pool?"

"What about it?"

"You said you'd fill it this weekend."

"Yeah, so?"

"It isn't filled."

"Is the weekend over yet? Let me check my calendar."

He doesn't move and Logan can't see a calendar. "Does that mean," she inquires, "that you'll fill it tomorrow?"

"Miss, do you have any idea how much *maintenance* is required? It ain't like no bathtub. You don't just plug it and go."

Logan can feel her mother getting steamed and knows that at any moment she could blow, which would definitely mean Mr. Bluxom won't fill the pool. "I could help," Logan offers. "I used to help measure the chlorine at the wading pool at our park."

Mr. Bluxom scratches under his armpit, then behind his ear. Logan can hear McKenna's breathing.

"Tell you what," Mr. Bluxom says, "you get your mother off my case about the washers and dryers and I'll see what I can do."

"That's blackmail," McKenna spits.

"You're welcome to leave anytime. Have a nice day." He grabs his remote and cranks the volume.

"What's wrong with going to a laundromat?" Logan asks over stir-fried vegetables.

"Don't let him fool you. That tub-o'-guts isn't going to fill the pool. I'm really sorry." McKenna hands her a bag. "This is for you. They didn't have whales. You like dolphins too, right?"

"Sure." Logan winds it up and watches the tail flap.

"It's grey, right?" McKenna asks.

Every time Logan forgets that her mother is colour-blind, something happens to remind her. "Yeah, it's grey."

"Because they had blue ones too, but I thought grey would be more authentic."

"Are you going to see another doctor about your eyes?"

"Not right away. They're busy. I don't know that there's a whole lot they can do."

"Maybe they could operate on them."

"I don't think it's that simple."

"They can transplant eyes now, take them out of dead people."

"I don't want somebody else's eyes."

"I'm not saying that, I just mean they can do all kinds of stuff."

Her mother's staring down at her plate picking out the water chestnuts. Logan's noticed that she's been eating only white or black food. It seems to her McKenna has been living on kalamata olives and feta cheese. Logan winds her dolphin again. She's trying not to obsess about the pool because the more upset she gets, the more her mother gets fussed. "Belugas keep washing up dead on the beaches of the St. Lawrence," she says to fill the silence. "They're getting cancer from the runoffs from the aluminum factories."

Her mother jabs a chunk of tofu but doesn't eat it.

"Did you buy sand for my sand turtle?"

"I forgot. We could still go look for some, after supper."

"That's okay. I'm too old for it anyway." She glides the dolphin through the air. "Was Dad here?"

"When? No. Why do you ask?"

"I was just wondering."

"Do you want him here?"

"Maybe he could talk to Mr. Bluxom. Maybe Mr. Bluxom's just a woman-hater."

"He is that, but your dad talking to him isn't going to make any difference."

When the phone rings, as usual her mother freezes like it's about to attack them. "Can I answer it?" Logan asks.

"If you want."

It's not her dad. It's some lady with an accent. "It's for you," Logan says, passing the receiver to her mother.

McKenna handles it like it might be dangerous. As she listens, her forehead creases as though she's having trouble understanding.

She says "Yes" a few times, and "When?" and "What do you mean?" and "How long?" Logan eats more snow peas. Some fall out of the pod. She mashes them with a fork. Her mother hangs up. "We have to go to the hospital," she says. "Something's happened to Grandpa."

Her mother wears her sunglasses in the hospital because of the lights. People stare at her as if she's a movie star or something. She's walking fast, faster than usual, and nearly bumps into a gurney with a dead-looking man on it. They take the wrong elevator and have to get out and find a different wing so they can get into the right elevator. They speed down one corridor, then another. McKenna tries to find a nurse but nobody is at the desk. She starts zooming into rooms filled with beds and sick people. The hospital smells sick. Logan suspects it has sick building syndrome, or at least some mutated SARS virus floating around. Perfectly healthy people get sick just by going to the hospital, inhaling the viruses coasting around on air particles. Logan feels sick and wonders if right this second the flesh-eating virus is entering her bloodstream.

Her mother didn't say anything during the drive, just swore at drivers. Logan brought the dolphin, keeps winding it up and watching the tail flap.

"I thought we weren't going to see Grandpa ever again," she tells the back of her mother's head.

"That was before he got hurt."

"How did he get hurt?"

"I'm trying to find that out." McKenna strides into another room and doesn't come out. Logan waits outside because she doesn't want to go in. She winds the dolphin again. An orderly pushes an old man in a wheelchair. The old man is shaking his fists and shouting, "I'm gonna get you, you motherfucker!" His feet in plaid slippers keep sliding off the footrests. The orderly repeatedly stops to fit them back on. He's wearing a headset and not even listening to the old man. Logan's feet are starting to hurt so she slides down the wall and sits on the floor. Her mother comes out and says, "Where's the frigging doctors? Did you see any doctors?"

"Is Grandpa in there?"

"Yes."

"Is he alright?"

"He's asleep. I have to find a doctor."

A guy in a labcoat turns the corner and McKenna charges after him. He says he can't help her. She tries a couple of nurses. Logan knows that if somebody doesn't help soon, her mother's going to start yelling. She plans to pretend she doesn't know her, that she's just hanging around waiting for someone. It's good that Grandpa is asleep, at least this means he isn't dead. Although if he were dead he couldn't hurt her mother anymore.

McKenna darts around another corner, out of sight, and Logan finds this strange because normally her mother would make sure Logan was with her. She always says that Logan must stay in sight. It's noisy in the hospital even though it's night. Machines hiss, whirr and beep. Periodically announcements are made over the intercom.

Her mother recruits some droopy doctor and fires questions at him, but all he says is, "Let me look at his chart." They go into the room together. Logan winds the dolphin again. She can't stop worrying about that North Atlantic right whale she saw on the news. For two days she's been snarled in fishing gear, trying to break free. Her mother's swimming around, calling to her. Researching her whale project, Logan learned that nearly one thousand whales, dolphins and porpoises drown every day in fishing nets.

Her mother and the droopy doctor come out of the room. McKenna bends down and takes Logan's hand. "Okay, monkey, we're outta here."

McKenna doesn't say much during the car ride back. Logan has to ask her what happened to Grandpa.

"He had a stroke."

"What is that exactly?"

"Something interferes with the blood getting to the brain."

"What does?"

"Plaque. Your arteries get clogged. It's like a heart attack only it's his brain."

"Is he going to die?"

"Don't know. He's in a coma."

Logan has seen these on TV; people lie stiff with all kinds of tubes and wires running in and out of them.

"So he could get better?" she asks.

"He could."

The dolphin swims really well in the bath. Logan would like to keep playing with it but her mother says they have to get some sleep. Logan knows that her mother won't sleep, she'll feed Fuzzball and go outside and sit in the lawn chair and talk to one of the no-lifers. When they got back from the hospital the pig woman was wearing her clown outfit and crying because she said her husband was over trying to beat her up. McKenna made her some tea and told her to calm down. Her red clown lips came off on the cup. McKenna told her she should call the police but the clown said they never do anything, by the time they show up he's long gone. When she left there was clown makeup on Kleenexes all over the floor.

While her mother brushes her teeth Logan takes a quick look under her bed and discovers that her father's suitcase is gone. She kneels on the floor and gropes around for it, thinking maybe it's been shoved to the back. Something like a fist is pushing inside her ribs, making it hard to breathe. She checks under her mother's bed, and in the closet. There is no suitcase.

Her father came and left without seeing her.

She gets into bed and tucks the covers around Tiger. When her mother comes out of the bathroom, she pretends to be asleep.

He came and left without seeing her, and he's not coming back.

27

I told him to drop dead and he did, or anyway tried it. We know what happens next: I mop up his drool and shit for the rest of my days.

I've never even heard of a brain stem. It's some essential widget in the computer, the link between the brain and the spinal cord. A "cerebrovascular accident"—try fitting your mouth around that one. I got the numbnuts to write it down. "Call it a massive stroke," he said.

"Massive strokes kill people," I pointed out.

"Not always," he said, "with improved resuscitation techniques."

Old Lester'd been at the supermarket selecting deli meats. Lots of people were around to prolong his death.

Chances are, if he comes out of it, he'll be paralyzed from head to toe. His mind will be intact, or anyway as intact as it was, meaning he'll be able to think but unable to speak or move. He'll be imprisoned in his own body. The numbnuts called it "locked-in syndrome."

How's it feel to be locked up, old man?

I hate him even more for this. Because it will weigh on me forever. Drop dead, I said. A day later he's on the floor covered in salami.

They've taped his eyes closed. Otherwise he'd be staring into space, drying up his eyeballs.

I call my brother. He's not there, or if he is, he has the phone turned down.

What happens in a coma, where are you? Up high looking down, trying to decide whether or not to fly back in there? Die, old man, you don't want the life that's left, trust me on this one.

I'd thought I was free of him finally, thought I'd "matured," accepted that he despises me and my daughter and that that's just dandy, why fight it, lose the savage and his bile. Save Logan from him. Save myself.

If he comes out of it they do rehab, prop him up and move him around. Keep the veggie active so he won't rot.

Die, old man, before they start shoving things up your butt, in your nose, into your veins. They've already made a hole in your throat so you can breathe; they'll be making more holes, trust me on this one. Let it go, you're not wanted here. I feel no pity when I look at your face that for once is free of malice because you're out of body. If it were me comatose, or my daughter, what would you do? Zip. Likewise, you'll get nothing from me. Stay locked in; I'm not looking for the key. Only those who love deserve to be loved. Only those who will throw themselves in front of a speeding car to save another. It is this selflessness that has freed me from you. I'd give my life for that "no-good bastard," bleed to death, watch my blood flow into her if I knew it would give her a life that was fading. You know none of this, old man. I don't know what's kept you going, what you've been feeding on. Die. There's nothing for you here.

"Good evening," Mr. Charm's muse says. "How's it goin'?"

I smell weed. "Not great. My father's in a coma."

The lawn chair squawks as she wriggles into it. She's got a roach between her fingers. "I'm sorry to hear that."

"Don't be."

She's cheerier tonight, probably because she's stoned, and because she didn't have to bang Bluxom. I can see his TV flickering. She offers me the joint. I shake my head while my mind's reaching for it.

"Nice night out anyway," she says. I breathe in the fumes, thinking grass isn't such a big deal. It's legal now for people with medical illnesses.

"That was some performance, with the clown," she adds. "Where's she get off making all that noise?"

"She was upset."

"Is that a reason to wake the neighbourhood? We all got bad

news, it's no reason to get hysterical. I seen her type my whole life. Everything's a tragedy. Someone should tell her to put a sock in it."

"She says he tried to set her clown wig on fire."

"Don't believe a word of it. Girls like her always make like somebody's after them, anything to get attention. The truth is, nobody'd look twice. Have you seen her legs? I got twenty years on that girl and she's the one with the orange peel."

My mother was in the room just now, looking at me as if I murdered him.

"You ever notice," the floozie continues, "it's the people who complain the most got the least problems? You ever noticed that?"

"Yup." Days ago this woman was sobbing into the night.

"I say, if you got a problem, fix it." Or smoke a joint.

"So you've never seen Allanah's husband?"

"Lord, no."

"She was really scared."

"Aren't we all. No, dear, didn't hear a thing, other than her getting hysterical. And the pig grunting. I say it's high time somebody converted that pig into bacon."

Why does this woman have no compassion for the other? Is she seeing her own weaknesses in her? Do we despise in others what we recognize in ourselves? When I see a junkie I want to kick him.

Smoke swirls from her nostrils. "That blond fella with the fancy car was around looking for you. He's cute. He your boyfriend?"

"When was he around?"

"This evening, asked me the time."

I don't like it that he's snooping.

"My name's McKenna. What's yours?"

"Shirley. Shirl. Do me a favour, McKenna, don't go telling Burt what I told you about the Human Rights Commission. He don't like me talking to the tenants. And don't tell him about the pot-smoking neither. Don't think he'd be too happy about it."

"My lips are sealed."

"Good girl. Have you met Troy?"

"Who?"

"The boy in room 6, wears white pants all the time. He's been passing me one every now and again. Makes a nice change from booze. He's a nice boy, keeps his clothes clean. Can't say the same for his visitors." She kicks off her pumps. "So, like, what are the doctors saying?"

"Not much."

"Never do. How'd it happen?"

"Stroke."

"Isn't that something. You never know what's coming down the pipe. So I guess you're pretty choked about it."

"Actually, I hate the buzzard."

"Is that so? Well, maybe it's just as well then."

A silence descends. The *hate* word tends to subdue chatter. I want her to go back inside. *I* can't because my useless-in-life-and-death mother is in there.

"He left a note for you," Shirl says, "the blond. Did you see it?" She points to a piece of paper wedged into the doorframe. I remove it and read Payne's twelve-year-old handwriting: *Dear M, some people are looking for me, it's no big deal, just don't tell them anything. Yours, P.*

Great. Somebody wants their money back.

"I wasn't too crazy about my dad neither," Shirl admits. "He used belts on us, clothespegs, hangers."

"Did you want him dead?"

"I wanted him tortured. Especially that water torture where they tie you down and drip water on your forehead till you die of thirst."

"How did he die?"

"In his sleep. A hundred and two."

"So much for the assholes getting it in the end."

"The assholes never get it," Shirl pronounces. "That's how they get to be assholes."

"My dad's getting it," I point out. "I wanted him dead."

"He ain't dead yet, dear." She flicks ash onto the pavement. "I seen people live like veggies for years. You might just have to pull that plug yourself."

"I looked for a plug, couldn't find it. He's hooked up to all kinds of devices."

"Go for the one in the throat. You pull that one out, he's history."

"And I go to prison."

She shrugs. "Pick your poison."

I sit in the bath in the dark. Mom's not around, has crawled back into her hole of reproach. Speaking of water torture, there's not one faucet in this shithole that doesn't drip. Bluxom could have filled the pool with all the wasted water.

I let my daughter down again, didn't even get it together to buy sand for the turtle. She was looking forward to the summer, the pool. It was all she had.

Why's she asking about her dad all the time, what's that about? I guess when you have your world torpedoed, you grab at anything familiar. I'm so out of bounds I wouldn't even recognize the familiar. We're not on the same plane, Logan and me, we're shooting off in different directions. It's getting hard to talk because I know I'll disappoint her, like I disappoint my mother. I'm talking to myself more, in the car, the can. Logan has noticed this. "Who are you talking to?" she demands in a tone that isn't admiring. A tone that reminds me of Payne when the ground started crumbling. At one point he said he couldn't get his former girlfriend out of his mind. I said, "What kind of line is that?" He had his back to me, was blow-drying his hair. For a second I saw myself in the mirror, desperate, grasping. A Francis Bacon.

Maybe the thing to do is to force them to spend time together, give her the opportunity to find out what a lowlife he is. I call his cell. It's out of service. So who's after him? I paid his debt once, out of ignorance, desperation, fear. He said his debtors were threatening to cut his face.

Allanah tonight, that was sad. Even sadder if she's making it up. She said her hubby started out charming, considerate, doted on her. It was after the pig that things got out of hand. I said, "Why didn't you get rid of it?" She said her husband *loves* Charleton.

I'm starting to think it's impossible to actually know anyone. You make up who they are, who you want them to be. When a bit of the real them shows up you tell yourself *that's not the real them*. You ignore the rough edges and go on your merry way until he tries to burn your hair.

Clients tell me all the time they thought some guy was really great, that they had the same values, goals, then he turned out to be a bigamist. So who's at fault, the man for being the jerk he is or the woman for using white-out? I mean, get a grip, he didn't turn into Bluebeard overnight.

Allanah said she was "batty" about her husband. I thought that was an interesting choice of word, what with bats being blinded by daylight—she couldn't even see the fucker. Like I didn't see Payne. I'm seeing him clearly now though, with no colour dazzle.

It's scaring me that I don't know my daughter. I don't even know what I used to think I knew. Colourless, it's hard to get a hold on her. She blends in. Unless I'm seeing who she really is. Maybe she's been growing distant for a while and I had to be colour-deprived to notice it. Maybe she despises me and it's only showing up now because there are no flowers to look at, no baby pictures, just us in monochrome. With no pool.

We buzz my brother from the lobby of his condo. He doesn't answer. We buzz more. I know he's in there, buying something on-line. When a dollybird on a cell phone exits the building, we grab the door on the rebound and head up to his apartment, bang on the door. The peephole darkens as Heathcliff glowers at us. "What do you want?" he says through the door.

"To come in."

"What for? I'm busy."

"Just let us in, alright?"

He does, wearing some gear he just acquired because it's still tagged. "What do you want? It's Sunday."

"I know and normally I wouldn't bother you but our father's in the hospital in a coma."

"Is he going to die?"

"I don't know. I thought you might like to go and see him."

The robot does not react, waits for programming. "Why?"

"Because he's your father. I don't want to do this by myself. You have to take some responsibility."

"Why? The hospital takes responsibility to avoid litigation."

He starts adjusting straps on the gear. It looks like some kind of body harness. Maybe he's planning to strap himself to a plane.

"So you're not going to do anything?" I stare into eyes that have always been opaque. Eyes that have never registered pain, or love.

"About what?"

"Our father is in critical condition."

"There's nothing to do. He'll die or he won't."

"If he lives he'll be paralyzed, a thinking veggie."

"There are facilities for that kind of thing. He must have savings. Sell the house. I have to steam some shirts. Do you want to see my new steamer, Logan? Twenty-nine ninety-five U.S. It burns my arm."

I grab Logan's hand. "Let's go."

I sit and stare at my father, who doesn't look like my father, just some old grey thing. I don't know what I'm waiting for, hoping for. Logan's in the hall eating a muffin because she says looking at him gives her the creeps. Also, the old fart in the next bed is in serious disrepair, garbling who knows what to invisible people. Meanwhile old Lester looks peaceful, almost friendly, completely not the person I know, or thought I knew. All last night I saw his face. Not the real one, this comatose one. This comatose one makes me wonder if I missed something.

28

The North Atlantic right whale died, of course. Her mother is still swimming around making whale sounds.

Overall it's been a pretty tense Sunday, what with doing laundry with Mr. Bluxom's dryers from 1952 plus dealing with some guy in white pants who kept using gallons of bleach even though Logan told him he was poisoning the water supply. He kept blabbing at McKenna, and laughing at her jokes about Bluxom and the washers. It bothered Logan that the guy was being so friendly when they didn't even know him. It drives her nuts the way her mother will talk to anybody. Anyway, after checking on Grandpa they went to the art gallery and looked at the Henry Moores again. Her mother likes to sit around looking at those big women. Logan doesn't mind it, if the security guard bugs off. It's very quiet except for the slapping of their running shoes against the granite floor. She likes Henry Moore's drawings of sheep, and people sleeping in the subway during the war. But her mother was so out of it she wasn't even looking at the sculptures. She just kept staring at patches of sunlight on the floor, and trying to touch shadows. The security guard wouldn't take his eyes off her. Logan hopes she isn't having a nervous breakdown or something. A kid from school's father had a nervous breakdown, became a stay-at-home dad so his wife could work. After a while he refused to leave the house. The girl had to take taxis to and from school. Everybody knew why and nobody wanted to talk to her because her dad was nuts. If McKenna goes nuts, there's nobody else. It's not like Payne would suddenly quit chasing jiggle-factor waitresses to take care of Logan. If McKenna goes nuts, Logan will have to look after herself. Which in some ways might be easier, as long as her mother's cared for in a good facility. At least then Logan wouldn't have to worry about her all the time. She's been thinking seriously about a line of work, she doesn't know what exactly, but there must be something. Boys mow lawns. She could try that. Once she washed Mrs. Pawusiak's windows for ten dollars. Mrs. Pawusiak wasn't too happy about it though. She said Logan left streaks.

McKenna acted almost normal at Wal-Mart when they bought sand for the turtle. She only tripped once. But then they stopped to look at the tropical fish, which they always do, and her mother gasped and fell back on some shelves, covering her eyes. Logan was afraid she'd start crying or something but McKenna just kept rubbing her eyes and saying the fluorescents were hurting. Logan suspected that her mother was upset because she couldn't see the fishes' colours. Normally McKenna loves looking at the fish. They never buy any because Logan thinks it's criminal to keep fish in tanks.

Logan's trying to decide if she wants her grandfather dead or alive. Dead, he wouldn't bother them, but he *is* family. If he is going to die she hopes it's soon because visiting the hospital is gross, not just because of the airborne viruses but because people croak there. Somebody sent a bunch of flowers to the dirty old man in the bed beside her grandfather's. Logan couldn't figure out why anyone would think the dirty old man wanted flowers. His lips are all scaly—somebody should send him some Chap Stick.

She's been trying not to think about her father, but of course she is. She keeps picturing him with the jiggle-factor waitress, laughing and eating pancakes. The waitress was wearing red lipstick, the kind Sheena smeared on Logan once. "Look at this *babe*," Sheena had remarked, brushing blush onto Logan's cheeks.

"*Serious* babe," Payne agreed. Logan left the makeup on because she thought it pleased him, but she hated the way it felt and tasted. She made sure she washed it off before McKenna saw her.

At the Lakeview she works on her bumblebee project while her mother goes over the list of claims again. McKenna keeps remembering things to add to it. She says that tomorrow the builders are going to start working on their house.

Logan thinks it's totally amazing that bumblebees beat their wings two hundred times per second. It's her hope that the project will make people understand how crucial bees are to human survival because they are highly efficient pollinators. In the right greenhouse conditions they can pollinate all year round. They're called the "mine canaries" of a greenhouse because if they get sick, growers know there's something wrong with the environment. With bees dying outside greenhouses, you'd think humans would figure out there's something wrong with the environment.

"There's somebody at the door, Mum."

"Ignore it."

"Hey, ladies," Vance says through the window. "What's shakin'? I brought you some kitten food I got dirt cheap. My treat."

"Let him in," McKenna grumbles.

Logan opens the door and tries to fry him with her eyes. She's found that staring at people sometimes makes them go away. One of the things Vance does that really irritates her is snapping his fingers. He'll be talking about something boring like a dog food special or something and snap go the fingers, like he thinks that makes what he's saying important. "I was having a chin wag with Bernice down at Pet Valu," he says, "and she said they got too much of a certain kitty food and I said"—snap go the fingers—"I got just the kitty for you. I told her about your circumstances, being homeless and so forth, and she made me a deal I couldn't refuse." *Snap.*

"Thanks, Vance," McKenna says.

Logan knows that Vance will keep talking because her mother isn't.

"Bernice got some old biddy in her building fined a hundred bucks for tying a kitten in a plastic bag and tossing it in a Dumpster. The old lady pleaded guilty to abandoning an animal in distress, said hard times forced her to throw away the kitty. I'm telling you, you don't want to mess with Bernice."

McKenna's eating kalamata olives again and frowning at the swirly carpet. Logan tries to focus on her bee project. Bumblebees are covered in fur and, although they shiver in the cold, they can work in cold and wet conditions that send honeybees back to their hives.

"There was some guy looking for you, McKenna," Vance says.

"Blond?"

"Nope. Black-haired. Looked like he could use a shave."

"What did you tell him?"

"Nothing. Said I walked your dog."

"Don't tell anyone where I work."

"Sure. No problem." He feels for his missing ear. "You in trouble or something?"

"Nope. Just want privacy."

"Right on. Okay, well, we'll see you a little later on."

"Yup."

Logan closes the door. "Who was looking for you?"

"Probably Tait."

"His hair's not black."

"Close enough." Her mother starts shaking her hands again.

"He already knows where you work."

"Maybe he forgot."

"He never forgets anything."

"Maybe it wasn't him, then."

"Who'd want to know where you work?"

"I have no idea."

"Maybe you're being sued for some reason," Logan suggests. "Maybe one of those people you nearly ran over is suing you."

"Can we not talk about this anymore?"

"Maybe it was the tax collector. Do you owe taxes?"

Her mother puts her hands over her ears and closes her eyes. "Just drop it, alright? It's time for bed."

The worst thing is when her mother tries to have meaningful conversations when Logan is in the bath because, as she's in the bath, there's no escape. These days her mother wears sunglasses during the meaningful conversations, which makes things even worse.

"I'm sorry I shouted at you," McKenna says.

"You didn't really shout."

"Whatever. I'm sorry. I wish you'd talk to me."

"I talk to you."

"Not about what's really going on. Not about what made you try to drown yourself."

"I wasn't drowning myself."

"Whatever. Something's not tickeyboo."

"I'm busy with my bee project."

"How's that going?"

"Did you know that bumblebees nest in the ground, in mouse holes and stuff?"

"Really? I thought they'd nest high up where they'd be safer."

"And they only sting in self-defence."

"Sounds reasonable."

Logan winds the dolphin.

Her mother takes off her glasses and squints at her. "Do you want to see your father again?"

"Why?"

"Because I'll find him if you want to see him."

"He doesn't want to see me."

"What makes you think that?"

Logan can't mention the suitcase. "He prefers girls."

"I think he's just busy trying to earn a buck. He's been short of cash lately."

"You don't want him around anyway."

"I don't mind having him around if you want him around."

"It's okay."

"You have to tell me what you want." McKenna puts the sunglasses back on. "Tomorrow, after I pick you up, we'll go see where they're at with our house."

"That would be excellent."

"And we should start looking at colours you want to paint it. Maybe we'll stop at a hardware store and look at samples. Would you like that?"

"Sure."

When they got home Logan checked under the bed to see if her father had put the suitcase back. It occurred to her that he might have taken it just for the night and brought it back while they were out. But it wasn't there and she told herself not to care.

Once she asked him why guys like women to wear lipstick. He told her there is no turn-on like lipstick marks on a cigarette. He'd quit smoking, so Logan found this weird. "Doesn't it come off on you when you kiss?" she asked.

"Sure."

"So isn't that gross?"

He shrugged. "You're wearing the woman."

Logan couldn't figure that one out, why you'd want to wear somebody. On the news there was a story about a dad who wanted to be a woman and wore his wife's clothes. Then his little boy decided he wanted to wear girls' clothes. His dad changed the boy's name to Aurora and told the teachers at school to treat him like a girl. The kid was put in a foster home. It seems to Logan wanting to wear your own clothes is the best policy.

A foster home, that's another possibility, if her mother goes nuts.

"Come on, monkey, bedtime."

"Mum . . . ?"

"Yes?"

"Can you comb my hair?"

"Of course, honeybun."

"You haven't combed it in a while. It's pretty matted."

It hurts as her mother combs out the knots. But Logan welcomes the pain. Because it is familiar; because it is her mother.

29

So I think I'm being followed, which explains why some black-haired dude was looking for me. Some black-haired dude who's looking for Payne and feels he should inform me that, if he finds him, he'll cut his face. "Go ahead," I'll tell him.

It's hard to be certain you're being followed when you can't see the colour of the car. It's one of those nondescript sedans. I can't tell what the driver is wearing, or his skin colour. He's not black-black, or even off-black, just grey. So he could be white or Asian or Hispanic. His hair's dull grey, not jet black, maybe brown, or dirty blond, or black with highlights. Or maybe really grey. Anyway, I'm trying not to get hyper about it; it's not me he wants. Payne makes these deals, stupid investments. He made a shitload of money on mood collars for pets once and never got over it. Things get tricky when he's hot to invest in something but has no capital. That's where the sharks come in.

I should feed Fuzzball, but Kristos insists we all admire his newly delivered Nazi car. We file out the back door into the lane littered with garbage and used condoms.

"Seelver," he tells us in case we hadn't noticed. "Six speed, eighteen-inch reems, thirty-series tires."

We all nod like this means something.

"Get een, get een."

I get sandwiched between French and Coco. Little Miss Spread-her-legs scores the front seat. Kristos feels her up while demonstrating the six-way adjustable *heated* sports seats with complementary piping.

"Cool," Little Miss Spread-her-legs says. "Do you have, like . . . airbags?"

"Of course. Lateral, plus traction control, plus leemeeted sleep traction management."

"That's awesome."

I say, "I personally wouldn't drive a car that doesn't have computerized engine management."

Kristos does a one-eighty to look at me. "Are you *crazy*? Of course I have computerized engeen management. Thees is a *Special Edition*."

"That's a relief."

Kristos fondles the buttons on the dash.

"They all have lights," Little Miss Spread-her-legs observes.

"So I can see in the dark. My glove compartment, how many times at night do you have to feel around for your glove compartment?"

"I hate when that happens," French says, pulling out his mickey and taking a swig.

"I like the white knobs," Coco comments, obviously bored out of his mind.

"Gauges," Kristos corrects, "they are optional white gauges."

"Whatever."

"And thees is a *carbon fibre* dashboard." Kristos runs his hand over it as though it's some woman's thigh.

"A thing of beauty," I say. "It's been a slice. Move over, boys." The three of us depart, leaving the boss and the slut to test the suspension.

"Hey, baby, what gives?" It's Julius, the new stylist. I've been avoiding him because he's on the make. At first, because he shaves his head and has multiple piercings, I figured he was gay. But he's been loitering and giving me "who loves ya baby" talk. He even dresses like Telly Savalas, close-fitting three-piece suits with that special seventies flavour that's currently hip.

"Your clients miss you, baby," he tells me. "I had two this morning. When I told them Mizz Mac was unavailable for an undisclosed period of time they looked like I'd just told them they had two minutes to live. Tragic, baby, tragic."

I'd told Kristos to tell the other hairdressers as well as the clients that I've developed an allergy to peroxide.

Julius trails me into the back room. As I mix up Fuzzball's formula he steps in front of me, thrusts his pelvis in my direction and starts singing, "You make me feel like dancing."

I had one of those Kafkaesque experiences at the insurance company this morning. I'd planned a surprise attack, had not expected to be blocked at reception by Hilda of the SS. My goal was to threaten the parasite insurance guy, a Mr. Kumpitch, with what I don't know exactly; I figured I'd think of something. But Hilda's one of those dutiful doggies who will not let go. So I had to sit in reception, staring at landscapes of grey skies and black oceans, waiting for Kumquat to appear. Usually I can forget about the strangeness of me. I don't dress like normal people: I streak my hair with whatever colours appeal to me that month, I wear sparkly shoes if I can find them, with mix-and-match laces, earrings, often feathered. Colour, I wear colour. So there I was in corporate central not feeling my colourful self, therefore muted, close to invisible in fact while Hilda in her all-consuming greyness barked into her headset. When Kumquat appeared he insisted that he was with a client and that the cheque, to the best of his knowledge, was in process. "Who has better knowledge?" I inquired.

"I beg your pardon?" Kumquat said. He had a sweep-over. My former self would have whipped out a comb and exposed his bald pate. But I had no juice, was just a shadow, could feel myself fading.

I have this idea that there are forces in your life that fuel you, negative and positive, that keep you in balance. When one of them loses strength you're thrown off. Like my hatred for my father, it was a power source I could count on. Now he's this helpless creature and I'm having trouble standing. Usually I can torque my loathing for him into fury with similar dirtbags, Kumquat for instance. If I get a burn going I can usually scare just about anybody.

But I just stood there feeling like a really stupid person in dire need of a corporate makeover.

"We'll be in touch," Kumquat said.

I ducked into a Starbucks and sat in the can in the dark until somebody started pounding on the door. I grabbed an espresso, thought maybe caffeine would help. A homeless guy was squatting outside the café, leaning against the window, eating the remnants of a Mars bar. After he finished, he headed for the trash can, I assumed to look for more food scraps. But no, he bunched up the wrapper and carefully pushed it through the flap. Life is full of surprises.

"So what do you say, baby," Julius says, "cold drinks on a hot night?"

"It's a bit early in the season for that, Jules." I feed the cat. Kojak hovers, smelling of a decent cologne, and I can't help noticing the maleness of him. Underneath the seventies garb beats a living, breathing, muscular, *available* heterosexual male body. It's not like I run into these kinds of opportunities often in the hair business, particularly as a single colour-blind mom. His baldness is an asset because it frees him of the grey-hair look, which is a turnoff from the get-go.

Sandrine/Akabar scampers in. "Ohmygod, ohmygod," she says. In her hands are foil balls with hair in them, hair that should be on the client's head. She holds them out as though they're spiders.

"Does the client know?" I ask.

She shakes her head. "Ohmygod, ohmygod."

"Throw them out," I say. "Calm down."

I find the client engrossed in *Vanity Fair*. She doesn't notice that it's me rather than Sandrine attending her. I get the foils off fast but with care. Fortunately the breaks are around the crown—with a good cut, she won't notice. I order Little Miss Spread-her-legs to wash her and then check back with Sandrine. She's sobbing with her head on Julius's shoulder. I would have thought he'd be groping her, but I guess she's not his type because only one arm is offered, the hand awkwardly patting the back of her head. "Can you cut her?" I ask Sandrine. She looks at me as though I've just asked her to walk through fire.

"She'll kill me," she gasps. "Do you know who that is? That's the carpet woman. You know, the *carpet* woman, that's her husband's company. She'll kill me. Ohmygod, ohmygod."

"What kind of cut did she want?"

"I don't know. The same. I don't know. Ohmygod."

"Okay," I say, "the story is you're having a bad period, cramps, puking your guts out, alright? Stay here."

To appease the bag of waste who's missing chunks of hair, I tell her she has copper in her eyes that brings out the hues in her skin and the golds in her highlights. I tell her she has beautiful skin, that she's lucky she doesn't need to paint up. I cut her hair as she's never seen before and convince her that it's youthful, brings out her bones. French, by now aware of what's going on, helps out by enthusing over the do, how it's the latest thing, some supermodel—he can't remember which one—started this look and they're all doing it now. It's almost the Farrah Fawcett thing all over again, people are crazy for it.

The truth is, when I'm done with her, the carpet woman looks good. She leaves a lousy tip, which I give to Sandrine of the blotchy face.

"You didn't dilute enough," I tell her.

"Like I don't know that."

"Then why'd you do it?"

"I'm just really stressed out right now, alright, with the move and everything. And my yoga teacher's moving to New York." She grabs my wrist and looks up at me with the eyes of a maiden about to be tossed to the minotaur. "Please don't tell Kristos, *please?*"

"Your secret's safe with me."

Not even so much as a thank-you. Amazing how the deluded continue to believe, after the age of thirty, that they're the centre of the universe.

"My knees are hurting," I comment, which they do sometimes.

"Your ego's in your knees," Sandrine advises me.

I sit in the dark in the can thinking about the joint Troy Boy gave me, how I didn't refuse it but tucked it away in a drawer. I think about how I'm weakening, how I can't feel my legs anymore, how Troy Boy knew, at a glance, that I was a potential customer.

Maybe I should fuck Julius, maybe he'll carry me away in those pumped-up arms of his, *who loves ya, baby*, and everything will be okay again. Maybe a purely animal act will help me see the light.

30

Occasionally Logan tries to determine what kind of man she's going to marry. He would have to be intelligent, but she wouldn't mind if he was also handsome. Russell, the fibre optic nerd, is probably intelligent but lacks depth in Logan's opinion, and he certainly isn't handsome. Curling Ellsworth, on the other hand, lacks intelligence and depth but is handsome in an average way. There's nothing unique about him though. Logan would prefer to marry someone unique. Her mother says that Armand who fixed scooters and made cheese was unique. McKenna says unique men are out there, but you're not going to find them in the Wal-Mart parking lot.

Logan can't believe that Mr. Beasley's in the can with Katey again. They've been in there for like twenty minutes and Logan needs to whiz. She knocks on the door again. "Hold your horses," Mr. Beasley says.

Dotty's going through something ultra-weird, all she does is make junk food—rice crispy squares in particular. If she shoves another rice crispy square at Logan, she's going to hurl big time. And brownies with gooey icing all over them. These are not healthy snacks in Logan's opinion. When parents sign up their kids at Dotty's, part of the deal is that their kids get healthy snacks. She pointed this out to Dotty, but Curling was present and shouted, "No like, no eat!" with a Chinese accent. He's been eating two brownies at a time, squeezed together like a sandwich. He gets totally hyper on them. When Logan was in the tree he ran around the trunk yowling through his vampire fangs.

Before Dotty started making rice crispy squares, she got it into her head that the kids should do crafts. She cut boys and girls out of construction paper. The boys had legs and the girls had skirts but no feet. She wanted the kids to decorate them with felt markers, sparkles and googly eyes. Logan complied because there was nothing else to do and because she likes the smell of glue. But all Curling did was stick a straw in the crotch of his paper doll and announce that it was a dick. That's when Dotty started melting marshmallows.

Finally Mr. Beasley and Katey come out of the bathroom. He looks sternly at Logan as if she's been misbehaving, when the fact is her bladder's about to explode.

Her bumblebee project didn't go over very well. Miss Spongle seemed interested and asked a few questions, but no one else did. And Nina was munching supplies from her desk the whole time and the sound of the cellophane wrapping kept distracting Logan. She couldn't believe Miss Spongle couldn't hear it. Curling put up his hand and said, "Excuse me, Miss, but is there anyone in this *entire* school who gives a goat's turd about bees?"

Miss Spongle stressed, as Logan had, that bees are important to the environment. But Logan suspected that something else was bothering Miss Spongle, because her engagement ring was missing. Logan noticed it when Miss Spongle was absently handling her model bees. Miss Spongle was supposed to marry Mr. Wagman the gym teacher. They'd been dating for eons and sometimes the kids would catch them frenching in the corridors. Mr. Wagman always wears tinted glasses, and there are rumours that he's an alcoholic. Personally, Logan finds him gross and thinks that Miss Spongle could do better. She wasn't sorry to see the missing ring although she was sorry for Miss Spongle. She also had a run in her nylons crawling up her leg.

Logan returns to the kitchen and sees that all her Play-Doh whales have been mashed. Dotty hasn't noticed, is too busy cutting up rice crispy squares. Logan balls the Play-Doh and fits it back into the containers. She really doesn't understand why Curling is so horrible to her. He's not nearly as horrible to anyone else. McKenna says it's because he knows he can't get at Logan, so he keeps trying. "It's the dog chasing the squirrel syndrome," she explained. "Shit-for-brains wanting to possess the nimble of mind and body. Ignore him."

McKenna's always telling Logan to ignore assholes, but McKenna never does. She goes after them. It doesn't seem to help though. Mr. Bluxom isn't going to fill the pool.

The clown was out with her pig this morning and acted like she hadn't been apoplectic about her husband trying to burn her wig. "Bee-ewtiful day, isn't it?" she kept saying. She was eating an Egg McMuffin and the ham was slipping out of it. "Days like this," she added, "make me feel like I'm a kid back in school, looking forward to the summer holidays." She did one of her rubbery-lipped smiles. The ham fell on the ground and the pig gobbled it.

"Cannibalism," Logan remarked. "Your hog's eating hog."

"Charleton, honey, bad, *bad* pig. You're a veggie, remember?"

Logan looked to see if her mother was ready yet. Logan always has to wait for her mother. McKenna hassles her to get ready but Logan inevitably ends up sitting around waiting for her. "Pigs will eat anything," Logan offers. "They get fed pigs' brains from slaughterhouses. That's how you get mad pig disease."

"Is that so?" the clown remarked. "Aren't you a mine of information."

Logan was thinking it wouldn't be bad if the husband offed the clown one of these days. The Lakeview's too crowded in Logan's opinion. Then she remembered God, and the truck and everything. "Forgive me," she whispered.

"Why are you always looking in the rearview mirror?" Logan asks her mother.

"I'm not *always* looking in the rearview mirror."

"Yes you are."

"No I'm not."

"Logan, I'm just trying to drive safely, alright? We can't afford an accident right now."

"Dad says slow drivers are more dangerous than fast ones."

"Yeah, well, what does he know? How many scrapes has *he* been in?"

"Just that dog. And the old lady. And she shouldn't have been crossing the street anyway. Dad said she should've been wearing a hearing aid."

"Don't quote your father to me, alright?"

"He's a good driver."

"I don't care, I don't want to hear about it."

"He parallel parks better than you."

"Do you want to get out and walk?"

"We're driving so slow people are staring at us."

"Let them."

There are times—now, for example—when Logan finds her mother extremely irritating. Or that time McKenna slashed a bunch of squad car tires because the police beat up a friend of hers. McKenna told Logan to wait in the car while she hammered nails into the tires. Her mother's friend was a hairdresser who was dying of AIDS. According to him the cops picked him up for no reason, got him in a van and kicked him, then took him to the station, locked him up and said, "See you in court." Logan didn't feel that slashing tires was an effective recourse. Her mother has no concept of procedure. It was a miracle that she didn't get caught. McKenna said the one thing you can be sure of about cops, they're not watching the street.

Logan holds the paint sample in front of her mother's nose. "This one's nice. Ancestry Violet."

Her mother squints at it. "Is it purple?"

"Definitely. Or Preservation Plum is cool, although I kind of like Pink Punch. What about Irish Acres for the bathroom?"

"Is it green? You want a *green* bathroom?"

"Or Leapfrog is nice." Logan shows her mother another sample. "What's that say?"

"Terra Verde."

"That's nice too. Softer. Then there's Celery Leaf, that's a bit brighter." Logan can't say that she was impressed by the progress on her house. Her mother said they had to do stuff to the foundation, clean it and spray it or something.

McKenna squints at the tiny print on the sample display. "I thought we were looking for purple."

"Maybe we should go for Electric Pink on the outside. That would put a bug up Mrs. Pawusiak's ass."

"Don't use that word."

"You use it all the time."

Her mother rubs her eyes, smearing her makeup. "We don't have to decide right away, we're just looking."

"I'd like yellow for the kitchen. Citrus is awesome, although maybe it's too lemony. What about Sunny or Daisy Chain?"

"Logan, I can't *see* the colours, remember?"

"Harvest Moon is nice. And we should do blue in the living room. Something like South Seas or Sea Strand. Oh look, Mum, Whispering Wind. That would be excellent."

"What kind of blue is it?"

"Sort of robin's eggy."

"You want a robin's eggy living room?"

"Your eyeliner's smeared," Logan points out. "You look like a coon."

Her mother wipes under her eyes with her fingers.

"Or Riverside," Logan adds.

"What kind of blue is that?"

"Darker robin's eggy."

"Pale blue makes me think of doctors' offices."

"You can't see it anyway."

In the wallpaper department, McKenna complains the patterns are giving her a migraine. And there's no dinosaur paper. Logan thinks that a zebra pattern might be nice, but her mother just starts rubbing her eyes again.

"What about a cow pattern?" Logan suggests. "That would be funky."

"We'll talk about this later."

Logan waits outside Grandpa's room. There's no way she could ever be a doctor and hang around a place like this. She takes shallow breaths to avoid inhaling viruses. A doctor goes into the room, which relieves Logan because this means her mother won't have to hunt one down. But then she hears her mother shout, "What the fuck do you think you're doing?" Logan, concerned that McKenna might kill the doctor and be put in prison for life, hurries in. He's poking a needle into one of Grandpa's eyelids. The skin stretches as he pulls the thread taut. "It's to protect the eye," the doctor explains, poking the needle into the eyelid again. He does this with practised ease, as though he's darning a sock. His hands are very hairy, hairier than his head. "Otherwise he will lose the eye. The lid won't stay closed."

"Tape it."

"The tape comes unstuck. We can take the stitches out at any time if he regains function."

Her mother, silenced, keeps her hand over her mouth while watching him stitch the eye closed.

All the flowers that somebody sent the dirty old man have wilted and there's a smell of rot beyond the usual stink of unwashed bodies and shit. Logan feels about to gag and takes her mother's hand. "Let's go, Mum."

"I was going to give him a shave," McKenna whimpers, not sounding like her mother but like some little girl who's been bad and wants forgiveness.

"Tomorrow," Logan says.

Logan makes them sandwiches on white bread. She's been noticing that her mother will eat white bread as long as what's on it is black or white. Cream cheese works well, and kalamata olive paste.

"I wonder when Tait's going to get me that laptop," Logan says. She's eating peanut butter and jelly. Normally her mother wouldn't allow this at dinner. "He said he'd get it to me this week. It's really hard to do homework without it."

Her mother phones Tait again. Logan knows he just isn't picking up. She doesn't know why he bothers having a phone, he never answers it.

"Do you think he'll ever get married?" Logan asks.

"If she's a cyborg." McKenna puts the phone down.

Logan feeds Stanley a piece of her sandwich. "They just cloned this bull," Logan says. "He's had two hundred thousand babies in more than fifty countries. Tait says most of the dairy cows on the planet are related to that bull." She feeds Stanley a kalamata olive. "I wonder when they'll start cloning humans. Dolly the sheep getting arthritis and dying has kind of cooled their jets. I guess they won't start seriously cloning humans until they figure that one out. How was your eye test? What happened?"

Her mother pulls her sandwich apart and examines the ingredients. "Nothing. They freeze your eyeballs, then put contact lenses on them and attach electrodes or something."

"That must've been weird."

McKenna shrugs, still staring at the pieces of her sandwich.

"Did they say they could do anything?" Logan asks.

"Nope. They say there's nothing wrong with my eyes."

Her mother puts the sandwich together but doesn't eat it. She leans her elbows on the table and covers her eyes with her hands. It looks a bit like she's shaking and Logan doesn't know if she's crying or what. They hear noises next door, furniture being moved and toilets flushing. Somebody turns on the shower. Logan doesn't know what to do about her mother.

"What colour's my hair?" McKenna asks.

"You've still got some purple in it, but there's a lot of roots."

"I want to touch it up. You have to help me, alright, because I can't tell what's my colour and what's purple. And I want to look like me. I can't stop looking like me."

Logan doesn't want to say that her mother hasn't looked herself since the accident, that the black clothes have made her almost invisible. Watching McKenna tremble, Logan becomes convinced that something has happened to her mother's body. It has shrunk, takes up less space. You wouldn't notice her on the subway.

Her mother stands at the bathroom sink, working colour into her hair with her fingers. Logan, kneeling on the counter, hands her the strands that have been previously coloured. "I should probably just dye it all black," McKenna says.

"No way you're going Goth." Logan lifts some hair off her mother's neck and notices the skin underneath, how white it is. She thinks about the necks of Henry VIII's wives who had their heads cut off—how white their necks must have been. What did the executioner feel looking at those necks? Did he have to force himself to do it, close his eyes at the last minute before the blood gushed out? Logan feels that her mother is as defenceless as those women. Her mother, who has always been so fearless, has the air of the condemned.

"You tell me if it doesn't come out my regular purple, alright? I don't want aubergine or something, I want my regular purple."

"Okay."

"I want to look like myself."

"Okay." Logan realizes that she will have to treat her mother as you would any disabled person. You don't stare at their deformity, you don't say, "Wow, what a drag it must be to live in a wheelchair," or, "What's it like being blind?" You're polite, you talk as if they're normal. You only stare at them when their backs are turned. Like now, when her mother's bent over the sink rinsing, Logan allows the loss of her mother to grip her face. Despair pulls down on her mouth and forces tears out of her ducts. But when her mother flips her hair back and reaches for a towel Logan tries to smile, or anyway look preoccupied—anything but sad. Sad would be an admission of loss and Logan doesn't want her mother to know that she's lost. She wants her mother to fight.

McKenna reaches for her sunglasses. "These lights are going to kill me."

31

She was here a minute ago. Mommy dearest. Sitting on her chair. I hissed, "What do you want?" Then suddenly she wasn't there, didn't fade away or anything, just vanished, couldn't take the heat. Whenever I confronted her in life, she headed for the door, or the medicine cabinet for prescribed dope. I think one of the reasons, since I've been clean, that I've become obsessed with getting to the nub of problems—confronting them, ejecting them, demolishing, whatever—is that my mother never acknowledged them. Which left me in this place with rubber walls, bouncing around, thinking, I must be crazy, there *is* no problem, I'm imagining it, exaggerating, get with the program, chill, grow up, get a life.

So maybe she's been refused admission on the other side because of some unfinished business down here, some *problem* she can't face. Ergo, she's lingering in ghostly torment, doing all that deaf and dumb nodding and crying.

Before her presence sent needles up my ass I was actually dreaming about her. We were in a laundromat watching my father being sloshed around in a washing machine. Through the porthole his face looked soft, like it does in the coma. I said, "He could drown. Maybe we should turn it off." Mom responded, "He'll be fine." On the spin cycle he really got going and his face kept smashing into the glass. He didn't try to protect himself; he seemed asleep, or dead—like he does now. "Shouldn't we turn it off?" I asked again. "He'll be fine," the loving wife said. Soon the glass was smeared with black blood.

Some poor nudnik with a scalp condition was bleeding black blood after Sandrine/Akabar had her way with him. When she started combing his hair, flakes of skin stuck to the comb. This happens, people get scalp conditions, there's not a whole lot they can do about it, it's not like they're lepers. He had wiry hair, hard to comb, and Akabar got pretty savage. Well, she freaks around blood, she cut her finger once and I had to drive her to Emerg because she was sure she needed a blood transfusion. So she starts gasping around the poor nudnik, and clutching her throat, and he's asking, "What's wrong?" thinking she's uncovered a melanoma or something, and the whole time I'm watching this black stuff ooze and thinking, That must be blood.

It was then I started dropping things. I'm not getting better at this. It's like my body's getting further and further away from me. It's taking longer for my brain to deliver the messages. I was in the middle of perming a windbag who felt I needed to know about her hemorrhoids and constipation. "Drink water, eat fibre," I said when she stopped to breathe. I dropped another roller, thinking, This is it, I'm losing my sense of touch, next go the ears. And then Coco started crying because he'd just watched some tennis sisters on his mini TV fight it out on the court for the cup or whatever you win in tennis. "They were absolutely stunning," he said, darting his tongue. "It was *so* touching, at the end, because they actually *hugged*. It was utterly moving."

I'm dropping things because, colourless, they don't seem real to me. It's the same feeling I had watching a drowning boy years ago, on one of those whitewater adventures that everybody was doing back then to remind themselves they were alive. It was after Payne, when inhaling water seemed like a good option. I kept hanging off the boat, leaning the wrong way. The instructor shouted at me to lean into the current, but I was drugged, on a mission. The raft behind us ran into trouble, which we only realized when they didn't show up downstream. After fifteen minutes we started looking questioningly at each other—the noise of the rushing water made conversation difficult. But by twenty we were shouting hysterically. The instructor, one of those thick-necked dudes who could get hit with a plank and not notice, scrambled up the bank carrying ropes. "Wait here," he commanded. But I, Action Woman, went after him. I remember the sting of nettles against my bare skin as we scaled the cliffs. I remember the sweet smell of moss and the warmth emanating from sun-drenched rock. I remember thinking, This must be one of the most beautiful places on earth.

The raft had capsized but it looked like everybody was okay; most of them were already on the shore. But out in the water, waist deep, was a boy of sixteen or so. He called out that his boot was caught between some rocks. This seemed like no big deal to me. We'd go and move the rocks, he was wearing a life jacket, the water was only waist deep, what was the problem? So Action Woman charged in. In seconds I lost my footing in the strong current and was swept downstream. I thought, Now's your chance, drown already. But, without my consent, my hands grabbed hold of some branches and hauled my ass to the bank. By this time the instructors were in the water. The boy watched them calmly, leaning into the current to prevent being dragged under. I thought about how his foot must have hurt. I thought about animals in traps gnawing off their paws.

The thick-necked instructor, Jimbo as he preferred to be called, approached him and held out his hand. But as the boy tried to grab it, he lost his balance and slipped under. Seconds passed while we all waited for him to surface. Abruptly the current whipped off his T-shirt and life jacket. We watched the orange nylon bobbing downstream, disbelieving that there was no body in it. Jimbo and the other instructor kept flailing around in the water in an effort to locate the boy. The rest of us stood on the bank, an anxious crowd waiting for the parade to begin. I refused to believe that the boy was lost. Jimbo would find him, I assured myself and anyone listening, Jimbo will drag him to shore and do mouth-to-mouth resuscitation. Instead Jimbo and his pal stayed in the water a long time, thrashing around. I suspect they knew early on that the boy was doomed but kept demonstrating heroic measures to satisfy us and themselves. Returning to dry land with anything but hypothermia would have meant they hadn't tried hard enough.

The body turned up days later, minus the boot.

Anyway, this feeling I have of not connecting with anything reminds me of the feeling I had watching the boy. It's almost as though I'm watching a movie, except that when you're watching a movie you know it's a movie. I knew that boy was drowning, but it felt like a movie. I know that I'm colour-blind, but it feels like a movie. It's a kind of suspension. I know I'm going to crash, am hovering above the disaster.

It's like that with Logan. I'm watching the most precious part of my life earnestly go about her business as though her mother isn't lost, as though her mother is going to surface and be resuscitated.

That's why we can't talk. I have to keep thrashing around, even though I've lost the body. I have to demonstrate heroic measures.

I tried to hold her hand. She pulled away from me. It sent me back years, to when Stanley was new to us and Logan wasn't sure of him yet and therefore allowed me to hold her hand—usually she'd charge ahead, climb fences, scale telephone poles. Feeling her little monkey grip in mine I understood that this was a fleeting moment, a rarity at that point, and I wanted to remember the feel of that palm in mine forever. I couldn't imagine what would fill my life when that little hand wasn't available. Now I know—smoke, shadows, black pools, rat-coloured flesh. A world full of the young looking old. A smear in which my daughter moves but does not shine. She could be anybody. Like any parent I was in the process of letting go, understanding that the moment they're born to you you're already starting to lose them. The moment they're born to you they're starting to die.

I lie beside her, close my eyes and smell her. Her scent I know. But even with my eyes closed I see her in grey. I used to judge her health by the colour of her skin.

It might come back, my sight. Be optimistic. French calls me a pessimist. I tell him optimists are loiterers who don't want to do the work, want to wait and see what happens, see if Santa shows up. It's the grasshopper versus the ant thing. The truth is, I've always wanted to be the grasshopper but couldn't cut it. Which is why I'm drawn to them like a fly to shit.

"You know those songs," Shirl says.

"What songs?"

"Those songs they're always playing." She kicks off her pumps.

"Who?" She's canned. Bluxom did her tonight. She's drinking it off.

"Everywhere you go they're playing those songs," she clarifies. "I can be standing at the checkout, minding my own beeswax, and some gal is belting out some tune about how you light up my life, and I'm thinking, I missed that. And I get misty."

I squeeze more formula into Fuzzball.

"They're like so corny, right," she continues, "like we know it don't happen like that, like I'll love you forever and all that BS. But the songs are always going on and on about it and it's like . . . I just get so pissed I have to listen to that shit. It fucks with your head."

I push my lawn chair into the reclining position. I came out because my mother was in, shedding crocodile tears. "Did you have to dance to that shit?"

"That is exactly right, can you believe it?" She wiggles around in her chair to suggest dancing. "*Give it to me, baby, nobody does it like you, you're the only one, do it to me one more time.*" She pokes her finger in her mouth and gags. "And that pole you're supposed clamp your thighs around and rub up against, it hurts. You get bruises."

"Maybe you should just go for severance. Forget going back to work."

"They won't pay me nothing." She smokes and I'm thinking about those songs. She's right, they fuck with your head, suck you back into some modified version of your *grande passion*, or worse, make you think you missed out on *la grande passion* and here you are buying revitalizing cream.

"I like music without words," Shirl says. "Soundtracks. Those are good."

My night vision reveals one of the number-one buzzcut dealers doing a hand-off with Troy Boy in the parking lot.

"I had *one* decent man in my life," Shirl adds. "And he went and died. Was playing baseball with his kids, keeled over, went to the hospital, never came out. Forty-two years old. What do you think his wife did?"

"When?"

"After he died."

"Weep?"

"She went to Costco. There he was, barely cold, and she was out shopping."

"Do you think it was decent of *him* to screw around on his wife?"

She lights up another butt. "There isn't one man going who hasn't screwed around on his wife after she hit fifty. And it's always some piece of ass he meets at work." She finishes her drink and looks reproachfully at her glass. "Anyway, they play those songs and I think of him and then I think, Would he have stayed decent?"

I shrug, look vague.

"That's where those songs fuck with your head," she reiterates. "Because the truth is—" she leans towards me to emphasize her point, "the truth is, he probably would've passed me over for some younger meat just like everybody else. So I'm minding my own beeswax eating bacon and eggs and those songs come on and fuck with my head."

"There should be a law," I say.

Troy Boy in the white pants swivels by. "Good evening, ladies." He has that easy charm that makes women creamy. There's not a whiff of drug dealer about him. He looks like a travel agent. "A hint of summer in the air," he says.

"About time," Shirl grumbles.

"You girls planning to hang by the pool?" He looks through me at the junkie cringing in the soles of my feet.

"There's no water in it," I say.

"That could be a problem. Did you see my bike?"

"What bike?" Shirl asks.

"The Harley, just got it." Meaning somebody just paid him off with their mode of transport. "Let me know if you want to go for a spin."

"You wouldn't catch me dead on one of them things," Shirl says.

He touches my shoulder, letting his hand linger. "What about you?"

"I used to own one."

"Seriously?"

I nod, remembering the feel of it between my legs. It gave me the illusion of power. And drove Lester wild. I used to tinker with it in the driveway, dripping oil on his immaculate tarmac.

"I know a guy busted his leg riding one of them things," Shirl says. "They had to stick it together without the knee."

He winks at me. "It happens." His cell rings. "Catch you later," he says, taking the call while ambling to room 6.

Shirl sucks on the ice her empty glass. "Nice fella. Nice buns."

Sex in a lawn chair—lots of squeaking and wobbling. I wasn't even awake for part of it. But then this feeling of being immersed in something warm, soothing, tactile, *real* slid under my skin, which was grey but whose isn't in the dark. So there we were, writhing around for the coons. He has a touch, a gift, doesn't mash your clitoris to a pulp or gnaw on your breasts. You want him inside you, to split you open, free you of yourself, your ugliness, your sorrow, your anger, your pain. You want it to go on forever and he doesn't rush you, waits for you, which in a way bugs you because it's obvious you need it more than he does. He's in control while you're a mass of live wires. I close my eyes and move with the currents, my torso undulating under him with my arms outstretched, like the drowning boy. I force myself not to think about the body, or who he is, was, what he's done, did. I force myself not to think about our child asleep behind the door.

32

"Where's your suitcase?" Logan asks.

Her father's waving his coffee cup at the older waitress, not the jiggle-factor one because she's not serving them. The older waitress has a cold. While she served their pancakes, she coughed all over them. She said it wasn't her fault she was spreading germs, she said if she didn't show up for work she wouldn't get paid. "No such thing as sick days in the service industry," she grumbled. Payne told her to take zinc lozenges, said he had an associate who swore by them.

"What associate?" Logan asked.

"A guy I work with."

"Where?"

"At the office."

"Why don't you ever take me there?"

"I will."

"When?"

"When it's convenient. Don't get pushy like your mother." He always says this when he wants her to drop a subject.

When Logan got up to watch the news this morning, and saw that her father was sleeping on the floor again, she wasn't exactly ecstatic. Her mother showered first, then her father. They barely spoke to each other, which Logan found strange, as normally they fight. She managed to get her mother to eat some plain yoghurt, and to take kalamata olives to work.

The older waitress, dripping snot, pours her father more coffee.

"Vitamin C's good too," Payne offers.

"I've taken so much of that crap I'm turning into an orange," the waitress says.

Sitting in the booth behind her father is a geezer who keeps making faces at Logan. He twists a napkin and holds it against his upper lip as though it's a moustache. Logan ignores him and looks at her dad again. "So where's your suitcase?"

"What suitcase?"

"The one that was under the bed."

"Oh that. I took it."

"Why?"

"I needed it, do you mind?"

"What was in it?"

"Clothes. Like what is this, an interrogation or something?"

The geezer curls his upper lip under the twisted napkin to hold it in place. He tries to twitch it but it falls off.

Logan has noticed that her father is having difficulty getting the attention of the jiggle-factor waitress. When they first came in he skibbled over to her and said something, but she wouldn't look at him.

"Are you staying with us now?" Logan persists.

"Lo, don't get clingy, alright? Eat your pancakes. You don't want to be late for school." He slides out of the booth and walks over to the coffee machine where the jiggle-factor waitress is fitting a new filter into a basket. He leans over and whispers something in her ear. She still doesn't look at him. The geezer tries to fit the twisted napkin over his upper lip again. Payne touches the jiggle-factor waitress's arm but she jerks it away, causing the ground coffee in her hand to spill all over the floor. She starts to cry. Payne puts his arms around her and she boohoos into his shoulder. Gag, Logan's thinking. The older waitress, blowing her nose, steps around them to reach a coffee pot. "Break it up," she says loudly. Payne and the jiggle-factor waitress scuffle towards the kitchen and huddle beside the swinging doors. She starts bawling again. He hugs her and kisses her forehead. The geezer winks at Logan, then sticks out his tongue and pulls on his ears. Logan leaves the restaurant. She doesn't look both ways before crossing the street. She stares straight ahead, daring metal to crush her bones.

Mrs. Pawusiak pushes the bag of Peek Freans at her again. Logan picks one with a raspberry centre. "I just don't get how God could let all that happen," she says.

"All vat?" Mrs. Pawusiak nibbles on a chocolate wafer.

"The Romans crucifying him and everything."

"He vas sent to suffer for our sins."

"I know that, but I mean, what good is he dead? It seems to me God should have offed Judas before he let them do that to Jesus."

"Vee learn from Jesus's suffering,"

"We don't learn anything. We're still bombing each other." Before Logan came here she went to the museum and sat with the dinosaurs. She was so angry, so disgusted with her father, that she wanted him not dead exactly but close. She wanted something horrible to happen to him. She wanted him to suffer. She doesn't see why he should be able to wander around Earth, hurting her mother and herself and the jiggle-factor waitress, and probably all kinds of other dipshits Logan doesn't know about, while Jesus had to die.

And if God has his eye on everything, why are two-thirds of the world's species extinct?

"I don't see how the meek are supposed to inherit the earth," she says. "If that was true it would've happened by now. All that happens is that the meek get tortured and killed."

Mrs. Pawusiak starts swatting flies again.

"And I don't see how," Logan adds, "if Jesus was just an ordinary man, he could make bread and fish out of nothing. And wine out of water."

"God helped him vis zat."

"Well, then why didn't he help him off the cross?"

"He gave him eternal life."

Sitting with the dinosaurs, Logan understood that it's just a matter of time before man devours himself. And he won't even realize he's doing it. He'll be chomping on his own leg, thinking it's a pretzel or something, watching sports or surfing the Net for porno or the best deal on Sea-Doos. Jesus could die all over again. Man wouldn't even notice.

"He's probably been and gone already," Logan says.

"Who?"

"The Messiah. We probably killed him without even noticing."

Before Mrs. Pawusiak insisted she come inside to get warm, Logan stared at the pit that was her house. Her mother had advised her that the builders would have to wait for the foundation water-proofing to dry. McKenna also said she wants to put brick siding on the house because it's less flammable. Logan pointed out that McKenna had promised her that she could choose the colour of the house—bricks are brown. "So, we'll paint the bricks purple," her mother said. Logan knows that isn't going to happen. Nobody paints brand-new bricks. Her house is going to be shit-coloured like everybody else's.

Mrs. Pawusiak swats a fly on the fridge, then picks it off the floor with a Kleenex. "Vy did you not die in ze fire?"

"Because we were on the deck."

Mrs. Pawusiak shakes her head and points the fly swatter at Logan. "You have been touched by Jesus."

Her mother doesn't know that Logan's skipped school, that she's spent her emergency money on cab fare, that outside the museum a homeless man practically assaulted her for money for a hot dog. "Buy me a fucking hot dog!" he shouted, lunging at her. She gave it to him, told him he didn't have to shout. He didn't even say thank you.

Logan counts what's left of her emergency money. She told Mrs. Pawusiak that her mother knew she was here and was going to pick her up. Fortunately, Mrs. Pawusiak has to take her miniature poodles and her cockapoo to the hairdresser. She chases them around the house before grabbing them and shoving them into their carriers.

Logan walks into the rain and stands where her mother's flower bed used to be. The dump trucks, backhoe and steam shovel have destroyed the lawn. Even McKenna's French lilac has been swiped. Logan tries to tear off some of the broken branches, but it requires clippers. The low-growing cedars and the mugo pines have been trampled. She remembers how happy her mother was when she bought them at an end-of-season sale. Logan couldn't figure out what she was so excited about. "Evergreens cost money, monkeypie,"

McKenna explained, piling them onto a cart. "These are a serious score." In the car Logan had to hold one on her lap and one between her feet because the back seat and trunk were full of them. The car smelled of forest. They planted them right away. "We have a copse now, sweetie bun," her mother stated proudly. They drank hot chocolate with marshmallows while they admired their copse. Now it would just look grey to her.

Her father held the jiggle-factor waitress's face tenderly between his hands before he kissed her forehead. Logan can't remember ever being kissed on the forehead by her father. Sometimes he kisses the top of her head but usually he just pats it.

It starts to rain harder, so Logan squelches through the mud to the little aluminum garden shed and stands under the eaves. She thinks about the monsoon flooding in India, the death toll now 355. They've opened the sluice gates of three major rivers to prevent the dams from bursting. That would be scary, watching water rushing towards you, gushing into your living room, climbing your stairs, rising up to your neck, filling your nose, your mouth, your ears, crushing you against the ceiling. Better just to have your house burn down.

Maybe she *was* touched by Jesus.

33

I'm back inside the inferno with my water pistol. Julius smells it on me: woman in heat. *Baby baby baby*.

"So Mizz Mac, to what music do you jive?"

"I hate music."

"Let me cook for you. A little pasta."

I'm doing a perm on a CEO's wife who's testy because the CEO discovered beetles on their kitchen counter and blamed the wife for it. "He said I don't know the meaning of clean," she tells me.

She's one of those steel-jawed matrons who bite off words. "They were tiny, grubby little beetles, under the bread, everywhere."

I'm light of limb, levitating, not even here actually but with Payne, on a raft somewhere, drifting. The relentless head-pounding of my life has taken a hiatus and I'm back to not knowing where my body ends and his begins.

"So guess what happens," the steel-jawed matron says. "I look in all the cabinets and find *more* bugs. And do you know why?" I shake my head. "Because he doesn't put things in jars. He's been taking cooking classes and going out and buying all these exotic grains. He uses what he needs for a recipe then just shoves them to the back of the cabinets."

It was the strength of him, over and around me. Shelter.

"*Without putting them in jars*," the CEO's wife bites. "Any idiot knows if you don't put grains in containers you're going to attract *parasites*."

I've surrendered, put down my weapons. My body told me I can be blind and belong. It was a silent truce; we didn't want to wake the baby.

"He told me it was like living in a slum and that I was a pathetic house cleaner. Well, I've got news for him, they're *his* grains, *his* bugs, he can deal with it."

French hears the *bug* word. "Chinese chalk," he advises. "Good for roaches, silverfish, anything that crawls."

I got up this morning and couldn't find the five-ton rock I'd been carting around. I looked for it because I wasn't sure how to stand without the strain of it. But he was still there on the floor, sleeping like Fuzzball, and I realized he'd replaced the rock. Or had been the rock but was now this live, warm, pulsing being. Or maybe he'd been the being all along and I'd been so tormented with jealousy and the usual baggage that I'd turned him to stone.

My first client this morning greeted me with a cheeriness I hadn't see in him for a year. He has colorectal cancer. They've cut out his colon, rectum and other pieces of his gut. Two months ago they told him to get his affairs in order. Now they're telling him that what they thought was the cancer spreading might just be scar tissue. Meanwhile he's spent all his money and said all his good-byes. "From now on I'm taking it a day at a time," he told me. I will do likewise, no more freaking out before shit happens. I've been thinking ahead too much. You keep looking ahead, you miss the bus. Logan wants him around, she's made that clear, maybe we can work something out in the new house.

I've stopped dropping things, can feel my hands.

Visited my dad before work, gave him a shave, told him I'd dreamed about somebody stitching *my* eyes closed. It was weird talking to him, I'm not used to it, usually he grows agitated before I finish a sentence. Early on I decided there was no point in finishing sentences because people were glad to do it for me. Except Payne. "Speak up, Mickey," he'd say, or "What are you trying to say, Mick?" or "Am I supposed to have ESP or something?"

I smell Julius.

"So what's the deal, baby, you can't find a babysitter?"

"Julius, I don't know if you've noticed, but I've got a client."

I started crying in the drugstore because of one of those mind-fucking tunes Shirl was talking about. The cashier looked ready to bolt. "It's alright," I said, "it's the song."

"Oh, Celine Dion," she said, nodding. "She's awesome."

The body in the bed next to Lester's was talking dirty, using the f-word, the c-word. I've noticed that demented old men talk about sex while demented old ladies talk about domestic details. A client brings her mother in from a residence once a month. The old bird burbles at me about her closet space. The men are hanging on to their sanity by talking dirty while the women are clinging to their former organizational skills. A tidy house is a tidy mind. Which brings to mind my mother, who showed up in a dream. We were in my father's house, which she always kept tidy but crammed with knick-knacks. Every windowsill, mantel, table, shelf had some porcelain waste-of-space on it. In the dream I started flinging my body around, which I always wanted to do because in reality I had to tread carefully to avoid knocking shepherdesses to the floor.

Anyway, in the dream I was letting loose on cherubs, deer, fishermen, unicorns, elves, doves. *Crash bang boom.* I woke up refreshed.

She really should stay dead because dead you can forgive them. Or anyway forget what they did or didn't do to you. Denial's easy when they're subterranean.

The point is, even the colourless world isn't too torturous today. It adds a sixties French movie flavour to the Payne event. It's all in how you look at it. Shit happens, you cry, consider suicide, eat chocolate, then say to yourself, "Look at it this way." And usually there's a glint there, some speck you can focus your hopes on until the next kneecapping. So far I've only made two visits to the can.

We hear a roar. Kristos has discovered the first scratch on his Nazi car. "I park for *two* minutes, leave the car for *two* minutes, and some guy, some *skullhead*, don't know how to park, swipes my car."

"How do you know it was a guy?" Coco inquires.

"Maybe a woman, I don't know, they shouldn't have a licence. In this country any skullhead gets a licence." He sits at the front desk with his head in his hands, grunting and moaning about "this country." In minutes he'll start telling us we all need a stint in the Greek army.

"It's just metal," I tell him as I take the steel-jawed matron's bill to the front. How can he be that old and that stupid? Isn't one of the good things about getting older that you want less stuff? I'm planning to have empty rooms in the new house, rooms in which I can fling my body around without causing breakage. Maybe I'll pad the walls.

"She's genetically bald," I hear French explain re an absentee client to a present client he is styling to look like French. "It's *genetic* baldness. She's afraid to blow-dry her hair because it will fall out."

I shove his debris collecting on my side of the counter to his side.

"She was infertile for years," French continues, jangling bangles, "then finally had a daughter and was like terrified to brush her hair, cut it or anything. I had to like beg to make the girl look presentable."

Julius grabs my ass en passant. I ignore him.

"So the girl's a teenager now," French adds, "and her mother's freaking out every time she sees her daughter's hair in the tub. At the same time, however, she tells the girl, 'We're not good looking, you and me.' I mean, *honestly*. So now the girl's bulimic and her teeth are rotting from having stomach acids in her mouth all the time."

"Get rid of advertising," I say. French and his client gawp at me. "Advertising tells her she has to be skinny. Get rid of it."

My next client is Asian and missing fingers on her right hand. She has a misshapen thumb and index finger and the rest are stumps. She doesn't try to hide this but lets her hand dangle from the armrest. I'm thinking Hiroshima, birth defect. I'm thinking this woman was cursed before she even got started. She doesn't speak much English and indicates with her stumpy hand how she'd like her hair styled. I try not to stare at the hand, or think about how the discovery of the atom went wrong, how every human advancement requires sacrifice and that the obvious question is, is it worth it? Then she smiles at me, this deformed soul, with such kindness, as though she alone understands how inflamed my heart and mind are at this moment, and that she forgives me for screwing the father with the child behind the door. I smile back, begin cutting into the black, thinking only that I've been given a second chance.

34

Mr. Beasley stands watching Logan change. "Take everything off," he tells her.

"My underpants aren't wet," she protests.

"Everything off, we'll put it in the wash so you'll be nice and fresh for your mama."

Logan came to Dotty's so her mother wouldn't have a cow about her missing school. She slips off her underpants and hands them to Mr. Beasley, who won't stop staring at her with his flat fishy eyes.

"Come here," he tells her, holding a towel.

"I can dry myself," Logan says.

"Don't be bossy." He pulls her towards him and rubs her with the towel.

"Where's Dotty?" Logan asks.

"She had to pick up a few things. She'll be back shortly."

He rubs Logan all over, more than is necessary in her opinion.

"That's fine," she says. "What am I supposed to wear?"

"Between your legs now," he says.

"What?"

"Let's dry your pussy."

"It isn't wet."

"Don't make trouble." He pushes the towel between her legs. She can feel his hand through the towel, his fingers pressing against her vagina.

"That's fine," she says, pushing his hand away.

Curling Ellsworth opens the door and shouts, "She's naked and she ain't got titties!"

Mr. Beasley slams the door and points to a drawer. "Dotty keeps spares in there. Get dressed." They can hear Curling chanting, "She's naked and she ain't got titties!" Mr. Beasley hurries out to tell him to sit on the quiet chair. When Curling doesn't button it on the quiet chair Mr. Beasley threatens to tell his father about him looking at naked girls and talking about titties. This shuts Curling up because when his dad is pissed at him he doesn't buy him stuff.

Logan can't find anything big enough in the drawer. She has to wear a T-shirt that exposes her midriff and sweatpants that are too short. She wants out of the bedroom in case Mr. Beasley returns but she knows that Curling is going to make smartass comments about her outfit. She grabs her wet clothes, which Mr. Beasley seems to have forgotten. "Are you going to wash these?" she asks him. He looks paler than he did a minute ago, as though he's just remembered something he shouldn't have forgotten. When Dotty comes in with groceries, he quickly explains why Logan's clothes need washing. Dotty stares at him as though she's not hearing what he's saying. He pushes the clothes at her, and she takes them. Logan steps between them. "They have to be dry before my mother gets here."

"Righto," Dotty says and goes down to the basement. One of her grocery bags falls over. Boxes of Rice Krispies and bags of marshmallows tumble out.

"More rice crispy squares," Curling shouts. "Cool!"

Her mother got a cheque from the parasite insurance guy and wants to buy clothes. She's trying on everything black in every store in the mall. "Does this look nice, monkey? I just want to look elegant, you know, for a change."

Since the fire her mother has been wearing mostly baggy clothes, but the outfits she's currently trying on cling to her. She looks tiny to Logan; either she's lost weight or the colourful clothes inflated her. McKenna keeps turning her back towards the mirror and looking at her butt. "Does it make me look fat?" she keeps asking. Or, "The neck makes me look old, doesn't it, it's an old-lady neck." Or, "It's too trendy, isn't it? I don't want to look like a trendoid." Logan despises the salesclerks. They smile like reptiles and tell her mother she looks good in everything, which she doesn't.

When Logan complains that she's starving, her mother hurriedly makes some purchases. They order from Mr. Greek in the food court. McKenna insists they have lemon rice soup and salad with their souvlaki. "The chicken broth will do us good," she says.

They drove by their house on the way to the mall. Lumber was stacked in the yard. Logan hoped her mother would express concern over the torpedoed copse, but she didn't notice it.

"Our new house is going to be great, sweetie bun," was all she said. "You wait and see."

"It's going to be brick."

"Brick is nice, we get to choose the brick."

"Brick is brick."

"No, there's different tones. *You're* going to have to choose. I won't be able to tell the difference."

Logan balances an olive pit on the edge of her paper plate. "Why are you always talking like you're going to be colour-blind forever? You're supposed to go see a neurologist."

"All neurologists do is prescribe drugs. They don't have a clue what's really going on so they dope you."

"How do you know?"

"One of my clients goes to one."

"What for?"

"Pain."

"So, that's different, that's not like an eye problem."

"I've made the appointment, alright? They have waiting lists."

"I just don't get why you're giving up."

"I'm not giving up. I'm trying to function. Logan, don't give me a hard time. It hasn't been a great day. Tell me about yours."

Logan doesn't want to tell her about hers, about her father kissing the jiggle-factor waitress, about getting soaked and having to take her clothes off in front of Mr. Beasley. She can still remember the feel of his fingers through the towel. "I just want to eat."

"Okay." Her mother doesn't eat but looks in her bags at her purchases, squinting at the labels. "This is all black, right?"

"Yes."

"No witch is sneaking navy past me again. Next we have to get something for you. What do you want?"

"Nothing."

"At least some jeans, and maybe some trackpants. You can't wear overalls every day."

A man with hair that hasn't been combed in years is sitting at the table beside them blowing on his plastic fork. Logan tries not to stare at him but she's never seen anyone blow on a plastic fork before. Still gripping the fork, he dips his finger into some ketchup in a little paper cup then immediately shakes his hand as though the ketchup is disgusting. He gets up and finds napkins, sits down again, wipes his finger with one napkin and the fork with the other. All he's got in front of him is fries and Logan can't figure out why he doesn't just eat them with his fingers instead of the fork. He gets up again and throws the dirty napkins into the trash can, sits back down and starts blowing on the fork again. After a while he dips his finger into the ketchup again and immediately shakes his hand as though the ketchup's disgusting. He gets up to find more napkins, sits back down, wipes his finger and the fork, stands back up to put the napkins in the trash can, sits back down and resumes blowing on the fork. He performs this ritual repeatedly while Logan eats her dinner.

"Why did Dad sleep over last night?"

"He needed somewhere to stay."

"I thought you didn't want him around."

"I thought *you* wanted him around."

Logan picks up grains of rice with her plastic fork. A girl and her dad were walking in front of her on her way to Dotty's. The dad had his arm around the girl's shoulders and was holding a big umbrella over both of their heads. They talked constantly and sometimes laughed. They walked into a house together.

"You said he has no brain," Logan points out.

"What's that got to do with him sleeping on the floor?"

Two tables over a family is unwrapping Wendy's takeout. The little boy is holding a fierce-looking action figure, which he keeps jabbing at his older sister. "Settle down," the dad says.

"There's a woman in England," Logan offers, because she doesn't want to talk about her father, think about her father, "who feels pain when she comes into contact with electricity. She's allergic to it." She knows that her mother's not really listening because she's squinting at labels on her new clothes again. "She can't wear a battery-driven watch. And her shoes are specially lined so she doesn't feel pain when she steps over underground electrical cables."

The Wendy's family eats in comfortable silence; they have shared takeout many times before and will do so many times again.

"She has to wrap herself in a survival blanket," Logan adds, "and wear rubber boots during electrical storms to stop the pain from becoming unbearable."

Her mother tears off a label with her teeth. "How did she become allergic to electricity?"

"She was caught in an electrical storm twenty years ago."

There was lightning today and Logan did not run from it. She felt it would be an opportune moment for God to snuff her if he felt it was appropriate. She has seen a tree struck by lightning, the flash then smoke and the sound of splitting wood. She imagined herself struck, cracked open, her spirit freed, drifting skyward. She imagined her father, on hearing the news, dropping to his knees on the concrete where she'd been fried, repenting.

McKenna has put on one of her new black outfits, a dress that's too short in Logan's opinion. She keeps looking towards the door as though expecting someone. When she isn't looking at the door she's glancing at herself in the mirror and fiddling with her hair. The phone rings and she leaps at it, which surprises Logan as normally her mother avoids it like a poisonous snake. It's a wrong number. She puts her shades on again. "Why did you puncture Allanah's balloon animals?"

"They irritated me."

"Why?"

"Because they're stupid human tricks." Her mother trails her into the bathroom and watches while Logan gets into the tub. Logan knows her mother is making sure she doesn't try to drown herself again. She grabs a washcloth and tries to scrub off the feel of Mr. Beasley.

"Why are you rubbing so hard?" McKenna asks.

Logan winds the dolphin. "Fifty-three melon-headed whales were found dead in China. Humans say they have no idea why, like poisoned water had nothing to do with it. Humans cut pieces off the whales and ate them."

Her mother takes off her glasses and rubs her eyes. "It's a tragedy, Logan, what am I supposed to do about it?"

Logan puts the dolphin in the water and watches it flap around. "Why are you dressed like that?"

"Like what?"

"Your skirt's too short."

Her mother puts her glasses back on. "Is it? Why didn't you say something about it in the store?"

"I didn't notice it till you started sitting down. You can practically see your pussy."

"My what?"

"Your vagina."

"Who called it pussy? Was it that Curling kid?"

"No."

"Where did you hear that?"

"At school. Everybody talks like that."

"Well, you're not everybody. *We* call sex organs by their names."

Logan submerges but her mother immediately pulls her up by the hair. "No goofing around," she warns.

"I was just rinsing."

"Use the faucet." McKenna sits on the edge of the tub and turns on the taps. "Put your head under." Logan does and feels her mother's strong fingers massaging her scalp. She closes her eyes and tries to get lost in her mother's grip, to be absorbed through her palms, to shed the skin that was touched by Mr. Beasley.

35

I've spent the entire day and night hoping that Payne, the beetle-brain, the shithead, the deadbeat, would call. I've evolved that much in eight years, attained that level of maturity. For two seconds I even indulged in the suicide fantasy again, imagining it would alert him to my presence. Does it get more jaundiced than that, more juvenile? Then, being a big girl now, I recognized that my death would be just another blip on the radar screen. It would leave no mark on him, or the world, would only destroy my retreating daughter. She doesn't want to be seen with me anymore. She stands about twenty feet from me at all times.

Shirl's on her lawn chair, painting her toenails black. "Next I caught him hittin' the kitty's head with a wooden spoon. Right then I knew I had a problem. Bad idea, shacking up with him. You just never know. They start out good as gold then turn rotten on you."

"You still want one though."

"Who, me?"

"You're always talking about them."

"Force of habit." Shirl lights up another smoke. "Obladi oblada life goes on." She shrugs. "I always try to keep an open mind. That's a trap a lot of girls fall into, they think they know all about a guy just by watching him eat. Candice, one of the girls at the club, said she could never marry Ernie because he picked his teeth with toothpicks. They've got two kids now. I was over there for a barbecue and sure enough there he was jabbing at his gums. Candy quit noticing. You can do that, decide not to notice something about a person."

"Until there's too many things not to notice."

"That happens. You see those couples in restaurants, staring past each other, like there's not one piece of them either of them can stand to look at anymore, and you have to ask yourself—" she stares hard at some trash cans as though she's about to ask them, "you have to ask yourself, 'Did they ever really love each other or was it just a convenience deal?'"

"Beats me," I say.

"Nine times out of ten it's a convenience deal, I seen it a hundred times. The girls ask me, 'Do you think I should marry him?' and I say, 'Do you think you can live without him? Because if you can live without him there's no point in doin' extra laundry.' It's got to be a life-and-death deal."

"Like in the songs that fuck with your head."

"That is exactly right."

In high school I read a story about a man who gets lost in South America and stumbles into an isolated valley where the natives have been blind for generations because of some disease. At first he pities them but gradually he starts to figure out that they don't miss sight, that their sensitive ears and fingertips provide all the stimulation they need, that they have imaginations beyond his imaginings. They pity *him* because he is distracted by the visual. They think he's wacko and suffering from hallucinations. When the guy falls in love with a native girl and decides he wants to stay in the valley and marry her, the elders agree on the condition that he allow them to gouge out his eyes.

So lust can blind you. Ergo, here I sit once again, duped, in my too-short, pussy-revealing dress. Obladi Oblada.

I even bought condoms, hadn't bought them for years. Fuck-with-your-head music was blaring all about never being able to forget your touch. I was standing at the cash, staring at Slim-Fast brochures, and this lyric struck me as deeply profound. Because the ugly truth is, you never do forget his touch, which doesn't mean you want to spend the rest of your life with the dullard—you know the conversation would kill you. But the feel of him never leaves you, even though you get busy with other things, like survival. You shove the touchy-feely stuff to the back of your underwear drawer along with the lingerie he bought you which you never had the guts to wear but can't bring yourself to throw out because it means somebody thought you were sexy once.

In a dream last night my father was sitting on a black horse wearing his mean face, not the new brain-dead peaceful one. I was standing on the ground pleading with him to take off his "mask," all the while wondering if the horse was going to trample me. Its bulky haunches pushed against me as I tried to reach up to Lester, who was muzzled by the mask. I figured he was trapped behind it, that he didn't want to be mean anymore, that he was yearning for his new without-attitude face. With superhuman strength I straddled the horse and started to pull off the mask. It was glued on. To take if off I'd have had to tear the skin off his face. I couldn't free him without drawing blood.

In my teens I figured out that he was claustrophobic. We never travelled as a family because he refused to get on planes—the über-pilot who was so proud of bombing people. He couldn't even handle movie theatres, parades, anything that involved crowds. A couple of years ago I cut a claustrophobic who was seeing a shrink because her "disorder" was starting to wear on her marriage. The shrink retrieved a childhood memory of her getting lost in a crowd at a circus and meeting up with a man in a clown suit who forced his penis in her mouth.

It made me wonder if a similarly nasty experience is buried in Lester's brain box. If so, let's hope it's repressed because otherwise how could he, the claustrophobic, lock his kid in a dark room?

"That was the other thing," Shirl says. "He put a blanket over my hamster cage. What kind of moron puts a blanket over a hamster cage? Four of the babies died. When I pulled the blanket off, the mother was eating them. That's what they do to protect the other babies from getting infected by the corpses. What a scene that was, trying to snatch the dead ones from her. She was never the same after that. That moron left his mark on my animals."

We call them morons and yet they fool us again and again. Who's the moron? One of my searching-for-Mr.-Right regulars informed me that she gets Botox injections in her armpits to stop her from sweating—$1,500 a pit every few months. "It doesn't hurt any more than a Brazilian bikini wax," she assured me. "And I'm dating a new guy right now and I was getting all sweaty around him. I was using like men's extra-strength Right Guard. Now I can use stuff that smells pretty." I looked at her closely to determine if more than her pits had been paralyzed, her frontal lobes for example. It's minutes away, I guess, that kind of psych surgery. You got an anxiety disorder? Paralyze it.

Who came up with the term *disorder* anyway? As though the brain's an ordered place. Those who fail to keep tidy brains shall forever be on drugs and couches. I haven't cut one shrink who didn't have a personality disorder.

"He hated his mother," Shirl says. "Most of them do even if they don't admit it. The deal was she was always after him to do this, that and the other thing, called him an idiot, jackass, was always checking his fingers to make sure he wasn't smoking, which he was. Anyways, he'd do anything for money, right, like take dares—since his mother was a tightwad. He told me, if the other boys paid him enough, he'd do it with animals."

"And they would watch?"

"They'd hold the animal down. He only told me that after we broke up. He told me he even did it with a cat."

"*Charmant*."

"He started out nice though. You just never know."

In the dungeon, in the dark, I discovered masturbation. It was a silent, throbbing revenge on my father. Afterwards the room didn't scare me as much but became a safe place for sin. And the sanctity of it became apparent, the fact that there was nothing I could do, that no amount of screaming, kicking, repenting would alter the situation. Recognition of this brought relief in itself. There is something to be said for confinement. You know your limitations, you don't have to imagine them, fear them. Kaspar must have figured this out, which is why he wanted to go back to his hole. We should be able to create this in ourselves, a place where nothing goes in or out; solitary confinement for the soul.

We're on the bathroom floor this time because it's raining out. He tells me I look fabulous, amazing, and I lap this up like a good little doggy. The too-short dress is over my head in seconds. I become supple in his grip, tension slips off me like sand. I see him better in the dark. I slide my hands up his torso, amazed that eight years later he can still be so smooth, and I just want him and revel in the knowledge that I will have him, because I must possess something he badly wants otherwise he wouldn't be here because, let's face it, it's not my body he's after. He holds back, gives us time, and I slide my mouth over him. When we kiss it is a rescue effort, sharing what's left of the oxygen because we know we're both doomed.

"Mickey," he says in the calm after the storm.

"What?"

"I'm scared."

"Are they offering to cut your face?"

"I don't think they're that serious."

"How serious are they?"

"I don't know."

I feel his breath on my neck. "What a good time to visit with your family."

"They won't hurt you. They're not those kinds of guys."

"What kind of guys are they?"

"Korean."

"Maybe I've seen too many movies but it seems to me Koreans are handy with knives."

"They're just sharks. The cops are after them. They want me to be a witness."

"Somebody was looking for you here."

"What'd you tell him?"

"Didn't get to meet him. He hasn't been back so maybe he figured out I'm broke." I listen to the dripping tap, wonder if Payne could fix it. "I think I'm being followed."

"You're not sure?"

"Nope."

"I'm so sorry, baby." He holds me closer. Whatever's going on here, it's definitely disorderly.

"Don't count on the cops saving your tushy," I say.

"I'm not counting on anything, just trying to keep moving. Don't want to stay anywhere too long."

"How much?"

"You don't have it."

All the tensions that recently vacated my body come surging back. "How can you be so stupid?"

"I ask myself that all the time."

I start to feel him again, grasp him, because I'm not willing to let it go yet, the sensation that connects my disenfranchised body, turns the wood of me into flesh, frees me from the five-ton rock. Soon it will be dawn, the count will be back in his coffin, and I'll be groping in the dark of day.

36

Logan notes that her mother isn't in bed yet, which means she's out talking to one of the rejects, or feeding the garbage cat. She looks around for Stanley, hoping to find an ally, but as usual he's right out, dreaming of meat. She's having trouble sleeping, and coming up with a reason for living. If Jesus was supposed to suffer for her sins, why does she have to? Especially as she's not even sure her sins qualify compared to Curling Ellsworth's. Or that girl who barbecued the pomeranian.

Mrs. Pawusiak said that God knew that men would never be able to stop sinning, so he sent Jesus among them so that his blood would serve as their salvation. Logan has difficulty with this concept as it suggests that sinners can go on sinning because Jesus will take the heat. Curling Ellsworth will be forgiven because God knows he's bad news and doesn't expect him to act like a decent human being. Which means there's absolutely no point in being a decent human being because the Curling Ellsworths can all of a sudden decide they believe in God and get accepted at the gates of heaven.

And this whole business of Jesus walking on water is a bit much. It just seems weird that he would perform all these tricks just to prove he was the saviour. Why would he waste his power on making wine for a wedding when there were children starving in the streets? And healing the Roman soldier's wound? Get serious, what a waste of a miracle.

She crawls into McKenna's empty bed. She misses her mother, the sound of her breathing, the snores. The skin under McKenna's eyes has become the colour of a bruise. She looks witchy in her black garb, and the squinting doesn't help. Watching her hunched over the steering wheel this evening, Logan expected her to emit witchy *hee hee hee* sounds. Instead McKenna started singing along with Louis Armstrong, which normally wouldn't bother Logan. But for some reason all those swinging, thrillin', my-blues-are-over lyrics really got up Logan's nostrils. Because none of it's true. Everybody knows Satchmo was a pothead.

If there is a God, and Logan feels there has to be *something*, that the universe didn't just happen, why would the creator demand that humans build churches to worship him/her/it in? And then allow dirtbags in the churches to make all these rules that people who don't work for the church have to obey but that the dirtbags in the church break all the time—raping little boys, for example. And if there is a God, it's pretty obvious it has to be the same creator for everybody, and Logan can't believe that he/she/it is happy about humans having wars over religion. She's beginning to think religion is just another stupid human trick. Humans can't deal with the fact that stuff happens so they came up with this guy in robes so they could fantasize about never-never land and have an excuse to kill each other when really all they want is each other's cash.

She hears something, hops out of bed and peeks through the venetian blinds. Her mother isn't out there. Logan calls, "Mum . . . ?" then "Mum!" again. McKenna comes out of the bathroom in her trashy dress. "What is it, love? Can't you sleep?"

"There's something outside. Like on the roof or something. I heard it."

"What?"

"Something."

"Probably a coon."

They hear clumping. McKenna grabs her baseball bat.

"I don't think you should go out there," Logan cautions.

"I'm just going to have a look." Her mother has always gone ahead and investigated potential intruders. She has no concept of procedure. "Stay here," she tells Logan, who watches her through the window until she's obscured by darkness. Logan decides she'll count to ten before dialling 911. But screams happen, then squeals, and all Logan can think is that she must save her mother. She runs towards the screams, suddenly imagining life without her mother, the abyss of it, and decides that she must die with her mother. She saw a mother and daughter die in a movie. They were black and had been shot nineteen times by a racist white man. They lay together, shivering and bleeding, and the mother said, "Don't worry, baby, the Lord's goin' to come down and lay a blanket over us and take us up to heaven." Logan liked this ending.

The black pig appears first, stumbling, dripping blood. Logan hears her mother shout, "Get the fuck out or I'll bust your skull!" Then a guy scrambles out wearing a baseball cap backwards and the kind of wispy moustache McKenna always wants to rip off.

"Somebody call the police!" the clown screams. "He cut my phone wire."

McKenna chases the moustached man, swinging her bat. She's barefoot and her newly purpled hair is sticking out all over her head. When the man hurdles the fence at the edge of the parking lot, McKenna stops and rests the bat against her shoulder as though she's waiting for a pitch. The clown drops to her knees beside the pig, who's on its back, squealing and groaning. "Oh Charleton, baby, baby, what has he done to you?"

"It's only his ear," Logan points out. "It's not like it's a mortal wound."

At the all-night clinic they have to sit around waiting for the vet to stitch it up. He said he'd never seen a miniature pig before and asked if it was allergic to any medication. The pig was hysterical and the vet wanted to dope it. "He's allergic to peanuts," the clown said, still bawling. The back seat of the car is covered with her teary Kleenexes, and pig shit, which the clown said she'd clean up in the morning. "He messes when he's stressed," she explained.

The only other customer is a wasted woman in beige. Even her hair and skin are as beige as her bloated cat. "He hasn't gone in days," she tells McKenna. Logan would really like to know what it is about her mother that makes people yabber at her. McKenna can be just anywhere, the subway, the supermarket, and people will start telling her about their indigestion or bunions or something.

"At first," the beige woman confides, "I thought he just needed fibre, so I gave him a little Metamucil, just a tad. Well, he just got worse."

"Could be a blocked bowel," the clown offers between sniffs. "I know somebody who had that and they had to cut him open to unblock it."

"Oh for lord's sake," the beige woman gasps, clutching her constipated cat.

"What about exercise?" McKenna offers. She's blinking a lot, which means the fluorescents are bugging her. "Does the cat just lie around all day?"

Logan can't believe her mother's even talking to these people. Just once she wishes her mother would meet somebody interesting who might have read a book once. Armand, who made cheese and fixed scooters, also wrote poetry, so he might have had a brain. Over the souvlaki at the mall Logan tried to explain to her mother about stars, that they are huge, hot shining balls of gas like the sun, and that some stars are trillions and trillions of miles away but are actually bigger than the sun even though they look smaller.

"If they're just gas," her mother replied, "what's the point of wishing upon them? Just so much hot air."

This only came up because Logan's space project would be considerably easier to complete if she had the laptop promised by Uncle Tait. But it was another example of how her mother has no concept. While McKenna was slurping her lemon rice soup she asked Logan why the planets don't crash into each other.

"Because the sun has an extremely powerful gravitational force and all the planets are moving at different speeds," Logan explained.

"So?"

"Centripetal force keeps them rotating and moving on different curved paths."

Her mother tore another label off a black garment with her teeth.

The fact is, Logan doesn't want McKenna to go to the parent-teacher interview with Miss Spongle, which is why she hasn't told her about it. All she needs is for Miss Spongle to figure out how totally weird and ignorant her mother is and notify the authorities.

"Have you given him prunes?" the clown asks the beige woman. "Because when Charleton has difficulty passing, I give him stewed prunes. It works a charm."

It seems to Logan that her mother is always rescuing people, cats, dogs. McKenna would throw somebody a life preserver before figuring out she was drowning herself. This isn't healthy in Logan's opinion.

She nearly trips over her father on the bathroom floor. "What's he doing here?"

"I guess he needed somewhere to sleep," her mother says. "Just leave him, sweetpea, let him sleep."

"I have to pee."

"Step over him."

While on the toilet she studies her father's face. He looks younger asleep, almost like a boy. His mouth is hanging open but he doesn't snore like her mother. She reaches down and touches his hair, just to feel it. She has never touched it before and its softness surprises her. Angel hair. She kneels beside him and touches his shoulder, very gently because she doesn't want to wake him, to have him look at her as though she's crazy, or clingy or pushy.

She told *him* about stars this morning, before he rushed off to do kissy-face with the jiggle-factor waitress. She explained that there are billions and billions of them, sharing the universe, unlike the billions of humans who are always crashing into each other. She told him that it takes billions of years for stars to use up their fuel. When they finally run out, they die. The biggest stars explode, while smaller ones flicker out slowly.

"We all got to go sometime" was all he said.

Quickly, lightly, she kisses his cheek. She can't remember the last time she kissed her father's cheek. Her lips taste salty afterwards.

37

Shaved my father with a straight-edge razor this morning, all the while hyper-aware of his carotid artery, how easy it would be to terminate the buzzard. I threw a knife at him once, didn't even realize I was doing it, just suddenly it was there, clattering on the floor. I walked out, determined never to return. I was only nine, spent a day in the dungeon as punishment, pissed in a corner when my bladder couldn't take it. Inhaling the stink of urine I felt ashamed, dirty, untouchable. I stared into the dark for what felt like forever until this sort of window opened in my mind. Because when you're in total darkness you don't know if you're in a finite or infinite space because you can't see anything. You could be trapped or completely free. Meaning *you* get to decide how to perceive the thing. I stopped thinking about confinement, stopped listening for footsteps above me and focused on outside noises: dogs barking, cars passing, kids playing. I decided I was part of *that* world, which was infinite. The dark one was a moment in passing. This blackness I'm in is no different. If I listen to distant sounds, I'm not trapped.

I turned on a car I thought was following me, stopped in the middle of the street and started screaming at him. It turned out it was some dweeb with bed head who wanted to warn me that one of my brake lights wasn't working.

"*I* didn't want to sell the house," my current bag of waste tells me, a colour client even though I told Pixie the squeeze receptionist not to send me colour clients. The bag of waste's colour card has vanished, which leaves room for error. "*He* wanted to sell the house," she says, "said it would resolve our financial difficulties. Well, I put my soul into that house, sponge-painted the walls, *made* the curtains."

"Oh sponge-painting is *totally* hard," French offers, because my client sells Mary Kay products and he wants referrals. "And curtains," he adds, "I mean, that's like work."

"Tell me about it, and it's not like they'd fit just any window."

"Of course not," French agrees, swallowing Tylenol number nine. "Honestly, I would have killed him. Especially over the sponge-painting because I've had personal experience with that. It's like slave labour. I couldn't lift my arms for days."

Julius, trailed by his cologne, passes by. "Hey, baby, nice outfit."

"Yeah, what's with the cling-fit, Mac?" French inquires. "Suddenly we can see your ass. Are you dieting again or something?"

I have noticed, in the mirror, that there is less of me, that I strike a clean line. Actually, everything is lines to me now—I'm seeing lines I didn't know existed.

Kristos storms in, throwing his dead-animal jacket at Pixie. "Somebody," he bellows, "stole my hood ornament!"

"That's tragic," Coco says.

"So now I have freakin' holes in my car."

"*My* ornaments have been stolen at least six times," the bag of waste says.

I cut a radiology technician this morning who runs ultrasound probes over suspicious masses. Sadness filled her face with lines I wanted to draw. This surprised me as I haven't wanted to draw in years. While asking my usual get-to-know-the-client questions, I watched as the lines merged, ebbed and flowed. Every week, she told me, she's finding more and more cancers. This very morning she found four tumours on the breast of a twenty-nine-year-old woman. "She doesn't know yet," the technician told me. "*I* know what's going to happen to her and she doesn't even *know* yet. She was telling me about her two-year-old. He calls elephants elphalants. She misses him constantly at work. And all the time I was looking at those tumours and thinking she's going to die before that child is five." She covered her eyes with her hand. I handed her a Kleenex and sent Little Miss Spread-her-legs out for java. While the technician was drying her tears I was mesmerized by the dark grey veins flickering in her light grey hands. She drank the coffee zombie-style. I tried to imagine sitting in front of a monitor that the patient can't see, or understand, exchanging small talk while measuring the shadows of death, and I felt fortunate to be a hairdresser listening to bags of waste grieving over sponge-painting and hood ornaments.

The sponge-painting expert is turning rancid. "Is this the same colour you did the last time?"

"Exactly," I lie.

"It looks orange to me."

"Coppery. It looks great on you, makes you look younger. Brings out your eyes."

"Kristos," she hollers, "this is not the same colour as last time!"

Kristos, always willing to prostrate himself in front of customers, starts grilling me about what products I used. I admit that I couldn't find her card. He grabs his chest in horror, the bag of waste starts pulling on her hair like she wants it off her head. "How many years have I been coming here," she cries, "and this is the treatment I get?"

"She'll fix it," Kristos assures her.

"No, I won't," I say, wondering if this is it, the showdown.

"What do you mean, 'no'?" the bag of waste demands.

"What do you mean, 'no'?" the Greek repeats.

I point to my eyes. "No can do." Kristos grabs my elbow, hauls me to the back room and starts yelling at me. I'm not used to this. His sweat's making the goat and garlic he ate at lunch ooze from his pores. He's doing his speech about the customer always coming first and how he started out washing heads and wouldn't be where he is today without putting the customer first. He hasn't shaved between his eyebrows lately and is looking apey. "I'm leaving," I tell him, suddenly wanting to be fired, imagining a life free of heads and personality disorders. His mouth keeps moving but I don't hear it. They all watch me walk between the chairs, the gunslinger leaving town.

Of course it takes me about five minutes to start freaking about finances. And what I'm going to tell Logan, who's guaranteed to write me off if she hears about it. I try to look sharp for Wolfgang Stumph, my contractor who's butt-ugly and mountainous. Some of his slopes jiggle, but my sense is there's muscle under there, that he can mash bolts with his fingers. He talks constantly on his cell phone, his most common refrain being "The bottom line is . . ." Another popular one is "He's just going to have to pony up and pay it." Wolf is strictly a money man, has no interest in discussing the aesthetic possibilities of my new home because the insurance company is paying him bottom-line dollars to build it. Any extras I'm going to have to pony up and pay for. He has conceded to a skylight at a bottom-line price. I'm hoping for another one and am therefore hanging around in my pussy-revealing dress while his workers install the support for our first floor. Watching them screw down the floor joists with power tools, I try to figure out how I'm going to pay for it. I picture the want ad: colour-blind hairdresser seeks full-time employment, cuts only.

"Wolf," I say, "I was wondering if you could squeeze in another skylight, in my daughter's room?"

He grunts, takes a call on his cell, argues with a cabinetmaker about kitchen cabinets. "The bottom line is they can't afford oak." He paces around his W. Stumph General Contracting sign that he's skewered into what was once my lawn. "So what if it's soft," he grumbles, "use pine." He leans on the sign. "That's not my problem, Luigi, they get what they pay for." He pushes the phone back in his pocket. "Fuckin' dagos."

"Wolf," I venture. "Did you hear what I said?"

He rubs his hand over his bottom-line barber job. "You're going to have to pony up and pay for it."

I found the keys for my father's house in his pants. I've been avoiding coming here because I knew there'd be food growing fungus, and assorted debris that I would feel compelled to clean up. Like an automaton I sweep up crumbs, hairs, salami rinds. I fill a garbage bag with empty Pot of Gold chocolate boxes. He's a Pot of Gold addict, although I've never actually caught him in the act. Always, when we visit, the lid's on it. Logan once asked if she could have one, which sent the old guy into convulsions. In the car later I said, "Don't ask Grandpa for chocolates, okay?"

"Why not? He can't eat all of them."

"Oh yes he can." What's he do, gobble them one after the other, recklessly leaving the lid off the box? Or does he deliberate over the orange cream versus the coconut, sneak one, then carefully fit the lid back on the box and tell himself he's not going to eat another? Until two minutes later.

There are animal products in the fridge I don't even recognize, except for the gangrenous ham. I dump everything, including the pies. If he knew I was invading his house it might goose him out of his coma. I'll tell him later, see if it gets a rise out of him.

In a box in the broom closet I find my mother's figurines. He'd told me he'd sold them. They're just piled on top of each other, and consequently some have busted hands or hooves. It's as though Lester was planning to junk them but couldn't bring himself to do it. I take them out and clean them, set them in their rightful places. The mantel and shelves are covered in junk mail. All the envelopes have been opened. I guess nobody else writes to him.

Why didn't he toss the figurines? Did he think they were worth money? He erased all other traces of my mother from the house, so why let the shepherdesses and deer linger? Was it because he couldn't face a life in which she'd never existed? Because without little reminders it is possible to forget? And if you do forget, it means you never meant anything to anybody. Nobody ever listened for your key in the lock, put the kettle on for you, set the table. You're just this everlasting human taking up space, choking on chocolates.

Maybe he didn't want to remember but *needed* to remember, which would explain the careful wrapping. He resented needing the memory of her to confirm that he did matter once. As I've resented needing Payne.

This morning, as we tried to detox my car of pig shit, Allanah was speaking as usual about her ex. "Roy knows how to get stains out of anything," she assured me while we sprayed chemicals on the piss marks. I considered reminding her that Roy had just tried to kill her and the pig, but decided against it because maybe she needs him in order to feel that she matters. Without him she's just another supermarket clown. Without Payne I'm just another loveless single mom.

Besides, Roy represents danger, and we all want a bit of that.

Little Miss Spread-her-legs was bitching about the guy who got her pregnant, said he was a walking hormone, was only twenty-two but had impregnated five girls. "If you knew that," I asked, "why did you sleep with him?"

She and the boys looked at me as though I was an old lady with a freeze-dried vagina.

"Desire," French explained. "Something you wouldn't know about."

Which makes me think of longing, that pit you fall into. I'm there again, on the edge looking down, not just with Payne but with the father I never had, the grey creature with the gentle face who's going to wake up and tell me I'm the bestest daughter ever.

And then there's Logan, doing the same dance around the man who, had he known, would have driven me to the abortion clinic.

In need of eye relief, I walk into the windowless room and close the door. The usual panic grabs my gut. I hear noises, real or imagined, my father's foot on the stair. It smells the same, damp and mouldy. He's stashed piles of boxes, which adds the sour stench of rotting cardboard to the mix. I sit with my back to the door as I always did, only now I can see in the dark. The shapes and varying tones of the boxes against the walls, pipes and ductwork make an interesting collage. Once I hid a flashlight down here. He found it, and from then on searched the place before locking me up.

I notice boards I've never seen before, nailed over a window, a tiny window I didn't know was there. Outside it must be hidden by my mother's cedars. I touch the boards, try to pry them loose, but they're nailed tight all these years later. I hear the hammering as he bashes in one nail after another. What was my mother doing? Ignoring the banging in the basement because she was busy banging Wally?

My father nailed the boards over the window to create a torture chamber specially for me.

I close my eyes and listen to faraway sounds. A siren, and a baby crying. I think of the twenty-nine-year-old soon-to-be cancer patient constantly missing her son, not knowing she's given life to four tumours, that her days are numbered, that her child will hardly remember her, that she must hold him to her heart.

I should have slit his throat.

38

Breakfast conversation with her father proves difficult. She tells him about the discovery of the oldest fossilized dinosaur vomit.

"It belonged to a large marine reptile that lived 160 million years ago. That's the Jurassic age. It had a long head and four flippers."

"I slept like shit last night," he says.

"That's because you were on the bathroom floor."

Something's bugging him about his hair; he keeps adjusting it.

"Why did you?" Logan asks.

"What?"

"Sleep on the bathroom floor."

"It wasn't like I knew I was on the bathroom floor. I just fell asleep."

"Were you drunk?"

"Drunk? When have you seen me drunk?"

"Never."

"Then why would you ask me that?"

"Because when people sleep on bathroom floors in movies it's usually because they're drunk and pass out."

"You've been watching too many of those." He waves his coffee cup at a waitress with minor jiggle-factor. When he reads Cherie on her name tag he starts singing "Ma Cherie Amour." After she pours his coffee, he asks her the time.

In an effort to prevent her father from running off to locate the major jiggle-factor waitress, Logan explains the difference between meteorites and Earth rocks. "They're denser, and almost all of them have a thin bluish-black crust a few millimetres thick."

"I hate metric," he says. "Like what's wrong with inches?"

"And they have no bubble holes, and are almost all magnetic."

He pours sugar into his coffee and stirs it around, keeping an eye on Cherie. "What is a meteorite anyway?"

"A chunk of a meteoroid."

"Which is?"

"A small celestial body that orbits the sun. When they enter the Earth's atmosphere they become visible as meteors."

"And crash down on people."

"Sometimes. Actually, recently a close-approaching asteroid measured 0.9 kilometres in diameter, which meant it was a big enough rock to cause catastrophe if it collided with Earth."

"How close was it?"

"Just 11.2 million kilometres, nearly twenty-four times the distance from the earth to the moon."

"Gee, glad I didn't lose sleep over that one. Eat up. I'll be back in two secs."

And he's off. Normally Logan loves pancakes but she's getting sick of them. What she would really like is to discover a meteor. Most of them turn a rusty brown if they've been on Earth for a long time. She imagines pressing her face against its smooth surface, contemplating where it's been. Nothing on Earth matters when she considers the vastness of outer space. Jupiter, now there's a planet. All the other planets and moons of the solar system could fit inside Jupiter.

"Honey," she hears her father say, "this is Cindy, a friend of mine. She's going to sit with us for a minute. Is that alright?"

"Why?"

"Don't be snarky, she hurt her ankle. I'm driving her home."

"Hi," the major jiggle-factor waitress squeaks with what McKenna would describe as an I-brush-with-Crest smile. She must be wearing one of those push-up bras because her boobs are bulging under the bib of her apron.

"How did you hurt your ankle?" Logan inquires.

"Carlos just did the floors and I slipped. It's my own dumb fault, I forgot my work shoes."

"You should elevate it," Logan says, hoping this will make her buzz off and get supine somewhere, but her father lifts the jiggle-factor waitress's foot off the floor, lays it across his lap and takes off her shoe, which McKenna would describe as a whore-heel. "How's that feel?" he asks.

"Better."

Next the jiggle-factor waitress starts talking about *The Horse Whisperer*, which she saw on TV last night and just can't get out of her mind. "It was awesome. Like *so* passionate, I just didn't know what to think, I mean, on the one hand I was hoping she'd stay with him, and on the other hand I just couldn't stop worrying about the girl. I mean, imagine growing up without a foot *and* a mother."

Logan also watched this movie and considered it retarded. She liked the idea of a movie about a man who has special relationships with horses, but this was a movie about two no-lifers who wanted to get laid. McKenna watched it because she was fascinated by Robert Redford's hair. "He must have his hair person on duty constantly," she remarked. "Between every take they must do a fluff-up. And what's with the blond, how old is this guy, sixty-something? Is there one white hair on his head, Logan?"

"No."

"Big bucks, that hair." And when Robert Redford took off his cowboy hat, McKenna practically jumped at the TV. "Did you see how carefully he did that so he wouldn't muss it? And no hat head. They must stop the cameras for this guy's do. Forget the acting, how did Bob's hair look?"

"I cried at the end," Cindy admits. "When she was driving away. I was like totally wrecked."

The whole time the jiggle-factor waitress is talking, Payne nods as though what she's saying is really interesting. "I mean," she continues, "how could she go back to her husband after that?"

"My mother said he was wearing a rug," Logan says, primarily to remind her father of the existence of her mother.

"Oh, so that's why his hair looked so odd," Cindy says. "I wondered."

Logan enjoyed watching the horses, wanted to be on one, galloping through Montana.

"Cindy rides horses," Payne informs Logan.

"I pay by the hour," Cindy admits modestly. "It's not like I own one."

"Logan was telling me," Payne says, "that millions of years ago horses were the size of dogs."

"No way," Cindy says.

Logan is well aware that her father wants her to bond with the jiggle-factor waitress. He always wants her to like his girlfriends. But she's not in the mood. "Earth's temperature is changing faster than anybody'd anticipated," she says. "In Antarctica 500 billion tonnes of ice has melted in less than a month."

"You won't find me complaining about warmer weather," Cindy says.

"Right on," her father agrees, "give me heat."

"Ninety per cent of the world's ice is in Antarctica," Logan explains. "If all of it melts, it will raise sea levels worldwide."

Her father gently removes the dip's knee-high nylon and starts massaging her foot. "That hurt?"

"Feels awesome," the dip says before doing her I-brush-with-Crest smile at Logan again. "Antarctica, that's like in the Arctic, right?"

"It's the South Pole."

"Kind of far away, Lo," her father says. "Like maybe you shouldn't sweat it."

Logan stares at the blood-red polish on the dip's toes. "It's not like the flooding's just going to happen in Bangladesh. London, New York and Tokyo will be submerged."

"Time to get a boat," her father says, winking at the jiggle-factor waitress, who giggles. A wisp of her hair has escaped her ponytail. Payne lifts it off her face and tucks it behind her ear. He has never done this to Logan.

Curling Ellsworth repeatedly flicks marshmallows across the kitchen behind Dotty's back. She can't hear the soft thud as they land because she's playing country western music and making rice crispy squares with multicoloured kernels. Logan is staying in the kitchen with Dotty because she prefers to keep her distance from Mr. Beasley, who called Dotty "lard-ass" again this afternoon. Unfortunately he comes into the kitchen with Katey, who's sucking on a popsicle. He makes Katey sit on his lap while he licks melted popsicle off her hands and face. Katey squirms but he holds her firmly. Sometimes he licks her popsicle, which makes her start to cry. "What a fussy little girl," he says.

"Why don't you get your own popsicle?" Logan asks.

"My *own* popsicle," Mr. Beasley says. "That's not nearly as much fun, is it?"

"Katey isn't having fun."

"Sure she is. You're having fun, aren't you, love? Unlike other children I could name, she likes to share, don't you, sweetie?" Katey doesn't answer, just sucks on her popsicle. Her eyes are large and full of darkness.

"What's that you're working on, princess?" Mr. Beasley asks. Logan decides to ignore him.

"Her *space project*," Curling says in a nasally voice. "Like anybody gives a goat's turd about space."

"Lots of people do," Dotty interjects. "Tell them about the comets, Logan. Go on, don't be shy."

"They're made of snow and dust," Logan mutters.

"And . . . ?" Dotty urges. "Show Mr. Beasley how clever you are."

Logan can smell the dead-ratness of him, can feel his flat-fish eyes through her clothes. "Their tails are formed when the sun warms them and forms gas. As a comet moves away from the sun, its tail disappears."

"I feel a better person for knowing that," Curling says.

"What's *your* project, young man?" Dotty asks.

"Haven't decided."

In the backyard Curling announced to Logan that his project was about shit, all different kinds. He was going to collect it and put it in ziplocked bags and asked Logan if she would give him a sample. Logan ignored him and climbed the tree. But she's having difficulty with the ignore concept, because they still get to you. Even if you don't look at your tormentors, they are still there. You feel them in your body, tensing your muscles, drying your mouth, making you sweat. Like right now she's trying to ignore Mr. Beasley but it's as though his hands are all over her. She saw a program about pain being imprinted on the brain, that even after the source of pain is healed, you can still feel it. She wonders if this is also true of people—long after they're gone they can still hurt you.

Vance, the clown and the woman who stinks of perfume are eating pizza and bowling in the parking lot. They use Coke bottles filled with sand for the pins and a soccer ball. Vance has a ghetto blaster tuned to some rock station. Between bowls he plays air guitar. All this activity will make working on her space project difficult.

"You folks want to chow down on some pizza?" Vance offers.

"Logan . . . ?" McKenna asks.

"Can we give some pepperoni to Stanley?"

"If it's off your slice, missy," Vance says. "It's like I always say, what you do with your pizza is your own biz." He hands her a slice with a flourish. Logan starts picking off the meat slices and feeding them to Stanley. She knows it will knock him out but he so rarely gets pizza. Her mother never orders it, says they're made by hairy, sweaty men who can't read signs that say Wash Hands Before Handling Food. Logan sits on a lawn chair to eat her slice and watch her mother bowl. Her mother's been cheery, which should be a positive thing except that there's something creepy about it, in the same way McKenna's new clothes are creepy. It's a forced cheeriness. Normally McKenna gets excited about something specific, like a full moon, a shooting star, Mars on a clear night. There's no way normally she'd get excited about bowling but here she is, waving her arms around every time she knocks over a bottle. "You've got a talent," Vance tells her, setting them up again.

"How was school today?" the perfume-stinking woman asks Logan. She's painting her toenails with glitter.

"Alright," Logan responds.

"You don't sound too excited about it."

"I'm not."

"It was the same deal for me. I hated school. It was like, why do I have to sit around eight hours a day with these goons? It was like prison only worse because you had to do homework."

"I beg to differ," the clown says. "Those were the happiest days of my life."

The perfume-stinking woman eyeballs her through cigarette smoke. "I thought you said the happiest days of your life was when you was in Florida with your husband who wants to kill you."

"That was our honeymoon. Everybody's happy on their honeymoon."

"I wouldn't know," the perfume-stinking woman says.

"There's killer algae in Florida," Logan tells them. "It's killing alligators, white pelicans, turtles, bass and domestic cats. Soon it's going to start killing people."

"That sounds like a movie, don't it?" the perfume-stinking woman comments.

"It's not a movie," Logan says. "It's another ecological disaster caused by human arrogance."

"What a serious little girl," the clown remarks.

Logan wakes Stanley and drags him into their unit. She pours water into his bowl because he's always thirsty after eating pepperoni. She hears her mother shout, "Aced it!" as she hits the bottles again. Logan pulls her space project out of her backpack and writes: *A comet orbits the sun anywhere from every few years to millions of years.*

"What's going on, monkeypie?"

"Nothing."

"You don't want to try bowling?"

"I have to do my space project."

Her mother flops down on the bed and starts to feed Fuzzball. Logan wishes she'd say something half normal, or at least stop squinting for five minutes.

"I wanted to ask you about those rings around Saturn," McKenna says. "What are they?"

Logan knows that her mother's just acting interested, just like she's acting cheery. "Billions of icy particles," Logan says. "Jupiter and Uranus also have rings but theirs are much thinner than Saturn's."

"How did you get to be so smart? It has to be your uncle's genes. I talked to him today. He's going to bring the laptop over on the weekend."

Logan knows he won't, that this is just another adult lie.

"I asked the contractor," her mother says, "to put a skylight in your room so you can see the stars."

"You can't see stars in the city."

"Sometimes you can. I can now, better than when I could see colour."

"You talk like you're glad you're colour-blind." Logan starts to colour her drawing of Jupiter with felt marker.

"I'm not glad. I'm just noticing the differences. Think of a black-and-white photograph, how stunning it can be, you see a subject in a completely different way."

Logan really doesn't want to talk about this—her mother in that other world where she bowls and wears slutty dresses and thinks piles of garbage are homeless people. This afternoon, in bright sunlight, they had to stop because McKenna thought a person was lying on the sidewalk and she always calls Outreach when she finds someone unconscious. "It's garbage," Logan told her. When McKenna got back in the car she kept feeling her face, as though making sure no parts were missing. Back at the Lakeview her mother felt she had to rescue the guy who wears white pants' motorbike. He'd parked it too close to one of Mr. Bluxom's weed beds and the kickstand had sunk into the dirt. The white pants guy saw her touching his bike and came out to make sure she wasn't trying to make off with it. "Nice ride," McKenna told him, bending down to get a better look at it. "Too bad it's been dropped a few times."

The guy looked worried. "What makes you say that?"

"The exhaust's dented, the pegs are worn, somebody's been riding hard on corners." She stuck her finger into one of the pipes then looked at the grime on it. "It's running rich, carboning up. Is it leaving puddles?"

"Puddles?"

"Of oil."

"Yeah, I guess it is."

"The chrome's turning blue, means it's been ridden hard."

Logan had never heard her mother use bike talk before. McKenna became quite animated and kept fondling the bike in various places. The white pants guy watched her anxiously, as if she were operating on it.

"What do you think it's worth?" he asked.

"It's a kick-starter, that's rare, it's all electrical these days. Does it start on the first kick?"

The white pants guy shook his head sadly. "I can't get it going."

"You're kidding."

"Do you think *you* might be able to?"

"You're not getting on that," Logan said loudly. "No way you're getting on that."

"She's right. It's been a while." Her mother peered closer at something on the bike. "It could use a timing change. Good-looking bike though. Too bad they beat the crap out of it."

"Anytime you want to try it . . . ," the white pants guy said.

"She's not getting on it," Logan repeated.

Logan starts to colour Venus. "You're not getting on that motorcycle, right?"

"Right."

"That would be like suicide with your eye problems."

"I know."

"Then why did you take the key?"

"What?"

"I saw him pass you the key."

"It doesn't mean I'm going to ride it. It probably doesn't even start. I was being polite." McKenna looks at the chart of the planets. "What's that one?"

"Venus."

"The love planet."

"It's covered by thick clouds of poisonous gas."

"Makes sense." McKenna lies back on the bed and rubs her arms, which get sore from work. "Did you and Dad have fun at breakfast?"

"He had some dipshit sit with us. She hurt her ankle. He drove her home."

Her mother sits up and squints at her. "What dipshit?"

"I don't know. The waitress there. Her name's Cindy. He's always talking to her."

"The one who served us the other day?"

"Yeah, her. They suck face by the coffee machines. It's gross."

"When?"

"What?"

"When did they suck face?" Her mother looks frightened.

"I don't know," Logan says. "Yesterday."

"Did they suck face today?"

"Maybe a little, in the car. I can't remember." Logan really can't see how this is important. Her father makes out with different dip-shits every day. Like her mother has said, sex is a drug and he's addicted.

"I'm going to have a bath," her mother says.

"Okay. Thanks for putting sand in the turtle."

"You're welcome. Let's hope cats don't shit in it."

Logan writes under Venus, *The second nearest planet to the sun, visible as a bright star.*

The water stops running and Logan thinks she hears her mother crying again. She has no idea why and does not go to comfort her because she has no idea how. She realizes that her mother, in the water, in the dark, thinks that she can't hear her sobs. Logan prefers it this way. She writes under Mars: *The fourth planet from the sun, has red dirt and pink sky, could have possible extraterrestrial life.*

Her mother stops crying, leaving only the sound of the dripping tap. At first this relieves Logan, but then it occurs to her that McKenna might be holding her head under water, that she will have to rescue her mother as her mother rescued her, drag her slippery body out of the bath, shake the water out of it. "Mum . . . ?" she calls.

"What is it?"

"Nothing."

39

Allanah, Shirl and I watch the bust. More undercovers show up with a van in which to store the busted. Bluxom's stomping around acting like this is the worst thing that's ever happened to him, that he's an innocent in a den of thieves. As the cops line up Troy Boy and company against the van, Bluxom spreads his cheeks on a lawn chair and shakes his head in what I'm assuming is intended to represent disbelief.

"Will they do anything to Mr. Bluxom?" Allanah inquires.

"Let's hope so," I say.

"I thought that boy was real cute," Shirl says. "Always polite. Would take a good look, mind you, but I'm used to that. After a certain age you take it as a compliment."

Troy Boy and his cohorts do not resist handcuffs or spit profanities, even though they must know what's coming—hours rolling around in the van as the undercovers meet their quota for the night. Then the strip search, fingerprinting and more hours in a crowded holding cell waiting for processing, inhaling the stench of the toilet and each other as they sit wedged on benches, wondering if anybody's going to try to snuff anybody.

"It's a shame young people today got nothing better to do than take drugs," Shirl says.

The obvious question is how is this different from getting polluted on rye, but I don't ask it. "Give them hope," I suggest.

"I got no time for people sitting around looking for hope."

"Hear, hear," Allanah says.

Somewhere in the hopeless eighties I got busted. It was at a party, I wasn't actually drugged but had a crack pipe on me. To improve my chances of prison survival I handed over all valuables, including earrings, to the corrections officer for lock-up, and maintained minimal eye contact with my sister captives. My thought was that not looking at a person would suggest fear, while looking too much would suggest a challenge, and I didn't want to challenge any of the street-worn in there. One of the partygoers, new to prison policy, became demented and kept throwing herself against the bars. I was amazingly calm about the whole deal, I guess because being locked up was old news to me. I fell asleep on the concrete floor.

"Troy helped me with my laundry the other day," Shirl says, "said I reminded him of his mama."

"Roy always says I remind him of his mother," Allanah offers.

"Does he try to kill her too?" Shirl asks.

"Other times he says I'm not half the woman his mother was."

"*He's* probably not half the man his mother was," Shirl suggests. "Any man beats up on a woman is no man in my book."

I want to be with Logan, hold her, tell her everything will be all right. She won't buy it. She didn't even kiss me good night, just pulled the covers over her ears. It feels like a hundred years since we've snuggled together. She used to rest her head on my shoulder then, in half-sleep, slide down until her head was on my stomach, rising and falling with my breathing. I wondered what the movement of my belly did for her, if she was back in the womb. Watching her peaceful face in sleep, I felt so incredibly lucky to be of service to her still, to be able to offer comfort with my body. I was brutally aware that this magical time would pass, and that I would have to find some other means of offering comfort. My belly still aches for her though. We want our children back. All they want is to go forward.

This may explain my current obsession with the man who'll fuck anything that moves. Logan no longer fills my life because she has her own, crowded with planets, dinosaurs and ecological disasters. Payne is more on my level; when there's nothing on the tube, the dull-witted seek solace in copulation.

So I'm crying over him again, even though I know I'm blind, deluded, depraved, whereas he's being true to himself. I'm a lie in a pussy-revealing dress, getting sucked down the expectation drain again. I can hear the sewage burping and farting around me.

The question is, what action to take? Baseball bat? Burn his hair?

"Your beau was by with flowers today," Shirl tells me.

"What beau?"

"The blond. He left them with Burt. I offered to take them but he didn't like the look of me. Nice buns."

I approach the bag of fat in the wife-beater. "Yo, Bluxom," I say. "That was some bust, like right out of a movie. It sure is amazing that they were doing deals right under your snout and you didn't even know about it."

"What do you want?"

"I heard you've got flowers for me."

With effort he heaves himself off his lawn chair. I follow him into the office, where porn grunts and moans from his TV. It's one of those hand-held jobs, the guy with the hard-on films his penis before jerking it into a K-Y jellied vagina. Sometimes I get so sad about the world.

"Here," Bluxom mutters, pushing a white box at me.

"Thank you so much. By the way, we're using the laundromat down the street. The deal was you'd fill the pool if I backed off about the washers and dryers." I say this knowing that I am speaking into the wind, that Bluxom is not a man of his word. On the screen the woman behind the vagina utters orgasmic cries. Bluxom pays her no mind but unwraps a stick of Dentyne and starts chewing on it. I guess it's important that he have fresh breath.

"The pool," I repeat. "You said you'd fill it if I stopped complaining about the laundry facilities."

"I didn't make no promises."

"A little girl is counting on it."

"Yeah, yeah, yeah."

I open the flowers in front of the girls. Black roses.

"Long stemmed," Allanah sighs, "how romantic."

"Those are beauties," Shirl says. "Nice buns *and* he sends you flowers. You've got it good, girl."

My father's jellied eye stares at me. I avoid it, am still scared of him, even though he's mummified. I don't tell him I got fired, that I can't even provide for my bastard. I put the black flowers in a cheap vase I lifted from the salon. I hold them in front of his eye, expecting what, that he'll say *gee thanks, how thoughtful*? He doesn't blink. I stand in front of his eye again and start acting retarded. *How are you feeling, Dad? We didn't know if you'd make it, it's great to see you, I guess you don't know you've been in a coma, you had a stroke, I guess you don't know that either.* It goes on and on, my yammering. My hope is that a doctor will show up and give him drugs or something, anyway, get the eye off me. It's hard to read the expression of an eye in a face that can't move, but my sense is, the old buzzard is not pleased to be alert in a corpse. The wingnut in the next bed begins one of his cunt monologues. I meet my father's eye. "Can you hear?" I ask it. It blinks. "Blink twice if you can hear," I say. He does. He's trapped but can listen to distant sounds.

"Is there anything I can get you?" I ask, realizing as the words leave my lips that he can make use of nothing—no deli meats or Pots of Gold can offer comfort. The man is stranded. Even so I find myself hating him because here I am once again, failing, at what I don't know exactly. But the eye says it all. There is no *Welcome, daughter*. He is unchanged, as I am. Were I the fallen, he would not have brought redirected roses. He would not have pretended, as I am doing, to care. He would be true to himself.

I've always suspected that whatever is said with conviction is a lie, protestations of love, for example, or honesty, trustworthiness, dependability, loyalty. If they have to say it, they don't mean it. They want you to believe it because it gives them a handle on you they can grab. The dense ones don't even realize they're lying, they just want to be liked, accepted. They'll say anything to keep you happy. And you want to believe it, because it gives you a reason for occupying space. How many times has my gut told me to run fast in the opposite direction while my brain kept stalling me, offering deep insights like, Maybe he didn't mean it, or, He's harbouring a lot of anger and resentment from his childhood, or—my personal favourite—maybe he's changed?

At least my father never lied.

Kristos phones and begs me to come back because "the crazy girl is going crazy." I try to act like I have to think about it. She's not crazy, she's got Tourette's syndrome, but is probably off her medication because she hates the side effects. When she heard I wasn't available she started poking people in the waiting area and shouting obscenities. She hugs me when she sees me, leaving no doubt that she's off her meds because she's energized, actually beautiful, even more so in black and white because her pale skin looks paler and her dark hair darker. She thinks she's ugly, avoids her eyes in the mirror as her head jolts back. The head jerk is her most noticeable tic and she does it frequently. I'm always afraid, during the jolt, I'm going to gouge one of her eyes. While she's in my chair the boys get edgy, yak even more than usual, the topic being snuff fiction. Rose, my client, jolts, then starts poking my stomach. It's like being pawed by a curious cat. Then she stops and says, "Sorry." I tell her it's okay. That's about all we say to each other. I dodge in and out of her tics while she pokes me or anyone else who comes close. It's good to be back at the job I hate because it's familiar and means money. Occasionally Rose swears or says something completely inappropriate or true that makes everyone gasp, then she says she's sorry. This is her life, apologizing for whatever pops out of her loose-edged mind. Kristos is doing a fluff 'n' puff on one of his Thornhill sowees who's complaining about taxes and welfare bums. Rose starts jolting again. I back off to give her space.

"Clearly they can't be relied upon to use contraception," the

Thornhill sowee declares. "One in four children living in poverty, is it any wonder?"

"Cow," Rose spits, then, "Stupid, stupid."

I hold her head firmly in my hands, which I've found helps to steady her. But this time, for some reason, I also kiss the top of her head. This stops her. Black-eyed, she stares at me in the mirror. I continue to steady her head while Kristos explains to the cow that my client is "a little . . ." and he does the old index-finger twirl at his temple.

"Oh," the bovine remarks, "don't get me started on that issue."

"Ignorant, ignorant," Rose sputters.

I kiss her again and, when I have her focused in my sightlines, I smile, and she smiles back. We are co-conspirators, the mad hairdresser and the client.

Payne phones, uses that intimate tone reserved for lovers. My brain's telling me "run" while my hormones are urging compromise. I don't know when or if to blast him. It's not like we're married, it's not like I was expecting we'd live happily ever after.

"They got the guys," he tells me.

"What guys?"

"The sharks. I had to pick them out of a lineup."

"Where are you?"

"At the station."

"Watch your tail."

"Mickey, it's over, they're toast. It's not like I'm the only witness. These guys have a history."

Don't we all. My body has ousted my mind, is caving into something dangerous, one of those cushy chairs that kill my back. I always think, Wow, this is so soft, let me luxuriate. Ten minutes later I'm a cripple.

"We should celebrate," he says. "Is it okay if I pick Logan up after school?"

She would love that, to be seen with her dad, to be spared Dotty's shelter for the dysfunctional. "Okay," I say. I hang up and check my pocket. Fuzzball, the dormouse, has opened her eyes. We stare at each other, trying to figure it out. *If you're my mother*, she's thinking, *where's your fur?* I'm trying to guess the colour of her eyes. I hope they're grey. If they're grey she will remain the one creature in my life I see as she is.

In my mind, my father's eye chases me like a follow spot.

40

"Let's go for a doughnut," her father said as soon as he saw her. Logan had been watching boys on bikes circling Nina and pelting her with tennis balls.

"Someone should stop them doing that to her," Logan told Payne.

"What?"

"They're hurting her."

"They're just fooling around. Let's go score some sugar."

McKenna would have interfered, chased the boys with her baseball bat. Logan suspects that her father is a coward. He bites on a jelly doughnut. "Cindy was pretty impressed by your knowledge of outer space. She asked me to ask you about the northern lights."

"Northern lights don't have anything to do with outer space."

"Seriously? I thought maybe they were like the Milky Way or something."

"They're caused by particles from the sun that strike gases in the atmosphere and make them glow."

"Isn't that something? She said she saw them once, up north, said they were mysterious and magical. She says ever since then she's understood that nature is bigger than we are."

"We're destroying nature. Climate change is causing death from heat stress, devastation from weather disasters, acute water shortages and rapid-progressing diseases." She had to memorize this for her environmental degradation project.

Her father's cherry doughnut bleeds. "Where are you getting this stuff, TV or something?"

"It's from a report endorsed by four hundred scientists and more than one hundred governments."

"Yeah, well, as soon as the government's involved you know it's bullshit."

"How would the government benefit from telling us we're causing our own extinction?"

"Get more taxes out of us. Give us your money or you'll croak."

"The fact is," Logan says, "humans have consumed more natural resources in the last forty years than in all the other centuries combined."

"Eat your doughnut, hon," her father says, leaving the table to get a refill. The girl behind the counter smiles at him when he asks her the time. He dawdles while opening his creamers and pretends to be interested in the details of the Souper Soup 'n' Sandwich special. When he sits back at the table he's perky. Logan wonders what it is about talking with dips that energizes him. Does he realize that they're even stupider than he is, which makes him feel smart?

"Do you ever dream, Lo?"

"You mean at night?"

"No, *dreams*, like what you want to be when you grow up."

"No."

"There, you see, that's a problem. You've got to have dreams."

"I dream that the planet will be saved."

"There you go with that planet stuff again."

"It's a dream."

"I'm talking about you personally."

"Personally we all need the planet. We're standing on it."

"I just wondered if you ever dream about getting married or anything like that. Or if your mother's turned you off that kind of thing."

"If I meet a smart man," Logan says, "I might marry him so our children won't be bastards." She watched *Anne of a Thousand Days* on TV recently. Every time Anne insisted that she would not divorce Henry because it would make Elizabeth a bastard, Logan cheered inwardly. Hearing the word *bastard* repeatedly was disturbing. The actress spat the word as though it were a curse. Logan kept assuring herself that things are different now, nobody talks about bastards, except her grandfather.

"Where'd you get the word *bastard*?" her father asks.

"A movie about Henry VIII. Anne let them cut her head off so Elizabeth wouldn't be a bastard."

"Huh." Her father avoids her eyes by bunching up the wax paper from his doughnut.

"I know I'm a bastard," Logan says.

"Who told you that?"

"I was born out of wedlock." She thinks the word *wedlock* is interesting, the idea that you're locked up once you're wed.

"Nobody talks about wedlock anymore," Payne says.

"I know. But I'm still a bastard. It's no big deal, I just am."

"Christ, where do you get this stuff? You're watching too much TV."

"You and Sheena were always watching it."

"Don't be a smartass."

She's not even sure she likes her father. She spends so much time wanting him to like her, she doesn't know what her true feelings are. But it's not as if he can be replaced. The mother of a five-year-old girl across the street died. The girl and her older sister found her body in the bathroom. The week after the death the girl had supper every night with Logan and McKenna because the father couldn't cope and McKenna wanted to help. Any time the girl heard a sound that might have been the front door, she asked if it was her mum. Even when the father came to pick her up, she asked if it was her mum.

At least Logan has a father.

At dinner, conversation is limited. Payne wanted to eat Hungarian, which Logan enjoys normally, particularly cabbage rolls. But a violin player keeps wending towards them, screeching strings. McKenna eats her mashed potatoes and the beet salad but doesn't touch the schnitzel Payne insisted she order. She's not wearing her concrete face exactly but she's definitely not happy. Payne keeps talking about things nobody's interested in, like the neighbour of his ex-boss who fell off a moped once and is brain-damaged.

"He swears all the time, right, like he thinks everybody's out to get him."

"How is that different from you?" McKenna asks.

"Excuse me?"

"You always seem to think somebody's gunning down your ass."

"That's a little different from being brain-damaged."

"Is it?"

When the waitress pours more wine, Payne asks her the time. She's wearing a uniform with puffy sleeves that keep slipping off her shoulders. When Payne isn't eating, he's watching the waitress.

Logan butters another roll. "How could somebody get brain-damaged from falling off a moped?"

"The thing is," Payne elaborates, "the nutter lets his dogs shit on his deck, then kicks the turds into my ex-boss's yard." Payne laughs hard at this, showing teeth and even his tongue. Logan has never seen him laugh this hard. McKenna just stares at him.

"My ex-boss is like a neat-freak, right, like lines his shoes up according to colour. So he gets tough with the guy, says he's going to do this, that and the other thing if he keeps kicking dog shit into his yard. Well, the guy has no short-term memory, right, my boss could threaten to cut off his balls and it would make no difference, the guy can't remember." Payne laughs so hard tears stream down his cheeks. McKenna stares at him.

Logan chews her roll, wondering how the dogs feel about shitting on a deck. It can't be comfortable for them. "Does he ever walk the dogs?" she asks.

"I don't know, it's not like he's a personal friend of mine."

"Because you should report him if he doesn't walk them."

"It's not my business, Lo."

"Dogs kept inside all the time go weird. Some dog bit through a can of hairspray causing a fireball that burned down a house. Two cats were killed and another dog died from smoke inhalation."

Her father looks at her as he often does now, as though he has no idea who she is. The puffy-sleeved waitress asks if she can get them anything else.

"We should get going," McKenna says. "We've got laundry to do."

"What, no dancing?" Payne asks. "Peachypie, don't you want some strudel?"

"I'm pretty full, actually."

"Can I drop by later?"

"Can he drop by later, Mum?"

"Whatever."

They leave him there, with the violin player. Logan sees him wave his coffee cup at the waitress. She hopes he has enough cash to pay the bill.

41

Laundromats signify renewal or despair, depending on your chemical mix at the moment. Tonight my head's in there, full of suds and dirty water, getting thumped around. Logan is completely into it. "There's an industrial-strength one that says you can wash carpets and stuff. That's way better for the environment than drycleaning."

A five-hundred-year-old man sits across from us sorting through bits of paper he discovers in his laundry and on his person. How many hours has *he* spent in laundromats? Or did he have a wifey to wash his shorts, his house, his kiddies? Did he labour hard at some shit job only to arrive here at Sudsorama? Did he fight in both wars? What gets him out of bed in the morning?

Why do I still want him when he is so obviously a moron and slobbers over waitresses? And why does Logan, who can see through anybody, even want to be in the same room with the cheesebrain? Are we so damaged that healing isn't an option, we'll take abuse forever because that's all we know? When nice guys used to chase me I thought they were weak. Something had to be wrong with them otherwise why would they want me? But that's me, the girl who was locked in darkness. Logan has lived in daylight. Logan should see better.

The five-hundred-year-old man starts fitting the little bits of paper back into his pockets. He throws nothing away. I throw everything away. I want no clutter around me, no reminders of opportunities lost. I discard people when it becomes obvious that they have bad intentions, that they just want to use me until they find some other sucker intent on self-battery. Nothing excites a human like kicking around another human. So why can't I discard Payne who'll live to be a hundred? I can see him being congratulated on one of those morning talk shows, under his toupé, asking the makeup girl for the time.

My daughter throws nothing away, collects pebbles, driftwood, the famous plastic animals. Now all burned. I can't even begin to imagine what this is doing to her.

"They're figuring out," she says, "that the Tyrannosaurus rex wasn't a vicious killer but a scavenger, like some gigantic vulture. He had a huge olfactory lobe on his brain to smell carrion. And he only had little stubby arms and two small claws. They were so short he couldn't even touch them together let alone kill anything. And he didn't have knife-like teeth for tearing flesh, just big jaws and rounded teeth for crushing bones."

"So he's been misunderstood."

"I just think it's weird that they've only just figured that out, that all this time he's been considered this tyrant when really he was just stomping around sniffing for corpses. It makes you wonder what other stuff they've got wrong."

"Probably plenty."

She sits on a washer. "Why were you pissed at Dad today?"

"Was I?"

"You were crabby at dinner."

"I'm tired."

"It bugged you when he was flirting with the waitress."

"No, it didn't."

"I don't get why it bothered you. He *always* flirts with waitresses."

"Why didn't you tell me about parent-teacher night?"

She swings her legs, thumping her heels against the washer. "I didn't think it was important."

"Why not?"

"It's not like I have problems."

I've been noticing, in her backpack, that she's started collecting garbage: broken pencils, bottle caps, bits of string and busted plastic toys. I'm wondering if this has to do with being homeless. "I'm going anyway."

"Can you not act weird?" she asks. "Like don't wear your sunglasses inside and stuff like that."

I yearn for the four-year-old who did not pass judgment. The past. Burn it. It's something to be shed. It hinders you because you long for this other time when your child adored you, when people hesitated before stepping over bodies in the street and didn't boast about spending six hundred dollars on dinner, drinking eighty-dollar bottles of wine, smoking forty-dollar cigars. There used to be shame attached to self-gratification overdrive. How did we come to lose that? Is it because we quit going to church? Without the fear of God there are no limits to what we'll do to get a buzz on. And we have to push harder at it—consume more wine, drugs, DVDs, screw more bodies until we notice we're all alone in Sudsorama fitting little bits of paper into our pockets.

Wolfgang has been laying studs for the first storey. Now the tilt-up panels are in place and the thing is starting to look like a house.

"We're getting a bigger window on the front, one that'll open. Won't that be nice, to get cross-breezes?" She's started chewing on her hair, which is driving me nuts. "What's bugging you?" I ask.

"What?"

"Something beyond the usual is bugging you." She's fidgety, keeps shifting her legs and arms around. She used to be comfortable in her body; now it's an obstacle course.

"It *bugs* me," she says, "when you keep asking me what's bugging me."

I can't believe how I'm hoping the man who fucks anything that moves will show up. I have no clear plan of action. I asked Logan to tell me about outer space, which helped with perspective. If Jupiter were hollow, more than thirteen hundred planet Earths could fit inside it. It's got sixteen moons, and an atmospheric pressure so great, a spaceship landing there would be crushed. Winds blow over it at four hundred miles an hour. I've been thinking of all the humans I'd like jettisoned to Jupiter. Payne, for example.

She's watching one of those romantic comedies that make me want to hurl bricks. Boy sees girl, can't have her, pursues her anyway, charms her with his persistence and delivery of flower arrangement. Into the sack they go without a thought to contraception or STDs. We all stare passively at them while they hump in beds, on tables, on motorcycles. Girl's hair and makeup remain intact as do boy's hair and muscles.

"Quit fidgeting, Mum," Logan commands.

"Why are you watching this?"

"There's no violence in it."

"Of the physical variety."

Romance is probably more damaging than action adventure. Romance leaves us fat on the couch, wondering where *our* persistent boy is and why, when we tried screwing the stand-in for boy on the table and the motorbike, it hurt and we got crabs.

"It's just a movie," Logan says.

"No, it's not. It's affecting you on some subliminal level. Quit chewing your hair."

She won't go to bed because she said her dad's coming. I said there were no guarantees. She said if I'd been nicer to him, he'd have shown up.

"Why do you want to see him?" I asked.

"He's my dad."

"Beyond that, Logan. There has to be something."

"Like what?"

"Do you enjoy talking to him?"

"It's okay, if there's no dipshit around. At least when he comes here there's no dipshit."

On TV they're necking again. Boy's sliding his hands up girl's blouse, under her skirt.

"I don't think you should be watching this," I say.

"Why not? It's a natural act. It's not like it's porn or something."

"It's not natural, it's staged. It's not like that."

"What's it like?"

"Complicated. Awkward. Over fast."

"So why do people do it?"

"Distraction."

"And because they love each other," she insists.

"That's the theory."

"You used to get it on with Dad."

"Yes."

"Didn't you like it?"

"Yeah, but it wasn't like in the movies. We fumbled around a lot." I can't meet her eyes, knowing we've been shagging in the can.

"Everybody knows movies aren't like life, Mum."

"I don't know that everybody does. There's a lot of boys with guns out there."

I look at my watch again, listen for sounds of him. I don't have a clue what the love word means where boy is concerned. There's been too much pushing and shoving, power plays, hooks and jabs.

The volts charge through me, leaving me sprawled on the tiles. Feeling his breath on my neck, I tell myself none of it matters: jiggle-factor waitresses, loan sharks, previous offences. The moment matters, sensation, being freed from smogland.

42

Logan tells herself not to care about the screams because it's probably the clown getting murdered by her husband. She's actually relieved to be awake and free of a nightmare in which she was walking naked to school, trying to cover herself with her hands.

The screaming stops and torques into familiar curses. "Burn in hell!" she hears her mother shout. At the window Logan sees her parents grabbing and jabbing at each other. Mr. Bluxom pulls them apart, also swearing. McKenna tolerates the referee but it is clear that, once the bell sounds, she will gouge Payne's eyes. "Stop it!" Logan shouts, pushing open the door, feeling her legs move under her at cheetah speed. They turn to her, her mother's face ugly with rage, her father looking dumbfounded, as though the surprise party was a surprise. Logan tackles her mother, causing them both to tumble to the pavement, reminding Logan of other times, picnics, when they would wrestle in the grass. She says "Mum" into her mother's ear but McKenna seems not to hear, only pushes her palms into her eyes, uttering jagged breaths that cause her body to shudder.

"Cool it, Mick. I said I'm sorry."

Her mother begins to bang her head into the tarmac.

"Fucking freaking out," Bluxom observes.

"Stop that!" Logan shouts, really scared now, because she's never seen her mother smack her head into pavement before. Unable to restrain her, Logan slides her legs between her mother's head and the ground. McKenna stops abruptly, with her head in her child's lap. Logan strokes her mother's hair as her mother has stroked hers. The father stands outside the circle, misunderstood—a Tyrannosaurus rex, sniffing for carrion, unable to do the killing himself.

"You'd better go, Dad," Logan says, although she doesn't want him to go, she wants him to pick her mother up in his arms and carry her tenderly into the Lakeview. She wants him to tell McKenna that he loves her more than any of the dipshits and that he wants to marry her and live with them happily ever after. "It's okay, Dad, we'll be okay."

He shrugs and walks away, loose-hipped, glancing around as though waiting for an invitation to some other party.

"Is she bleeding or anything?" Bluxom asks.

"I'm not sure. Can we just stay here for a minute?"

"You tell your mother I'm not putting up with any more of this shit. That's it, no Mr. Nice Guy."

"Good night, Bluxom," McKenna says, sounding weary but almost normal. "Let us know how you get on with the police investigation. They were around again today, weren't they?"

"You stay out of it," he warns and shuffles off.

A trash can lid clatters to the ground as a raccoon searches for his supper. He looks disinterestedly at the humans before tearing open a bag of chicken remains.

"Tell me more about space, monkey. I need to hear about space."

Logan watches the minutes flick past on the clock radio. She dozes off periodically but then starts awake, afraid that her mother has left her again, to do something strange, dangerous, fatal. McKenna makes no sound. Now and again Logan checks to make sure she's breathing. She thinks about her father, what he can be doing, where he can be sleeping. But she's willing to sever the limb to save the body. She tells God if she never sees her father again but gets to keep her mother, she will be thankful.

She persuaded McKenna to put ice on her head and to eat some kalamata olives. She told her about Europa, one of Jupiter's moons that's a bit smaller than Earth's and one of the few places in the solar system scientists think might be warm and wet enough to support life.

"Let's go there," her mother mumbled.

After the olives McKenna had a bath, in the dark. Sitting on the toilet, guarding her, Logan felt compelled to talk, to pretend things were normal.

"Jupiter's got this Great Red Spot on it. It's a huge storm, a super-hurricane big enough to hold two planet Earths inside it. Sometimes it's small and pink, other times it's big and red, but it never changes its position on Jupiter. And it's always oval. It hasn't changed its shape for centuries, ever since Galileo saw it."

For the longest time her mother didn't speak and Logan wondered if she was falling asleep. She leaned close to see if her eyes were open.

"I'm sorry I fought with your father," McKenna murmured. "I don't think he'll be back."

"I know."

The tap dripped. Logan thought maybe her mother was crying, she wasn't sure.

"It was a super-hurricane," McKenna said.

"You could have hurt each other."

"We did that already. It's you I'm worried about."

"Lots of kids don't have fathers."

Curling Ellsworth, after he asked Logan to have sex for the hundredth time, told her that he was going golfing with his father on the weekend. Logan couldn't imagine having a firm plan with her father, driving to a predetermined destination to partake of an activity that required booking ahead.

"You're the best thing he ever did," McKenna said. "Too bad he's got gonads for brains."

"He prefers girls."

"One day he'll be sorry."

"Maybe not."

"Oh yes he will, and it will be too late."

"I want to stay with you tomorrow," Logan said. "I don't want to go to school."

"Okay. I'm doing a wedding."

"Gross."

"Jewish so there'll be food."

"Egg salad sandwiches."

"You can tell me what colour the dresses are." Her mother became silent again, which worried Logan. She wanted her mother to gab like usual. She leaned forward again to make sure McKenna's eyes were still open. They were but had that body-snatched look about them.

"It's kind of gross," Logan said to chase away the silence, "that we're cluttering outer space with all these burned-out spaceships. I mean, I'm all for exploration but it's kind of like littering." Her mother didn't respond. "I guess it's the only way we'll find out though," Logan added. She heard someone coughing next door, and slamming drawers.

"Why do we have to find out?" McKenna asked.

"If people didn't find out stuff we'd still think the world was flat."

"It looks flat from here."

Which made Logan consider the phrase *what you don't know can't hurt you*—like a dead father rather than a live one. A father who died before you were born, whose grave you could visit. In movies people are always talking to headstones; it looks comforting, particularly if you've never met the person and can imagine all kinds of nice things about them.

"What's on your mind?" her mother asked as she often does, as if Logan would tell her.

“The Great Red Spot. Nobody can explain it.”

“Explanations dull the wonder.”

Logan has understood for some time that her mother has limited knowledge and wants to keep it that way. But for the first time Logan perceived this as an asset. Her mother has a certain density.

Logan helped her mother out of the bath and wrapped her in towels. She searched the drawers for one of the oversized T-shirts McKenna uses as a nightshirt. “Where do you think he went?”

“Oh, somebody’s bedroom.” McKenna pulled the T-shirt over her head.

“It’s going to be harder to pick up girls when he’s older.”

“Harrison Ford’s still at it.” Her mother sat on the bed and stared without blinking at the zigzaggy wallpaper. She looked as if somebody’d died.

“Aren’t you going to sleep?” Logan asked.

“Sure.”

“When?”

“When my eyes close.”

Logan tried to stay awake, to wait for her mother’s eyes to close, to ensure that her mother would not do anything strange, dangerous or fatal.

43

I lie still so she’ll think I’m sleeping, but it’s a straitjacket. I want to bust out, flail around, scream, tear my hair, his hair. I can’t stand the neediness of me, the stench of my cunt that has his garbage in me, can’t stand the taste of him in my mouth, his filth under my fingernails. My flesh revolts me, the hairs on my thighs, the puckers on my belly, the calluses on my feet, the bristle on my armpits, the sag of my ass, my anus, the shit in my gut. My tongue disgusts me, the plaque on my teeth, the pores on my nose. I’m putrefying.

The decaying corpses are back, lunging at me, shouting, You stupid fuck, you asshole, you no-good useless twat. I'm hazardous to the angel beside me. I will demolition-ball her life. I'm toxic. I dig Troy Boy's gift out of the drawer, with the matches I pocketed while not eating baby cow. I want out of this.

I sit on the lawn chair, clenched, waiting for it to kick in. I inhale harder, hold on to it longer. Dogs bark, babies cry, engines rev, televisions drone, husbands beat their wives. I start to walk, run, to get away from the pustule that is my body. Rat-coloured arms and legs flail around me. I stumble over something and land flat on my face. It's easier face down on the ground, a car could run me over. Blood trickles from my chin. I taste it, to see if it's blood and not some noxious fluid. It's the stupidity, over and over again, the same mistakes. I smack my head into the tarmac again. You fuck-head, moron, dipshit, loser. A vomit's pending; drowning face down in vomit. A car could run me over, its tires squeezing the rot out of me.

"What do you think *you're* doing?" It's Bluxom, stinking of toilet.

"I fell."

"Well maybe you want to pick yourself up."

"In a moment."

"I don't tolerate wackos around here."

"Only drug dealers."

"Don't try your little blackmail numbers on me."

"Ditto, Bluxo." He looms large above me. I grab his ankle, want to push him over, wrestle his flab in the dirt.

"Get up or I'll call the cops."

"Close personal friends of yours." I try to bite him. He kicks himself loose and starts to scramble.

"Trash like you makes me sorry I got into this business."

A door slams. Quiet again. Spaceship Earth pulses beneath me.

I see the bike.

44

At first Logan figures her mother is in the bathroom. She waits for the sound of flushing and the tap. It's possible, she knows, that her mother is sitting in the dark crying again. Logan doesn't have the energy to deal with this right now. She listens for voices outside, thinking that maybe McKenna's outside with the no-lifers. Or having another fight with her father in the parking lot. But it's very quiet, she can't even hear anybody's TV or plumbing. The digital clock reads 3:42. "Mum . . . ?" she says. "Mum . . . ?" Another possibility is that the bathtub is filled with blood and her mother's body. Logan saw this in a movie; a woman cut her wrists in the tub and watched the blood swirl into the water.

She grips Tiger as she walks to the bathroom. It takes forever and she's finding it hard to breathe. She can't turn the lights on because it will freak out her mother. "Mum . . . ?" She peers into the darkness, hearing only the dripping tap. She flips the lightswitch and sees that the bath is empty. This relieves her, until she realizes that this means her mother has left her alone. Her mother never leaves her alone.

The lawn chairs are vacant, lights are out, even Mr. Bluxom's Office sign. Logan checks the pool, thinking maybe it's been filled and her mother's at the bottom of it. She's seen this in movies too; dead bodies at the bottom of pools, their hair snaking around them. The pool is empty. A thumping so violent begins in Logan's chest that she crosses her arms tightly over her ribs to keep them from cracking. "Mum . . . ?" she calls into the darkness. "Mum!"

She doesn't understand what Mr. Bluxom is doing in the perfume-stinking woman's unit.

"What now?" he grumbles.

"Have you seen my mother?"

"She was face down on the pavement. Maybe a truck ran her over."

"What do you mean, she was face down on the pavement?"

"I mean she was face down on the pavement. Don't bother me." He closes the door. Logan tries to compute why her mother would be face down on the pavement. She must have tripped again, which means she must be hurt. Maybe somebody called an ambulance.

The clown doesn't look too happy about being woken either.

"Have you seen my mother?"

"No. Are you sure she's not in your room?"

"Did you see her fall or anything?"

"Maybe she went to the store and will be back in a couple of minutes."

"At four in the morning?"

"Maybe her period started and she had to get Kotex."

"She has a whole package of it." Logan can hear the pig grunting.

"Look, I'd like to help you but I need my sleep, I have a show in the morning."

McKenna used to read Logan a story about a baby bird who falls out of a nest and spends the entire book asking other animals if they've seen his mother. It bothered Logan that the mother bird didn't notice that the baby bird had fallen from the nest. McKenna explained that the mother bird had to leave the nest to find food for the baby bird. The mother bird wasn't even there when the baby bird fell out of the nest. Logan tries to believe that McKenna is out getting food. Her mother's so weird now, anything's possible. She tries to sit on a lawn chair and wait but the thumping makes it uncomfortable. She phones her father's cell but it's out of service. She calls Uncle Tait but he's not answering. She tries to wake Stanley but he's right out because she fed him bacon.

She grabs the skipping rope from the Jump for the Heart fundraiser. The sound of it slapping against the tarmac is louder than her heart. She counts as she skips. She skips even when her chest begins to hurt, even when her legs begin to burn, because she doesn't want to listen to her heart. When she reaches 581 she sees that the motorcycle is gone. She drops the rope, understanding that her mother is dead. She sees the mangled body on the highway. Her heart no longer thumps, her legs lose power. She falls face down on the pavement.

Hot liquid dripping on her face wakes her: her mother's tears, her mother who is rocking on her knees beside her with blood on her face. "I'm so sorry, baby," she says between gasping sobs that Logan has never heard before, sobs that sound as though she's choking on her heart. "Please forgive me, angel. I don't deserve you, I only hurt you. I'm so sorry, baby. Please forgive me, I'll do anything, please believe me, angel." The tears sting Logan's eyes, forcing her to turn her face away. McKenna drops her forehead onto Logan's chest.

"What happened to your face?" Logan asks.

"I fell, stumbled over something I couldn't see. I hate my eyes. They lie."

"Where did you go?"

"For my last ride."

"You promised you wouldn't."

Her mother doesn't move, seems hardly to breathe. "I needed to find out I didn't want to die."

Logan stares up at the moon, which is full and sorrowful. "We should go inside. We don't want to wake up Mr. Bluxom."

In electric light Logan sees that her mother has pulled jeans over her nightshirt and that one of the pant legs is shredded, that there is blood on the side of her leg, hand and forearm. "You had an accident."

"Some old guy pulled a right out of a left-hand lane. I slid the bike. It's just road rash."

"It could get infected."

"Whatever."

"I have to clean it." Logan leads her mother by the hand into the bathroom. "Take your pants off and sit on the edge of the tub with your legs in." Her mother moves slowly, as if in pain. "Does it hurt?"

"Nope. I'm fine."

Logan knows she isn't fine. She runs warm water and gently bathes the scrapes with washcloths.

"Bluxom's not going to be too happy about bloodstains on his bleached whites," McKenna says.

"He can shove them up his ass."

Her mother doesn't tell her not to use that word. "There's no way I can work tomorrow."

"Yes, you can. Kristos will have a cow if you don't. Weddings are easy."

"I hate them, fucking delusional."

"I have to put Polysporin on this."

"Do we have any?"

"We bought a first-aid kit."

"We did?"

"You wouldn't believe me when I said it was red."

McKenna stares at the box as though it's a UFO.

"It's got gauze in it," Logan says. "We're going to need a lot of gauze." She starts to bathe her mother's chin. "You better not pick on this when you get a scab or you'll get a scar."

"Battle scar."

Logan dabs Polysporin on her mother's chin. "You found out you don't want to die, right?"

"Right."

"That was your last ride, right?"

"Right."

Logan begins to unravel gauze. "No man's worth dying over."

45

It's *Dynasty* time, a Big Hair-athon. The soon-to-be-wed's mothers are neck and neck in the trashiest fluff 'n' puff competition. Their sequinned gowns could stand without them. Zipped, they can hardly breathe or walk in the heels intended to raise them above the other. Even colour-blind, I know we're dealing with variations on bombshell blond. Some gals will not let it go, no matter how tactfully we hairdressers try to bring them around to platinum. Bombshells don't go grey, just more blond. They all stare at my gauze. I tell them I had a rollerblading accident.

Kristos had the grand idea of pairing me up with Julius for this event. Telly incarnate is wearing more cologne than any of the wedding posse, and has stripped down to a black T-shirt rolled up at the sleeves to display his flexing muscles as he brushes and teases. The women go mute around him. With me they rattle on about how there's nowhere to shop but Holt's anymore, that if you want decent clothes you have to go to New York. Privately, the groom's camp kvetch about the ungrateful bride. Privately, the bride's camp kvetch about the stinginess of the groom's camp. I've seen it all before, know how it ends. They'll pop babies, hire nannies. Hubby will work late, ding his secretary. Wifey will work out, complain about the fat under her arms while drinking skinny lattes with equally rich and neglected wives. They'll bitch about their husbands and their wrinkles, then show up at the salon expecting miracles from the likes of me and Jules.

I had this idea once that I would get married, in a field or something. I wanted to make my mother happy, and to stop my father calling me a slut. I had a dress planned, the music, the florist, the caterer, just no groom.

Then there was Payne. I went electric with hatred, sparks were shooting off my fingernails. There was no remorse, not even a hint of recognition that banging me and the perky waitress in quick succession might not be tickeyboo. I was crying in the bath, silent gutter tears, not for him but for Logan, because life is pain and she's starting to know it. I don't think she noticed my dribbling. She has no idea how warped her parents are. Her whole childhood I've read her picture books about animals falling in love and getting married. The donkey romance in particular was her favourite, the donkeys dancing the tango and spawning little donkeys. Happy endings—there must be some.

No man's worth dying over.

The grass didn't help, made me feel like my tires had no traction. I stopped at the Gerrard Square walkway and did some screaming, even though there were no trains. I screamed until my throat felt bloody and black boys in hoods were coming at me. Then I saw Logan drowning in the bath and it was as if I was in one of those nightmares I've had since she was born, where I lose her in some public place, can't find her, start screaming for her, only this time it was real and I couldn't move because I knew the black boys were going to rape and strangle me. I stared into outer space, wanted to be there on that planet Logan was talking about, wanted to be there with Logan, away from the toxic dump that is our life. They walked by me without a word, creating a breeze.

She's been keeping a close eye on me, giving me colour cues and handing me pins, making sure I don't take off again. I'm trying to blow volume into the groom's porky little sister. I've tried to explain to her that you can't make voluptuous hair out of a pixie cut but she's not hearing me. She's been drinking ice water nonstop, is on an ice water diet, says it makes her body burn calories trying to heat up. While I work a can of mousse into her she eats a bag of potato chips, insisting it's her treat for the week.

The bride charges in, using the f-word repeatedly. "I can't find the dress!" she shrieks.

"What do you mean, you can't find the dress?" her mother demands.

"It's not in the room!"

"What do you mean, it's not in the room?"

"It's not in the room!"

"Of course it's in the room."

The mother chases bridey out. The groom's mother, flipping through *Cosmopolitan*, grumbles, "She can't look after a dress, how's she supposed to look after a family?" Sheldon the Wonder Dud, she means. He's losing his hair already; I'm convinced it's the hormones in the meat scalping these boys. She calls him on her cell. "Sheldon," she pronounces, "she lost the dress." A whiff of victory there.

Kojak gropes me again. "Hands off," I say, louder than I'd expected. I've been noticing he's been touching Logan; little pats and cuddles.

"Take it easy, Mac."

"Hands off me and my daughter," I say even louder, "or I cut off your balls." I flash scissors at him. The wedding party gasps. Logan chews on her hair.

Eventually they find the dress, in bridey's suitcase in the room of a Chinese salesman who shares Deb's taste in luggage. But time's running out and Deb's taking it out on the help. The makeup girl endures abuse while trying to supply the little oinker with cheekbones and full lips. I arm myself with hot rollers and the curling iron. Deb's face is bottom heavy so an updo should help, but I need time and she's not giving it. I grab her head in the same manner I grabbed my Tourette's syndrome client's. In a vise she can't twitch her piggy eyes away from me. "You behave," I tell her, "or I make you look like dog doodoo." This cools her jets, the mouth stops frothing, and she makes nice even though she wants me crucified. All things considered I make her look "babe," pin the veil on her and off she goes down the yellow brick road without so much as a thank you. No matter, we did a lot of heads today, Kristos shall reap our reward. I tell Jules to go feel up the bridesmaids, only one of us needs to stick around for the photos. I take Logan to the Queen Mother for lunch because she loves the desserts there. I make her eat soup and salad first. She's been engrossed in an *Archie* comic she scored off one of the mini-bridesmaids. The fact that the Betty and Veronica thing is still going is an indication that we've come to the end of history. It's reruns from here on in, and not even the good stuff.

"Why's Veronica so popular?" I ask.

"Because she's rich."

"Lots of rich people aren't popular. I bet it has more to do with big boobs."

"Betty has big boobs too," Logan says. "It's not about breasts, Mother."

"What is it, then? Her bitchiness? Do you admire that?"

"I think *Archie* sucks."

"Then why are you reading it?"

"Because there's nothing else."

"I always preferred Betty."

She's eating a massive piece of vanilla layer cake. "Why did you have to shout at that guy?"

"What guy?"

"The guy who was feeling you up."

"What do you know about feeling up?"

"Duh, like his hand was on your ass."

"Don't use that word."

"You use it all the time," she says. "Anyway, you shouldn't go shouting at people. You're always shouting now, at Dad and Mr. Bluxom, and Grandpa. It makes you look psycho."

"Sorry."

"You always tell *me* to ignore people but *you* never do, you're always shouting at them."

"I'm not *always* shouting. There are many people I don't shout at."

"It makes you look crazy. Those wedding people thought you were nuts."

"I don't care what people think."

"Yes, you do. You say you don't but you do. Everybody does."

It's almost like she hates me. I don't know how to deal with this venom. There's icing on her nose I'd like to kiss off but I'm afraid she'll push me away.

"Was her dress ever tacky," she says. "She looked like a cake ornament."

"She was trying to be his princess."

She forks more cake. "A study showed that human relationships based on sex end after four years. The brain chemicals that make them fall in love run out after thirty-six months, then it takes another year for them to get divorced."

Why is she telling me this? To justify the loss of her father?

"Sometimes the males want to stick around anyway," she adds, "because human females have sex whether they're fertile or not. Same with birds and porcupines."

"What's the deal with donkeys?" I ask. "Remember that donkey book you wanted me to read all the time? The donkeys who tangoed and lived happily ever after?"

"A male donkey will fuck anything," she says.

So much for happy endings.

I can't believe I'm lost in the hospital again. We try another elevator.

"Take your sunglasses off," Logan orders. "People are staring at you."

"No, they aren't. Logan, why do you think people are always staring at me? People don't care, they've got their own problems." I take the glasses off anyway.

"Don't shout at the doctors, alright?"

"Why would I shout at the doctors?"

"You always shout at the doctors."

We find the old buzzard surrounded by whitecoats. They're putting clothes on him, twisting his dead-weight limbs into his plaid shirt and grease-stained pants. "What's going on?" I inquire. "Who's in charge here?"

"I am," a petite, bobbed missy tells me. "And you are . . . ?"

"His daughter. Is he going somewhere?"

"We've found that clothing patients in their own apparel is good for morale. It's time he were up and about." She enunciates her t's very carefully, unlike us plebs who let t's degenerate into d's.

Two attendants seize the veggie by the shoulders and feet, hoist him off the bed and dump him in the wheelchair. The functioning eye is turned away from me. I stare at the stitched one, having no idea how this is going down with him. "I'm missing something," I say. "I mean, he can't feel anything."

Missy shoves a cushion behind his head, presumably to stop it from wobbling around. "We're trying to determine if the seated position will trigger uncontrollable spasms."

"Nice," I say.

Off they go, the team, with Dad in the lead. I'm trying to figure out if he's graduated from being a patient with an uncertain prognosis to an official quadriplegic. I can't ask this in front of him. He was up and about in a dream last night, accusing me of being confrontational. "Nobody likes you," he told me, "figure it out." I said, "You rose from the dead just to give me a hard time?" When I woke, my mother was on her chair playing the distressed lass in her silent movie. "Get a death," I told her.

The team whisks him back. "He can handle the wheelchair," the bobbed missy tells me.

"Is that supposed to be a positive thing?"

She sniffs. "It's a start. We'll see how he does with physiotherapy."

"Why don't you talk to *him*? He can hear."

Logan had the TV blaring this morning informing us that a woman had locked her eighteen-year-old daughter in a windowless basement for three weeks as punishment for skipping school. This was after beating her with a clothes hanger. Made me think better of Lester.

Three orderlies deposit the stiff back on the bed. The bobbed missy doesn't talk to him, has no time for such frivolities, but marches off with her troops, leaving me and the old guy eye to eye.

"That was fun," I say. "Can't wait for the physio to start. Maybe they'll roll you around on a ball or something. Do you want the TV on? Blink if you want it on." He does. I switch it on; some ancient Burt Lancaster movie—I try to guess how many tubes of Brylcreem went into that hair. "Blink if you want to watch this," I say. He doesn't. One after the other we try the channels. No blinks. We end up back at Burt getting hot and heavy with Rita Hayworth. "Do you want me to turn it off? Blink if you want me to turn it off." He doesn't. "Is the volume okay?" He blinks. We're communicating. After all these years.

"Can we go now?" Logan asks. She's been leaning against the wall, keeping an eye on the cunt-monologue neighbour who can't stop scratching his balls. He's watching a sitcom. The laugh track accompanies my father's stare. "Is there anything else I can do for you?" I ask his eyeball. *Ha ha ha.* "Blink if there is." No blink, just the old how-did-scum-like-you-spring-from-my-loins stare. *Ha ha ha.* I'd say our bonding potential is limited. I try to tell myself this doesn't matter in a world where birds and porcupines are going at it. I keep wanting to rescue him and be forgiven. Who needs the rescuing?

46

Logan pretends to be looking at the bulk foods while her mother feels and sniffs her way through the produce section. People stare at her but McKenna is oblivious. She leans over a pile of mangoes, her nose inches from the fruit. Logan can tell her mother doesn't know what they are. McKenna's so busy sniffing and feeling she doesn't notice she's knocked a bunch of mangoes off the pile. Logan tries to look interested in mixed nuts. She can't stop thinking about the humpbacked whale getting decapitated by the cruise ship full of whale-watching no-lifers. She hears her mother calling her but she doesn't respond, doesn't want to be any part of the mess she's making. She leans over the honey-roasted peanuts. Her mother calls louder, so loud that people stop pushing their shopping carts to stare at her. Logan stands straight so McKenna can see her but McKenna looks through her. "My daughter," she's screaming, "someone's taken my daughter!" Everybody starts talking at once and looking around the produce section. Logan shouts, "I'm here," but McKenna doesn't hear above all the people freaking out.

She's shouting, "Logan!" and running around the store. Logan doesn't understand how she could not have seen her. She starts chasing her, finally spots her at the opposite end of the personal needs aisle. "Mum!" she shouts. "I'm here!" She waves her arms as though she's on a lifeboat trying to flag down a chopper. Her mother squints at her. "It's me," Logan says. Her mother strides towards her as she used to stride towards her when Logan did something seriously bad, like smear grease on the couch. Her mother grabs her wrist. "How many times have I told you to stay in sight?"

"I *was* in sight."

"A ten-year-old girl was kidnapped and cut to pieces and thrown in the lake."

"I know that, it's not like it's news."

"Don't act smart, don't you *dare* act smart with me." She's gripping Logan's wrist so tightly it burns. "Half the time I don't know where you are anymore," McKenna says. "From now on you stay close or no TV. None."

"I *was* in sight. I was in the bulk section. I could see you. If I could see you, you could see me." The slap on her face is so sudden that it takes her a moment to recognize that her mother has hit her. Her mother has never hit her. McKenna, also stunned, stands rigid, blinking, with her hands over her mouth. It's as though they've watched someone jump in front of a train. It's too late to stop it.

Vance, the perfume-stinking woman and the clown are drinking Bacardi Breezers and talking about love gone wrong. "Cry me a river, I told him," the perfume-stinking woman says. "You can't go running around dippin' your wick and expect me to be home cooking taties."

An electric fan attached to an extension cord blows hot air on them. It is unseasonably warm for May. Logan knows this is due to global warming. She mentioned this to the no-lifers when they were discussing the most recent deaths due to contaminated water. They weren't too interested. The perfume-stinking woman lit another cigarette and the clown drank more Mountain Dew. McKenna seems to have passed out on the recliner. She begged Logan's forgiveness again, hugged her till she could hardly breathe while people with shopping carts stared at them. Logan doesn't know if she can forgive her mother anymore. She figures keeping her distance is the best policy. She tried watching a Stallone movie where he kept almost falling off a mountain while bad guys were chasing him, but it's stinking hot in the Lakeview.

Vance is talking about his brief marriage to his high-school sweetheart. "There's no love like the first one," he assures them.

"What happened," the perfume-stinking woman asks, "she bite your ear off?"

"That's not funny," the clown says.

"Well, ex*cuse* me for having a sense of humour."

McKenna, still motionless in the recliner, holds up her hand. "I'm for hearing about the high-school sweetheart." She speaks slowly, as though she's having trouble getting her mouth around the words.

"She had thirty-three cats," Vance says, like this explains everything.

Logan's noticed that, since the motorcycle accident, her mother has been doing everything slower.

"Her house stank of piss."

"You didn't have to bunk at her house," the perfume-stinking woman points out.

"She wasn't going no place without those felines."

Logan starts to worry that maybe her mother's experiencing heatstroke. Her great-grandfather was a roofer and got heatstroke, fell off a roof and died. As much as her mother is acting psycho, Logan doesn't want her dead. Bluxom claims he's got a repairman coming to fix the air conditioners, but nobody believes him.

Logan's been trying to forget about her father because she feels that this is necessary. She doesn't understand what went on between her parents last night but she does know that he walked. Her telling him to go away didn't justify his leaving in her opinion. She's been keeping her mind on other things, the 130-million-year-old fossil of a dromaeosaur, for example. It proves that some non-avian dinosaurs were covered in feathers. The fossil was a two-legged predator just like the Tyrannosaurus rex. Which means that some theropods looked more like weird birds than giant lizards. Everybody's been going around making like rexes were these vicious beasts and it turns out they were just carrion-sniffing grounded birds.

She was considering telling her mother that Mr. Beasley slid his hand under her shirt but since the freak-out in the supermarket, Logan doesn't feel this would be appropriate. And anyway, it's possible the shirt slipped up and his hand just happened to be there. He didn't take his hand away though, but left it there, on the small of her back, and when she moved to get away from him, the hand slid down and patted her bum. She can still feel its slimy trail on her skin.

"Burn in hell!" her mother shouted at her father. Logan can't imagine hating someone so much that she would want them to suffer this fate. She thinks of the oversized, under-brained dinosaurs writhing in red-hot ash, not understanding that their role in evolution was over. Or that they would be remembered forever, although misunderstood.

She knows she will never forget her father.

She would like to know how many other facts, scientific or otherwise, will shift with time and prove to be false. She's not convinced that there's any point in learning anything because she'll probably just have to unlearn it. She's not convinced that there's any point in getting to know people when what you think you know about them will probably prove untrue. Her father, for instance. Ever since she can remember, she's been trying to get to know him. She didn't know he had the power to make her mother slam her head into pavement. She didn't know he could walk away from her mother distraught on the ground. She didn't know he was cruel.

She didn't know her mother could hit her.

Not once today, in her slow-motion state, has McKenna mentioned Payne. Logan has been waiting for it, some kind of explanation. Her mother always feels she has to explain.

"He was cleaning his mother's kitchen," the perfume-stinking woman says, "and fell onto the open door of the dishwasher. Two pointy utensils in the cutlery tray stabbed him. I always told him he shouldn't go cleaning his mother's kitchen, but there you have it, a mama's boy."

"Was he okay?" the clown asks, patting her pig.

"You kidding? He was one dead layabout."

"No offence intended," the clown says, "but have all your former lovers suffered violent deaths?"

"One of them's a Mountie."

"No shit," Vance says. "That is one cool job."

"Mum? The phone's ringing."

"What phone?"

"In our unit," Logan explains. "Can I answer it? It might be Tait about the laptop."

"Whatever."

But it isn't, it's some breathy woman asking for McKenna.

"It's for you," Logan tells her.

"I don't want to talk to anybody."

"I already told her you were here."

"Her? Probably some twat selling something." Her mother stumbles out of the lawn chair and it occurs to Logan that she is drunk from the Bacardi Breezers. Her mother doesn't drink and never stumbles. She has trouble opening the door to the unit because it sticks—another thing Bluxom said he'd fix. "Fuck," she grumbles. Normally McKenna doesn't swear.

"Allow me," Vance says, yanking it open.

Logan's been trying to forget the news item about the U.S. military training dolphins to act like humans, to attack enemy divers with harpoons strapped to their backs, or to drag them to the surface to be taken prisoner. They showed soldiers releasing dolphins into mine-infested waters harnessed with sonar equipment to neutralize mines. If a dolphin gets blown up they just send another one. It seems to Logan dolphins should be training humans.

"Let's go, Logan," McKenna says, kicking the sticking door open.

"Where?"

"I'll explain in the car."

She doesn't though, McKenna is very quiet, driving fast because it's night and she can see.

"Who was on the phone?" Logan asks finally.

"Cindy the dipshit waitress."

"Why?"

"Your father's had an accident and Miss Jiggly Jugs can't cope."

"What kind of accident?"

"He's been burned. He was mowing the dipshit's mother's lawn, lit a cigarette and kaboom."

Logan can't picture this, her father in flames. "He doesn't smoke."

"He was lighting it for the dipshit. She's been trying to quit but says it makes her fat."

"Is *she* burned?"

"Not a blister."

They have to sit in the visitors' lounge surrounded by jerks with hockey hair discussing subways they have known. "In Hong Kong they got people who push you in, like guys get *paid* to stuff you in like sardines."

Sixty per cent of her father's body is burned, including his face. He's in the hydrotherapy room getting hosed down. They have to remove the dead tissue to prevent infection. They've already hooked him up to a ventilator, a heart monitor, an oximeter to measure the oxygen in his blood, two IV pumps, and a catheter so his urine goes into a bag.

"At least he's still got a penis," McKenna remarked.

"Excuse me?" the only nurse who would speak with them said. McKenna had already decided she was an uptight cow because of her barely visible lips and power blunt. "A fugitive from the eighties," McKenna told Logan, explaining that everybody was power-blunting back then. Logan has thought of suggesting to her mother that she not judge people by their hairstyle, but she knows this would be pointless.

"Is he getting morphine?" McKenna asked.

The power blunt nodded, then explained that the doctor would have to assess Payne's burn and determine his fluid requirements. "His head will be shaved," she added.

"Is he getting enough morphine to knock him out?" McKenna asked.

"He's in critical condition," the power blunt replied. "If he regains consciousness it will not be for some time. We can't treat burn victims when they're conscious. That would be torture."

By this time Miss Jiggly Jugs was back from the can where she'd been barfing because the burn unit smells of charred human meat.

"Let's go get a coffee," McKenna said. Logan had no idea why her mother even wanted to talk to this person who'd caused her father's suffering. Logan wanted to grab the dipshit by the tits and hurl her in front of a passing car. There is no room in their world for can't-quit-smoking morons who blunder into people's lives causing death and destruction.

The cafeteria smells of food that's been wrapped in plastic for ten years. Sick people lean over paper plates, gripping plastic forks. Her mother offers the dipshit without a blister a Kleenex to wipe her snot. Logan wants to shove it down her throat, plug her trachea.

"I'm so sorry," Jiggly Jugs blubbers. "So sorry."

"It wasn't your fault," McKenna says, and Logan wonders if the alcohol is still affecting her brain. Of course it's the dipshit's fault, it was *her* mother's lawn, *her* stinking gas mower, *her* stinking cigarette.

"Was it a match or a lighter?" Logan demands.

"Matches, but you know those little eensy-weensy ones that are hard to light. My nails are too long for those. That's why Payne had to do it."

Logan expects McKenna to fly over the table and box the dip's ears but she only stares at her as though she's having trouble placing her.

"Had you just fucked him or what?" she asks.

Jiggly Jugs sits a little straighter and flicks her hair. McKenna despises hair-flicking, says it's a come-on. McKenna watches couples in restaurants and predicts when the chickybabe is going to flick.

"Did we just make love, you mean?" the dip inquires. "Yes, as a matter of fact."

An old woman dragging an IV pole hunches on a seat beside them and starts picking raisins out of a muffin. A slightly younger old woman joins her and talks loudly to her about gardening while eating a Danish with four pounds of icing on it.

Jiggly Jugs rests her feet on her chair and her chin on her knees. She hugs her legs as though they're cute dogs. "He was always talking about you, Mac," she says. "He said there was nobody else like you."

McKenna stares at her as if she's just remembered who she is but isn't too excited about it. The Danish-munching old lady leans towards the raisin-picking one and almost shouts, "Would you believe those damn squirrels ate my hostas?" The other old lady doesn't seem to hear, or care.

McKenna puts her dark glasses on. "Are you going to look after him? Are you and mama going to take him in?"

"We can't . . . I mean, we hardly know him."

"Just his cock. Get out of my face before I start screaming."

The dip grabs her purse and takes off. The Danish-munching woman shouts, "It goes without saying the little vermin will eat the tulips, but the *hostas*?"

Logan waits for some indication from her mother regarding

their next plan of action. But McKenna only raps her index finger against her coffee cup.

"I put hot pepper out to burn the little bastards," the Danish-munching woman shouts. "That'll teach them."

"Astronomers have discovered," Logan begins, knowing that talking about outer space will calm her mother, "that all the gold in the universe was forged in a collision between two neutron stars. It only occurs about once every ten million years in any given galaxy."

"All the gold in the world," her mother repeats.

"In the universe. Atoms of iron are bombarded with so many neutrons, they build up to form heavy elements, like platinum and gold."

Her mother takes off her glasses and rubs her eyes. "One big chemical reaction." She puts the glasses back on. "Meanwhile we keep running around thinking we're in charge."

Logan drains her Sprite. "Do you think Dad's going to die?"

"No. He wouldn't do that."

"Why not?"

"He's too stupid to let go."

The Danish-munching woman starts hacking, reminding Logan of the viruses floating on air particles. "Mum, we should go."

"Where?"

Logan gets her to drive them to the Dairy Queen and orders two Pecan Mud Slides. Cop cruisers crowd the strip mall across the street. The hair-twirling server explains that a woman was just beaten with a mallet and raped behind O'Malleys tavern.

"Just another day on planet Earth," McKenna remarks.

"We should change your gauze when we get back," Logan says.

"Whatever." McKenna stares hard at something Logan can't see. "I'm so sorry I hit you. I'll cut off my hands before I hit you again."

Logan says nothing. There is nothing to say. They sit on stools and watch the fat cops across the street cross their arms and lean against their cars. One of them points to the Dairy Queen and starts walking towards it.

"Tomorrow we'll go back and see Dad," McKenna says, "if you want."

"Is he going to be blind?"

"Don't know."

The hair-twirling server takes a call on her cell and starts giggling. Logan picks at a pecan piece stuck between her teeth. "You said you wanted him to burn in hell."

"I did."

"That was like a curse."

McKenna digs around in her Pecan Mud Slide with her spoon but doesn't eat any. "Don't blame me for this."

"I'm not."

"You are."

"I'm not." Logan swings her legs so that her Nikes bump against the plate glass window. "It was just a chemical reaction."

47

Fingernails. He had a thing about them, the longer, the trashier, the better. She could have the face of a weasel but if she had the nails he'd stuff her. Don't want to think about it, feel like a bag of hammers, clanging around. I shouldn't drink. Shouldn't care. What does it matter? He walked out, was gone, history, led by his gonads to hell. It wasn't my business, I didn't care anymore, had figured it out. Grown up.

He is, always has been, a problem. He is, always has been, worthless.

Without his face he will be lost.

After I hit her it was like I was falling through ice, black cold dragging me down.

Logan's teacher approaches in pedal-pushers, shoulder-length hair, bangs like a twelve-year-old. She'll wear her hair like this to her coffin, believing it makes her look younger. In colour I remember she wears too much pink blush and lipstick. Can't see the pink anymore, she just looks chalky. She smiles the meaningless smile she offers all parents while condemning Logan's photographic memory. "I wish it could be more selective," she says.

"It's very selective."

"Such horror stories she remembers."

"There *is* horror in the world."

"I realize that, I just think, for her own sake . . ."

"The rest of us forget too easily. That's what got us into this mess."

Why do schools smell of sickness and garbage? I started smoking so I wouldn't have to smell them.

"For her sake," Ms. Pedal-Pusher says, "I wish she'd socialize more with the other children."

"Why?"

This stumps her. Her forty-year-old eyebrows fuse beneath her twelve-year-old bangs. "Normally children socialize."

"Well, forget normal. Are her assignments good?"

"Oh yes. A little over-researched, perhaps, for her age."

"Forget her age."

"She's very worried about the environment."

"Shouldn't she be?"

She smiles the smile reserved for the learning disabled. "It's a lot to carry on such young shoulders."

"They're the only ones who can save us. Did you know our house burned down?"

"No. I'm so sorry."

"She hasn't said anything?"

"She doesn't talk much."

"Maybe you should try talking to *her*." I take off my sunglasses because Logan asked me to. White blotches multiply. I rub my eyes but try not to "act weird" as per my daughter's request.

"With thirty-two students," Ms. Pedal-Pusher says, "it's difficult to give individual attention."

"You could try saying, 'Logan, I'm sorry to hear that your house burned down.' Something like that." I'm so tired of teachers. I couldn't stand them then, can't stand them now. They know everything, have seen it all, have tenure and the biggest pension plan going. I cut a few teachers; all they do is whine about marking papers—they of the short workday and summers off.

Ms. Pedal-Pusher adjusts her bangs, making sure her wrinkles are covered. "I'll certainly mention it."

"She's without a computer at the moment," I say, "which is stressing her out. And her father's been burned."

"Burned?"

"He may not live."

"I'm so sorry. Was he in the house?"

"What house?"

"Your house that burned down."

I hadn't made the connection. I'm being chased by wildfire. "No," I say, wanting to light a match to her hair, to burn the smug so the rest of us can get on with it. Instead I smile meaninglessly back at the woman who spends more waking hours with my daughter than I do.

"That really is unfortunate," she observes and I see her in her house with the two-car garage, the pesticided lawn, the swing set for the kiddies, the mini fire extinguishers on every floor, and I just want her to go away, far from my daughter of the original mind who will never under-research enough.

"Goodbye," I say and head for the garbage-stinking corridor.

I have no difficulty understanding why kids shoot guns at school. If I had a piece I'd fire a few at the scuzzy walls covered in "art work" that all looks the same. I had *one* teacher who was emotionally connected to what he was teaching, who lived and breathed mathematics, made it real. He got us all excited about the guy who figured out how to measure the circumference of the earth. The rest were toads watching their backs, paying union dues.

Logan hates school. I know this but don't know what to do about it. Burn it down. I need to whiz, and locate a staff washroom, but it's locked. I give up, lean against a Coke machine, stare at an overflowing trash can, regretting that I don't have matches on me.

Second- and third-degree burns all over. His face and arms will need grafting. They cut skin off the thigh and calf of his unharmed leg. They mesh the skin and stretch it. It's patchwork. Every day they will apply new dressings, pick off the scabs with blades and hose him down. Every day he will experience excruciating pain. A nice little Asian nurse assured me that enough morphine to kill the pain would kill the patient.

He is suffering now. This is what I wanted.

"What did she say?" Logan asks. She's been in the car with the doors locked reading a book about the great apes.

"She says you're doing great."

"She did not."

"What do you think she said?"

"I bet she said I'm negative. She always going on about approaching things positively."

"She didn't say anything about negative. She said you don't have to research your projects so hard if you don't want to."

"I want to." She rests her feet on the dash. "She's just ticked off because Mr. Wagman dumped her."

"I thought she was married."

"Who would marry her? She's gross."

"She's alright."

"You hate her hair."

I whiz in my father's house, eat Chinese takeout. My fortune tells me that nothing is impossible for my willing heart. Logan's says her personal finances will improve.

"The flesh of apes and monkeys is being sold as bushmeat," Logan tells me while chewing on a vegetarian spring roll. "One species of monkey was eaten to extinction last year. Conservationists figure gorillas, bonobos and chimpanzees have only ten years left."

"I say bring back cannibalism."

"It's not funny."

"I didn't say it was."

We eat in that deafening silence that's become habit lately.

"I have to go in the basement for a couple of minutes," I tell her.

"Why?"

"I'm looking for something."

She turns on the TV which I truly believe is destroying civilization but I can't stop her because I can't offer an alternative. I'm dried up, it's a desert in here. I close the door and sit in the dark. I'm thinking they should die, both of them, buzzard and superdick. Because they've lost their power. Powerless they will be grovelling in mud. People will step on their hands and faces.

I should feel something. Victorious.

My father, the first time he kicked me out for glue-sniffing, was wearing one of those wash-and-wear shirts with little epaulettes. "Aye aye, captain," I said. Just before he slammed the door in my face he said, "Don't come back." I hung out at the mall till closing time with other kids whose parents hadn't kicked them out. I said, "Can I sleep at your house?" I did it doggy-style with a rich kid who had Peter Frampton hair and the run of his mansion while his parents were at the cottage. He'd obviously always dreamed of doing a girl up the ass and got all wide-eyed and macho about it. It hurt but I didn't care. The dirtier it got the more I hurt my father. That's what I thought.

Chances are they're currently shoving things up *his* butt. I have a client whose mother has been getting radiation on a tumour in her mouth. They put her on codeine to relieve the pain from the burns inside and outside her mouth. The hitch is the drug is constipating her. So my client has to give her mother enemas several times a day. My client is accustomed to being able buy her way out of anything and could not believe she couldn't take her mother somewhere to get an enema, a kind of enema drive-through, like a quick-lube. The first round she gave her two enemas in a row because one got no response. The second flush caused an "accident." I said, "That's an interesting reversal though. I mean, she used to clean up your shit and now you're mopping up hers." The client didn't think it was interesting.

I wonder if I would get a kick out of shoving a nozzle up Lester's ass.

You want them to burn and they do and you're left holding the stick of dynamite. You don't know what to do with it because you've been clutching it all these years. You look around for a place to stash it because you can't dump it just anywhere, it could hurt somebody. So you stick it in your mouth.

Fuzzball surfaces for the first time of her own free will. She climbs down my body and sniffs around on the floor. Her greyness stands out against the black. She leaps onto one of the old boxes and starts to purr. She likes it here, in my dungeon.

If I could forget, if it weren't all plastered inside my skull, removable only by drilling. A client told me about some guy who woke up with a broken nose and no memory. The medical establishment views this as a tragedy but I'm thinking, Hey, no hard feelings, let's play again. What's to stop him? Start over, make stuff up, write yourself a good part this time, not one of these I-never-got-over-my-parents/my first-grade teacher/my first fuck/my first husband. This same client told me about an acquaintance of hers, a "pleasant woman," she said, who got murdered by her own son. He stabbed her and her husband to death, then jumped in front of a train. "I don't know how he knew a train was coming," she said. "I guess he'd looked at a schedule." She sipped on her decaf espresso. "Imagine that, your child coming at you with a knife."

I don't find that hard to imagine. Parents know you better and worse than anyone. You've got a record with them.

I hit my daughter.

"What are you doing in there?" she asks, pushing open the door.

"Nothing."

"It's dark."

"I know."

She squints. "I can't see."

"I can."
"What?"
"Baggage."
"Did you find it?"
"What?"
"What you were looking for?"
"No."

Kristos has lined up Jules and me to do a rock video. It's amateur hour but they're dentists and therefore loaded. They've called their band ReVerb and want big and wild hair. I use about ten pounds of moulding paste on the bass player, who wants to look like Rod Stewart. "Did you know that the Guess Who are all fat now?" he asks me. "Total butterballs."

The dentists are all stooped from leaning over mouths and look feeble clutching guitars. Their teeth gleam as they try to look intense. It appears to be a drug-free environment, which is good because Logan's in the green room continuing her great apes/bushmeat reading. She told me they share ninety-eight per cent of the DNA in humans. Aside from being eaten, war and destruction of habitat have pushed them to the brink of extinction. "Soon we'll just have the nature shows," Logan told me. "The animals will all be dead and we won't care because we'll still be able to watch them on reruns." She's got a point: what does it matter what's *really* out there? Why should you care when you can see them aping around in digital clarity? Seeing is believing. Just turn on the Discovery channel and have yourself another beer.

The dentists start to spin outside their dental uniforms, which makes me wonder if they aren't popping a few pharmaceuticals. One of them won't stop rubbing oil on his weedy biceps to make them glisten. The Rod Stewart wannabe is having trouble clipping on earrings.

Julius keeps sniffing one of the backup singers/dental assistants. He starts backcombing, watching her cleavage. I start Frenchlacing the other one, who's worried about her cat who won't stop meowing. "The vet says he's bored," she tells me.

"Get him another cat."

"There is another cat. He's obese and lies around all day."

I check on Logan. She's watching reality television and nods at bikinied girls on the screen. "Which one do you think he's going to fuck?" she asks me.

"Why are you talking like that?"

"That's all anybody cares about. Who's fucking who. In the entire world. That's all anybody thinks about."

I try to compute this. According to mass media she has a point. What's *People Magazine* if not a who's-fucking-who update? "Well," I say, "you said yourself porcupines and birds go at it non-stop."

"They don't have brains like ours. We're supposed to use our *brains*."

I'm trying to figure out if this is about the father being led by his dick to hell. "The truth is," I explain, "humans don't go at it non-stop. They watch it on TV or get it off the Net. The real thing's too messy."

"If it's so messy then why were you always doing it?"

"When?"

"Grandpa says you were a slut and couldn't keep your legs crossed."

I sit beside her on the leather couch, listen to it squawk. "I wanted to be loved."

"Were you?"

"Of course not."

"So why did you keep doing it?"

"Because I kept wanting to be loved."

"Did Dad love you?"

"Nope."

"I bet he did. The dip said he was always talking about you. She said he said there was nobody else like you."

"Since when do we believe the dip? She said that so we would take him off her fingernails."

One of the dentists has produced a punch bowl of vodka. In the bowl, frozen in a block of ice, is a pair of black lace panties. The other dentists grunt and whistle.

I've waited all day for her to talk about her father. She said she doesn't want to see him and yet keeps bringing him up—a child trying to place things in her life. She wants her parents to have a love story even if it has to have a sad ending. These happen and people still pay to see them. Sad love stories are marketable. Zero love stories are not.

"He's not dead yet," she tells me.

"Nobody said he was."

"You want him dead."

"I didn't say that."

"Say you don't want him dead."

"I can't say that until I know what kind of shape he's going to be in."

"I hate you." She tries to run from me but I grab her, pull her to me, feel her tears against my neck. The dentists stop drinking vodka.

"Carry on," I tell them.

48

Logan tried to change her mother's bandages again but McKenna kept flipping out because pulling the adhesive tape off hurt her skin. It's pretty obvious that her mother doesn't care if she gets gangrene and dies. Which means she doesn't care if Logan is left alone, which isn't surprising considering she's abandoned *and* hit her in the last forty-eight hours. Logan's watching a movie about retarded people falling in love and slobbering all over each other while her mother flops on furniture like some kind of wounded animal. Logan's given up on the idea of her mother ever acting normal again. They stopped at the hospital to check on Grandpa. McKenna had a bird when she discovered bedsores on him. She charged around the hospital until she found somebody to chew out about it. Nobody cared, that was obvious. "He can't feel anything," a squat Jamaican lady pointed out.

"That's not the point," McKenna fired back, insisting that she wouldn't leave the hospital until someone dressed his sores. "Suit yourself," the lady said. Logan wasn't even sure she was a nurse, probably just an aide.

So they waited. There wasn't much action. It's a floor full of people waiting to die. Nobody's too interested. A man with a stick body came to visit the dirty old man in the next bed. He brought chocolates and Logan could hear them slurping them. They talked about people they knew who were dead and what shitfuckers they were. The stick-body man said his mother *almost* died, was attacked through a hole in the floor by a python in Kuala Lumpur. She was too fat to fit through the hole so the snake just bit her foot then slithered away. The dirty old man found this funny and laughed so hard he farted. The stick-body man didn't laugh but looked around as though hoping no one was listening. Logan kept staring at him, which caused one side of his face to twitch. Meanwhile McKenna was having one of her blink once for yes, twice for no conversations with Grandpa. Logan wondered if he could smell the chocolates and was craving Pots of Gold. On TV a woman with what McKenna would describe as Barbie hair was winning a game show and getting hysterical. Logan just wanted everybody to be quiet. She thought about dolphins again, under the sea, quiet, intelligent. Their sonar is so powerful it can discover an embryo in a woman before she even knows she's pregnant. Meanwhile another dolphin just bit the dust at Marineland, just days after being captured in the Black Sea. Even a dolphin *born* at Marineland died after eighteen days. It doesn't take a rocket scientist to figure out dolphins don't belong in tanks.

What is it about ignorance, Logan would like to know, that makes humans cling to it no matter what? They'll kill each other rather than smarten up. How can anybody with half a brain figure it's okay to go on burning fossil fuels? All summer long smog alerts tell parents to keep their kids indoors—like staying inside is going to stop the stuff from screwing up their lungs. And now everybody's getting excited about nuclear reactors again, like they've forgotten that nuclear waste kills and deforms forever. It seems to Logan there's no question that *Homo sapiens* are accelerating their own destruction. If they wanted to do something about it they could, but they'd have to stop shopping and watching other people have sex.

Vance is barbecuing and the truth is, Logan wouldn't mind a hot dog, and one for Stanley. So she sits on a lawn chair and tries to look friendly. She thinks the business about the great apes having dark tissue around their irises is interesting, and the fact that they will do anything to avoid eye contact with fellow troop members. Meeting an ape's gaze can infuriate them, and trigger an attack. Unlike humans who are always looking into each other's eyes. Humans are the only primates who have white scleras, which exaggerates the direction of their gaze and is supposed to aid in communication. Humans are the only primates who lie.

They looked at their house on the way back from the hospital. Logan figured her mother thought it would make her feel better. It didn't. It's just a house she'll have to live in with her crazy mother. The framing for the upper floor was finished but McKenna didn't do her usual isn't-it-going-to-be-great-sweetpea yabbering. She didn't even get out of the car, just did her body-snatched stare. After a while she reached for Logan's hand and squeezed it. Logan squeezed back but it felt fake. She doesn't even know her mother anymore. Like right now McKenna's comatose on the bed with a facecloth over her eyes. In the middle of the night she was talking to the chair they moved against the wall to hide the dent from the frying pan. "What do you want from me?" she kept hissing at the chair. Logan pretended to be asleep but it was scary. At one point her mother got out of bed and waved her arms over the chair. "See, you don't exist," she said. And then, "Go fuck yourself."

"You want mustard and relish on your dog?" Vance asks her.

"Please. Stanley will take his straight." Logan takes a wiener and blows on it to cool it. Stanley sits before her, drooling.

It seems pretty obvious to Logan that her mother is freaked that her father was burned, even though she told him to burn in hell.

The perfume-stinking woman peers through cigarette smoke at Logan. "I bet *you* could tell me how fish breathe under water."

"They use their gills," the clown interjects.

"I know that part, but how does it work exactly? I bet the kid knows."

"Why are you interested?" Logan asks.

"I got me two goldfish to soothe my nerves and I can't figure it out."

"They open their mouths to let water in, then close them, which pushes the water between their gills," Logan explains. "The blood inside the gills takes the oxygen from the water and carries it through their bodies. Extra water goes out the gill openings." Stanley falls asleep. Logan pats his head. "Can I see your fish?"

"Go ahead."

Inside the perfume-stinking woman's unit clothes are strewn over every surface. Pink, red, black and purple bras and underpants hang from lampshades, over chairs. Logan spots the aquarium by the TV. She pulls up a chair and watches the fish dart in and out of the shipwreck, swishing backwards and forwards, up and down.

Her mother forgot to pack her a lunch again today. That's two days in a row. She'll pack her own tomorrow. And she told her mother that from now on she's picking the fruits and vegetables at the supermarket.

The police have uncovered a pedophile ring of religious fanatics. They pushed candles up naked boys' rectums and lit them. Mr. Beasley can't be a pedophile in Logan's opinion because he lives with Dotty. Pedophiles are weird guys who live alone. Besides, Mr. Beasley isn't religious.

A fish flits up to the glass and appears to be watching her, wondering what she's doing out there when it's so cool and finite in here.

If Mr. Beasley touches her again she'll bite his hand. Human bites can be deadly.

49

I'm supposed to be eternally grateful that they had a cancellation. I'm supposed to sit here mute, reading grubby magazines for three hours. Within fifteen minutes the potato-faced receptionist had my number and now ignores me. I said, "If you can give me an estimate of how long it's going to be, I could grab a coffee or something."

"I have no way of knowing," she snipped. She's wearing a pageboy gone wrong, must have told her hairdresser she wanted to look like Audrey Hepburn and the hairdresser, in need of cash, did not say, "Have you looked in the mirror lately?"

The patients leaving the examining room clutch prescriptions. *That drug didn't make you normal, try this one.*

I have a client, cheerleader pretty, who showed up at the salon this morning with a rash all over her body and bumps on her tongue—side effects from an antidepressant. I said, "What are you taking?" because I know something about the drugs as most of my clients are on them. "I don't know," she said. "They're purple."

"Why are you taking them?" I asked.

"My psychiatrist thinks I should."

"Why?"

"I don't know. She says there's some kind of chemical imbalance in my brain." She kept scratching her arms. "She just switched me to the purple ones."

"Why?"

"I don't know. They make my gums stick to my teeth. I think they're necessary because I used to get really depressed about stuff and now I'm just sad."

I think we have to rethink the "depression" word. I think we have to recognize that if you're walking around smiling in a world that's hurtling towards self-destruction you're missing bolts. There's suffering out there that makes the put-on-a-happy-face mode obscene. This idea that you're sick if you happen to notice life is spooky is perverted.

Another patient comes out gripping a prescription. Only half of her face moves as she says "Have a nice day" to the spud-head, who doesn't look up from her monitor.

I'm trying to figure out how I became a child-beater. Logan's stopped looking at me when she talks to me, *if* she talks to me. She's disappearing behind clouds. If I had a rocket I could do something about it, but I'm grounded, can barely bring myself to move one leg in front of the other. I don't know why this is. The assholes in my life have been felled. The manacles are off. I should be doing song-and-dance numbers.

I dropped in on Payne, stared at him through the window. He's bloated beyond recognition, one big festering blister, naked except for gauze. If I could see red, I wouldn't be able to stomach it.

Dr. Angst—that's really his name—is shorter than I am, which means right off the top we have a problem because short guys always have something to prove. I sit ASAP. He stands behind his desk and I'm thinking stunted growth. Because I'm not exactly tall, towering over guys has never been one of my problems. He wants my history and I give it to him. He appears to be listening although mostly he stares at something behind me. When I finish he asks me to name colours around the room. Of course I can't. This bugs him. He asks me to describe a painting on the wall. I can't, there's not enough contrast in it. "Is it a setting sun?" I ask.

"What else?"

"I don't know. An ocean?"

"What else?"

"A boat?"

"You're guessing." He starts speaking unintelligibly into his Dictaphone about "the patient." Next he does what I guess is your basic neurological exam, wagging fingers in front of me, shining widgets in my eyes and testing reflexes. I find myself itching to draw his face. He's got dark triangles for cheeks, dark circles for temples and black eyebrows scribbled over his eyes. The charcoal lines on either side of his double-barrelled nose pin his mouth down; the lines on either side of his eyes shoot back into his streaked black hair. Sun damage has mottled the general greyness of him but has left the tip of his nose paler than the rest of him. I find myself staring at it, wanting to touch it to see if it's a soft animal nose.

"Your electroretinograms were normal," he tells me.

"Is that what those were?" Behind him a black plant is growing up and up towards the ceiling.

"Which indicates that all three cone mechanisms in the retina are intact."

"Is that good?"

The nostrils flare slightly. "It means your achromatopsia is of cerebral origin. It's possible you sustained tiny areas of brain damage as a result of the concussion. Or you could have had a small stroke either following or precipitating the accident. Do you smoke?"

"A hundred years ago."

"Nicotine can dim vision and sometimes cause achromatopsia."

"I used to take drugs, mostly cocaine." It's been one of my fears, that I brought this on myself.

"No connection proven there." He tells his Dictaphone about the drug use. "We'll get you set up for some brain imaging, certainly an MRI."

"I don't want to do that."

"Why not?"

"I'm claustrophobic, I'll freak out."

"They give you sedatives."

"The thing is, what's the point? I mean, you can't fix brain damage, right? And if it's hysterical, you can't fix that either. So I go through all these tests and end up where I started. I don't think so."

He leans back in his chair and puffs out air, erasing the black triangles from his cheeks. "Why are you here?"

"My daughter."

"Talk it over with her."

"She's eight."

The triangles reappear, and some new vertical lines on his brow.

"The other thing is," I mumble, "I'm seeing things, like I think I'm seeing my mother, only she's dead. Do you think that might be related?"

"Hallucinations are common as sight diminishes. The mind compensates, sending images that either your conscious or unconscious mind is anticipating. You see something you think should be there even though it isn't. I wouldn't worry about it." He talks to his Dictaphone about the hallucinating. I look up at the growing plant, wait for it to swoop down and throttle me.

"I'm scared I'm going to go completely blind."

"That's unlikely." He stands again and I remember that he's short. He'd enlarged behind the desk.

"You can't say for certain though."

"Nothing's for certain."

I leave without a prescription, without hope of a cure.

On the subway, I draw Dr. Angst on the back of a flyer soliciting Single Nature Lovers. I miss charcoal, rubbing it into paper, the feel of it in my hands. After working with charcoal I'd have black smears on my forehead, cheeks and chin because I couldn't draw without grabbing at my face in frustration. Because it never worked out the way I thought it would. But what does? Now in my world things are constantly changing. The grey tones are never static. The lights and darks fluctuate with different illumination whereas the coloured world I can only vaguely remember is stable, constant. Dull.

If I can catch the light, stop worrying about what it represents but just draw what I see, it could be interesting. Like living without fear of the before and after.

50

Dotty's old-lady neighbour has a gold tooth and does her laundry by hanging her dirty clothes on the line and hosing them down. Logan watches her from the tree while Curling slaughters worms. "They don't have eyes and ears," Logan advises him, "but earthworms can see light and detect vibrations."

"I did not know that," Curling responds, hacking away at another one.

"The narrow, slightly pointed end is the front of the worm's body."

Curling holds up a wriggling, decapitated worm. "Do they have dicks is what I want to know."

The old lady with the gold tooth starts beating her soaked sheets with a wooden spoon. Her cell rings and she shouts into it in a foreign language.

Mr. Beasley was playing freeze tag with them earlier. Any time a child ran to him he would position himself so that their hand would land near his crotch. When Logan didn't try to tag him, he called her a spoilsport. When Mr. Beasley was "it" he would tag the children on their bums. Logan has no doubt that if she told people that Mr. Beasley was positioning himself in freeze tag so that the children would touch his penis, they wouldn't believe her.

Curling digs around for more worms. Logan wants to stop his massacre but doesn't know how, just as she doesn't know how to stop Mr. Beasley from taking Katey into the washroom.

The old lady hangs up some underpants with skid marks on them and starts to hose them down.

Another North Atlantic right whale has a marine line hanging from both sides of her mouth, and wounds on her head from being hit by ships. The line has cut through her skin and blubber, causing severe infection. She's losing colour, is almost entirely white. Humans are trying to shoot her up with sedatives and harness her tail so they can loosen the line. The whale's frightened and won't let them near her.

Curling pulls a leg off a daddy-long-legs.

Logan saw Dotty taking pills. She didn't make rice crispy squares, just sat staring at the TV. When Curling asked why she wasn't making rice crispy squares, Dotty said she'd heard about a three-year-old boy choking on a marshmallow and dying because it blocked his windpipe.

Katey has started to pee her pants rather than go to the washroom with Mr. Beasley.

Logan watched *Schindler's List* last night. So did her mother because it was in black and white. "I still don't understand how that could happen," McKenna kept saying. "I mean, how could people let that happen?" Nazi movies always upset her mother. But Logan understands how it could happen and that it could happen again, that you do not like those you envy, that you would rather see them slaughtered in the streets than recognize the cheapness inside you.

She does nothing as Curling pulls another leg off the daddy-long-legs. It drags its body backwards, still trying to escape, still believing it has a life worth saving.

"Curling," Mr. Beasley calls, "your mother's here for you."

"Bye, toots," Curling says.

The old lady with the gold tooth starts thwacking the skid-marked underpants with her spoon.

Logan climbs down from the tree to examine the daddy-long-legs. Without front legs it has lost its bearings. The back legs drag the body in circles. Logan never kills insects because she knows they serve a purpose, that the global bug shortage is destroying crops around the world. She searches the sky for a bird who might put the daddy-long-legs out of its misery. The old lady's cell rings again and she resumes shouting into it. Mr. Beasley comes into the backyard to get Logan, she knows, to slide his hands under her clothes, to rub his penis against her. She prepares to bite him but first she steps on the daddy-long-legs. She does not look to see if it's still twitching.

"Your mother's here," Mr. Beasley says.

"Who's that?" Logan asks.

"My neurologist. Do you like it?"

"He's ugly."

"I know, but the drawing's alright, isn't it?"

"Since when do you draw?" Logan has never been in an art supply store before. Her mother fingers and sniffs everything, paper, pencils, brushes. Fortunately the salesclerk hasn't noticed because he's eating Burger King takeout which he has stashed under the counter. When he thinks no one's looking he stuffs his face, then quickly wipes his hands on his jeans before ringing up another sale. Logan ponders the bacteria crawling around on the money, how it's currently entering the clerk's intestines.

"What happened with the neurologist?" Logan asks.

"He said I might get my sight back."

"When?"

"He doesn't know."

"Did he say you might not get it back?"

"Nothing's certain, he said."

"Can't he do anything?"

"They can determine cause with x-rays and crap but they can't do anything." Her mother feels more paper.

"So what are you supposed to do?"

"Nothing."

"You can't do nothing."

"Why not?"

"You can't live like this."

"Like what?" Her mother sniffs some erasers.

"You're *totally* weird now."

"It's the same me, Logan. Just because I can't see colour doesn't mean I'm different."

"You *are* different. I hate being with you." She immediately regrets saying this, sees that she has dealt a body blow. McKenna drops the brushes and fumbles around in her pockets for cash to pay for the pad and pencils. Her hands tremble as she hands the money to the guy eating Burger King. Logan doesn't understand why she's hurting the only person on planet Earth who cares about her. "I'm sorry," she says on the sidewalk, knowing that apologies work like bandaids.

"It's alright."

"It's just you never even comb my hair anymore. And you're always shouting or looking spooked or something."

"I'm sorry."

"I just want you to get better."

"Sometimes we don't get better, Logan. Sometimes we just get different."

They keep walking, Logan doesn't know where. She's afraid her mother doesn't know either.

McKenna squints at the bowl of soup. "It looks like worms."

"Eat the broth and the water chestnuts," Logan advises. She suggested they go for Chinese food because rice is white. She has ordered strictly vegetarian dishes because a health inspector discovered squirrel and cat carcasses outside a Chinese restaurant recently. She still has the smell of hospital in her nostrils. When they got there a physiotherapist with large breasts was massaging Grandpa's face and hands. Logan was certain the breasts would get some action out of Lester because he always refers to jugs and bazookas when he describes women. Logan kept waiting for him to say, “Nice hooters,” or something. Or at least for his hand to twitch as he pondered fondling them. He drools all the time now so the saliva trickling down his chin didn’t signify anything. “Try to squeeze my hand,” the physiotherapist kept saying. Try asking him to squeeze your tit, Logan wanted to suggest. The physiotherapist replaced his inert hand on a foam pad. After she left, Logan saw one side of his mouth move. “His mouth moved,” she said.

“Are you serious?” McKenna asked.

“It did, I saw it.”

“Move your mouth, Dad, can you move your mouth?”

He just stared at them again, with that eye that belongs to a rhino who’s been shot by poachers, who isn’t dead yet but knows what’s coming and is mighty pissed about it.

“These are red peppers, right?” her mother asks, forking them.

“Yeah. Eat those.”

Her mother shaved him, got him all foamed up. He had to close his eye. Logan ran towels under warm water to lay on his face. There was no way of knowing if he was enjoying any of this. He said yes in blink language but everybody says yes when they don’t mean it, when they can’t be bothered to say no. He communicated in blinks that he wanted to watch a reality television show in which a guy with Ken hair was made to eat octopus eyes. Meanwhile the dirty old man was on the phone with somebody called Fawney who he called honey and baby. “Fawney, baby, please, honey,” he kept saying. “I know I was a prick, baby, please, honey . . .” Logan wanted to go home but her mother just stared at Grandpa watching the Ken-haired guy swallow the eyeballs.

Last night her mother kicked the chair she’s been talking to, and turned it upside down. Logan pretended to be asleep.

They were still only working on the interior partitioning today but they went to look at the house anyway. Wolfgang said they were going to start framing the roof tomorrow. Mrs. Pawusiak came out and complained that the new house is going to be taller than the old one and therefore shade her tomato plants. Even when McKenna explained fifty times that the new house was being built to the exact dimensions of the old house, Mrs. Pawusiak looked suspicious and brought up the delphinium again, the one she thinks McKenna stole.

Logan wishes her mother would eat a water chestnut or something. Instead McKenna picks up one of the sketch pads she bought and starts drawing the compulsive eater at the next table who doesn't appear to be swallowing food but funnelling it in.

"Did you see Dad today?" Logan asks.

"Yes."

"Is he any better?"

"He's still critical. Do you want to see him?"

Logan's afraid to see him, charbroiled, oozing pus. If he's going to die, she wants to remember him as he was, with angel hair and smooth skin.

"He isn't conscious," McKenna says. "There's not much to see. He's having surgery tomorrow, on his arms and face."

The compulsive eater inhales a mango shake. Logan keeps expecting him to notice her mother drawing him, to swivel around and plug her one. The smell of barbecued pork nauseates her, because it smells of her father. On the news she saw Iranian men set fire to themselves. They ran in flames, as though the fire could be escaped. Did her father do this? Did he scream at Jiggly Jugs to get a hose? Did he cry out in horror and agony as his skin blistered and crackled? Did he hear his subcutaneous fat, once exposed, spit like bacon grease into the flames? On a show about survivors of trauma Logan saw a woman talk about being burned in a car accident. She was pregnant at the time so they couldn't do much to her without harming the fetus inside her. As the baby grew, the scar tissue on the woman's belly wouldn't stretch like normal skin. It split open and there was nothing anybody could do about it except try to stop the bleeding. She couldn't even take painkillers. After the baby was born the woman lost her job as a hotel manager because her scarring scared the guests. She started selling life insurance by phone. Her baby wasn't afraid of her. They showed the toddler on TV kissing her hideous face and holding her hideous hands that could barely move because of the scar tissue. The woman said she wouldn't have wanted to live if it weren't for her baby. She has chronic pain and can't ride in cars. Sometimes she imagines herself like she was, forgets that she's ugly, then sees the revulsion in people's faces. She doesn't like going out of the house, because she knows people will gawp at her. She's putting on weight because of the lack of exercise, and the fat is making her skin split open again. She's thinking of getting one of those stomach stapling operations.

Logan can't see her father staying inside, getting fat, selling life insurance by phone. And she can't see herself being the reason he wants to go on living. She can't see herself kissing his hideous face or holding his hideous hands.

51

I'm in a bar with Julius, who's just told me he was married once, to a girl with cystic fibrosis. He knew she had cystic fibrosis when he married her, knew she was going to die. "I wouldn't give up those years for anything," he tells me. He still puts holly on her grave at Christmas and roses on her birthday. He will always love her, he says. I'm trying to compute this, Jules, the man with the Home of the Whopper underpants, being committed to a dying girl.

"You thought you had my number," says Kojak.

Kristos fired him today, the excuse being Jules has stood up too many clients. We all know this isn't the real reason because clients love being stood up by Jules, they'll sit around waiting for hours, imagining he's licking caviar off a runway model. The truth is, Kristos axed Julius because there's only room for one stud in the salon. Consequently, I felt sorry for the guy and agreed to have a drink with him. Plus, feeling rejected and dejected myself, I'm hoping bar activity will offer diversion.

"I thought that was a childhood disease," I say.

"Some make it to their thirties."

"Did she know when she was a kid she was going to die young?"

"You can know it and not know it, you know what I'm saying?" He drains his brew. "She didn't waste time. She had wisdom."

"How long were you married?"

"Four years."

"Were you faithful?"

"What's faithful? I *loved* her."

"Did she know you were screwing around?"

He holds up his hands like I'm about to arrest him. "What kind of person do you think I am?"

"I'm just curious, can behaviour change?"

"When you're facing death, anything's possible."

"Does it last though?"

"Shit, no. It's like you forget everything you learned in high school."

I can't get the overcooked sausage that is my former lover out of my head. Mostly I just stared at him, smelled him. They let me in the room, masked, gloved and gowned; memories of my quarantined cancer-blasted mother. They've put some kind of cotton toque on him and burn pads over the gauze. They're grafting him now, as we speak, cutting little squares off his leg and stretching them over his face. I can't imagine what he'll look like at the end of it, if he lives. I see napalm victims, children running with burning bodies. The ones who survived never had skin again. He will look in the mirror and wish he were dead.

"How did your wife deal with losing her looks?"

He shrugs. "We put the mirrors away."

I've had this experience before, when someone I thought was an asshole turned out to be capable of a humane act.

It was so weird watching the buzzard's eyeball watching the Ken doll eat the octopus's eyeballs. Old Les wanted to make sure he got it all down, just as he used to make sure I swallowed the kidneys. Facing death, I don't see his behaviour changing.

The pool, Bluxom's filled it. I'm so excited I chase him down to hug his blubber. He's watching porn again, silicone tits plug the screen. He glances at me, then stares back at the box. "What do *you* want?"

"To thank you for filling the pool."

"Don't go thinking I'm doin' anything about the washers."

Back at the ranch, Logan stalls. "What's up?" I ask her. "Where'd you put your suit?"

"I don't want to go in," she says without looking at me.

"Why not?"

She sits on the floor beside the dog. "There's men out there."

"What men?"

"I don't know. They're drinking beer."

"So, who cares? We'll have a dip and come back in." At dinner she told me a new study says dinosaurs' nostrils were near the end of their snouts, not at the top of their heads and close to their eyes as previously thought. "They're always getting it wrong," she grumbled.

"Who?"

"Scientists."

"Well, isn't part of the learning process making mistakes?"

"Fuck that shit."

I made no comment because her house burned down and her father may be dying.

"Well," I say, "I'm going for a swim."

The "men" are Mexicans, sun damaged, missing chunks of ears and noses that surgeons have cut off to save their lives. They've got a boom box playing Latino music. They're harmless touristos, displaying merchandise recently purchased with cheap Canadian dollars. I go back to the room to tell Logan. She's on the floor hugging the dog. "Baby, what is it?" I ask. "They're doofuses, please come and swim, you'll feel better."

She walks as though she's ashamed of her body. I'd expect this if she were hitting puberty, but the girl is eight. She paddles around briefly, then swaddles herself in a towel and huddles on a chair. I sit beside her, ask for an outer space update since she won't tell me what's really going on. One of the Mexicans is crashing around on new rollerblades.

"A cataclysmic storm has hit Mars," she informs me. "White water-ice clouds and swirling orange dust storms, winds gusting up to 320 kilometres an hour."

José the Mexican blader slams into the Lakeview.

"The dust circles the entire planet," Logan says. "The sun's heat, trapped by dust particles, raises the planet's overall temperature by thirty degrees."

"Hope the Martians have sunscreen."

"It's not funny. It's happening here. Greenhouse gases are trapped in our atmosphere."

"It's kind of like we've sealed the garage and have started the car."

"Except we don't want to die."

"Maybe we do." José's amigos thrust kneepads at him. "Or maybe we should."

"Did you visit Dad?"

"Yes. He's had the face graft, and the arm. He was in surgery for eight hours. I called. He's okay."

"What if he lives?"

"I don't know."

"Nobody will want to fuck him anymore."

"Why are you using that word?"

"All he ever does is fuck waitresses. What else is he supposed to do, wash cars? Nobody's going to give him any work, except maybe as a night janitor. He should just die. Why doesn't he just die?"

I reach for her hand but she pulls away from me. I kneel in front of her, wrap my arms around her bony knees so she can't escape. She hides her face in the towel. She's spent her entire life chasing a father's love and now he's a freak, a liability. She wants him dead, thinks that out of his body he will be out of her mind. I can't tell her that if he dies she will wear the guilt to her grave, that dead or alive he will be her burden. She's too young for this.

52

Logan can't sleep. She zonked out for about two minutes and dreamed Mr. Beasley was on top of her, fingering her, squeezing the breath out of her. Normally, when she has a nightmare, she gets into bed with her mother and they talk about the nightmare until its reality fades. But she can't tell her mother about this nightmare because then she'd have to tell her about Mr. Beasley. Besides, McKenna's out with the no-lifers again.

That North Atlantic right whale died of course.

If her father lives Logan will have to pretend that it doesn't make her gag to look at him. She doesn't understand why her mother's going to see him all the time since she's the one who wanted him burned alive in the first place. Logan goes outside and sits on a lawn chair because she's afraid if she goes back to sleep she'll meet up with Mr. Beasley. Her mother has her sketch pad out and is drawing the no-lifers in the dark. The drawing thing is getting out of control in Logan's opinion, especially as her mother always draws ugly people. Earlier she was drawing the pig.

Logan stares up at the sky and tries to spot Uranus 1.8 billion miles away. Sixty Earths could fit inside it. Beneath Uranus's thick atmosphere is a deep ocean of water and icy gases.

Two children suffocated in a sandpit today. They were visiting their grandparents, digging a cave in the sandpit with coffee cans. When they didn't come home the grandparents went out to look for them, saw the little footprints going into the sandpit but none coming out.

And yet some stinking Nazi just celebrated his hundredth birthday. This is where Logan continues to have a problem with the God concept, what with the kids suffocating, and her father burning, and Mr. Beasley hurting Katey, and all the bombing going on of innocent people and animals, and that lady drowning her five kids in the bathtub, and those families living on garbage dumps—how could any decent god let any of this happen?

The no-lifers are discussing whether or not they could eat a human if they were in a shipwreck or something.

"I heard," Vance says, feeling for his ear, "human meat tastes like pork."

"Who told you that?" the perfume-stinking woman asks. "You been hanging out with Pygmies?"

"When Franklin screwed up finding the Northwest Passage," Logan tells them, "his men ate each other. And the Huron and the Iroquois used to eat captives."

"So what's your point?" the perfume-stinking woman asks.

"We could all do it. We may have to when agriculture goes tits up because there's no water."

What she can't stop doing is replaying in her head what happened before her father got burned. If she had behaved better, if her mother hadn't told him he had no brain, there's no question things would have panned out differently. She's not sure how exactly. Maybe they could have come to some arrangement. Maybe her parents would have figured out that they loved each other.

Her grandfather wasn't in his bed when they got there, which made her mother hysterical because she assumed he was dead. She charged around looking for a whitecoat to shout at. Logan couldn't figure out why McKenna should care if he was dead since he was so shitty to her all the time. Logan stayed in the room watching the dirty old man sleep. His scaly lips were hugging his gums because his teeth were out. One of his hands kept twitching. They wheeled her grandfather back in wearing a fresh diaper. His staring eye was wide open and tearing. Logan wondered if he was crying because he had to be diapered like a baby. They flipped him onto the bed and took off, leaving Logan alone with the rhino eye. "Hi," she said to it. "Mom was looking for you. She was afraid you were dead." The eye didn't blink, just stared at her. Logan stared right back until it closed.

She wants the no-lifers to go inside so she can find out about her father. She tells them about the rabid coyote with sores on its back who's in the neighbourhood making off with cats. "It's because we've taken away their forest," Logan points out. "I just hope it doesn't get wind of your pig." This works as a direct hit. The clown excuses herself and the pig, and the other two, fearing coyote bites, come up with reasons for calling it a night.

"Why are you visiting Dad all the time?" Logan asks.

"Somebody has to."

"He wouldn't visit you if you were bacon."

"Is that a reason not to visit him?"

Logan isn't sure. She personally doesn't give anything away for nothing. Because no matter what you give, they'll take more, and they won't thank you for it.

Her mother looks asleep or dead. Logan wants her awake. "They're saying the moon was sprung from one big collision," she says loudly, "between the earth and a Mars-sized planet 4.5 billion years ago. There was all this vaporized rock kicked out from the crash that cooled and started orbiting and became the moon. It took a hundred years."

They hear a howling, which could be the coyote or just some dog.

"I think I should see Dad tomorrow."

53

This treadmill we call life. I dropped her off at school this morning and felt no better about dropping her off at school than I did that first day of kindergarten, when she cried and clung to my legs. Usually I speed off without looking back because I can't stand it. Today I watched as she stood alone in the yard by a black and grey tree. I wanted her back. But once that bell tolls and those doors clang shut, you can never have them back. Not as they were. She was whimpering in her sleep last night. I tried putting my arms around her but she squirmed and said, "What?"

"You had a bad dream."

She burrowed into the pillow, away from me.

So I carry around this missing piece that was my child before "socialization" got ahold of her, and hope that one day it'll fit again. It won't of course. I used to think that, as she got older, I'd agonize less over her life away from me, get used to it. That didn't happen. I've just learned to live with it, like any chronic pain. Like colour-blindness.

She used to wake from dreams terrorized because I'd been featured as a corpse. "I'm not going to die," I'd tell her, knowing full well that it was entirely possible; cancer could strike, as could a car, a plane piloted by terrorists, a chunk of plaque in an artery. Then she'd dream that I went away. "I will never leave you," I'd tell her.

I don't think she's smiled once since the fire. I can't remember the last time she laughed. Something is broken and I can't fix it, can't even see the crack.

There's some kind of infection going on with Payne. They call it sepsis. He's got a high fever, his blood pressure's dropping. They're dripping antibiotics into him. Through all this he has to endure the twice-daily dressing changes, the picking and hosing-down of wounds. Gloved, gowned and masked, I told him what's going on, even though he's supposed to be out of it. I told him what's going on so he can feel free to exit.

I order pancakes from Miss Jiggly Jugs. She pretends she doesn't recognize me, that I'm just another deadbeat female customer who'll take forever over coffee and leave a lousy tip. A construction crew is chowing down at the next table. She fawns over them, shaking her booty. How could he ruin his life for this? Why do the rest of us have to grow up, figure out there's more to life than pussy, like enjoying responsibility because it means somebody needs you, cares about you, will visit you in the home? Aren't you supposed to figure out who you are after a few decades, make the same mistakes until finally you go, Okay, that's it, no more, I know where that one goes?

She won't give me a refill. I don't actually want one, just want to rattle her chain, keep waving my cup at her. I've been up against girls like her my whole life—blondes with attitude. Her hair's a box job, you can be sure her bush is brown; doesn't matter in the dark. I've always had to work overtime around girls like her. I've had to be smarter, sparkier, funnier. A better lay. Girls like her kicked people around in concentration camps, pulled the levers in the gas chambers. Eventually her tits will fall and the perky nose will look like a snout, but this offers me no comfort. She has years ahead of her of setting men on fire.

I want him to die. But not for the old reasons. I'm in this different space, above and beyond our sordid history. There's a stillness here, in black and white. Even the blonde, dulled, has lost her power. I stiff her.

The daughter, chewing her hair, looks at her charred father through the window. Critical-burn victims get private rooms with windows facing the corridor so nurses can keep an eye on them without actually going in. What does this say to the patient? would be my question. *We don't want to go near you, just stare at you through glass.*

They won't let us in either because, they say, with the infection, he's even more vulnerable to bacteria. It's probably just as well. Logan would probably pass out from the heat and the stench of decay. I guess they have to keep the room hot because the burn victim's naked except for gauze.

"Can he feel anything?" she asks.

"A little. They dope him as much as they can."

"Is he blind?"

"No."

"How do you know for sure?"

"He looked at me."

"When?"

"Last visit. I talked to him."

"What did he say?"

"Nothing."

"So how do you know he heard you?"

"I just know."

She stares at the heart monitor, watches his pulse. I didn't tell her about the blood pressure drop, the possible descent into death. I just told her about the infection and the fever. They've hooked him up to more pumps. The pageboy-gone-wrong told me we have to take it one day at a time.

"Why's his face grey?" Logan asks.

"Is it? It's all grey to me."

"His face is almost black in places. It looks leathery."

"I guess that's how it heals."

"He's oozing pus."

"Means he's fighting it."

She rests her forehead against the glass. "He's going to die, isn't he?"

"It's possible."

The roof trusses are up, wood, which scares me. "Why not steel?" I asked Wolf when I was by earlier and trying to avoid getting run over by the mobile crane. He snorted. "The gusset plates on the corners are steel," he said, like that helps in a fire.

"Aren't you glad the roof's up?" I ask her, knowing she can't be glad about anything with her father dying and her mother totally weird all the time.

Mrs. Pawusiak is on the prowl. Earlier she was ranting about how Wolf broke her fence, the fence that divides our backyards, which is two thousand years old and already busted in places.

"Did you talk to heem?" she demands.

"Haven't had a chance."

"You *must* talk to heem. All day zey are zrowink garbage on my lawn."

What I'd like to know is if owning a tiny plot of dirt and warring over it extends your life. There has to be something to it because there are a lot of lawn freaks out there—Lester, for example—who live forever. His hatred for me today was smoking out his socket. My guess is he's added resentment to the mix, because I'm up and about, able to savour Pots of Gold. I'm thinking maybe I should munch a box in front of him, let cherry syrup dribble down my chin. I'm thinking maybe I should do something to deserve his abuse.

It's peaceful by the pool. Water laps. With eyes closed we can pretend we're somewhere else.

"They're including do-it-yourself pregnancy kits in the medical packs aboard the International Space Station," Logan tells me. "If they want to have sex in space they have to have a third person hold one of the others down while they're going at it. Up there among the planets, and all they want to do is fuck."

"Whoops, there goes that word again."

More lapping. I try to put myself beside a calm sea. I've been thinking it's fortunate I don't love him. There was a hairdresser at the salon who lost her husband in a car crash. She stopped eating and developed "symptoms"—she spent all her time going to doctors getting tested for every disease going. Watching her waste away, I told myself I was lucky I wasn't pinned to a man I could lose in a car crash.

"Dad's going to die because all he wanted to do was fuck."

"He did it well. We all want to do what we're good at. Or die trying."

"I can't believe how you don't care if he dies."

"Did I say that?"

She twists away from me on her lawn chair. The cat jumps out of my pocket and trots to the water, dunks her paw in and leaps backwards.

"Wasn't it you," I ask, "who said he should die because his only job option was night-time janitor?"

She's very still, glaring at her toes. "I want it to be like it was."

"That doesn't happen under any circumstances." We all fall into this one, remember how it "was" when the truth is, while we were living "was" we were dreaming about some other "was," or some "going to be." You get rid of one problem, you can always find another.

I know I should say something motherly like, "It's going to be alright, honey," but I've never lied to her. "Stop chewing your hair."

She does but closes her eyes as though there's something she doesn't want to see. "I'm not sure I want him to die."

"Fortunately, you don't get to make that decision."

"Why did you want him to burn in hell?"

I can't say because he lied to me, because he didn't. And I can't say because he betrayed me, because no deal was made, no vows were sworn. "He was unreliable," I say.

"You wanted him to burn in hell because he hurt you, and you said you can only get hurt by people you care about, which means you care about him." She pushes her recliner back and frowns at the stars. "I bet you love him and just aren't admitting it."

Here we go searching for happy endings again.

"You must love him," she persists, "otherwise why would you be going to the hospital all the time?"

"Because nobody else is."

"There's all kinds of people in hospitals who don't get visitors, why don't you visit them, start up a voluntary visitors association?"

"That's a thought. And when they kick off I can take the flowers home."

A breeze sends an empty chip packet into the water. I watch it sail, think about boats, being on one.

She starts chewing on her hair again. "I bet you still love him and just aren't admitting it. I bet if you told him you love him, he'd get better."

More Hollywood brainwashing.

"When they let me in there," she says, "I'm going to tell him you still love him."

I say nothing, don't want to torch her hope, if that's what this is.

"I'd like to bomb Jiggly Jugs," she says. "Palestinians put bombs in watermelons. Israelis buy them at the market and blow up. I'd like to do that to her."

The cat falls in, of course. I jump up and grab her. She scratches me, not understanding what's hit her, which is what we all do, strike out when we don't understand, dream of bombs. I hold her until she's calm. Back inside my pocket, she starts to purr. The only creature in my life I can still save.

54

The thing about ants that Logan particularly admires is that they look after each other. Wounded ants are never deserted. Even if they die, the other ants carry them to the morgue. Another thing she admires is that they kill off the males after they've used them for mating.

The carpenter ants she is currently watching live in Dotty's back porch. They have tunnelled a comfortable home in one of the support beams. Logan has been careful to watch them only when no one else is around because she is quite certain that, should Mr. Beasley see them, he would get out the Raid. And Curling Ellsworth would definitely try to roast them with his Bic. Logan's aware that the ants don't appreciate her studying them because they become agitated when they smell her. Although she's been careful not to block their entryways, she has scraped the nest slightly with a stick in order to see the inner passageways. There's a nursery in there, and the queen's lodging, and dormitories. Ants always look busy because they work in shifts, but each ant actually works only thirty per cent of the time and rests for the remaining seventy. Logan thinks if humans could get as organized as ants, they too could rest for most of the day and not become psychotic. Worker ants are assigned jobs by the queen's drones and they don't argue. They develop special skills, which they teach younger ants. Assigned skills change as they age and become less able to do certain tasks. In other words, old ants don't get shit on like old humans.

She wonders if planet Earth would be in better shape if the males were killed off after mating. Certainly there would be fewer wars because women don't enjoy wars. During wars women lose their homes and get raped, and watch their children starve and get mutilated and murdered. If their husbands survive, they come back missing parts, and toxic with revenge. Women don't want revenge. They want homes and food for their children. Which must be why the female ants kill off the males. They off them before they can start wars. Some warrior ants survive, but the queen sends them away to fight elsewhere, far from the nest.

The trick to getting rid of ants is to kill the queen. Without the queen the workers go mental, become disoriented and die. What Logan can't understand is why the queen bites off her own wings after she proves her superiority. Maybe because she knows she must always remain in the nest to keep order, and therefore has no use for her wings. Maybe it's a symbolic gesture of sacrifice.

It bothered Logan today when Oscar was aiming spitballs at Nina. During recess he took a drink from the fountain and spit water at her. Nina started to cry, snot was dripping from her nose. The teacher on duty didn't see Oscar spitting, and Nina didn't tell on him, probably because she knew there'd be no point. All that would happen would be that Oscar would be sent to the principal's office again. This wouldn't stop him spitting at her. In retaliation, Logan stole his New York Yankees cap. They're not supposed to wear them in school but he brings his anyway and puts it on the minute he's off the premises. Logan saw it sticking out of his backpack and snatched it. It's in the lunchroom garbage can, covered in sandwich crusts.

Every minute she's wondering if her father's dead yet. She's still not convinced that this would be bad in the long term. At first she knows she'd be upset, but she'd get over it, and at least then she wouldn't have to touch his skin or anything. Because if he lives she'll have to kiss him; it would be cruel not to. Maybe this is why her mother isn't too concerned about him dying, even though she loves him. Although McKenna doesn't touch him anyway, just pushes him around when they argue. She would have to look at him though. Logan's been thinking about *Phantom of the Opera*, and how the girl loved him even though he was hideous. She hopes it was based on a true story. She saw a movie about a guy who got mauled by factory equipment and sued the company. His wife left him because he'd lost his hands, but his occupational therapist fell in love with him while she was showing him how to use artificial hands. He won the lawsuit and they bought a yacht together. That was based on a true story.

Dotty said that Curling Ellsworth was projectile vomiting last night, which is why he isn't here on Logan's case. Logan has the yard to herself, except that the old lady with the gold tooth is hosing down her skid-marked underpants again and listening to the all-news station. There's been another oil spill. Nobody's too concerned about it because the stock market crashed again. Logan pictures the sea mammals coming up for air, gulping crude oil. When the oil coats their fur they can no longer swim. The fish can no longer breathe. The birds can no longer fly. They all die slowly, washing up on the shore, food for maggots.

It starts to rain, but Logan doesn't go inside because Mr. Beasley's in there. Dotty is making cupcakes and getting the kids to decorate them with jelly worms.

The ants file into the entryways to escape the rain. Logan covers the area of the nest she investigated with rotten leaves and dirt.

"What you got there, princess?"

"Nothing."

Mr. Beasley pushes the dirt away with his shoe, destroying one side of the nest. The ants scramble for cover, suddenly disorganized. "Bloody hell," he says, stomping on them.

"Don't!" Logan shouts, trying to shield them with her body.

"Get out of the way, girl."

Logan drops to her knees in front of them, holding her arms over the rotten beam.

"Move it," he says, nudging her with his foot. She doesn't. She looks down at the trodden ants. Most of them are still moving. Other ants have turned back from the entryways and are trying to rescue the wounded.

At first the hand down her track pants doesn't register. But then his finger is pushing into her rectum and she starts to scream. He uses his other hand to cover her mouth but she bites hard. The sharp taste on her tongue must be his blood, she realizes. She continues to bite even after his finger is out of her anus. While he howls and tries to jerk his hand free, she feels a piece of his skin tear in her mouth. The rotten-fish taste of his flesh makes her want to vomit but she does not let go, even when he hits her, for if she lets go he will be free to harm her, and the ants. He actually looks frightened while she is forced to swallow his blood, blood she does not want in her body. She worries that she will have to swallow a chunk of his skin as well, and that the cells will mutate inside her, make her evil, with flat fishy eyes. The old lady with the gold tooth looks over the fence and starts shouting at them in her language.

Dotty appears, hands coated in chocolate icing. "What in heaven's name . . . ?"

Logan lets go and spits out his flesh and blood. "Call my mother," she says.

"He's going to have to have stitches," her mother says. Rain blurs the windshield; everywhere cars seem to be honking. Logan closes her eyes and rests her head against the car door. The ants, she knows, will be massacred. She has betrayed them.

"Are you going to tell me why?" McKenna asks.

"He was rude."

"How rude?"

"He's always pushing us around."

"Why didn't you tell me this before?"

"I didn't think it was important."

"It was important enough that you felt you needed to bite him. Which must be pretty important considering you've never bitten anyone in your entire life."

Logan pretends to be asleep. Her mother can't do much to her while she's driving because, in the rain, she has to lean over the wheel and practically press her nose against the windshield.

"Logan . . . ?"

The bathwater doesn't clean her. She will never be clean again, she knows. She still has the taste of him in her mouth. She doesn't know if God had anything to do with this but she's decided that if there is a God, she hates him. From now on she will be an agnostic. You never hear about agnostics starting wars, bombing civilians, drowning children because they think they're possessed by Satan. Agnostics don't have anything to prove to anybody. They mind their own business.

Her mother won't take her squinty eyes off her.

"There has to be more to this story," McKenna says.

There is no doubt in Logan's mind that, if she tells her mother about Mr. Beasley molesting the children, McKenna will storm over to the police and make a scene and Logan will have to testify and the whole school will know that Mr. Beasley had his finger up her ass. She cannot live with this. On the other hand, she does not want to go to Dotty's ever again, and must come up with a good reason for her mother finding an alternative at such short notice.

"How's Dad?"

"Don't change the subject."

"Is he still alive?"

"Yes. What happened at Dotty's?"

"He hit me."

"*After* you bit him. Why did you bite him? Was he hurting you?"

"Kind of."

"What was he doing?"

"He stepped on my ants. There's an ant nest there I was studying."

Her mother stands abruptly, leans over the sink and throws cold water on her face. As she pats her face dry, Logan can see her concrete face forming. "Don't lie to me, Logan."

"He hurt me."

"How did he hurt you? What did he do?"

Logan tries to immerse herself in the water but her mother grabs her by the hair. "*What* did he do to you?"

Only now does Logan start to cry, because it's so impossible, so relentless, so senseless, so brutal. She thinks of her ants, carefully rebuilding their nest, unaware that tomorrow they will be sprayed with poison.

Her mother holds her face in a vise grip. "Tell me what he did to you."

Logan vomits the words, as she wants to vomit the taste of his blood and skin. She begins to shake. Everything, everything that's wrong in the world is contained in her body, which she loathes. She would like to explode, to have every piece of her gone. The sobs scrape her throat, her lungs, her gut. Her mother pulls her out of the bath and wraps her in a towel. She lifts her onto her knees and rocks her. "Don't tell anyone," Logan pleads. Her mother kisses her head, her face, her eyelids, and she rocks her.

55

They're in there. I can see the TV through the venetians. They're not answering. I tap on the picture window. He pushes back the blinds and I smile meekly, apologetically. The bat feels hot in my hand. The sweat on my palm is loosening my grip. I wipe my hand on my jeans. I must not kill him. I wait patiently by the door, hoping to appear repentant, while waves crash inside my skull. I must not kill him and go to prison for life. Lightning blinds me as he switches on the porch light. I blink, holding my hands behind my back, a defenceless pose. "Sorry to bother you," I say. "I just wanted to let you know how sorry I am."

He shrugs, watching me for signs of knowledge. "We would prefer," he tells me, "that you place her elsewhere. She's been violent before. The pencil incident at school."

"I understand. Did they give you stitches?"

"Eight."

"I'm so sorry. May I see it?" The bat moves at high speed. The hand cracks like a hardball. The bat swings back then stops inches from his face. I try to savour his look of terror, the pooling eyes, the mouth stretching into yowls, but all I can see are the children, cowering, maimed, shamed, lost, without hope. I jerk the bat again as he begs for mercy, grasping behind him for the doorknob with his functional hand. I shove the bat under his chin, pinning him against the door. Like the children, he does not know what his abuser will do, can only wait, in pain and fear, for it to end. I push hard with the bat, causing his head to bang against the door. "What's it feel like, fuckhead?" I know that if I strike his skull there will be brain damage, maybe death, and that this would leave my daughter alone. "You go near her again," I say into his whimpers, "and it'll be your head."

I don't go home right away, can't face her. Shirl's watching over my unconscious child. I left her in a sleep from which she won't want to wake. At first it will seem like a bad dream, something to be left behind after the Cheerios. But then the reality will spread and she will want to be free of her body, to be free of his filth.

I want him dead.

I stop in a strip mall parking lot. It's over, who she was. She will be different now, forever. Distrust and fear will rule her days. And I was there, blind, too busy chasing dollars and fucks.

She's been there five days a week for two years. I did not look closely because it was what I could afford. I was thankful that the woman spoke English and did not have the TV on constantly, and did crafts with popsicle sticks and pipe cleaners. I gave the woman a wedding present. "Congratulations," I said, thinking it was a miracle that any man would want such a woman. Now I know he didn't.

My father is watching wrestling. Beefy men straddle and strangle each other, bounce off ropes. He doesn't notice me. I don't know what I'm doing here. Looking for continuity? Your child gets ripped apart while your father breathes on. Savagery happens; children survive war, abuse, mutilation. Baby girls get raped in Africa by relatives who think sex with virgins will protect them from AIDS. Nine-month-old babies are raped.

He did not rape her. If he had raped her he would be dead.

Savagery happens. She will have birthday parties, move into new decades.

To stop the noise in my head I ask the buzzard how it's going. He doesn't look thrilled to see me and I tell myself this is the last time. I tell him about Mom appearing and ask if he's seen her. He blinks no and stares back at the TV. I turn it off because I want him to look at me. I want to be sure there is no one there I need to know.

"Did you enjoy locking me in that room?" I ask. Isn't that what the shrinks tell you to do? "*Talk* to your father, tell him how you *feel*." He's pissed about the TV. I clutch at the bed rails—straws. "Did you hear me screaming, and feel nothing? Not a hint of doubt that locking a child in a dark room for hours might not be a bit extreme? Because I think it screwed me up for life. I think it's why I can't trust a living soul." If he could walk he would be in the yard by now, bonding with the mower. "Can't trust the dead ones either," I add. The eyeball's looking a little frenzied. He's afraid I'm going to do something to him, pull his plug or something. I lean over him, eyeball to eyeball. "My daughter was violated today. The daughter I would kill for. Some fuck, some cruel, sick fuck put his finger up her ass. Does this mean anything to you?" He blinks but it's not a "yes" blink, it's an animal-caught-in-trap wince. I could do anything to him, roll him off the bed, smother him with a pillow, shove implements up his orifices. Revenge is within my grasp and he smells it. "Do you care at all that some sick fuck shoved his finger up your granddaughter's rectum?" He blinks yes but it's a lie. "You think it's my fault, right?" I say. "I should never have been a mother, should have had her scraped out of me, right? Should have kept my legs crossed. Right?" No blink, just the stare that has undermined whatever faith I have ever been able to muster. I clap my hand over it, darken his window. He can't squirm, or turn his face away. He is my captive. His eyelashes buzz against my palm. "How does it feel to be locked up, old man?" I wait. Something has to give, with the role reversal or whatever it's called. I should get some kind of charge out of this, some kind of growth spurt, leave the buzzard behind, vanquished, move onward in my journey of self-discovery. But of course I just feel like a shit for tormenting a cripple. The oppressed oppress; this is no news. The eyelashes stop buzzing and I wonder if I've shocked him into another stroke. If I take my hand away I'm going to see a rolling eyeball, disconnected, already sinking into his skull. I'm sweating, probably dripping into his socket, burning him. A code blue is announced over the P.A. system and I'm thinking how do they know already? Is he wired to some central unit? Are they going to charge in here, with the police in tow? A mercy killing, I'll lie. "Tell that to the jury," they'll sneer. My little girl will visit me behind bars, with her foster mother standing beside her, clutching Barbies. "Time to go, dear," she'll tell my silent child, who will never forgive me for abandoning her.

A client told me that in India they trap monkeys by poking holes in coconuts, draining the milk and popping in peanuts. The monkeys grab the coconuts and shake them around to figure out what's inside. They squeeze their hands through the hole and wrap their greedy fingers around the peanut, trying to pull it out. But the fist won't fit through the hole. Do the monkeys let go of the peanut to free their hand as their captors bear down on them? Of course not, they hang on, because that's all they know. I saw a photograph in the paper of a four-year-old girl in the arms of a cop. The girl was naked, covered in cigarette burns and knife wounds. On the other side of the cop was the child's mother in cuffs, scowling, smoking a butt. The child was crying and reaching towards her mother. We all want what we know.

I could be in this dark pit forever, raging.

I take my hand off his eye. Immediately the eyeball's on me, still alive, still scared. Like the little girl who was let out of the dungeon, he knows it could happen again. With one quick movement I could slam him back into darkness.

"Don't worry about it," I tell him. "It's over."

I beg the nurse to let me in there. I tell her it's a family emergency, that even if he's going to die, he would want to know. She's tired, overworked, wearing a badge that reads "Your Tax Cuts At Work." She gives me the gloves, the mask, the gown. The stench of fermenting pus; even in black and white I can see he's festering. Machines buzz, hum, beep. A nurse client once told me that the more lines they've got in them, the more likely it is they're going to die.

I tell him that our daughter has been destroyed, knowing he can't possibly understand in his narcotic haze. I tell him because he's the only person who might care. And because he will listen, won't finish my sentences for me, won't think he can read my mind. I lean my head against the bed rail—bars—knowing he has no comfort to give. He is far away, making bad deals on the other side.

"She needs you," I try to say, although the words jam my throat and years of restrained tears drizzle out of me. The ventilator wheezes through my sorrow. I don't want him to see me cry, even though he's not looking. I keep my head down and watch tiny pools form on the floor. I imagine his hand stroking my hair. He would do that, nurse me out of bad trips. He never scolded me for taking drugs, just told me, "You don't need that shit." A show of faith I could not find in myself.

I lie carefully beside her, afraid that any sudden moves will wake her, bring her back screaming to ground zero. I inch towards her, barely breathing, shifting my weight an ounce at a time. On contact, I freeze, fearing she'll push me away. My mother is there, on her chair, nodding and crying. Maybe she knew all along, maybe she was warning me. Torment breeds solidarity. I too start to dribble again. Her presence no longer creeps me out. She's become just another shadow who will follow me, who will live in my closets forever, not to be forgotten but abided. You can't escape who you are.

I fit my body around my baby, tuck my knees behind hers, feel my belly warm her back, and cautiously wrap an arm around her and Tiger, who she hugs to her chest even in sleep. She doesn't move and I tell myself it could have been so much worse. I tell myself that the wounded can recover. I make lists in my head of all the things I must and must not do for her, for myself. I make lists knowing that they will be forgotten, that we will continue to stumble, that there will always be obstacles at our feet. I make lists until we breathe as one.

56

They've found a fossil of a cockroach the size of a bird. It lived three hundred million years ago, before the dinosaurs even evolved. That makes the cockroach one of the longest-surviving species. They had them at the Lakeview. Her mother got hysterical until Logan explained to her that the toxins left behind by the exterminator would be far more dangerous than the cockroaches. So they worked out a compromise. Logan would turn the lights on early to make the cockroaches scatter before her mother got out of bed. Also, Logan would check all foodstuffs regularly and make certain they were stored in airtight containers. Logan quite admires cockroaches, because they have been persecuted for millions of years and have survived.

Meanwhile humans continue to plunder Earth. Even the United Nations is admitting that the destruction of the planet has to stop to avoid worldwide disaster. Logan has no problem with humanity erasing itself. Evolution has always ensured the destruction of any species that becomes too dominant. There will still be cockroaches.

She has several ant colonies in her backyard, which puts a bug up Mrs. Pawusiak. Logan figures Mrs. Pawusiak is going to hyperventilate one of these days and croak. She hopes to be there to see it.

They planted another copse but had to pay full price for the evergreens because it wasn't the end of the season. Her mother dug up some of Mrs. Pawusiak's shasta daisies one night and planted them in a bed she's started near the sand turtle. She said Mrs. Pawusiak wouldn't miss them, that she was weeding them out anyway. This made Logan wonder if her mother did, in fact, steal Mrs. Pawusiak's delphinium.

Her mother sometimes talks about what happened. She says that Logan must not think of herself as a victim, that she would have kicked Mr. Beasley in the gonads if she hadn't been protecting the ants. McKenna stresses that he abused her physically but that that doesn't mean he deserves to live inside her head. He is a pathetic, disturbed roach of a man who should be exterminated, her mother says. McKenna has made it her mission to ensure that no more children come under his care. She stalks Dotty's every morning before going to work. Anytime she sees a drop-off, she chases down the parents, explains that she hasn't reported Beasley to the police because her child does not want to be interviewed. McKenna has told Logan that she mustn't feel guilty about not wanting to go public, that she would feel the same way, that even if enough evidence were put together to lock him up he'd be out again in a couple of years. McKenna says she's going to haunt him for the rest of her days. One night each week, because she sees in the dark, she soaps PEDOPHILE on their front-porch window. She keyed his car and said that that made her feel a lot better. Logan suspects she'll slash his tires one of these days.

Logan doesn't mind her father being around. It means she doesn't have to go to daycare. At least he's got some hair now. And he's taught her how to play poker, which she quite enjoys. But it's a little weird the way he never goes out. Sometimes, late at night, the three of them go for walks. He doesn't like going anywhere where there's lights because people will see him, and her mother doesn't like going anywhere where there's lights because it blinds her. So they walk in the ravine, which Stanley prefers anyway. Sometimes, if they want ice cream or something, they have to walk in residential areas to find corner stores. They always send Logan in for the treats while they wait outside, her father with his baseball cap pulled low over his face, and her mother shielding her eyes from the streetlight. This is the closest Logan has ever come to having two parents. Sometimes she walks between them holding their hands. Her father's left hand is normal, but sometimes she holds his right just to prove to him that she's not repulsed by his skin. It took a while though. At first she thought she'd never be able to look at him without barfing. The first graft on his face didn't take so they had to do the patchwork all over again, which meant he had to stay in the hospital even longer. The second graft worked but was still unbelievably gross. His skin was all bumpy, darker than normal, crusted with dried pus and blood. He got pneumonia and had to have secretions suctioned out of his lungs. He couldn't breathe on his own for weeks. McKenna got the idea that they should take turns holding his good hand even though he was totally out of it. By the time they took the breathing tube out of him, he was psycho. The nurses said he was just confused from the medication. They started giving him less, which meant he had more pain, but at least then he recognized them. McKenna had to explain to him about sixty times exactly what had happened. Even then he didn't seem to get it.

Logan spoke to him about different things. He was particularly interested in the Dog Boy in Chile, who grew up with a pack of dogs and ran from humans. Authorities took him away from the dogs, which totally freaked the boy out. He kept escaping from the group home. Unfortunately it was easy for the authorities to find him because all they had to do was track a pack of dogs. Logan wished the Dog Boy and dogs would have run to the mountains, but they were scavengers and needed the city to live. Eventually the authorities locked the boy up. Her father still mentions him, says he's wondering how the Dog Boy's doing. Logan knows he probably isn't doing well, that he has probably stopped eating, that he probably howls, smashing his limbs into the walls that confine him, that he's probably being drugged. She doesn't say this to her father; she says things like, "I bet he escaped again," or "He's probably gnawing on a bone." She tries to protect her father.

Her mother has hidden all the mirrors, and papered over the one in the bathroom, which makes flossing awkward. Occasionally, when he's alone, Payne tears the paper off the medicine cabinet. They know when he's done this, even before they use the bathroom, because he gets into bed and won't talk. At first McKenna tried to lure him out with food or a DVD or something, but leaving him alone seems to be the best policy. McKenna says his mother spent most of her life in bed, and that Payne always used to say at least he knew where his mother was. This is not unlike what Logan is currently feeling about her father. At least she knows where he is.

Her mother still acts weird sometimes but Logan's getting used to it. At least she's taking better care of herself, showering regularly and combing her hair. She's even remembering to comb Logan's hair. Payne has taken over packing Logan's lunches, which is great because he puts cool stuff in them like Fruit to Gos and yoghurt cups.

That stone cross killing the little French girl made her definitely feel she's made the right choice in going agnostic. The girl's baby brother had died and she was taking flowers to his grave with her parents when the cross fell from an old tomb and crushed her. It took her two days to die in the hospital. When Logan thinks about what Beasley did to her, she remembers the little French girl. And the Dog Boy. And those Palestinian children who got bombed on the way to school. Their mothers are still searching for bits of bodies and school books.

The good thing is, Logan doesn't feel like dying anymore. She still remembers the feel of him though, doesn't think she'll ever be free of that. But people adapt to worse, she knows. There's a new boy at school who sawed off half his index finger. At first the kids thought his stump was creepy but then he started doing finger tricks, sticking it into his eye and up his nose. This made him very popular.

That eight-year-old boy whose arm was reattached after a shark attack is awake. It bugs Logan how everybody's hysterical about sharks all of a sudden when the fact is, sharks would rather eat a mullet than a human. They only bite humans because they're hunting for fish along their northward migratory route. Once they figure out they've got a human in their mouth they spit it out and go back to hunting for mullet. It seems to Logan humans are always getting hysterical about things that don't matter, like if their cable got cut off or their garbage wasn't picked up or something, when the fact is 2.4 acres of rain forest—the planet's lungs—are being destroyed *every second*, which means 78 million acres a year. The fact is, it's getting harder to breathe.

Her ladybug project is going quite well. She thinks it's interesting that the larvae grow into pupae, and that a pupa looks defenceless but, in fact, can pivot around or jerk up and down even though it's attached to a leaf. The jerking startles its enemies, and makes them leave the pupa alone. But even more impressive is that, once the ladybug exits the pupa, a bitter orange liquid automatically bleeds from its legs when it's threatened. The oozing warns its predators that ladybugs taste gross. This is not unlike what McKenna describes as don't-fuck-with-me energy. McKenna says you can ward off assholes just by feeling strong. But Logan's system, and it seems to be working, is to imagine that her legs are bleeding bitter orange liquid that kills on contact.

She's quite enjoyed choosing colours for the house. Her mother asked that the living room and kitchen be black and white but said that Logan could go crazy with the rest of the house. She's not sure about the Terra Verde in the bathroom. Her dad says he feels like he's walking into a bar of Irish Spring.

The family karate classes have been interesting, more for her mother than herself in Logan's opinion, because her mother holds a lot of aggression. But Logan enjoys the discipline and concentration required in karate, and hitting the dummy. There are stupid boys, of course, who want to kick all the time, but if they try anything—like pulling on her ponytail or something—she just stares them down and imagines she's bleeding bitter orange liquid that kills on contact.

57

I won't call it forgiveness; more like I let go of the peanut. At some point you figure out the anger is burning holes through you and not even heating up their backsides.

I draw him all the time. He likes it, says, "You're the only one who can look at me, Mick." Which is true. In colour I probably couldn't stomach him; in monochrome he's textured, challenging. I start him in darkness, completely charcoal the page, then slowly bring in light with the putty. He's no bowl of fruit, the lines are always changing, nothing stays the same. I don't try to control it, just draw. He doesn't look at the pictures. I hide them in closets.

The physio has been hard for him. She's the kind of box job who used to go creamy around him. Now he's just another burn victim. He doesn't talk about it. Miss Jiggly Jugs sent flowers and threatened to "pop by and see how you're doing." She hasn't though. He feels ugly and cursed, as I have felt ugly and cursed. So we sit, the rejected, in silence except for the shuffle of charcoal. I don't know what's to become of him, if he'll always live under my roof, staring up at the skylight, invisible to the street but open to the universe. I don't know if I could stand this. He still is who he was, minus the skin. But there's a humility there that's new, maybe temporary. It could easily morph into resentment. Nothing stays the same.

He doesn't watch TV anymore, doesn't like watching smooth skin, except for cooking shows because he says they have some good ideas. Unasked, he's taken to doing cooking and housework. All those years ago I kept pushing him to get off his ass, now I do nothing and he's the model house-hubby. He orders groceries from Gateway, has them left on the porch, then scurries out to get the supplies in and start baking apples or something. He's adapted. He's done this all his life, lived in the present, used whatever was available, human or otherwise, while I've always been looking over my shoulder or the next guy's, trying to outsmart the next twist of fate.

Sometimes we sit on the porch late at night, Batwoman and the Phantom. There's no hurry. We talk or we don't. We've walked through fire together.

What's interesting is Logan. She has a different kind of confidence. She's always known she's smart, but anybody could undermine her with the "Where's your dad?" line of questioning. Now she talks about him to anybody who'll listen: garbagemen, dog walkers, bank tellers. And she reads to him, whatever's going: outer space news, war, famines, natural disasters, human slaughter. He's never read a paper in his life and here he is getting up to speed on current events. I caught them laughing together. She was telling him about life on spaceships, the assisted screwing, and shitting into a vacuum. Apparently you have to get suctioned onto the pot if you plan to stay there. A flip of a switch spins you into space again. The two of them were in hysterics over this and I just knew it couldn't get better than this, listening to the two of them roar.

A client of mine is a bingo addict, not your church basement bingo but the real thing, where you lose thousands of dollars. Her mother's a senior with minimal savings but the bingo addict borrowed her money and lost it. She was in the salon today blithering about it. She has a good job, makes good money, and yet had to steal from her mother. I said, "Why do you think you need that shit?" which is what Payne said to me years ago re drugs.

"Everybody wants money," she said.

I told her about my nurse client who told me nobody on their deathbed says they wished they'd made more money. It's always they wished they'd spent more time with their kids, less time at the office, less time up their own assholes.

So then at the dollar store I hear the cashier giving this teenager the lowdown on how to become a supermodel. The cashier is around sixty with big hair and boobs and sparkles on her cleavage. I watch the girl get this idea that if she loses fifty pounds as per the cashier's instructions, life will be her oyster. If only. How many times are we sitting around thinking things would be great *if only*? Bite it, is my response. Because *if only* isn't going to happen. What's happening is happening and if you don't notice it you'll be on your deathbed making wishes.

Because of Logan I did the brain-imaging tests, ended up in a windowless room with some doctor with ear hair. He told me there was an operation that might possibly give me back colour. "Might possibly" didn't sound too promising to me. Then there was the problem of digging around in my brain, causing who knows what other damage. So then I started thinking, What do I need colour for anyway? This black-and-white world has slowed me down, made me notice. I can't grab at things anymore. I have to stop and look at them, figure it out. I can't assume anything. I actually have to taste my food, smell my fruit, feel my clothes, *listen* to what's going on. Tunnel vision doesn't work for the colour-deprived. We need context, we have to look at the whole picture to appreciate the detail.

So I look around me at these mortals getting wound up about their hair, their cars, their taxes, their zits, wrinkles, fat, central vacs, sex, bad nights out, movies, stocks, diets, what so-and-so said or didn't, the weather, the way so-and-so looked at them or didn't, their computers, their schedules—and I just think, You fools, you've lost it.

I hug him a lot. This is weird. Because I used to crave him. It started with restraining him because he'd wake up screaming, flailing, dreaming of flames and dressing changes. I'd hold him and tell him he wasn't dead, that we were all here, together in the house. If his screams woke Logan she would join in the hug, and we'd just stay there, feeling each other's hearts beating. When he had pneumonia in both lungs, when the nurses stopped making eye contact with me, I figured out I wanted him to live. Because we're bound by our daughter's DNA. Because our world would be smaller without him. Because nobody's perfect, because nothing stays the same.

My father is another story. I don't know what put him in that box but I can't get him out of it. I tap on it, let him know somebody's out there, check his tracheostomy, make sure the alarm on the machine regulating his feeding tube isn't beeping into a void and that his urinary catheter hasn't become detached, soaking him in piss. He has to endure rehab daily. They flip him onto a vertical board and wait to see if he moves. Afterwards they park him by his bed where he has to wait for nurses' aides to swing him back between the sheets. He was supposed to die, is lost, forever drooling, and I want to ask him why he won't let them shut down the respirator. But this would be too intimate for us. We blink TV channels and bodily needs. I look into that deranged eye and think it could have been me locked in there. I don't smile or play devoted daughter outside the box anymore. I watch for change but expect nothing. I go home and taste the vegetables I've grown in my garden and watch my daughter climb a tree and know that it doesn't get better than this. I lie with her under her skylight and see the stars vanish behind clouds then reappear with renewed twinkle. I listen to her explanations about the ever-changing universe and know that this will not last, that nothing stays the same, that I must live in this moment, because there may not be another.